THE COMPLETE TALES OF HENRY JAMES
VOLUME SIX: 1884–1888

THE COMPLETE TALES OF

HENRY JAMES

EDITED WITH AN
INTRODUCTION BY
LEON EDEL

6

1884–1888

J. B. LIPPINCOTT COMPANY

PHILADELPHIA AND NEW YORK

CONTENTS

INTRODUCTION: 1884–1888

FOUR of the six tales gathered in this volume were planned or written by Henry James during a sojourn in northern Italy in 1886 and 1887. He occupied rooms in an old Florentine villa on Bellosguardo, overlooking the valley of the Arno; later he worked in Venice, in the Palazzo Barbaro on the Grand Canal. In Tuscany and Venetia James recovered again, after a long lapse, his cherished "sense of Italy"; and he wrote in a happy freedom of the demands of his London life, where during the preceding two and a half years he had completed his long novels of the mid-1880's, *The Bostonians* and *The Princess Casamassima*. To this new period of happy creation—which I have elsewhere called his "Italian phase"—belong "The Aspern Papers," "Louisa Pallant," "Mrs Temperly," "The Liar" and certain other tales included in the next volume of this series. "A massing of masterpieces," said William Dean Howells, as the stories began to appear in the magazines during 1888. And he likened them to the fresh and brilliant paintings of a master hung for exhibition after a period of sustained creative effort.

They are indeed masterpieces. And the most remarkable of the group is the narrative of "The Aspern Papers," a veritable *tour de force* of story-telling. Related by an unnamed narrator, it is composed of distinctly romantic elements: a quest for the papers of a long-dead American poet named Aspern, the survival of the poet's aged mistress into a new time, in a mouldering Venetian palace, and the clash between the hunter and the hunted, the cat-and-mouse drama between the acquisitive narrator and the ancient lady seeking to protect her private life.

These are the essential elements of James's drama. What gives it a strange power is the writer's haunting sense of the

7

past and the way in which he melts the Venetian setting into his tale. He was to make a fine distinction years later between a past that is remote and a past that is "visitable." The remote past was a jumble of disconnected, odd facts, which man pieces together into a rough mosaic; the "visitable past" was a past still close enough to contain a fund of human detail. The story of Juliana living in her palace with her old memories of Jeffrey Aspern was distinctly visitable; and it contained within it "the poetry of the thing outlived and lost and gone."

The thing outlived and lost and gone. James drew not only upon the historical past of a Venice he intimately knew, but upon an actual piece of literary history—that of Jane Clairmont (who had called herself Claire), Byron's quondam mistress, mother of the poet's daughter Allegra. What fired James's imagination, early in 1887 on his hilltop of Bellosguardo, was his discovery that Claire Clairmont had lived to a ripe old age in Florence (she died at 91), and that he had often passed her door in the Via Romana in the 1870's. There was also an anecdote of an old Boston sea-captain named Silsbee, an admirer of Shelley, who knew Miss Clairmont possessed Shelley as well as Byron papers. He had gained admission to her home on the footing of a lodger, hoping to obtain some relics of his favourite poet. "The Aspern Papers" grew out of this episode and James's most imaginative stroke lay in moving the scene of the story from Florence to Venice. The water-city best served the counterpoint of incident and place: an old lady, an old palace, an old city—old grandeurs still visitable, living into a new and heedless age, Juliana in her ancient home with its garden on the canal, feeding on old memories in a city whose fading marble and musty decay are mocked by a perpetual iridescence of sea and sky.

The narrator is the key to the tale: we are not told his name and, as with the governess of "The Turn of the Screw," we shall never know it. We must identify him for ourselves, from the story he tells. And he tells a sufficiently damning story, a chronicle of subterfuge and duplicity, recounted lightly and with a grand air of innocence. We begin by accepting the narrator's insincerities—he is so obsessively sincere in proclaiming them. He worships the memory of Aspern, and to that memory he is prepared to sacrifice everything. He has charm; he seems an artist *manqué*; he is a critic, a zealous editor of documents, a biographer. As we listen to him, he fascinates us by his devotion and his ardour, and he involves us promptly in his battle of wits with the old lady. Then we begin to have doubts. He is too ingenuous, too ready to trifle with the old lady's grand-niece, Miss Tita,* a plain, middle-aged woman for whom the presence of a man in the palace is a major event in a long humdrum life. Yet to the narrator she is simply a fortuitous instrument to be used in his game of outwitting the old lady. It is difficult to accept the narrator's behaviour to Miss Tita, and the pathos of her final scene opens our eyes to his brutal egotism. Juliana had called him a "publishing scoundrel." We are quite ready to call him an unfeeling cad.

The tale thus holds up to our inspection an invader of privacy, a meddler in the lives of others. And yet James tells a story which casts a spell. We are in the city of *Othello* and of *The Merchant of Venice*; of *Volpone* and *Venice Preserved*. The image of the dying woman driving her bargains with her unscrupulous tenant can claim a distinct kinship with Jonson's comedy of Venetian cupidity. Indeed "The Aspern Papers" derives its highest moments of drama from a series of bargaining episodes: Juliana bargaining for the apartment, or attempting to obtain a good price for a miniature of Aspern from the unusually interested stranger; and above all Miss Tita, at the end, seeking to barter the Aspern papers for a hope of love. But the motives of Juliana and Miss Tita are honest; they have something to offer and expect the highest price in exchange.

* In his late revision of the tale James changed her name to Miss Tina.

The motives of the narrator are more mixed: his obsession with the dead poet; his overriding need to obtain, at the cost of deception and fraud, some relics of him; and above all a blind egotism that will stop at nothing. And this in Venice: we can hear, as it were, the chink of ducats between the lines; and we see the shimmering light in the canals. Small wonder that the narrator, when he comes to the end of his stratagem, ruefully studies the statue of Bartolommeo Colleoni, on its great horse, turning stony eyes into the Venetian sunset. In the image of the true *condottiere* this would-be pirate recognises certain affinities, and fixes the scale of his own predatory impulses.

"The Aspern Papers" lives in the vividness of its detail and the measured tread of its narrative. There is not a false footstep in it. A superb sense of time prevails in each of its nine leisurely sections. We feel the unhurried passage of the Venetian spring; the narrator cultivates his roses and gazes at the shuttered rooms of the old ladies which guard their old mysteries; he waits and hopes for the moment when he will search for the Aspern papers. And we experience to the full the drama of his rising and declining hopes. With this tale James claimed Venice for his fiction as the Elizabethans had claimed it for transcendent poetry and drama, and as Proust and Mann would claim it after him. "The Aspern Papers" is an extraordinary time-vision, an invocation of the muse of history to serve the ends of fiction. "History is after all the true poetry," Carlyle had said. Henry James showed that the poetry of place and of the past was also a certain kind of human history.

The other stories of James's Italian phase tend to be overshadowed by the Venetian tale; however, they are lacquered with the same fine brush of his prose, and they are woven of the same moral stuff. "Mrs Temperly" is a graceful anecdote of a pleasant lady of many accomplishments, largely of an administrative order, in her own widowed household, who, behind her genteel and competent façade, conceals a will of iron. She has mapped the lives of her children and they are allowed no other course. The way in which this becomes apparent to the young suitor of one of the daughters is the essence of the tale; it is he who can give us the finished portrait of Mrs Temperly.

"Louisa Pallant" is also a portrait of a "hard" woman—a woman, to be sure, who repents of her hardness, when she sees how it has moulded her daughter into an image of herself. This is her punishment, and in her struggle with her guilt she warns off her daughter's young suitor. The reader is left with the uneasy feeling that the mother has compounded her complicated history by a grossly meddlesome act.

Finally, in "The Liar" James offers the bewilderment of a portrait-painter (named Lyon) who encounters an easygoing English Munchausen, a minor teller of "tall" tales. The drama derives from Lyon's discovery that this man is married to a woman he himself once loved. He cannot tolerate the thought that a creature he deemed so fine should now be married to an individual so coarse, a man who is nothing more nor less than a "liar." The painter sets out to discover whether the woman he loved is blind to her husband's weakness, or has been debased by her marriage. When she herself tells a lie in the liar's defence, this is proof to Lyon only of her moral collapse. He is unable to grasp the simple truth that she loves her husband.

The same moral search is to be found in the two tales of the early 1880's. "A New England Winter" treats of a mother's elaborate diplomacy to find a wife of her choosing for her son; it gives us charming scenes of Beacon Street filled with snow and a feminised Boston. "The Path of Duty" is a study in the psychology of self-deception—of two lovers who make an excessive virtue out of their virtuous attachment. "Georgina's

Reasons" is a Jamesian curiosity, written (with "Pandora")
for an unusual medium—serialisation in a group of Sunday
newspapers. The story of Georgina and her strange behaviour
—she treats her legitimate child as if it were illegitimate,
keeps her marriage secret and then commits bigamy—was
James's attempt to meet the supposed fictional taste of his
newspaper audience. For readers of the later James the most
interesting part of the tale is that in which Georgina's husband, a naval officer, encounters in Italy the sisters Kate and
Mildred Theory—an early foreshadowing of Kate Croy and
Milly Theale of *The Wings of the Dove*.

Long ago, James had said he hoped to become the "moral
portrait painter" of his time. In these tales he paints his moral
pictures; and for all his "objectivity" his feelings emerge
clearly enough. He shows the mischief created by those who
meddle in other people's lives, and by the invaders of the
private life. And he tells his little dramas without preaching;
the moral lesson is to be understood through his subtle
feeling for the ironies of his human comedy.

LEON EDEL

Gay Head, 1962

GEORGINA'S REASONS

I

SHE was certainly a singular girl, and if he felt at the end that
he didn't know her nor understand her, it is not surprising
that he should have felt it at the beginning. But he felt at the
beginning what he did not feel at the end, that her singularity
took the form of a charm which—once circumstances had
made them so intimate—it was impossible to resist or conjure
away. He had a strange impression (it amounted at times to a
positive distress, and shot through the sense of pleasure,
morally speaking, with the acuteness of a sudden twinge of
neuralgia) that it would be better for each of them that they
should break off short and never see each other again. In
later years he called this feeling a foreboding, and remembered
two or three occasions when he had been on the point of
expressing it to Georgina. Of course, in fact, he never expressed it; there were plenty of good reasons for that. Happy
love is not disposed to assume disagreeable duties; and
Raymond Benyon's love was happy, in spite of grave presenti-
ments, in spite of the singularity of his mistress and the in-
sufferable rudeness of her parents. She was a tall, fair girl, with
a beautiful cold eye, and a smile of which the perfect sweetness, proceeding from the lips, was full of compensation; she
had auburn hair, of a hue that could be qualified as nothing
less than gorgeous, and she seemed to move through life
with a stately grace, as she would have walked through an
old-fashioned minuet. Gentlemen connected with the navy
have the advantage of seeing many types of women; they are
able to compare the ladies of New York with those of Val-
paraiso, and those of Halifax with those of the Cape of Good

Hope. Raymond Benyon had had these opportunities, and, being fond of women, he had learned his lesson; he was in a position to appreciate Georgina Gressie's fine points. She looked like a duchess—I don't mean that in foreign ports Benyon had associated with duchesses—and she took everything so seriously. That was flattering for the young man, who was only a lieutenant, detailed for duty at the Brooklyn navy-yard, without a penny in the world but his pay; with a set of plain, numerous, seafaring, God-fearing relations in New Hampshire, a considerable appearance of talent, a feverish, disguised ambition, and a slight impediment in his speech. He was a spare, tough young man; his dark hair was straight and fine, and his face, a trifle pale, smooth and carefully drawn. He stammered a little, blushing when he did so, at long intervals. I scarcely know how he appeared on shipboard, but on shore, in his civilian's garb, which was of the neatest, he had as little as possible an aroma of winds and waves. He was neither salt nor brown nor red nor particularly "hearty." He never twitched up his trousers, nor, so far as one could see, did he, with his modest, attentive manner, carry himself as a person accustomed to command. Of course, as a subaltern, he had more to do in the way of obeying. He looked as if he followed some sedentary calling, and was indeed supposed to be decidedly intellectual. He was a lamb with women, to whose charms he was, as I have hinted, susceptible; but with men he was different, and, I believe, as much of a wolf as was necessary. He had a manner of adoring the handsome, insolent queen of his affections (I will explain in a moment why I call her insolent); indeed, he looked up to her literally, as well as sentimentally, for she was the least bit the taller of the two.

He had met her the summer before on the piazza of an hotel at Fort Hamilton, to which, with a brother-officer, in a dusty buggy, he had driven over from Brooklyn to spend a tremendously hot Sunday—the kind of day when the navy-yard was loathsome; and the acquaintance had been renewed by his calling in Twelfth Street on New Year's day—a considerable time to wait for a pretext, but which proved the impression had not been transitory. The acquaintance ripened, thanks to a zealous cultivation (on his part) of occasions which Providence, it must be confessed, placed at his disposal none too liberally; so that now Georgina took up all his thoughts and a considerable part of his time. He was in love with her, beyond a doubt; but he could not flatter himself that she was smitten with him, though she seemed willing (what was so strange) to quarrel with her family about him. He didn't see how she could really care for him—she was marked out by nature for so much greater a fortune; and he used to say to her, "Ah, you don't—there's no use talking, you don't—really care for me at all!" To which she answered, "Really? You are very particular. It seems to me it's real enough if I let you touch one of my finger-tips!" That was one of her ways of being insolent. Another was simply her manner of looking at him, or at other people, when they spoke to her, with her hard, divine blue eye—looking quietly, amusedly, with the air of considering, wholly from her own point of view, what they might have said, and then turning her head or her back, while, without taking the trouble to answer them, she broke into a short, liquid, irrelevant laugh. This may seem to contradict what I said just now about her taking the young lieutenant in the navy seriously. What I mean is that she appeared to take him more seriously than she took anything else. She said to him once, "At any rate you have the merit of not being a shop-keeper;" and it was by this epithet she was pleased to designate most of the young men who at that time flourished in the best society of New York. Even if she had rather a free way of expressing general indifference, a young lady is supposed to be serious enough when she consents to marry you. For the rest, as regards a certain haughtiness that might be observed in Georgina

Gressie, my story will probably throw sufficient light upon it. She remarked to Benyon once that it was none of his business why she liked him, but that, to please herself, she didn't mind telling him she thought the great Napoleon, before he was celebrated, before he had command of the army of Italy, must have looked something like him; and she sketched in a few words the sort of figure she imagined the incipient Bonaparte to have been—short, lean, pale, poor, intellectual, and with a tremendous future under his hat. Benyon asked himself whether he had a tremendous future, and what in the world Georgina expected of him in the coming years. He was flattered at the comparison, he was ambitious enough not to be frightened at it, and he guessed that she perceived a certain analogy between herself and the Empress Josephine. She would make a very good empress—that was true; Georgina was remarkably imperial. This may not at first seem to make it more clear why she should take into her favour an aspirant who, on the face of the matter, was not original, and whose Corsica was a flat New England seaport; but it afterwards became plain that he owed his brief happiness—it was very brief—to her father's opposition; her father's and her mother's, and even her uncles' and her aunts'. In those days, in New York, the different members of a family took an interest in its alliances; and the house of Gressie looked askance at an engagement between the most beautiful of its daughters and a young man who was not in a paying business. Georgina declared that they were meddlesome and vulgar; she could sacrifice her own people, in that way, without a scruple; and Benyon's position improved from the moment that Mr Gressie—ill-advised Mr Gressie—ordered the girl to have nothing to do with him. Georgina was imperial in this —that she wouldn't put up with an order. When, in the house in Twelfth Street, it began to be talked about that she had better be sent to Europe with some eligible friend, Mrs Portico for instance, who was always planning to go and who wanted as a companion some young mind, fresh from manuals and extracts, to serve as a fountain of history and geography—when this scheme for getting Georgina out of the way began to be aired, she immediately said to Raymond Benyon, "Oh yes, I'll marry you!" She said it in such an off-hand way that, deeply as he desired her, he was almost tempted to answer, "But, my dear, have you really thought about it?"

II

THIS little drama went on, in New York, in the ancient days, when Twelfth Street had but lately ceased to be suburban, when the squares had wooden palings, which were not often painted, when there were poplars in important thoroughfares and pigs in the lateral ways, when the theatres were miles distant from Madison Square, and the battered rotunda of Castle Garden echoed with expensive vocal music, when "the park" meant the grass-plats of the City Hall, and the Bloomingdale road was an eligible drive, when Hoboken, of a summer afternoon, was a genteel resort, and the handsomest house in town was on the corner of Fifth Avenue and Fifteenth Street. This will strike the modern reader, I fear, as rather a primitive epoch; but I am not sure that the strength of human passions is in proportion to the elongation of a city. Several of them, at any rate, the most robust and most familiar—love, ambition, jealousy, resentment, greed—subsisted in considerable force in the little circle at which we have glanced, where a view by no means favourable was taken of Raymond Benyon's attentions to Miss Gressie. Unanimity was a family trait among these people (Georgina was an exception), especially in regard to the important concerns of life, such as marriages and closing scenes. The Gressies hung together; they were accustomed to do well for themselves and for each

other. They did everything well: got themselves born well
(they thought it excellent to be born a Gressie), lived well,
married well, died well, and managed to be well spoken of
afterwards. In deference to this last-mentioned habit, I must
be careful what I say of them. They took an interest in each
other's concerns, an interest that could never be regarded as
of a meddlesome nature, inasmuch as they all thought alike
about all their affairs, and interference took the happy form
of congratulation and encouragement. These affairs were in-
variably lucky, and, as a general thing, no Gressie had anything
to do but feel that another Gressie had been almost as shrewd
and decided as he himself would have been. The great exception to that, as I have said, was this case of Georgina, who
struck such a false note, a note that startled them all, when she
told her father that she should like to unite herself to a young
man engaged in the least paying business that any Gressie
had ever heard of. Her two sisters had married into the most
flourishing firms, and it was not to be thought of that—with
twenty cousins growing up around her—she should put down
the standard of success. Her mother had told her a fortnight
before this that she must request Mr Benyon to cease coming
to the house; for hitherto his suit had been of the most public
and resolute character. He had been conveyed up-town, from
the Brooklyn ferry, in the "stage," on certain evenings, had
asked for Miss Georgina at the door of the house in Twelfth
Street, and had sat with her in the front parlour if her parents
happened to occupy the back, or in the back if the family
had disposed itself in the front. Georgina, in her way, was a
dutiful girl, and she immediately repeated her mother's
admonition to Benyon. He was not surprised, for, though he
was aware that he had not, as yet, a great knowledge of society,
he flattered himself he could tell when and where a polite
young man was not wanted. There were houses in Brooklyn
where such an animal was much appreciated, and there the
signs were quite different.

They had been discouraging, except on Georgina's part, from the first of his calling in Twelfth Street. Mr and Mrs Gressie used to look at each other in silence when he came in, and indulge in strange perpendicular salutations, without any shaking of hands. People did that at Portsmouth, N. H., when they were glad to see you; but in New York there was more luxuriance, and gesture had a different value. He had never, in Twelfth Street, been asked to "take anything," though the house had a delightful suggestion, a positive aroma, of sideboards, as if there were mahogany "cellarettes" under every table. The old people, moreover, had repeatedly expressed surprise at the quantity of leisure that officers in the navy seemed to enjoy. The only way in which they had not made themselves offensive was by always remaining in the other room; though at times even this detachment, to which he owed some delightful moments, presented itself to Benyon as a form of disapprobation. Of course, after Mrs Gressie's message, his visits were practically at an end: he wouldn't give the girl up, but he wouldn't be beholden to her father for the opportunity to converse with her. Nothing was left for the tender couple—there was a curious mutual mistrust in their tenderness—but to meet in the squares, or in the topmost streets, or in the sidemost avenues, on the spring afternoons. It was especially during this phase of their relations that Georgina struck Benyon as imperial. Her whole person seemed to exhale a tranquil, happy consciousness of having broken a law. She never told him how she arranged the matter at home, how she found it possible always to keep the appointments (to meet him out of the house) that she so boldly made, in what degree she dissimulated to her parents, and how much, in regard to their continued acquaintance, the old people suspected and accepted. If Mr and Mrs Gressie had forbidden him the house, it was not, apparently, because they wished her to walk with him in the Tenth Avenue or to sit at his side under the blossoming lilacs in Stuyvesant Square.

He didn't believe that she told lies in Twelfth Street; he thought she was too imperial to lie; and he wondered what she said to her mother when, at the end of nearly a whole afternoon of vague peregrination with her lover, this rustling, bristling matron asked her where she had been. Georgina was capable of simply telling the truth; and yet if she simply told the truth it was a wonder that she had not been still more simply packed off to Europe. Benyon's ignorance of her pretexts is a proof that this rather oddly-mated couple never arrived at perfect intimacy, in spite of a fact which remains to be related. He thought of this afterwards, and thought how strange it was that he had not felt more at liberty to ask her what she did for him, and how she did it, and how much she suffered for him. She would probably not have admitted that she suffered at all, and she had no wish to pose for a martyr.

Benyon remembered this, as I say, in the after years, when he tried to explain to himself certain things which simply puzzled him; it came back to him with the vision, already faded, of shabby cross-streets, straggling toward rivers, with red sunsets, seen through a haze of dust, at the end; a vista through which the figures of a young man and a girl slowly receded and disappeared, strolling side by side, with the relaxed pace of desultory talk, but more closely linked as they passed into the distance, linked by its at last appearing safe to them—in the Tenth Avenue—that the young lady should take his arm. They were always approaching that inferior thoroughfare; but he could scarcely have told you, in those days, what else they were approaching. He had nothing in the world but his pay, and he felt that this was rather a "mean" income to offer Miss Gressie. Therefore he didn't put it forward; what he offered, instead, was the expression— crude often, and almost boyishly extravagant—of a delighted admiration of her beauty, the tenderest tones of his voice, the softest assurances of his eye, and the most insinuating pressure of her hand at those moments when she consented to place it in his arm. All this was an eloquence which, if necessary, might have been condensed into a single sentence; but those few words were scarcely needed when it was as plain that he expected, in general, she would marry him, as it was indefinite that he counted upon her for living on a few hundred a year. If she had been a different girl he might have asked her to wait, might have talked to her of the coming of better days, of his prospective promotion, of its being wiser, perhaps, that he should leave the navy and look about for a more lucrative career. With Georgina it was difficult to go into such questions; she had no taste whatever for detail. She was delightful as a woman to love, because when a young man is in love he discovers that; but she could not be called helpful, for she never suggested anything. That is, she never had done so till the day she really proposed—for that was the form it took —to become his wife without more delay. "Oh yes, I will marry you:" these words, which I quoted a little way back, were not so much the answer to something he had said at the moment as the light conclusion of a report she had just made (for the first time) of her actual situation in her father's house.

III

"I am afraid I shall have to see less of you," she had begun by saying. "They watch me so much."

"It is very little already," he answered. "What is once or twice a week?"

"That's easy for you to say. You are your own master, but you don't know what I go through."

"Do they make it very bad for you, dearest? Do they make scenes?" Benyon asked.

"No, of course not. Don't you know us enough to know

how we behave? No scenes; that would be a relief. However, I never make them myself, and I never will—that's one comfort for you, for the future, if you want to know. Father and mother keep very quiet, looking at me as if I were one of the lost, with little hard, piercing eyes, like gimlets. To me they scarcely say anything, but they talk it all over with each other, and try and decide what is to be done. It's my belief that my father has written to the people in Washington—what do you call it?—the Department—to have you moved away from Brooklyn—to have you sent to sea."

"I guess that won't do much good. They want me in Brooklyn; they don't want me at sea."

"Well, they are capable of going to Europe for a year, on purpose to take me," Georgina said.

"How can they take you if you won't go? And if you should go, what good would it do if you were only to find me here when you came back, just the same as you left me?"

"Oh, well!" said Georgina, with her lovely smile, "of course they think that absence would cure me of—— cure me of——" And she paused, with a kind of cynical modesty, not saying exactly of what.

"Cure you of what, darling? Say it, please say it," the young man murmured, drawing her hand surreptitiously into his arm.

"Of my absurd infatuation!"

"And would it, dearest?"

"Yes, very likely. But I don't mean to try. I shall not go to Europe—not when I don't want to. But it's better I should see less of you—even that I should appear—a little—to give you up."

"A little? What do you call a little?"

Georgina said nothing for a moment. "Well, that, for instance, you shouldn't hold my hand quite so tight!" And she disengaged this conscious member from the pressure of his arm.

"What good will that do?" Benyon asked.

"It will make them think it's all over—that we have agreed to part."

"And as we have done nothing of the kind, how will that help us?"

They had stopped at the crossing of a street; a heavy dray was lumbering slowly past them. Georgina, as she stood there, turned her face to her lover and rested her eyes for some moments on his own. At last, "Nothing will help us; I don't think we are very happy," she answered, while her strange, ironical, inconsequent smile played about her beautiful lips.

"I don't understand how you see things. I thought you were going to say you would marry me," Benyon rejoined, standing there still, though the dray had passed.

"Oh yes, I will marry you!" And she moved away across the street. That was the way she had said it, and it was very characteristic of her. When he saw that she really meant it, he wished they were somewhere else—he hardly knew where the proper place would be—so that he might take her in his arms. Nevertheless, before they separated that day he had said to her he hoped she remembered they would be very poor, reminding her how great a change she would find it. She answered that she shouldn't mind, and presently she said that if this was all that prevented them the sooner they were married the better. The next time he saw her she was quite of the same opinion; but he found, to his surprise, it was now her conviction that she had better not leave her father's house. The ceremony should take place secretly, of course; but they would wait awhile to let their union be known.

"What good will it do us, then?" Raymond Benyon asked.

Georgina coloured. "Well, if you don't know, I can't tell you!"

Then it seemed to him that he did know. Yet, at the same time, he could not see why, once the knot was tied, secrecy should be required. When he asked what especial event they

were to wait for, and what should give them the signal to
appear as man and wife, she answered that her parents would
probably forgive her if they were to discover, not too abruptly,
after six months, that she had taken the great step. Benyon
supposed that she had ceased to care whether they forgave
her or not; but he had already perceived that the nature of
women is a queer mosaic. He had believed her capable of
marrying him out of bravado, but the pleasure of defiance
was absent if the marriage was kept to themselves. It now
appeared that she was not especially anxious to defy; she was
disposed rather to manage and temporise.

"Leave it to me; leave it to me. You are only a blundering
man," Georgina said. "I shall know much better than you
the right moment for saying, 'Well, you may as well make the
best of it, because we have already done it!'"

That might very well be, but Benyon didn't quite understand, and he was awkwardly anxious (for a lover) till it came
over him afresh that there was one thing at any rate in his
favour, which was simply that the finest girl he had ever seen
was ready to throw herself into his arms. When he said to her,
"There is one thing I hate in this plan of yours—that, for
ever so few weeks, so few days, your father should support
my wife"—when he made this homely remark, with a little
flush of sincerity in his face, she gave him a specimen of that
unanswerable laugh of hers, and declared that it would serve
Mr Gressie right for being so barbarous and so horrid. It was
Benyon's view that from the moment she disobeyed her father
she ought to cease to avail herself of his protection; but I am
bound to add that he was not particularly surprised at finding
this a kind of honour in which her feminine nature was little
versed. To make her his wife first—at the earliest moment
—whenever she would, and trust to fortune and the new influence he should have, to give him, as soon thereafter as
possible, complete possession of her: this finally presented itself to the young officer as the course most worthy of a lover

and a gentleman. He would be only a pedant who would take nothing because he could not get everything at once. They wandered further than usual this afternoon, and the dusk was thick by the time he brought her back to her father's door. It was not his habit to come so near it, but to-day they had so much to talk about that he actually stood with her for ten minutes at the foot of the steps. He was keeping her hand in his, and she let it rest there while she said—by way of a remark that should sum up all their reasons and reconcile their differences—

"There's one great thing it will do, you know: it will make me safe."

"Safe from what?"

"From marrying any one else."

"Ah, my girl, if you were to do that——!" Benyon exclaimed; but he didn't mention the other branch of the contingency. Instead of this, he looked aloft at the blind face of the house (there were only dim lights in two or three windows, and no apparent eyes) and up and down the empty street, vague in the friendly twilight; after which he drew Georgina Gressie to his breast and gave her a long, passionate kiss. Yes decidedly, he felt they had better be married. She had run quickly up the steps, and while she stood there, with her hand on the bell, she almost hissed at him, under her breath, "Go away, go away; Amanda's coming!" Amanda was the parlour-maid; and it was in those terms that the Twelfth Street Juliet dismissed her Brooklyn Romeo. As he wandered back into the Fifth Avenue, where the evening air was conscious of a vernal fragrance from the shrubs in the little precinct of the pretty Gothic church ornamenting that pleasant part of the street, he was too absorbed in the impression of the delightful contact from which the girl had violently released herself to reflect that the great reason she had mentioned a moment before was a reason for their marrying, of course, but not in the least a reason for their not making it public. But, as I said in the opening lines of this chapter, if he did not understand his mistress's motives at the end, he cannot be expected to have understood them at the beginning.

IV

MRS PORTICO, as we know, was always talking about going to Europe; but she had not yet—I mean a year after the incident I have just related—put her hand upon a youthful cicerone. Petticoats, of course, were required; it was necessary that her companion should be of the sex which sinks most naturally upon benches, in galleries and cathedrals, and pauses most frequently upon staircases that ascend to celebrated views. She was a widow with a good fortune and several sons, all of whom were in Wall Street, and none of them capable of the relaxed pace at which she expected to take her foreign tour. They were all in a state of tension; they went through life standing. She was a short, broad, high-coloured woman, with a loud voice and superabundant black hair, arranged in a way peculiar to herself, with so many combs and bands that it had the appearance of a national coiffure. There was an impression in New York, about 1845, that the style was Danish; some one had said something about having seen it in Schleswig-Holstein. Mrs Portico had a bold, humorous, slightly flamboyant look; people who saw her for the first time received an impression that her late husband had married the daughter of a bar-keeper or the proprietress of a menagerie. Her high, hoarse, good-natured voice seemed to connect her in some way with public life; it was not pretty enough to suggest that she might have been an actress. These ideas quickly passed away, however, even if you were not sufficiently initiated to know—as all the Gressies, for instance, knew so well—that her origin, so far from being enveloped in mystery, was almost the sort of thing she might have boasted of. But, in spite of the high pitch of her appearance she didn't boast of anything; she was a genial, easy, comical, irreverent person, with a large charity, a democratic, fraternising turn of mind, and a contempt for many worldly standards, which she expressed not in the least in general axioms (for she had a mortal horror of philosophy), but in violent ejaculations on particular occasions. She had not a grain of moral timidity, and she fronted a delicate social problem as sturdily as she would have barred the way of a gentleman she might have met in her vestibule with the plate-chest. The only thing which prevented her being a bore in orthodox circles was that she was incapable of discussion. She never lost her temper, but she lost her vocabulary, and ended quickly by praying that heaven would give her an opportunity to act out what she believed. She was an old friend of Mr and Mrs Gressie, who esteemed her for the antiquity of her lineage and the frequency of her subscriptions, and to whom she rendered the service of making them feel liberal—like people too sure of their own position to be frightened. She was their indulgence, their dissipation, their point of contact with dangerous heresies; so long as they continued to see her they could not be accused of being narrow-minded—a matter as to which they were perhaps vaguely conscious of the necessity of taking their precautions. Mrs Portico never asked herself whether she liked the Gressies; she had no disposition for morbid analysis, she accepted transmitted associations, and found, somehow, that her acquaintance with these people helped her to relieve herself. She was always making scenes in their drawing-room, scenes half indignant, half jocose, like all her manifestations, to which it must be confessed that they adapted themselves beautifully. They never "met" her, in the language of controversy; but always collected to watch her, with smiles and comfortable platitudes, as if they envied her superior richness of temperament. She took an interest in Georgina, who seemed to her different from the others, with suggestions about her of being likely not to marry so unrefreshingly as her sisters had done, and of a high, bold standard of duty. Her sisters had married from duty, but Mrs Portico would rather have chopped off one of her large plump hands than behave herself so well as that. She had, in her daughterless condition, a certain ideal of a girl who should be beautiful and romantic, with wistful eyes, and a little persecuted, so that she, Mrs Portico, might get her out of her troubles. She looked to Georgina, to a considerable degree, to give actuality to this vision; but she had really never understood Georgina at all. She ought to have been shrewd, but she lacked this refinement, and she never understood anything until after many disappointments and vexations. It was difficult to startle her, but she was much startled by a communication that this young lady made her one fine spring morning. With her florid appearance and her speculative mind, she was probably the most innocent woman in New York.

Georgina came very early, earlier even than visits were paid in New York thirty years ago; and instantly, without any preface, looking her straight in the face, told Mrs Portico that she was in great trouble and must appeal to her for assistance. Georgina had in her aspect no symptom of distress; she was as fresh and beautiful as the April day itself; she held up her head and smiled, with a sort of familiar challenge, looking like a young woman who would naturally be on good terms with fortune. It was not in the least in the tone of a person making a confession or relating a misadventure that she presently said, "Well, you must know, to begin with—of course, it will surprise you—that I am married."

"Married, Georgina Gressie!" Mrs Portico repeated, in her most resonant tones.

Georgina got up, walked with her majestic step across the room, and closed the door. Then she stood there, her back pressed against the mahogany panels, indicating only by the distance she had placed between herself and her hostess the consciousness of an irregular position. "I am not Georgina Gressie—I am Georgina Benyon; and it has become plain, within a short time, that the natural consequence will take place."

Mrs Portico was altogether bewildered. "The natural consequence?" she exclaimed, staring.

"Of one's being married, of course; I suppose you know what that is. No one must know anything about it. I want you to take me to Europe."

Mrs Portico now slowly rose from her place and approached her visitor, looking at her from head to foot as she did so, as if to measure the truth of her remarkable announcement. She rested her hands on Georgina's shoulders a moment, gazing into her blooming face, and then she drew her closer and kissed her. In this way the girl was conducted back to the sofa where, in a conversation of extreme intimacy, she opened Mrs Portico's eyes wider than they had ever been opened before. She was Raymond Benyon's wife; they had been married a year, but no one knew anything about it. She had kept it from every one, and she meant to go on keeping it. The ceremony had taken place in a little Episcopal church at Haarlem, one Sunday afternoon, after the service. There was no one in that dusty suburb who knew them; the clergy-man, vexed at being detained, and wanting to go home to tea, had made no trouble; he tied the knot before they could turn round. It was ridiculous how easy it had been. Raymond had told him frankly that it must all be under the rose, as the young lady's family disapproved of what she was going. But she was of legal age, and perfectly free; he could see that for himself. The parson had given a grunt as he looked at her over his spectacles; it was not very complimentary, it seemed to say that she was indeed no chicken. Of course she looked old for a girl; but she was not a girl now, was she? Raymond had certified his own identity as an officer in the United States navy

(he had papers, besides his uniform, which he wore), and
introduced the clergyman to a friend he had brought with
him, who was also in the navy, a venerable paymaster. It was
he who gave Georgina away, as it were; he was a dear old
man, a regular grandmother, and perfectly safe. He had been
married three times himself, and the first time in the same
way. After the ceremony she went back to her father's; but
she saw Mr Benyon the next day. After that she saw him—for
a little while—pretty often. He was always begging her to
come to him altogether; she must do him that justice. But she
wouldn't—she wouldn't now—perhaps she wouldn't ever.
She had her reasons, which seemed to her very good but were
very difficult to explain. She would tell Mrs Portico in plenty
of time what they were. But that was not the question now,
whether they were good or bad; the question was for her to
get away from the country for several months—far away from
any one who had ever known her. She should like to go to
some little place in Spain or Italy, where she should be out
of the world until everything was over.

Mrs Portico's heart gave a jump as this serene, handsome,
domestic girl, sitting there with a hand in hers and pouring
forth her extraordinary tale, spoke of everything being over.
There was a glossy coldness in it, an unnatural lightness,
which suggested—poor Mrs Portico scarcely knew what.
If Georgina was to become a mother it was to be supposed
she would remain a mother. She said there was a beautiful
place in Italy—Genoa—of which Raymond had often spoken,
and where he had been more than once, he admired it so much;
couldn't they go there and be quiet for a little while? She was
asking a great favour, that she knew very well; but if Mrs
Portico wouldn't take her she would find some one who
would. They had talked of such a journey so often; and, certainly, if Mrs Portico had been willing before, she ought to be
much more willing now. The girl declared that she *would* do
something, go somewhere, keep, in one way or another, her

situation unperceived. There was no use talking to her about telling; she would rather die than tell. No doubt it seemed strange, but she knew what she was about. No one had guessed anything yet—she had succeeded perfectly in doing what she wished—and her father and mother believed—as Mrs Portico had believed, hadn't she?—that, any time the last year, Raymond Benyon was less to her than he had been before. Well, so he was; yes, he was. He had gone away—he was off, goodness knew where—in the Pacific; she was alone, and now she would remain alone. The family believed it was all over, with his going back to his ship, and other things, and they were right; for it was over, or it would be soon.

V

MRS PORTICO, by this time, had grown almost afraid of her young friend; she had so little fear, she had even, as it were, so little shame. If the good lady had been accustomed to analysing things a little more, she would have said she had so little conscience. She looked at Georgina with dilated eyes —her visitor was so much the calmer of the two—and exclaimed, and murmured, and sank back, and sprang forward, and wiped her forehead with her pocket-handkerchief. There were things she didn't understand; that they should all have been so deceived, that they should have thought Georgina was giving her lover up (they flattered themselves she was discouraged or had grown tired of him) when she was really only making it impossible she should belong to any one else. And with this, her inconsequence, her capriciousness, her absence of motive, the way she contradicted herself, her apparent belief that she could hush up such a situation for ever! There was nothing shameful in having married poor Mr Benyon, even in a little church at Haarlem, and being given away by a paymaster; it was much more shameful to be in such a state without being prepared to make the proper ex-planations. And she must have seen very little of her husband; she must have given him up, so far as meeting him went, almost as soon as she had taken him. Had not Mrs Gressie herself told Mrs Portico, in the preceding October it must have been, that there now would be no need of sending Georgina away, inasmuch as the affair with the little navy-man—a project in every way so unsuitable—had quite blown over?

"After our marriage I saw him less—I saw him a great deal less," Georgina explained; but her explanation only appeared to make the mystery more dense.

"I don't see, in that case, what on earth you married him for!"

"We had to be more careful; I wished to appear to have given him up. Of course we were really more intimate; I saw him differently," Georgina said, smiling.

"I should think so! I can't for the life of me see why you weren't discovered."

"All I can say is we weren't. No doubt it's remarkable. We managed very well—that is, I managed; he didn't want to manage at all. And then father and mother are incredibly stupid!"

Mrs Portico exhaled a comprehensive moan, feeling glad, on the whole, that she hadn't a daughter, while Georgina went on to furnish a few more details. Raymond Benyon, in the summer, had been ordered from Brooklyn to Charles-town, near Boston, where, as Mrs Portico perhaps knew, there was another navy-yard, in which there was a temporary press of work, requiring more oversight. He had remained there several months, during which he had written to her urgently to come to him, and during which, as well, he had received notice that he was to rejoin his ship a little later. Before doing so he came back to Brooklyn for a few weeks, to wind up his work there, and then she had seen him—well, pretty often.

That was the best time of all the year that had elapsed since their marriage. It was a wonder at home that nothing had then been guessed, because she had really been reckless, and Benyon had even tried to force on a disclosure. But they were dense, that was very certain. He had besought her again and again to put an end to their false position, but she didn't want it any more than she had wanted it before. They had had rather a bad parting; in fact, for a pair of lovers, it was a very queer parting indeed. He didn't know, now, the thing she had come to tell Mrs Portico. She had not written to him. He was on a very long cruise. It might be two years before he returned to the United States. "I don't care how long he stays away," Georgina said, very simply.

"You haven't mentioned why you married him. Perhaps you don't remember!" Mrs Portico broke out, with her masculine laugh.

"Oh yes; I loved him."

"And you have got over that?"

Georgina hesitated a moment. "Why, no, Mrs Portico, of course I haven't. Raymond's a splendid fellow."

"Then why don't you live with him? You don't explain that."

"What would be the use when he's always away? How can one live with a man who spends half his life in the South Seas? If he wasn't in the navy it would be different; but to go through everything—I mean everything that making our marriage known would bring upon me: the scolding and the exposure and the ridicule, the scenes at home—to go through it all just for the idea, and yet to be alone here, just as I was before, without my husband after all, with none of the good of him"—and here Georgina looked at her hostess as if with the certitude that such an enumeration of inconveniences would touch her effectually—"really, Mrs Portico, I am bound to say I don't think that would be worth while; I haven't the courage for it."

"I never thought you were a coward," said Mrs Portico.

"Well, I am not, if you will give me time. I am very patient."

"I never thought that either."

"Marrying changes one," said Georgina, still smiling.

"It certainly seems to have had a very odd effect upon you. Why don't you make him leave the navy and arrange your life comfortably, like every one else?"

"I wouldn't for the world interfere with his prospects— with his promotion. That is sure to come for him, and to come immediately, he has such talents. He is devoted to his profession; it would ruin him to leave it."

"My dear young woman, you are a living wonder!" Mrs Portico exclaimed, looking at her companion as if she had been in a glass case.

"So poor Raymond says," Georgina answered, smiling more than ever.

"Certainly, I should have been very sorry to marry a navy-man; but if I had married him I would stick to him, in the face of all the scoldings in the universe!"

"I don't know what your parents may have been; I know what mine are," Georgina replied, with some dignity. "When he's a captain we shall come out of hiding."

"And what shall you do meanwhile? What will you do with your children? Where will you hide them? What will you do with this one?"

Georgina rested her eyes on her lap for a minute; then, raising them, she met those of Mrs Portico. "Somewhere in Europe," she said, in her sweet tone.

"Georgina Gressie, you're a monster!" the elder lady cried.

"I know what I am about, and you will help me," the girl went on.

"I will go and tell your father and mother the whole story—that's what I will do!"

"I am not in the least afraid of that—not in the least. You will help me; I assure you that you will."

"Do you mean I will support the child?"

Georgina broke into a laugh. "I do believe you would, if I were to ask you! But I won't go so far as that; I have something of my own. All I want you to do is to be with me."

"At Genoa; yes, you have got it all fixed! You say Mr Benyon is so fond of the place. That's all very well; but how will he like his baby being deposited there?"

"He won't like it at all. You see I tell you the whole truth," said Georgina, gently.

"Much obliged; it's a pity you keep it all for me! It is in his power, then, to make you behave properly. *He* can publish your marriage, if you won't; and if he does you will have to acknowledge your child."

"Publish, Mrs Portico? How little you know my Raymond! He will never break a promise; he will go through fire first."

"And what have you got him to promise?"

"Never to insist on a disclosure against my will; never to claim me openly as his wife till I think it is time; never to let any one know what has passed between us if I choose to keep it still a secret—to keep it for years—to keep it for ever. Never do anything in the matter himself, but to leave it to me. For this he has given me his solemn word of honour, and I know what that means!"

Mrs Portico, on the sofa, fairly bounced.

"You do know what you are about! And Mr Benyon strikes me as more demented even than yourself. I never heard of a man putting his head in to such a noose. What good can it do him?"

"What good? The good it did him was that it gratified me. At the time he took it he would have made any promise under the sun. It was a condition I exacted just at the very last, before the marriage took place. There was nothing at that moment he would have refused me; there was nothing I

couldn't have made him do. He was in love to that degree—
but I don't want to boast," said Georgina, with quiet grandeur.
"He wanted—he wanted——" she added; but then she
paused.

"He doesn't seem to have wanted much!" Mrs Portico
cried, in a tone which made Georgina turn to the window,
as if it might have reached the street. Her hostess noticed the
movement and went on, "Oh, my dear, if I ever do tell your
story I will tell it so that people will hear it!"

"You never will tell it. What I mean is that Raymond
wanted the sanction—of the affair at the church—because he
saw that I would never do without it. Therefore, for him, the
sooner we had it the better, and, to hurry it on, he was ready
to take any pledge."

"You have got it pat enough," said Mrs Portico, in homely
phrase. "I don't know what you mean by sanctions, or what
you wanted of 'em."

Georgina got up, holding rather higher than before that
beautiful head which, in spite of the embarrassments of this
interview, had not yet perceptibly abated its elevation. "Would
you have liked me to—to not marry?"

Mrs Portico rose also, and, flushed with the agitation of
unwonted knowledge—it was as if she had discovered a
skeleton in her favourite cupboard—faced her young friend
for a moment. Then her conflicting sentiments resolved themselves into an abrupt question, implying, for Mrs Portico,
much subtlety: "Georgina Gressie, were you really in love
with him?"

The question suddenly dissipated the girl's strange, studied,
wilful coldness; she broke out, with a quick flash of passion—
a passion that, for the moment, was predominately anger,
"Why else, in heaven's name, should I have done what I
have done? Why else should I have married him? What under
the sun had I to gain?"

A certain quiver in Georgina's voice, a light in her eye

which seemed to Mrs Portico more spontaneous, more human, as she uttered these words, caused them to affect her hostess rather less painfully than anything she had yet said. She took the girl's hand and emitted indefinite admonitory sounds. "Help me, my dear old friend, help me," Georgina continued, in a low, pleading tone; and in a moment Mrs Portico saw that the tears were in her eyes.

"You are a precious mixture, my child!" she exclaimed. "Go straight home to your own mother and tell her everything; that is your best help."

"You are kinder than my mother. You mustn't judge her by yourself."

"What can she do to you? How can she hurt you? We are not living in pagan times," said Mrs Portico, who was seldom so historical. "Besides, you have no reason to speak of your mother—to think of her even—so! She would have liked you to marry a man of some property; but she has always been a good mother to you."

At this rebuke Georgina suddenly kindled again; she was, indeed, as Mrs Portico had said, a precious mixture. Conscious, evidently, that she could not satisfactorily justify her present stiffness, she wheeled round upon a grievance which absolved her from self-defence. "Why, then, did he make that promise, if he loved me? No man who really loved me would have made it, and no man that was a man as I understand being a man! He might have seen that I only did it to test him—to see if he wanted to take advantage of being left free himself. It is a proof that he doesn't love me—not as he ought to have done; and in such a case as that a woman isn't bound to make sacrifices!"

Mrs Portico was not a person of a nimble intellect; her mind moved vigorously, but heavily; yet she sometimes made happy guesses. She saw that Georgina's emotions were partly real and partly fictitious, that, as regards this last matter especially, she was trying to "get up" a resentment, in order

to excuse herself. The pretext was absurd, and the good lady
was struck with its being heartless on the part of her young
visitor to reproach poor Benyon with a concession on which
she had insisted, and which could only be a proof of his devotion, inasmuch as he left her free while he bound himself.
Altogether, Mrs Portico was shocked and dismayed at such
a want of simplicity in the behaviour of a young person whom
she had hitherto believed to be as candid as she was stylish,
and her appreciation of this discovery expressed itself in the
uncompromising remark, "You strike me as a very bad girl,
my dear; you strike me as a very bad girl!"

VI

It will doubtless seem to the reader very singular that, in
spite of this reflection, which appeared to sum up her judgment
of the matter, Mrs Portico should in the course of a very
few days have consented to everything that Georgina asked
of her. I have thought it well to narrate at length the first
conversation that took place between them, but I shall not
trace further the successive phases of the girl's appeal, or the
steps by which—in the face of a hundred robust and salutary
convictions—the loud, kind, sharp, simple, sceptical, credu-
lous woman took under her protection a damsel whose
obstinacy she could not speak of without getting red with
anger. It was the simple fact of Georgina's personal condition
that moved her; this young lady's greatest eloquence was the
seriousness of her predicament. She might be bad, and she
had a splendid, careless, insolent, fair-faced way of admitting
it, which at moments, incoherently, inconsistently, irresistibly,
transmured the cynical confession into tears of weakness; but
Mrs Portico had known her from her rosiest years, and when

Georgina declared that she couldn't go home, that she wished
to be with her and not with her mother, that she couldn't
expose herself—she absolutely couldn't—and that she must
remain with her and her only till the day they should sail,
the poor lady was forced to make that day a reality. She was
over-mastered, she was cajoled, she was, to a certain extent,
fascinated. She had to accept Georgina's rigidity (she had
none of her own to oppose to it—she was only violent, she
was not continuous), and once she did this it was plain, after
all, that to take her young friend to Europe was to help her,
and to leave her alone was not to help her. Georgina literally
frightened Mrs Portico into compliance. She was evidently
capable of strange things if thrown upon her own devices.
So, from one day to another, Mrs Portico announced that she
was really at last about to sail for foreign lands (her doctor
having told her that if she didn't look out she would get too
old to enjoy them), and that she had invited that robust Miss
Gressie, who could stand so long on her feet, to accompany
her. There was joy in the house of Gressie at this announcement, for, though the danger was over, it was a great general
advantage to Georgina to go, and the Gressies were always
elated at the prospect of an advantage. There was a danger that
she might meet Mr Benyon on the other side of the world;
but it didn't seem likely that Mrs Portico would lend herself
to a plot of that kind. If she had taken it into her head to favour
their love-affair she would have done it openly, and Georgina
would have been married by this time. Her arrangements
were made as quickly as her decision had been—or rather
had appeared—slow; for this concerned those mercurial
young men down town. Georgina was perpetually at her
house; it was understood in Twelfth Street that she was
talking over her future travels with her kind friend. Talk
there was, of course, to a considerable degree; but after it was
settled they should start nothing more was said about the
motive of the journey. Nothing was said, that is, till the night

before they sailed; then a few plain words passed between them. Georgina had already taken leave of her relations in Twelfth Street, and was to sleep at Mrs Portico's in order to go down to the ship at an early hour. The two ladies were sitting together in the firelight, silent with the consciousness of corded luggage, when the elder one suddenly remarked to her companion that she seemed to be taking a great deal upon herself in assuming that Raymond Benyon wouldn't force her hand. He might choose to acknowledge his child, if she didn't; there were promises and promises, and many people would consider they had been let off when circumstances were so altered. She would have to reckon with Mr Benyon more than she thought.

"I know what I am about," Georgina answered. "There is only one promise for him. I don't know what you mean by circumstances being altered."

"Everything seems to me to be altered," poor Mrs Portico murmured, rather tragically.

"Well, he isn't, and he never will! I am sure of him, as sure as that I sit here. Do you think I would have looked at him if I hadn't known he was a man of his word?"

"You have chosen him well, my dear," said Mrs Portico, who by this time was reduced to a kind of bewildered acquiescence.

"Of course I have chosen him well. In such a matter as this he will be perfectly splendid." Then suddenly, "Perfectly splendid, that's why I cared for him," she repeated, with a flash of incongruous passion.

This seemed to Mrs Portico audacious to the point of being sublime; but she had given up trying to understand anything that the girl might say or do. She understood less and less after they had disembarked in England and begun to travel southward; and she understood least of all when, in the middle of the winter, the event came off with which in imagination she had tried to familiarise herself, but which, when it occurred, seemed to her beyond measure strange and dreadful. It took place at Genoa; for Georgina had made up her mind that there would be more privacy in a big town than in a little; and she wrote to America that both Mrs Portico and she had fallen in love with the place and would spend two or three months there. At that time people in the United States knew much less than to-day about the comparative attractions of foreign cities; and it was not thought surprising that absent New Yorkers should wish to linger in a seaport where they might find apartments, according to Georgina's report, in a palace painted in fresco by Vandyke and Titian. Georgina, in her letters, omitted, it will be seen, no detail that could give colour to Mrs Portico's long stay at Genoa. In such a palace—where the travellers hired twenty gilded rooms for the most insignificant sum—a remarkably fine boy came into the world. Nothing could have been more successful and comfortable than this transaction—Mrs Portico was almost appalled at the facility and felicity of it. She was by this time in a pretty bad way; and—what had never happened to her before in her life—she suffered from chronic depression of spirits. She hated to have to lie, and now she was lying all the time. Everything she wrote home, everything that had been said or done in connection with their stay in Genoa, was a lie. The way they remained indoors to avoid meeting chance compatriots was a lie. Compatriots in Genoa, at that period, were very rare; but nothing could exceed the business-like completeness of Georgina's precautions. Her nerve, her self-possession, her apparent want of feeling, excited on Mrs Portico's part a kind of gloomy suspense; a morbid anxiety to see how far her companion would go took possession of the excellent woman who, a few months before, hated to fix her mind on disagreeable things. Georgina went very far indeed; she did everything in her power to dissimulate the origin of her child. The record of his birth was made under a false name, and he was baptized at the nearest church by a Catholic priest. A magnificent contadina was brought to light by the doctor in a village in the hills, and this big, brown, barbarous creature, who, to do her justice, was full of handsome, familiar smiles and coarse tenderness, was constituted nurse to Raymond Benyon's son. She nursed him for a fortnight under the mother's eye, and she was then sent back to her village with the baby in her arms and sundry gold coin knotted into a corner of her pocket-handkerchief. Mr Gressie had given his daughter a liberal letter of credit on a London banker, and she was able, for the present, to make abundant provision for the little one. She called Mrs Portico's attention to the fact that she spent none of her money on futilities; she kept it all for her small pensioner in the Genoese hills. Mrs Portico beheld these strange doings with a stupefaction that occasionally broke into passionate protest; then she relapsed into a brooding sense of having now been an accomplice so far that she must be an accomplice to the end.

VII

THE two ladies went down to Rome—Georgina was in wonderful trim—to finish the season, and here Mrs Portico became convinced that she intended to abandon her offspring. She had not driven into the country to see the nursling before leaving Genoa; she had said that she couldn't bear to see it in such a place and among such people. Mrs Portico, it must be added, had felt the force of this plea, felt it as regards a plan of her own, given up after being hotly entertained for a few hours, of devoting a day, by herself, to a visit to the big contadina. It seemed to her that if she should see the child in the sordid hands to which Georgina had consigned it, she would become still more of a participant than she was already. This young woman's blooming hardness, after they got to Rome, acted upon her like a kind of Medusa-mask. She had seen a horrible thing, she had been mixed up with it, and her motherly heart had received a mortal chill. It became more clear to her every day that, though Georgina would continue to send the infant money in considerable quantities, she had dispossessed herself of it for ever. Together with this induction a fixed idea settled in her mind—the project of taking the baby herself, of making him her own, of arranging that matter with the father. The countenance she had given Georgina up to this point was an effective pledge that she would not expose her; but she could adopt the poor little mortal without exposing her, she could say that he was a lovely baby—he was lovely, fortunately—whom she had picked up in a wretched village in Italy, a village that had been devastated by brigands. She could pretend—she could pretend; oh, yes, of course, she could pretend! Everything was imposture now, and she could go on to lie as she had begun. The falsity of the whole business sickened her; it made her so yellow that she scarcely knew herself in her glass. None the less, to rescue the child, even if she had to become falser still, would be in some measure an atonement for the treachery to which she had already surrendered herself. She began to hate Georgina, who had dragged her into such an abyss, and if it had not been for two considerations she would have insisted on their separating. One was the deference she owed to Mr and Mrs Gressie, who had reposed such a trust in her; the other was that she must keep hold of the mother till she had got possession of the infant. Meanwhile, in this forced communion, her detestation of her companion increased; Georgina came to appear to her a creature of clay and iron. She was exceedingly afraid of her, and it seemed to her now a wonder of wonders that she should ever have trusted her enough to come so far. Georgina showed no consciousness of the change in Mrs Portico, though there was, indeed, at present, not even a pretence of confidence between the two. Miss

Gressie—that was another lie to which Mrs Portico had to
lend herself—was bent on enjoying Europe, and was especially delighted with Rome. She certainly had the courage of her
undertaking, and she confessed to Mrs Portico that she had
left Raymond Benyon, and meant to continue to leave him, in
ignorance of what had taken place at Genoa. There was a
certain confidence, it must be said, in that. He was now in
Chinese waters, and she probably should not see him for
years. Mrs Portico took counsel with herself, and the result of
her cogitation was that she wrote to Mr Benyon that a
charming little boy had been born to him, and that Georgina
had put him to nurse with Italian peasants; but that, if he
would kindly consent to it, she, Mrs Portico, would bring
him up much better than that. She knew not how to address
her letter, and Georgina, even if she should know, which was
doubtful, would never tell her; so she sent the missive to the
care of the Secretary of the Navy, at Washington, with an
earnest request that it might immediately be forwarded. Such
was Mrs Portico's last effort in this strange business of
Georgina's. I relate rather a complicated fact in a very few
words when I say that the poor lady's anxieties, indignations,
repentances, preyed upon her until they fairly broke her down.
Various persons whom she knew in Rome notified her that the
air of the Seven Hills was plainly unfavourable to her; and
she had made up her mind to return to her native land when
she found that, in her depressed condition, malarial fever had
laid its hand upon her. She was unable to move, and the matter
was settled for her in the course of an illness which, happily,
was not prolonged. I have said that she was not obstinate, and
the resistance she made on the present occasion was not worthy
even of her spasmodic energy. Brain-fever made its appearance, and she died at the end of three weeks, during which
Georgina's attentions to her patient and protectress had been
unremitting. There were other Americans in Rome who, after
this sad event, extended to the bereaved young lady every

comfort and hospitality. She had no lack of opportunities for returning under a proper escort to New York. She selected, you may be sure, the best, and re-entered her father's house, where she took to plain dressing; for she sent all her pocket-money, with the utmost secrecy, to the little boy in the Genoese hills.

VIII

"WHY should he come if he doesn't like you? He is under no obligation, and he has his ship to look after. Why should he sit for an hour at a time, and why should he be so pleasant?"

"Do you think he is very pleasant?" Kate Theory asked, turning away her face from her sister. It was important that Mildred should not see how little the expression of that charming countenance corresponded with the inquiry.

This precaution was useless, however, for in a moment Mildred said, from the delicately draped couch on which she lay at the open window, "Kate Theory, don't be affected."

"Perhaps it's for you he comes. I don't see why he shouldn't; you are far more attractive than I, and you have a great deal more to say. How can he help seeing that you are the cleverest of the clever? You can talk to him of everything: of the dates of the different eruptions, of the statues and bronzes in the museum, which you have never seen, *poverina*, but which you know more about than he does, than any one does. What was it you began on last time? Oh yes, you poured forth floods about Magna Græcia. And then—and then——"

But with this Kate Theory paused; she felt it wouldn't do to speak the words that had risen to her lips. That her sister was as beautiful as a saint, and as delicate and refined as an angel—she had been on the point of saying something of that sort. But Mildred's beauty and delicacy were the fairness of

mortal disease, and to praise her for her refinement was just
to remind her that she had the tenuity of a consumptive. So,
after she had checked herself, the younger girl—she was
younger only by a year or two—simply kissed her tenderly
and settled the knot of the lace handkerchief that was tied
over her head. Mildred knew what she had been going to say,
knew why she had stopped. Mildred knew everything, without ever leaving her room, or leaving, at least, that little *salon*
of their own, at the pension, which she had made so pretty
by simply lying there, at the window that had the view of the
bay and of Vesuvius, and telling Kate how to arrange and how
to rearrange everything. Since it began to be plain that
Mildred must spend her small remnant of years altogether in
warm climates, the lot of the two sisters had been cast in the
ungarnished hostelries of southern Europe. Their little sitting-
room was sure to be very ugly, and Mildred was never happy
till it was remodelled. Her sister fell to work, as a matter of
course, the first day, and changed the place of all the tables,
sofas, chairs, till every combination had been tried and the
invalid thought at last that there was a little effect.

Kate Theory had a taste of her own, and her ideas were not
always the same as her sister's; but she did whatever Mildred
liked, and if the poor girl had told her to put the door-mat on
the dining-table, or the clock under the sofa, she would have
obeyed without a murmur. Her own ideas, her personal tastes,
had been folded up and put away, like garments out of season,
in drawers and trunks, with camphor and lavender. They
were not, as a general thing, for southern wear, however
indispensable to comfort in the climate of New England,
where poor Mildred had lost her health. Kate Theory, ever
since this event, had lived for her companion, and it was
almost an inconvenience for her to think that she was attractive to Captain Benyon. It was as if she had shut up her house
and was not in a position to entertain. So long as Mildred
should live, her own life was suspended; if there should be

any time afterwards, perhaps she would take it up again; but for the present, in answer to any knock at her door, she could only call down from one of her dusty windows that she was not at home. Was it really in these terms she should have to dismiss Captain Benyon? If Mildred said it was for her he came she must perhaps take upon herself such a duty; for, as we have seen, Mildred knew everything, and she must therefore be right. She knew about the statues in the museum, about the excavations at Pompeii, about the antique splendour of Magna Græcia. She always had some instructive volume on the table beside her sofa, and she had strength enough to hold the book for half-an-hour at a time. That was about the only strength she had now. The Neapolitan winter had been re-markably soft, but after the first month or two she had been obliged to give up her little walks in the garden. It lay beneath her window like a single enormous bouquet; as early as May, that year, the flowers were so dense. None of them, however, had a colour so intense as the splendid blue of the bay, which filled up all the rest of the view. It would have looked painted if you had not been able to see the little movement of the waves. Mildred Theory watched them by the hour, and the breathing crest of the volcano, on the other side of Naples, and the great sea-vision of Capri, on the horizon, changing its tint while her eyes rested there, and wondered what would become of her sister after she was gone. Now that Percival was married—he was their only brother, and from one day to the other was to come down to Naples to show them his new wife, as yet a complete stranger, or revealed only in the few letters she had written them during her wedding-tour —now that Percival was to be quite taken up, poor Kate's situation would be much more grave. Mildred felt that she should be able to judge better after she should have seen her sister-in-law how much of a home Kate might expect to find with the pair; but even if Agnes should prove—well, more satisfactory than her letters, it was a wretched prospect for

Kate—this living as a mere appendage to happier people. Maiden-aunts were very well, but being a maiden-aunt was only a last resource, and Kate's first resources had not even been tried.

Meanwhile the latter young lady wondered as well, wondered in what book Mildred had read that Captain Benyon was in love with her. She admired him, she thought, but he didn't seem a man that would fall in love with one like that. She could see that he was on his guard: he wouldn't throw himself away. He thought too much of himself, or at any rate he took too good care of himself, in the manner of a man to whom something had happened which had given him a lesson. Of course what had happened was that his heart was buried somewhere, in some woman's grave; he had loved some beautiful girl—much more beautiful, Kate was sure, than she, who thought herself meagre and dusky—and the maiden had died, and his capacity to love had died with her. He loved her memory; that was the only thing he would care for now. He was quiet, gentle, clever, humorous, and very kind in his manner; but if any one save Mildred had said to her that if he came three times a week to Posilippo, it was for anything but to pass his time (he had told them he didn't know another lady in Naples), she would have felt that this was simply the kind of thing—usually so idiotic—that people always thought it necessary to say. It was very easy for him to come; he had the big ship's boat, with nothing else to do; and what could be more delightful than to be rowed across the bay, under a bright awning, by four brown sailors with *Louisiana* in blue letters on their immaculate white shirts and in gilt letters on their fluttering hat-ribbons? The boat came to the steps of the garden of the pension, where the orange-trees hung over and made vague yellow balls shine back out of the water. Kate Theory knew all about that, for Captain Benyon had persuaded her to take a turn in the boat, and if they had only had another lady to go with them he could have conveyed her to the ship and shown her all over it. It looked beautiful, just a little way off, with the American flag hanging loose in the Italian air. They would have another lady when Agnes should arrive; then Percival would remain with Mildred while they took this excursion. Mildred had stayed alone the day she went in the boat; she had insisted on it, and, of course it was really Mildred who had persuaded her; though now that Kate came to think of it, Captain Benyon had, in his quiet, waiting way—he turned out to be waiting long after you thought he had let a thing pass—said a good deal about the pleasure it would give him. Of course, everything would give pleasure to a man who was so bored. He was keeping the *Louisiana* at Naples, week after week, simply because these were the commodore's orders. There was no work to be done there, and his time was on his hands; but of course the commodore, who had gone to Constantinople with the two other ships, had to be obeyed to the letter, however mysterious his motives. It made no difference that he was a fantastic, grumbling, arbitrary old commodore; only a good while afterwards it occurred to Kate Theory that, for a reserved, correct man, Captain Benyon had given her a considerable proof of confidence in speaking to her in these terms of his superior officer. If he looked at all hot when he arrived at the pension she offered him a glass of cold "orangeade." Mildred thought this an unpleasant drink—she called it messy; but Kate adored it and Captain Benyon always accepted it.

IX

THE day I speak of, to change the subject, she called her sister's attention to the extraordinary sharpness of a zigzaging cloud-shadow on the tinted slope of Vesuvius; but Mildred remarked in answer only that she wished her sister would marry

the Captain. It was in this familiar way that constant medi-
tation led Miss Theory to speak of him; it shows how constantly she thought of him, for, in general, no one was more
ceremonious than she, and the failure of her health had not
caused her to relax any form that it was possible to keep up.
There was a kind of slim erectness even in the way she lay
on her sofa; and she always received the doctor as if he were
calling for the first time.

"I had better wait till he asks me," Kate Theory said.
"Dear Milly, if I were to do some of the things you wish
me to do, I should shock you very much."

"I wish he would marry you, then. You know there is very
little time, if I wish to see it."

"You will never see it, Mildred. I don't see why you should
take so for granted that I would accept him."

"You will never meet a man who has so few disagreeable
qualities. He is probably not very well off. I don't know what
is the pay of a captain in the navy——"

"It's a relief to find there is something you don't know,"
Kate Theory broke in.

"But when I am gone," her sister went on, calmly, "when
I am gone there will be plenty for both of you."

The younger girl, at this, was silent for a moment; then
she exclaimed, "Mildred, you may be out of health, but I don't
see why you should be dreadful!"

"You know that since we have been leading this life we
have seen no one we liked better," said Milly. When she spoke of
the life they were leading—there was always a soft resignation
of regret and contempt in the allusion—she meant the southern
winters, the foreign climates, the vain experiments, the lonely
waitings, the wasted hours, the interminable rains, the bad
food, the pottering, humbugging doctors, the damp pensions,
the chance encounters, the fitful apparitions of fellow-travellers.

"Why shouldn't you speak for yourself alone? I am glad you
like him, Mildred."

"If you don't like him, why do you give him orange-ade?"

At this inquiry Kate began to laugh, and her sister continued—

"Of course you are glad I like him, my dear. If I didn't like him, and you did, it wouldn't be satisfactory at all. I can imagine nothing more miserable; I shouldn't die in any sort of comfort."

Kate Theory usually checked this sort of allusion—she was always too late—with a kiss; but on this occasion she added that it was a long time since Mildred had tormented her so much as she had done to-day. "You will make me hate him," she added.

"Well, that proves you don't already," Milly rejoined; and it happened that almost at this moment they saw, in the golden afternoon, Captain Benyon's boat approaching the steps at the end of the garden. He came that day, and he came two days later, and he came yet once again after an interval equally brief, before Percival Theory arrived with Mrs Theory from Rome. He seemed anxious to crowd into these few days, as he would have said, a good deal of intercourse with the two remarkably nice girls—or nice women, he hardly knew which to call them—whom in the course of a long, idle, rather tedious detention at Naples, he had discovered in the lovely suburb of Posilippo. It was the American consul who had put him into relation with them. The sisters had had to sign in the consul's presence some law-papers, transmitted to them by the man of business who looked after their little property in America, and the kindly functionary, taking advantage of the pretext (Captain Benyon happened to come into the consulate as he was starting, indulgently, to wait upon the ladies) to bring together "two parties" who, as he said, ought to appreciate each other, proposed to his fellow-officer in the service of the United States that he should go with him as witness of the little ceremony. He might, of course, take

his clerk, but the Captain would do much better; and he represented to Benyon that the Miss Theorys (singular name,
wasn't it?) suffered, he was sure, from a lack of society; also
that one of them was very sick, that they were real pleasant
and extraordinarily refined, and that the sight of a compatriot
literally draped, as it were, in the national banner would
cheer them up more than most anything, and give them a sense
of protection. They had talked to the consul about Benyon's
ship, which they could see from their windows, in the distance,
at its anchorage. They were the only American ladies then at
Naples—the only residents, at least—and the Captain wouldn't
be doing the polite thing unless he went to pay them his
respects. Benyon felt afresh how little it was in his line to call
upon strange women; he was not in the habit of hunting up
female acquaintance, or of looking out for the particular emotions which the sex only can inspire. He had his reasons for this
abstention, and he seldom relaxed it; but the consul appealed
to him on rather strong grounds. And he suffered himself to
be persuaded. He was far from regretting, during the first
weeks at least, an act which was distinctly inconsistent with
his great rule—that of never exposing himself to the danger of
becoming entangled with an unmarried woman. He had been
obliged to make this rule, and had adhered to it with some
success. He was fond of women, but he was forced to restrict
himself to superficial sentiments. There was no use tumbling
into situations from which the only possible issue was a
retreat. The step he had taken with regard to poor Miss
Theory and her delightful little sister was an exception on
which at first he could only congratulate himself. That had
been a happy idea of the ruminating old consul; it made
Captain Benyon forgive him his hat, his boots, his shirt-front
—a costume which might be considered representative, and the
effect of which was to make the observer turn with rapture
to a half-naked lazzarone. On either side the acquaintance had
helped the time to pass, and the hours he spent at the little

pension at Posilippo left a sweet, and by no means innutritive, taste behind.

As the weeks went by his exception had grown to look a good deal like a rule; but he was able to remind himself that the path of retreat was always open to him. Moreover, if he should fall in love with the younger girl there would be no great harm, for Kate Theory was in love with her sister, and it would matter very little to her whether he advanced or retreated. She was very attractive, or rather she was very attracting. Small, pale, attentive without rigidity, full of pretty curves and quick movements, she looked as if the habit of watching and serving had taken complete possession of her, and was literally a little sister of charity. Her thick black hair was pushed behind her ears, as if to help her to listen, and her clear brown eyes had the smile of a person too full of tact to carry a sad face to a sick-bed. She spoke in an encouraging voice, and had soothing and unselfish habits. She was very pretty, producing a cheerful effect of contrasted black and white, and dressed herself daintily, so that Mildred might have something agreeable to look at. Benyon very soon perceived that there was a fund of good service in her. Her sister had it all now; but poor Miss Theory was fading fast, and then what would become of this precious little force? The answer to such a question that seemed most to the point was that it was none of his business. He was not sick—at least not physically —and he was not looking out for a nurse. Such a companion might be a luxury, but was not, as yet, a necessity. The welcome of the two ladies, at first, had been simple, and he scarcely knew what to call it but sweet; a bright, gentle, jocular friendliness remained the tone of their intercourse. They evidently liked him to come; they liked to see his big transatlantic ship hover about those gleaming coasts of exile. The fact of Miss Mildred being always stretched on her couch —in his successive visits to foreign waters Benyon had not un-learned (as why should he?) the pleasant American habit of using the lady's personal name—made their intimacy seem greater, their differences less; it was as if his hostesses had taken him into their confidence and he had been—as the consul would have said—of the same party. Knocking about the salt parts of the globe, with a few feet square on a rolling frigate for his only home, the pretty flower-decked sitting-room of the quiet American sisters became, more than any-thing he had hitherto known, his interior. He had dreamed once of having an interior, but the dream had vanished in lurid smoke, and no such vision had come to him again. He had a feeling that the end of this was drawing nigh; he was sure that the advent of the strange brother, whose wife was certain to be disagreeable, would make a difference. That is why, as I have said, he came as often as possible the last week, after he had learned the day on which Percival Theory would arrive. The limits of the exception had been reached.

He had been new to the young ladies at Posilippo, and there was no reason why they should say to each other that he was a very different man from the ingenuous youth who, ten years before, used to wander with Georgina Gressie down vistas of plank-fences brushed over with advertisements of quack medicines. It was natural he should be, and we, who know him, would have found that he had traversed the whole scale of alteration. There was nothing ingenuous in him now; he had the look of experience, of having been seasoned and hardened by the years. His face, his complexion, were the same; still smooth-shaven and slim, he always passed, at first, for a decidedly youthful mariner. But his expression was old, and his talk was older still—the talk of a man who had seen much of the world (as indeed he had to-day) and judged most things for himself, with a humorous scepticism which, what-ever concessions it might make, superficially, for the sake of not offending, for instance, two remarkably nice American women who had kept most of their illusions, left you with the conviction that the next minute it would go quickly back to its own stand-point. There was a curious contradiction in him; he struck you as serious, and yet he could not be said to take things seriously. This was what made Kate Theory feel so sure that he had lost the object of his affections; and she said to herself that it must have been under circumstances of peculiar sadness, for that was, after all, a frequent accident, and was not usually thought, in itself, a sufficient stroke to make a man a cynic. This reflection, it may be added, was, on the young lady's part, just the least bit acrimonious. Captain Benyon was not a cynic in any sense in which he might have shocked an innocent mind; he kept his cynicism to himself, and was a very clever, courteous, attentive gentleman. If he was melancholy, you knew it chiefly by his jokes, for they were usually at his own expense; and if he was indifferent, it was all the more to his credit that he should have exerted himself to entertain his countrywomen.

X

THE last time he called before the arrival of the expected brother he found Miss Theory alone, and sitting up, for a wonder, at her window. Kate had driven into Naples to give orders at the hotel for the reception of the travellers, who required accommodation more spacious than the villa at Posilippo (where the two sisters had the best rooms) could offer them; and the sick girl had taken advantage of her absence, and of the pretext afforded by a day of delicious warmth, to transfer herself for the first time in six months to an arm-chair. She was practising, as she said, for the long carriage-journey to the north, where, in a quiet corner they knew of, on the Lago Maggiore, her summer was to be spent. Raymond Benyon remarked to her that she had evidently turned the corner and was going to get well, and this gave her a chance to say various things that were in her mind. She had various things on her mind, poor Mildred Theory, so caged and restless, and yet so resigned and patient as she was; with a clear, quick spirit, in the most perfect health, ever reaching forward, to the end of its tense little chain, from her wasted and suffering body; and, in the course of the perfect summer afternoon, as she sat there, exhilarated by the success of her effort to get up and by her comfortable opportunity, she took her friendly visitor into the confidence of most of her anxieties. She told him, very promptly and positively, that she was not going to get well at all, that she had probably not more than a twelvemonth yet to live, and that he would oblige her very much by not forcing her to waste any more breath in contradicting him on that head. Of course she couldn't talk much; therefore she wished to say to him only things that he would not hear from any one else. Such for instance was her present secret—Katie's and hers—the secret of their fearing so much that they shouldn't like Percival's wife, who was not from Boston but from New York. Naturally, that by itself would be nothing, but from what they had heard of her set— this subject had been explored by their correspondents— they were rather nervous, nervous to the point of not being in the least reassured by the fact that the young lady would bring Percival a fortune. The fortune was a matter of course, for that was just what they had heard about Agnes's circle— that the stamp of money was on all their thoughts and doings. They were very rich and very new and very splashing, and evidently had very little in common with the two Miss Theorys, who, moreover, if the truth must be told (and this was a great secret), did not care much for the letters their sister-in-law had hitherto addressed them. She had been at a French boarding-school in New York, and yet (and this was the greatest secret of all) she wrote to them that she had per-formed a part of the journey through France in a "diligance"! Of course, they would see the next day; Miss Mildred was sure she should know in a moment whether Agnes would like them. She could never have told him all this if her sister had been there, and Captain Benyon must promise never to tell Kate how she had chattered. Kate thought always that they must hide everything, and that even if Agnes should be a dreadful disappointment they must never let any one guess it. And yet Kate was just the one who would suffer, in the coming years, after she herself had gone. Their brother had been everything to them, but now it would all be different. Of course it was not to be expected that he should have remained a bachelor for their sake: she only wished he had waited till she was dead and Kate was married. One of these events, it was true, was much less sure than the other; Kate might never marry, much as she wished she would. She was quite morbidly unselfish, and didn't think she had a right to have anything of her own—not even a husband.

Miss Mildred talked a good while about Kate, and it never occurred to her that she might bore Captain Benyon. She didn't, in point of fact; he had none of the trouble of wondering why this poor, sick, worried lady was trying to push her sister down his throat. Their peculiar situation made everything natural, and the tone she took with him now seemed only what their pleasant relations for the last three months led up to. Moreover, he had an excellent reason for not being bored: the fact, namely, that, after all, with regard to her sister, Miss Mildred appeared to him to keep back more than she uttered. She didn't tell him the great thing—she had nothing to say as to what that charming girl thought of Raymond Benyon. The effect of their interview, indeed, was to make him shrink from knowing, and he felt that the right thing for him would be to get back into his boat, which was waiting at the garden-steps, before Kate Theory should return from Naples. It came over him, as he sat there, that he was far too interested in knowing what this young lady thought of him. She might think what she pleased; it could make no difference to him. The best opinion in the world—if it looked out at him from her tender eyes—would not make him a whit more free or more happy. Women of that sort were not for him, women whom one could not see familiarly without falling in love with them, and whom it was no use to fall in love with unless one was ready to marry them. The light of the summer-afternoon, and of Miss Mildred's pure spirit, seemed suddenly to flood the whole subject. He saw that he was in danger, and he had long since made up his mind that from this particular peril it was not only necessary but honourable to flee. He took leave of his hostess before her sister reappeared, and had the courage even to say to her that he should not come back often after that; they would be so much occupied by their brother and his wife! As he moved across the glassy bay, to the rhythm of the oars, he wished either that the sisters would leave Naples or that his confounded commodore would send for him.

When Kate returned from her errand, ten minutes later, Milly told her of the Captain's visit, and added that she had never seen anything so sudden as the way he left her. "He wouldn't wait for you, my dear, and he said he thought it more than likely that he should never see us again. It is as if he thought you were going to die too!"

"Is his ship called away?" Kate Theory asked.

"He didn't tell me so; he said we should be so busy with Percival and Agnes."

"He has got tired of us; that is all. There is nothing wonderful in that; I knew he would."

Mildred said nothing for a moment; she was watching her sister, who was very attentively arranging some flowers. "Yes, of course, we are very dull, and he is like everybody else."

"I thought you thought he was so wonderful," said Kate—"and so fond of us."

"So he is; I am surer of that than ever. That's why he went away so abruptly."

Kate looked at her sister now. "I don't understand."

"Neither do I, *cara*. But you will, one of these days."

"How, if he never comes back?"

"Oh, he will—after a while—when I am gone. Then he will explain; that, at least, is clear to me."

"My poor precious, as if I cared!" Kate Theory exclaimed, smiling as she distributed her flowers. She carried them to the window, to place them near her sister, and here she paused a moment, her eye caught by an object, far out in the bay, with which she was not unfamiliar. Mildred noticed its momentary look, and followed its direction.

"It's the Captain's gig going back to the ship," Milly said. "It's so still one can almost hear the oars."

Kate Theory turned away, with a sudden, strange violence, a movement and exclamation which, the very next minute, as she became conscious of what she had said—and, still more, of what she felt—smote her own heart (as it flushed her face) with surprise and with the force of a revelation. "I wish it would sink him to the bottom of the sea!"

Her sister stared, then caught her by the dress, as she passed from her, drawing her back with a weak hand. "Oh, my darling dear!" And she drew Kate down and down toward her, so that the girl had nothing for it but to sink on her knees and bury her face in Mildred's lap. If that ingenious invalid did not know everything now, she knew a great deal.

XI

MRS PERCIVAL proved very pretty; it is more gracious to begin with this declaration, instead of saying, in the first place, that she proved very vapid. It took a long day to arrive at the end of her silliness, and the two ladies at Posilippo, even after a week had passed, suspected that they had only skirted its edges. Kate Theory had not spent half an hour in her company before she gave a little private sigh of relief; she felt that a situation which had promised to be embarrassing was now quite clear, was even of a primitive simplicity. She would spend with her sister-in-law, in the coming time, one week in the year; that was all that would be mortally possible. It was a blessing that one could see exactly what she was, for in that way the question settled itself. It would have been much more tiresome if Agnes had been a little less obvious; then one would have had to hesitate and consider and weigh one thing against another. She was pretty and silly, as distinctly as an orange is yellow and round; and Kate Theory would as soon have thought of looking to her to give interest to the future as she would have thought of looking to an orange to impart solidity to the prospect of dinner. Mrs Percival travelled in the hope of meeting her American acquaintance, or of making acquaintance with such Americans as she did meet, and for the purpose of buying mementos for her relations. She was perpetually adding to her store of articles in tortoise-shell, in mother-of-pearl, in olive-wood, in ivory, in filigree, in tartan lacquer, in mosaic; and she had a collection of Roman scarfs and Venetian beads which she looked over exhaustively every night before she went to bed. Her conversation bore mainly upon the manner in which she intended to dispose of these accumulations. She was constantly changing about, among each other, the persons to whom they were respectively to be offered. At Rome one of the first things she said to her husband after entering the Coliseum had been, "I guess I will give the ivory work-box to Bessie and the Roman pearls to Aunt Harriet!" She was always hanging over the travellers' book at the hotel; she had it brought up to her, with a cup of chocolate, as soon as she arrived. She searched its pages for the magical name of New York, and she indulged in infinite conjecture as to who the people were—the name was sometimes only a partial cue—who had inscribed it there. What she most missed in Europe, and what she most enjoyed, was the New Yorkers; when she met them she talked about the people in their native city who had "moved" and the streets they had moved to. "Oh yes, the Drapers are going up town, to Twenty-fourth Street, and the Vanderdeckens are going to be in Twenty-third Street, right back of them. My uncle, Mr Henry Platt, thinks of building round there." Mrs Percival Theory was capable of repeating statements like these thirty times over—of lingering on them for hours. She talked largely of herself, of her uncles and aunts, of her clothes—past, present and future. These articles, in especial, filled her horizon; she considered them with a complacency which might have led you to suppose that she had invented the custom of draping the human form. Her main point of contact with Naples was the purchase of coral; and all the while she was there the word "set"—she used it as if every one would understand—fell with its little flat, common sound upon the ears of her sisters-in-law, who had no sets of anything. She cared little for pictures and mountains; Alps and Apennines were not productive of New Yorkers, and it was difficult to take an interest in Madonnas who flourished at periods when apparently there were no fashions, or at any rate no trimmings.

I speak here not only of the impression she made upon her husband's anxious sisters, but of the judgment passed on her (he went so far as that, though it was not obvious how it mattered to him) by Raymond Benyon. And this brings me at a jump (I confess it's a very small one) to the fact that he did, after all, go back to Posilippo. He stayed away for nine days, and at the end of this time Percival Theory called upon him to thank him for the civility he had shown his kinswomen. He went to this gentleman's hotel, to return his visit, and there he found Miss Kate, in her brother's sitting-room. She had come in by appointment from the villa, and was going with the others to look at the royal palace, which she had not yet had an opportunity to inspect. It was proposed (not by Kate), and presently arranged, that Captain Benyon should go with them; and he accordingly walked over marble floors for half an hour, exchanging conscious commonplaces with the woman he loved. For this truth had rounded itself during those nine days of absence; he discovered that there was nothing particularly sweet in his life when once Kate Theory had been excluded from it. He had stayed away to keep himself from falling in love with her; but this expedient was in itself illuminating, for he perceived that, according to the vulgar adage, he was locking the stable-door after the horse had been stolen. As he paced the deck of his ship and looked toward Posilippo his tenderness crystallised; the thick, smoky flame of a sentiment that knew itself forbidden, and was angry at the knowledge, now danced upon the fuel of his good resolutions. The latter, it must be said, resisted, declined to be consumed. He determined that he would see Kate Theory again, for a time just sufficient to bid her good-bye and to add a little explanation. He thought of his explanation very lovingly, but it may not strike the reader as a happy inspiration. To part from her dryly, abruptly, without an allusion to what he might have said if everything had been different—that would be wisdom, of course, that would be virtue, that would be the line of a practical man, of a man who kept himself well in hand. But it would be virtue terribly unrewarded—it would be virtue too austere even for a person who flattered himself that he had taught himself stoicism. The minor luxury tempted him irresistibly, since the larger—that of happy love—was denied him; the luxury of letting the girl know that it would not be an accident—oh, not at all—that they should never meet again. She might easily think it was, and thinking it was would doubtless do her no harm. But this wouldn't give him his pleasure—the platonic satisfaction of expressing to her at the same time his belief that they might have made each other happy and the necessity of his renunciation. That, probably, wouldn't hurt her either, for she had given him no proof whatever that she cared for him. The nearest approach to it was the way she walked beside him now, sweet and silent, without the least reference to his not having come back to the villa. The place was cool and dusky, the blinds were drawn to keep out the light and noise, and the little party wandered through the high saloons, where precious marbles and the gleam of gilding and satin made reflections in the rich dimness. Here and there the cicerone, in slippers, with Neapolitan familiarity, threw open a shutter to show off a picture or a tapestry. He strolled in front with Percival Theory and his wife, while this lady, drooping silently from her husband's arm as they passed, felt the stuff of the curtains and the sofas. When he caught her in these experiments the cicerone, in expressive deprecation, clasped his hands and lifted his eyebrows; whereupon Mrs Theory exclaimed to her husband, "Oh, bother his old king!" It was not striking to Captain Benyon why Percival Theory had married the niece of Mr Henry Platt. He was less interesting than his sisters—a smooth, cool, correct young man, who frequently took out a pencil and did a little arithmetic on the back of a letter. He sometimes, in spite of his correctness, chewed a toothpick, and he missed the American papers, which he used to ask for in the most unlikely places. He was a Bostonian converted to New York; a very special type.

"Is it settled when you leave Naples?" Benyon asked of Kate Theory.

"I think so; on the twenty-fourth. My brother has been very kind; he has lent us his carriage, which is a large one, so that Mildred can lie down. He and Agnes will take another; but of course we shall travel together."

"I wish to heaven I were going with you!" Captain Benyon said. He had given her the opportunity to respond, but she did not take it; she merely remarked, with a vague laugh, that of course he couldn't take his ship over the Apennines.

"Yes, there is always my ship," he went on. "I am afraid that in future it will carry me far away from you."

They were alone in one of the royal apartments; their companions had passed, in advance of them, into the adjoining room. Benyon and his fellow-visitor had paused beneath one of the immense chandeliers of glass, which in the clear, coloured gloom, through which one felt the strong outer light of Italy beating in, suspended its twinkling drops from the decorated vault. They looked round them confusedly, made shy for the moment by Benyon's having struck a note more serious than any that had hitherto sounded between them, looked at the sparse furniture, draped in white overalls, at the scagliola floor, in which the great cluster of crystal pendants seemed to shine again.

"You are master of your ship—can't you sail it as you like?" Kate Theory asked, with a smile.

"I am not master of anything. There is not a man in the world less free. I am a slave. I am a victim."

She looked at him with kind eyes; something in his voice suddenly made her put away all thought of the defensive airs that a girl, in certain situations, is expected to assume. She perceived that he wanted to make her understand something, and now her only wish was to help him to say it. "You are not happy," she murmured simply, her voice dying away in a kind of wonderment at this reality.

The gentle touch of her words—it was as if her hand had stroked his cheek—seemed to him the sweetest thing he had ever known. "No, I am not happy, because I am not free. If I were—if I were, I would give up my ship, I would give up everything, to follow you. I can't explain; that is part of the hardness of it. I only want you to know it, that if certain things were different, if everything was different, I might tell you that I believe I should have a right to speak to you. Perhaps some day it will change; but probably then it will be too late. Meanwhile, I have no right of any kind. I don't want to trouble you, and I don't ask of you—anything! It is only to have spoken just once. I don't make you understand, of course. I am afraid I seem to you rather a brute, perhaps even a humbug. Don't think of it now; don't try to understand. But some day, in the future, remember what I have said to you, and how we stood here, in this strange old place, alone! Perhaps it will give you a little pleasure."

Kate Theory began by listening to him with visible eagerness; but in a moment she turned away her eyes. "I am very sorry for you," she said, gravely.

"Then you do understand enough?"

"I shall think of what you have said—in the future."

Benyon's lips formed the beginning of a word of tenderness, which he instantly suppressed; and in a different tone, with a bitter smile and a sad shake of the head, raising his arms a moment and letting them fall, he rejoined, "It won't hurt any one, your remembering this!"

"I don't know whom you mean." And the girl, abruptly, began to walk to the end of the room. He made no attempt to tell her whom he meant, and they proceeded together in silence till they overtook their companions.

XII

THERE were several pictures in the neighbouring room, and Percival Theory and his wife had stopped to look at one of them, of which the cicerone announced the title and the authorship as Benyon came up. It was a modern portrait of a Bourbon princess, a woman young, fair, handsome, covered with jewels. Mrs Percival appeared to be more struck with it than with anything the palace had yet offered to her sight, while her sister-in-law walked to the window, which the custodian had opened, to look out into the garden. Benyon noticed this; he was conscious that he had given the girl something to reflect upon, and his ears burned a little as he stood beside Mrs Percival and looked up, mechanically, at the royal lady. He already repented a little of what he had said; for, after all, what was the use? And he hoped the others wouldn't observe that he had been making love.

"Gracious, Percival! Do you see who she looks like?" Mrs Theory said to her husband.

"She looks like a lady who has a big bill at Tiffany's," this gentleman answered.

"She looks like my sister-in-law; the eyes, the mouth, the way the hair's done—the whole thing."

"Which do you mean? You have got about a dozen."

"Why, Georgina, of course—Georgina Roy. She's awfully like."

"Do you call her your sister-in-law?" Percival Theory asked. "You must want very much to claim her."

"Well, she's handsome enough. You have got to invent some new name, then. Captain Benyon, what do you call your brother-in-law's second wife?" Mrs Percival continued, turning to her neighbour, who still stood staring at the portrait. At first he had looked without seeing; then sight, and hearing as well, became quick. They were suddenly peopled with thrilling recognitions. The Bourbon princess—the eyes, the mouth, the way the hair was done, these things took on an identity, and the gaze of the painted face seemed to fasten itself to his own. But who in the world was Georgina Roy, and what was this talk about sisters-in-law? He turned to the little lady at his side a countenance unexpectedly puzzled by the problem she had lightly presented to him.

"Your brother-in-law's second wife? That's rather complicated."

"Well, of course, he needn't have married again," said Mrs Percival, with a small sigh.

"Whom did he marry?" asked Benyon, staring. Percival

Theory had turned away. "Oh, if you are going into her relationships," he murmured, and joined his sister at the brilliant window, through which, from the distance, the many-voiced uproar of Naples came in.

"He married first my sister Cora, and she died five years ago. Then he married *her;*" and Mrs Percival nodded at the princess.

Benyon's eyes went back to the portrait; he could see what she meant—it stared out at him. "Her? Georgina?"

"Georgina Gressie! Gracious, do you know her?"

It was very distinct—that answer of Mrs Percival's, and the question that followed it as well. But he had the resource of the picture; he could look at it, seem to take it very seriously, though it danced up and down before him. He felt that he was turning red, then he felt that he was turning pale. "The brazen impudence!" That was the way he could speak to himself now of the woman he had once loved, and whom he afterwards hated, till this had died out too. Then the wonder of it was lost in the quickly growing sense that it would make a difference for him—a great difference. Exactly what, he didn't see yet; only a difference that swelled and swelled as he thought of it, and caught up, in its expansion, the girl who stood behind him so quietly, looking into the Italian garden.

The custodian drew Mrs Percival away to show her another princess, before Benyon answered her last inquiry. This gave him time to recover from his first impulse, which had been to answer it with a negative; he saw in a moment that an admission of his acquaintance with Mrs Roy (Mrs Roy!—it was prodigious!) was necessarily helping him to learn more. Besides, it needn't be compromising. Very likely Mrs Percival would hear one day that he had once wanted to marry her. So, when he joined his companions a minute later he remarked that he had known Miss Gressie years before, and had even admired her considerably, but had lost sight of her entirely in later days. She had been a great beauty, and it was

a wonder that she had not married earlier. Five years ago, was
it? No, it was only two. He had been going to say that in so
long a time it would have been singular he should not have
heard of it. He had been away from New York for ages; but
one always heard of marriages and deaths. This was a proof,
though two years was rather long. He led Mrs Percival insi-
diously into a further room, in advance of the others, to
whom the cicerone returned. She was delighted to talk about
her "connections," and she supplied him with every detail.
He could trust himself now; his self-possession was complete,
or, so far as it was wanting, the fault was that of a sudden
gaiety which he could not, on the spot, have accounted for.
Of course it was not very flattering to them—Mrs Percival's
own people—that poor Cora's husband should have consoled
himself; but men always did it (talk of widows!) and he had
chosen a girl who was—well, very fine-looking, and the sort
of successor to Cora that they needn't be ashamed of. She
had been awfully admired, and no one had understood why
she had waited so long to marry. She had had some affair as a
girl—an engagement to an officer in the army—and the man
had jilted her, or they had quarrelled, or something or
other. She was almost an old maid—well, she was thirty, or
very nearly—but she had done something good now. She
was handsomer than ever, and tremendously striking. William
Roy had one of the biggest incomes in the city, and he was
quite affectionate. He had been intensely fond of Cora—he
often spoke of her still, at least to her own relations; and her
portrait, the last time Mrs Percival was in his house (it was at
a party, after his marriage to Miss Gressie), was still in the
front parlour. Perhaps by this time he had had it moved to the
back; but she was sure he would keep it somewhere, anyway.
Poor Cora had had no children; but Georgina was making
that all right; she had a beautiful boy. Mrs Percival had what
she would have called quite a pleasant chat with Captain
Benyon about Mrs Roy. Perhaps *he* was the officer—she

never thought of that! He was sure he had never jilted her? And he had never quarrelled with a lady? Well, he must be different from most men.

He certainly had the air of being so before he parted that afternoon with Kate Theory. This young lady, at least, was free to think him wanting in that consistency which is supposed to be a distinctively masculine virtue. An hour before he had taken an eternal farewell of her; and now he was alluding to future meetings, to future visits, proposing that, with her sister-in-law, she should appoint an early day for coming to see the *Louisiana*. She had supposed she understood him, but it would appear now that she had not understood him at all. His manner had changed too. More and more off his guard, Raymond Benyon was not aware how much more hopeful an expression it gave him, his irresistible sense that somehow or other this extraordinary proceeding of his wife's would set him free. Kate Theory felt rather weary and mystified, all the more for knowing that henceforth Captain Benyon's variations would be the most important thing in life for her.

XIII

THAT officer, on his ship in the bay, lingered very late on the deck that night—lingered there, indeed, under the warm southern sky, in which the stars glittered with a hot, red light, until the early dawn began to show. He smoked cigar after cigar; he walked up and down by the hour; he was agitated by a thousand reflections; he repeated to himself that it made a difference—an immense difference; but the pink light had deepened in the east before he had discovered in what the change consisted. By that time he saw it clearly—it consisted in Georgina's being in his power now, in place of his being in hers. He laughed as he sat alone in the darkness at the thought of what she had done. It had occurred to him more than once that she would do it; he believed her capable of anything; but the accomplished fact had a freshness of comicality. He thought of William Roy, of his big income, of his being "quite affectionate," of his blooming son and heir, of his having found such a worthy successor to poor Mrs Cora. He wondered whether Georgina had mentioned to him that she had a husband living, but was strongly of the belief that she had not. Why should she, after all? She had neglected to mention it to so many others. He had thought he knew her, in so many years, that he had nothing more to learn about her, but this ripe stroke revived his sense of her audacity. Of course it was what she had been waiting for, and if she had not done it sooner it was because she had hoped he would be lost at sea in one of his long cruises and relieve her of the necessity of a crime. How she must hate him to-day for not having been lost, for being alive, for continuing to put her in the wrong! Much as she hated him, however, his own loathing was at least a match for hers. She had done him the foulest of wrongs—she had ravaged his life. That he should ever detest in this degree a woman whom he had once loved as he loved her he would not have thought possible in his innocent younger years. But neither would he have thought it possible then that a woman should be such a cold-blooded devil as she had been. His love had perished in his rage, his blinding, impotent rage, at finding that he had been duped and measuring his impotence. When he learned, years before, from Mrs Portico, what she had done with her baby, of whose entrance into life she herself had given him no intimation, he felt that he was face to face with a full revelation of her nature. Before that it had puzzled him, it had mocked him; his relations with her were bewildering, stupefying. But when, after obtaining, with difficulty and delay, a leave of absence from Government, and betaking himself to Italy to look for the child and assume possession of it, he had encountered absolute failure and defeat,

then the case presented itself to him more simply. He perceived that he had mated himself with a creature who just
happened to be a monster, a human exception altogether.
That was what he couldn't pardon—her conduct about
the child; never, never, never! To him she might have done
what she chose—dropped him, pushed him out into eternal
cold, with his hands fast tied—and he would have accepted it,
excused her almost, admitted that it had been his business to
mind better what he was about. But she had tortured him
through the poor little irrecoverable son whom he had never
seen, through the heart and the human vitals that she had not
herself, and that he had to have, poor wretch, for both of
them.

All his effort, for years, had been to forget those horrible
months, and he had cut himself off from them so that they
seemed at times to belong to the life of another person. But
to-night he lived them over again; he retraced the different
gradations of darkness through which he had passed, from
the moment, so soon after his extraordinary marriage, when
it came over him that she already repented and meant, if possible, to elude all her obligations. This was the moment when
he saw why she had reserved herself—in the strange vow she
extracted from him—an open door for retreat; the moment,
too, when her having had such an inspiration (in the midst of
her momentary good faith, if good faith it had ever been)
struck him as a proof of her essential depravity. What he had
tried to forget came back to him: the child that was not his
child produced for him when he fell upon that squalid nest of
peasants in the Genoese country, and then the confessions,
retractations, contradictions, lies, terrors, threats, and general
bottomless, baffling mendacity and idiocy of every one in the
place. The child was gone; that had been the only definite
thing. The woman who had taken it to nurse had a dozen
different stories, her husband had as many, and every one
in the village had a hundred more. Georgina had been sending

money—she had managed, apparently, to send a good deal—
and the whole country seemed to have been living on it and
making merry. At one moment, the baby had died and received a most expensive burial; at another, he had been entrusted (for more healthy air, Santissima Madonna!) to the
woman's cousin, in another village. According to a version
which for a day or two Benyon had inclined to think the least
false, he had been taken by the cousin (for his beauty's sake)
to Genoa, when she went for the first time in her life to the
town to see her daughter in service there, and had been confided for a few hours to a third woman, who was to keep him
while the cousin walked about the streets, but who, having
no child of her own, took such a fancy to him that she refused
to give him up, and a few days later left the place (she was a
Pisana) never to be heard of more. The cousin had forgotten
her name—it had happened six months before. Benyon spent
a year looking up and down Italy for his child, and inspecting
hundreds of swaddled infants, inscrutable candidates for recognition. Of course he could only get further and further from
real knowledge, and his search was arrested by the conviction that it was making him mad. He set his teeth and made
up his mind, or tried to, that the baby had died in the hands
of its nurse. This was, after all, much the likeliest supposition,
and the woman had maintained it, in the hope of being rewarded for her candour, quite as often as she had asseverated
that it was still somewhere, alive, in the hope of being remu-
nerated for her good news. It may be imagined with what
sentiments toward his wife Benyon had emerged from this
episode. To-night his memory went further back—back to
the beginning and to the days when he had had to ask himself,
with all the crudity of his first surprise, what in the name of
perversity she had wished to do with him. The answer to this
speculation was so old, it had dropped so out of the line of
recurrence, that it was now almost new again. Moreover, it
was only approximate, for, as I have already said, he could

comprehend such baseness as little at the end as at the beginning. She had found herself on a slope which her nature forced her to descend to the bottom. She did him the honour of wishing to enjoy his society, and she did herself the honour of thinking that their intimacy, however brief, must have a certain consecration. She felt that with him, after his promise (he would have made any promise to lead her on), she was secure, secure as she had proved to be, secure as she must think herself. That security had helped her to ask herself, after the first flush of passion was over, and her native, her twice-inherited worldliness had had time to open its eyes again, why she should keep faith with a man whose deficiencies (as a husband before the world—another affair) had been so scientifically exposed to her by her parents. So she had simply determined *not* to keep faith; and her determination, at least, she did keep.

By the time Benyon turned in he had satisfied himself, as I say, that Georgina was now in his power; and this seemed to him such an improvement in his situation that he allowed himself, for the next ten days, a license which made Kate Theory almost as happy as it made her sister, though she pretended to understand it far less. Mildred sank to her rest, or rose to fuller comprehensions, within the year, in the Isle of Wight; and Captain Benyon, who had never written so many letters as since they left Naples, sailed westward about the same time as the sweet survivor. For the *Louisiana* at last was ordered home.

XIV

CERTAINLY, I will see you if you come, and you may appoint any day or hour you like. I should have seen you with pleasure any time these last years. Why should we not be friends, as we used to be? Perhaps we shall be yet. I say "perhaps" only, on purpose, because your note is rather vague about your state of mind. Don't come with any idea about making me nervous or uncomfortable. I am not nervous by nature, thank heaven, and I won't, I positively won't (do you hear, dear Captain Benyon?) be uncomfortable. I have been so (it served me right) for years and years; but I am very happy now. To remain so is the very definite intention of yours ever

GEORGINA ROY.

This was the answer Benyon received to a short letter that he despatched to Mrs Roy after his return to America. It was not till he had been there some weeks that he wrote to her. He had been occupied in various ways: he had had to look after his ship; he had had to report at Washington; he had spent a fortnight with his mother at Portsmouth, N. H.; and he had paid a visit to Kate Theory in Boston. She herself was paying visits; she was staying with various relatives and friends. She had more colour—it was very delicately rosy— than she had had of old, in spite of her black dress; and the effect of her looking at him seemed to him to make her eyes grow still prettier. Though sisterless now, she was not without duties, and Benyon could easily see that life would press hard on her unless some one should interfere. Every one regarded her as just the person to do certain things. Every one thought she could do everything, because she had nothing else to do. She used to read to the blind, and, more onerously, to the deaf. She looked after other people's children while the parents attended anti-slavery conventions.

She was coming to New York, later, to spend a week at her brother's, but beyond this she had no idea what she should do. Benyon felt it to be awkward that he should not be able just now to tell her; and this had much to do with his coming to the point, for he accused himself of having rather hung fire. Coming to the point, for Benyon, meant writing a note to Mrs Roy (as he must call her), in which he asked whether she would see him if he should present himself. The missive was short; it contained, in addition to what I have hinted, little more than the remark that he had something of importance to say to her. Her reply, which we have just read, was prompt. Benyon designated an hour, and rang the door-bell of her big modern house, whose polished windows seemed to shine defiance at him.

As he stood on the steps, looking up and down the straight vista of the Fifth Avenue, he perceived that he was trembling a little, that he was nervous, if she were not. He was ashamed of his agitation, and he pulled himself vigorously together. Afterwards he saw that what had made him nervous was not any doubt of the goodness of his cause, but his revived sense (as he drew near her) of his wife's hardness, her capacity for insolence. He might only break himself against that, and the prospect made him feel helpless. She kept him waiting for a long time after he had been introduced; and as he walked up and down her drawing-room, an immense, florid, expensive apartment, covered with blue satin, gilding, mirrors and bad frescoes, it came over him as a certainty that her delay was calculated. She wished to annoy him, to weary him; she was as ungenerous as she was unscrupulous. It never occurred to him that, in spite of the bold words of her note, she, too, might be in a tremor, and if any one in their secret had suggested that she was afraid to meet him, he would have laughed at this idea. This was of bad omen for the success of his errand; for it showed that he recognised the ground of her presumption—his having the superstition of old promises. By the time she appeared he was flushed, very angry. She closed the door behind her, and stood there looking at him, with the width of the room between them.

The first emotion her presence excited was a quick sense of the strange fact that, after all these years of loneliness, such a magnificent person should be his wife. For she was mag-nificent, in the maturity of her beauty, her head erect, her complexion splendid, her auburn tresses undimmed, a certain plenitude in her very glance. He saw in a moment that she wished to seem to him beautiful, she had endeavoured to dress herself to the best effect. Perhaps, after all, it was only for this she had delayed; she wished to give herself every possible touch. For some moments they said nothing; they had not stood face to face for nearly ten years, and they met now as adversaries. No two persons could possibly be more interested in taking each other's measure. It scarcely belonged to Georgina, however, to have too much the air of timidity, and after a moment, satisfied, apparently, that she was not to receive a broadside, she advanced, slowly, rubbing her jewelled hands and smiling. He wondered why she should smile, what thought was in her mind. His impressions followed each other with extraordinary quickness of pulse, and now he saw, in addition to what he had already perceived, that she was waiting to take her cue: she had determined on no definite line. There was nothing definite about her but her courage; the rest would depend upon him. As for her courage, it seemed to glow in the beauty which grew greater as she came nearer, with her eyes on his and her fixed smile; to be expressed in the very perfume that accompanied her steps. By this time he had got a still further impression, and it was the strangest of all. She was ready for anything, she was capable of anything, she wished to surprise him with her beauty, to remind him that it belonged, after all, at the bottom of everything, to him. She was ready to bribe him, if bribing should be necessary. She had carried on an intrigue before she was twenty; it would be more, rather than less, easy for her now that she was thirty. All this and more was in her cold, living eyes, as, in the prolonged silence, they engaged themselves with his; but I must not dwell upon it, for reasons extraneous to the remarkable fact. She was a truly amazing creature.

"Raymond!" she said, in a low voice—a voice which might represent either a vague greeting or an appeal.

He took no heed of the exclamation, but asked her why she had deliberately kept him waiting, as if she had not made a fool enough of him already. She couldn't suppose it was for his pleasure he had come into the house.

She hesitated a moment, still with her smile. "I must tell you I have a son, the dearest little boy. His nurse happened to be engaged for the moment, and I had to watch him. I am more devoted to him than you might suppose."

He fell back from her a few steps. "I wonder if you are insane," he murmured.

"To allude to my child? Why do you ask me such questions then? I tell you the simple truth. I take every care of this one. I am older and wiser. The other one was a complete mistake; he had no right to exist."

"Why didn't you kill him then with your own hands, instead of that torture?"

"Why didn't I kill myself? That question would be more to the point. You are looking wonderfully well," she broke off, in another tone; "hadn't we better sit down?"

"I didn't come here for the advantage of conversation," Benyon answered. And he was going on, but she interrupted him.

"You came to say something dreadful, very likely; though I hoped you would see it was better not. But just tell me this, before you begin. Are you successful, are you happy? It has been so provoking, not knowing more about you."

There was something in the manner in which this was said that caused him to break into a loud laugh; whereupon she added—

"Your laugh is just what it used to be. How it comes back to me! You *have* improved in appearance," she continued.

She had seated herself, though he remained standing; and she leaned back in a low, deep chair, looking up at him, with her arms folded. He stood near her and over her, as it were, dropping his baffled eyes on her, with his hand resting on the corner of the chimney-piece. "Has it never occurred to you that I may deem myself absolved from the promise I made you before I married you?"

"Very often, of course. But I have instantly dismissed the idea. How can you be 'absolved'? One promises, or one doesn't. I attach no meaning to that, and neither do you." And she glanced down at the front of her dress.

Benyon listened, but he went on as if he had not heard her. "What I came to say to you is this: that I should like your consent to my bringing a suit for divorce against you."

"A suit for divorce? I never thought of that."

"So that I may marry another woman. I can easily obtain a divorce on the ground of your desertion. It will simplify our situation."

She stared a moment, then her smile solidified, as it were, and she looked grave; but he could see that her gravity, with her lifted eyebrows, was partly assumed. "Ah, you want to marry another woman!" she exclaimed, slowly, thoughtfully. He said nothing, and she went on, "Why don't you do as I have done?"

"Because I don't want my children to be——"

Before he could say the words she sprang up, checking him with a cry. "Don't say it; it isn't necessary! Of course I know what you mean; but they won't be if no one knows it."

"I should object to knowing it myself; it's enough for me to know it of yours."

"Of course I have been prepared for your saying that."

"I should hope so!" Benyon exclaimed. "You may be a bigamist, if it suits you, but to me the idea is not attractive. I wish to marry——" and, hesitating a moment, with his slight stammer, he repeated, "I wish to marry——"

"Marry, then, and have done with it!" cried Mrs Roy.

He could already see that he should be able to extract no consent from her; he felt rather sick. "It's extraordinary to me that you shouldn't be more afraid of being found out," he said, after a moment's reflection. "There are two or three possible accidents."

"How do you know how much afraid I am? I have thought of every accident, in dreadful nights. How do you know what my life is, or what it has been all these horrid years? But every one is dead."

"You look wasted and worn, certainly."

"Ah, don't compliment me!" Georgina exclaimed. "If I had never known you—if I had not been through all this—I believe I should have been handsome. When did you hear of my marriage? Where were you at the time?"

"At Naples, more than six months ago, by a mere chance."

"How strange that it should have taken you so long! Is the lady a Neapolitan? They don't mind what they do over there."

"I have no information to give you beyond what I have just said," Benyon rejoined. "My life doesn't in the least regard you."

"Ah, but it does from the moment I refuse to let you divorce me."

"You refuse?" Benyon said, softly.

"Don't look at me that way! You haven't advanced so rapidly as I used to think you would; you haven't distinguished yourself so much," she went on, irrelevantly.

"I shall be promoted commodore one of these days," Benyon answered. "You don't know much about it, for my advancement has already been extraordinary rapid." He blushed as soon as the words were out of his mouth. She gave a light laugh on seeing it; but he took up his hat and added, "Think over a day or two what I have proposed to you. It's a perfectly possible proceeding. Think of the temper in which I ask it."

"The temper?" she stared. "Pray, what have you to do with temper?" And as he made no reply, smoothing his hat with his glove, she went on, "Years ago, as much as you please! you had a good right, I don't deny, and you raved, in

your letters, to your heart's content. That's why I wouldn't
see you; I didn't wish to take it full in the face. But that's all
over now; time is a healer; you have cooled off, and by your
own admission you have consoled yourself. Why do you
talk to me about temper? What in the world have I done to
you but let you alone?"

"What do you call this business?" Benyon asked, with his
eye flashing all over the room.

"Ah, excuse me, that doesn't touch you; it's my affair. I
leave you your liberty, and I can live as I like. If I choose to
live in this way, it may be queer (I admit it is, tremendously),
but you have nothing to say to it. If I am willing to take the
risk, you may be. If I am willing to play such an infernal trick
upon a confiding gentleman (I will put it as strongly as you
possibly could), I don't see what you have to say to it except
that you are exceedingly glad such a woman as that isn't
known to be your wife!" She had been cool and deliberate
up to this time, but with these words her latent agitation broke
out. "Do you think I have been happy? Do you think I have
enjoyed existence? Do you see me freezing up into a stark
old maid?"

"I wonder you stood out so long," said Benyon.

"I wonder I did! They were bad years."

"I have no doubt they were!"

"You could do as you pleased," Georgina went on. "You
roamed about the world, you formed charming relations. I am
delighted to hear it from your own lips. Think of my going
back to my father's house—that family vault—and living
there, year after year, as Miss Gressie! If you remember my
father and mother—they are round in Twelfth Street, just
the same—you must admit that I paid for my folly!"

"I have never understood you; I don't understand you
now," said Benyon.

She looked at him a moment. "I adored you."

"I could damn you with a word!" he exclaimed.

XV

THE moment he had spoken she grasped his arm and held
up her other hand, as if she were listening to a sound outside
the room. She had evidently had an inspiration, and she
carried it into instant effect. She swept away to the door,
flung it open, and passed into the hall, whence her voice
came back to Benyon as she addressed a person who apparently
was her husband. She had heard him enter the house at his
habitual hour, after his long morning at business; the closing
of the door of the vestibule had struck her ear. The parlour
was on a level with the hall, and she greeted him without
impediment. She asked him to come in and be introduced to
Captain Benyon, and he responded with due solemnity. She
returned in advance of him, her eyes fixed upon Benyon and
lighted with defiance, her whole face saying to him vividly,
"Here is your opportunity; I give it to you with my own
hands. Break your promise and betray me if you dare! You
say you can damn me with a word; speak the word and let us
see!"

Benyon's heart beat faster, as he felt that it was indeed a
chance; but half his emotion came from the spectacle, magnificent in its way, of her unparalleled impudence. A sense of
all that he had escaped in not having had to live with her
rolled over him like a wave, while he looked strangely at Mr
Roy, to whom this privilege had been vouchsafed. He saw in
a moment his successor had a constitution that would carry it.
Mr Roy suggested squareness and solidity; he was a broad-
based, comfortable, polished man, with a surface in which
the rank tendrils of irritation would not easily obtain a foot-
hold. He had a broad, blank face, a capacious mouth, and a
small, light eye, to which, as he entered, he was engaged in

adjusting a double gold-rimmed glass. He approached Benyon
with a prudent, civil, punctual air, as if he habitually met a
good many gentlemen in the course of business, and though,
naturally, this was not that sort of occasion, he was not a
man to waste time in preliminaries. Benyon had immediately the impression of having seen him, or his equivalent,
a thousand times before. He was middle-aged, fresh-coloured,
whiskered, prosperous, indefinite. Georgina introduced them
to each other—she spoke of Benyon as an old friend, whom
she had known long before she had known Mr Roy, who had
been very kind to her years ago, when she was a girl.

"He is in the navy. He has just come back from a long
cruise."

Mr Roy shook hands—Benyon gave him his before he
knew it—said he was very happy, smiled, looked at Benyon
from head to foot, then at Georgina, then round the room,
then back at Benyon again—at Benyon, who stood there,
without sound or movement, with a dilated eye and a pulse
quickened to a degree of which Mr Roy could have little idea.
Georgina made some remark about their sitting down, but
William Roy replied that he hadn't time for that, if Captain
Benyon would excuse him. He should have to go straight into
the library and write a note to send back to his office, where,
as he just remembered, he had neglected to give, in leaving
the place, an important direction.

"You can wait a moment, surely," Georgina said. "Captain
Benyon wants so much to see you."

"Oh yes, my dear; I can wait a minute, and I can come
back."

Benyon saw, accordingly, that he was waiting, and that
Georgina was waiting too. Each was waiting for him to say
something, though they were waiting for different things. Mr
Roy put his hands behind him, balanced himself on his toes,
hoped that Captain Benyon had enjoyed his cruise—though
he shouldn't care much for the navy himself—and evidently

wondered at the vacuity of his wife's visitor. Benyon knew
he was speaking, for he indulged in two or three more observations, after which he stopped. But his meaning was not
present to our hero. This personage was conscious of only
one thing, of his own momentary power, of everything that
hung on his lips; all the rest swam before him; there was
vagueness in his ears and eyes. Mr Roy stopped, as I say,
and there was a pause, which seemed to Benyon of tremendous
length. He knew, while it lasted, that Georgina was as conscious as himself that he felt his opportunity, that he held it
there in his hand, weighing it noiselessly in the palm, and that
she braved and scorned, or rather that she enjoyed, the danger.
He asked himself whether he should be able to speak if he
were to try, and then he knew that he should not, that the
words would stick in his throat, that he should make sounds
which would dishonour his cause. There was no real choice
nor decision, then, on Benyon's part; his silence was after all
the same old silence, the fruit of other hours and places, the
stillness to which Georgina listened while he felt her eager
eyes fairly eat into his face, so that his cheeks burned with the
touch of them. The moments stood before him in their turn;
each one was distinct. "Ah, well," said Mr Roy, "perhaps I
interrupt; I will just dash off my note." Benyon knew that he
was rather bewildered, that he was making a protest, that he
was leaving the room; knew presently that Georgina again
stood before him alone.

"You are exactly the man I thought you!" she announced,
as joyously as if she had won a bet.

"You are the most horrible woman I can imagine. Good
God, if I had to live with you!" That is what he said to her in
answer.

Even at this she never flinched; she continued to smile in
triumph. "He adores me—but what's that to you? Of course
you have all the future," she went on; "but I know you as if I
had made you!"

Benyon considered a moment. "If he adores you, you are all right. If our divorce is pronounced you will be free, and then he can marry you properly, which he would like ever so much better."

"It's too touching to hear you reason about it. Fancy me telling such a hideous story—about myself—me—me!" And she touched her breasts with her white fingers.

Benyon gave her a look that was charged with all the sickness of his helpless rage. "You—you!" he repeated, as he turned away from her and passed through the door which Mr Roy had left open.

She followed him into the hall, she was close behind him; he moved before her as she pressed. "There was one more reason," she said. "I wouldn't be forbidden. It was my hideous pride. That's what prevents me now."

"I don't care what it is," Benyon answered, wearily, with his hand on the knob of the door.

She laid hers on his shoulder; he stood there an instant, feeling it, wishing that her loathsome touch gave him the right to strike her to the earth, to strike her so that she should never rise again.

"How clever you are, and intelligent always, as you used to be; to feel so perfectly and know so well—without more scenes—that it's hopeless—my ever consenting! If I have, with you, the shame of having made you promise, let me at least have the profit!"

His back had been turned to her, but at this he glanced round. "To hear you talk of shame——!"

"You don't know what I have gone through; but, of course, I don't ask any pity from you. Only I should like to say something kind to you before we part. I admire you so much. Who will ever tell her, if you don't? How will she ever know, then? She will be as safe as I am. You know what that is," said Georgina, smiling.

He had opened the door wide while she spoke, apparently

not heeding her, thinking only of getting away from her for ever. In reality he heard every word she said, and felt to his marrow the lowered, suggestive tone in which she made him that last recommendation. Outside, on the steps—she stood there in the doorway—he gave her his last look. "I only hope you will die. I shall pray for that!" And he descended into the street and took his way.

It was after this that his real temptation came. Not the temptation to return betrayal for betrayal; that passed away even in a few days, for he simply knew that he couldn't break his promise, that it imposed itself on him as stubbornly as the colour of his eyes or the stammer of his lips; it had gone forth into the world to live for itself, and was far beyond his reach or his authority. But the temptation to go through the form of a marriage with Kate Theory, to let her suppose that he was as free as herself and that their children, if they should have any, would, before the law, have a right to exist—this attractive idea held him fast for many weeks, and caused him to pass some haggard nights and days. It was perfectly possible she might never learn his secret, and that, as no one could either suspect it or have an interest in bringing it to light, they both might live and die in security and honour. This vision fascinated him; it was, I say, a real temptation. He thought of other solutions—of telling her that he was married (without telling her to whom), and inducing her to overlook such an accident and content herself with a ceremony in which the world would see no flaw. But after all the contortions of his spirit it remained as clear to him as before that dishonour was in everything but renunciation. So, at last, he renounced. He took two steps which attested this act to himself. He addressed an urgent request to the Secretary of the Navy that he might, with as little delay as possible, be despatched on another long voyage; and he returned to Boston to tell Kate Theory that they must wait. He could explain so little that, say what he would, he was aware that he could not make his conduct seem natural, and he saw that the girl only trusted him, that she never understood. She trusted without understanding, and she agreed to wait. When the writer of these pages last heard of the pair they were waiting still.

A NEW ENGLAND WINTER

I

MRS DAINTRY stood on her steps a moment, to address a parting injunction to her little domestic, whom she had induced a few days before, by earnest and friendly argument—the only coercion or persuasion this enlightened mistress was ever known to use—to crown her ruffled tresses with a cap; and then, slowly and with deliberation, she descended to the street. As soon as her back was turned, her maidservant closed the door, not with violence, but inaudibly, quickly, and firmly; so that when she reached the bottom of the steps and looked up again at the front—as she always did before leaving it, to assure herself that everything was well—the folded wings of her portal were presented to her, smooth and shining, as wings should be, and ornamented with the large silver plate on which the name of her late husband was inscribed—which she had brought with her when, taking the inevitable course of good Bostonians, she had transferred her household goods from the "hill" to the "new land," and the exhibition of which, as an act of conjugal fidelity, she preferred—how much, those who knew her could easily understand—to the more distinguished modern fashion of suppressing the domiciliary label. She stood still for a minute on the pavement, looking at the closed aperture of her dwelling and asking herself a question; not that there was anything extraordinary in that, for she never spared herself in this respect. She would greatly have preferred that her servant should not shut the door till she had reached the sidewalk and dismissed her, as it were, with that benevolent, that almost maternal, smile with which it was a part of Mrs Daintry's religion to encourage and reward her domestics. She liked to know that her door was being held open behind her until she should pass out of sight of the young woman standing in the hall. There was a want of respect in shutting her out so precipitately; it was almost like giving her a push down the steps. What Mrs Daintry asked herself was, whether she should not do right to ascend the steps again, ring the bell, and request Beatrice, the parlourmaid, to be so good as to wait a little longer. She felt that this would have been a proceeding of some importance, and she presently decided against it. There were a good many reasons, and she thought them over as she took her way slowly up Newbury Street, turning as soon as possible into Commonwealth Avenue; for she was very fond of the south side of this beautiful prospect, and the autumn sunshine to-day was delightful. During the moment that she paused, looking up at her house, she had had time to see that everything was as fresh and bright as she could desire. It looked a little too new, perhaps, and Florimond would not like that; for of course his great fondness was for the antique, which was the reason for his remaining year after year in. Europe, where, as a young painter of considerable, if not of the highest, promise, he had opportunities to study the most dilapidated buildings. It was a comfort to Mrs Daintry, however, to be able to say to herself that he would be struck with her living really very nicely— more nicely, in many ways, than he could possibly be accommodated—that she was sure of—in a small dark *appartement de garçon* in Paris, on the uncomfortable side of the Seine. Her state of mind at present was such that she set the highest value on anything that could possibly help to give Florimond a pleasant impression. Nothing could be too small to count, she said to herself; for she knew that Florimond was both fastidious and observant. Everything that would strike him agreeably would contribute to detain him, so that if there were only enough agreeable things he would perhaps stay four or five months, instead of three, as he had promised—the three that

were to date from the day of his arrival in Boston, not from
that (an important difference) of his departure from Liverpool,
which was about to take place.

It was Florimond that Mrs Daintry had had in mind when,
on emerging from the little vestibule, she gave the direction to
Beatrice about the position of the door-mat—in which the
young woman, so carefully selected, as a Protestant, from the
British Provinces, had never yet taken the interest that her
mistress expected from such antecedents. It was Florimond
also that she had thought of in putting before her parlour-
maid the question of donning a badge of servitude in the shape
of a neat little muslin coif, adorned with pink ribbon and
stitched together by Mrs Daintry's own beneficent fingers.
Naturally there was no obvious connection between the
parlour-maid's coiffure and the length of Florimond's stay;
that detail was to be only a part of the general effect of American life. It was still Florimond that was uppermost as his
mother, on her way up the hill, turned over in her mind that
question of the ceremony of the front-door. He had been
living in a country in which servants observed more forms,
and he would doubtless ·be shocked at Beatrice's want of
patience. An accumulation of such anomalies would at last
undermine his loyalty. He would not care for them for himself, of course, but he would care about them for her; coming
from France, where, as she knew by his letters, and indeed by
her own reading—for she made a remarkably free use of the
Athenæum—that the position of a mother was one of the most
exalted, he could not fail to be *froissé* at any want of consideration for his surviving parent. As an artist, he could not make
up his mind to live in Boston; but he was a good son for all
that. He had told her frequently that they might easily live
together if she would only come to Paris; but of course she
could not do that, with Joanna and her six children round in
Clarendon Street, and her responsibilities to her daughter
multiplied in the highest degree. Besides, during that winter

she spent in Paris, when Florimond was definitely making up
his mind, and they had in the evening the most charming
conversations, interrupted only by the repeated care of wind-
ing-up the lamp, or applying the bellows to the obstinate little
fire—during that winter she had felt that Paris was not her
element. She had gone to the lectures at the Sorbonne, and she
had visited the Louvre as few people did it, catalogue in hand,
taking the catalogue volume by volume; but all the while she
was thinking of Joanna and her new baby, and how the other
three (that was the number then) were getting on while their
mother was so much absorbed with the last. Mrs Daintry,
familiar as she was with these anxieties, had not the step of a
grandmother; for a mind that was always intent had the effect
of refreshing and brightening her years. Responsibility with
her was not a weariness, but a joy—at least it was the nearest
approach to a joy that she knew, and she did not regard her
life as especially cheerless; there were many others that were
more denuded. She moved with circumspection, but without
reluctance, holding up her head and looking at every one she
met with a clear, unaccusing gaze. This expression showed
that she took an interest, as she ought, in everything that concerned her fellow-creatures; but there was that also in her
whole person which indicated that she went no farther than
Christian charity required. It was only with regard to Joanna
and that vociferous houseful—so fertile in problems, in opportunities for devotion—that she went really very far. And now
to-day, of course, in this matter of Florimond's visit, after an
absence of six years; which was perhaps more on her mind
than anything had ever been. People who met Mrs Daintry
after she had traversed the Public Garden—she always took
that way—and begun to ascend the charming slope of Beacon
Street, would never, in spite of the relaxation of her pace as
she measured this eminence, have mistaken her for a little old
lady who should have crept out, vaguely and timidly, to inhale
one of the last mild days. It was easy to see that she was not

without a duty, or at least a reason—and indeed Mrs Daintry had never in her life been left in this predicament. People who knew her ever so little would have felt that she was going to call on a relation; and if they had been to the manner born they would have added a mental hope that her relation was prepared for her visit. No one would have doubted this, however, who had been aware that her steps were directed to the habitation of Miss Lucretia Daintry. Her sister-in-law, her husband's only sister, lived in that commodious nook which is known as Mount Vernon Place; and Mrs Daintry therefore turned off at Joy Street. By the time she did so, she had quite settled in her mind the question of Beatrice's behaviour in connection with the front-door. She had decided that it would never do to make a formal remonstrance, for it was plain that, in spite of the Old-World training which she hoped the girl might have imbibed in Nova Scotia (where, until lately, she learned, there had been an English garrison), she would in such a case expose herself to the danger of desertion; Beatrice would not consent to stand there holding the door open for nothing. And after all, in the depths of her conscience Mrs Daintry was not sure that she ought to; she was not sure that this was an act of homage that one human being had a right to exact of another, simply because this other happened to wear a little muslin cap with pink ribbons. It was a service that ministered to her importance, to her dignity, not to her hunger or thirst; and Mrs Daintry, who had had other foreign advantages besides her winter in Paris, was quite aware that in the United States the machinery for that former kind of tribute was very undeveloped. It was a luxury that one ought not to pretend to enjoy—it was a luxury, indeed, that she probably ought not to presume to desire. At the bottom of her heart Mrs Daintry suspected that such hankerings were criminal. And yet, turning the thing over, as she turned everything, she could not help coming back to the idea that it would be very pleasant, it would be really delightful, if Beatrice herself, as a

result of the growing refinement of her taste, her transplanta-
tion to a society after all more elaborate than that of Nova
Scotia, should perceive the fitness, the felicity, of such an
attitude. This perhaps was too much to hope; but it did not
much matter, for before she had turned into Mount Vernon
Place Mrs Daintry had invented a compromise. She would
continue to talk to her parlour-maid until she should reach the
bottom of her steps, making earnestly one remark after the
other over her shoulder, so that Beatrice would be obliged to
remain on the threshold. It is true that it occurred to her that
the girl might not attach much importance to these Parthian
observations, and would perhaps not trouble herself to wait
for their natural term; but this idea was too fraught with embarrassment to be long entertained. It must be added that this
was scarcely a moment for Mrs Daintry to go much into the
ethics of the matter, for she felt that her call upon her sister-
in-law was the consequence of a tolerably unscrupulous
determination.

II

LUCRETIA DAINTRY was at home, for a wonder; but she
kept her visitor waiting a quarter of an hour, during which
this lady had plenty of time to consider her errand afresh. She
was a little ashamed of it; but she did not so much mind being
put to shame by Lucretia, for Lucretia did things that were
much more ambiguous than any she should have thought of
doing. It was even for this that Mrs Daintry had picked her
out, among so many relations, as the object of an appeal in its
nature somewhat ambiguous. Nevertheless, her heart beat a
little faster than usual as she sat in the quiet parlour, looking
about her for the thousandth time at Lucretia's " things," and
observing that she was faithful to her old habit of not having

her furnace lighted until long after every one else. Miss Daintry had her own habits, and she was the only person her sister-in-law knew who had more reasons than herself. Her taste was of the old fashion, and her drawing-room embraced neither festoons nor Persian rugs, nor plates and *plaques* upon the wall, nor faded stuffs suspended from unexpected projections. Most of the articles it contained dated from the year 1830; and a sensible, reasonable, rectangular arrangement of them abundantly answered to their owner's conception of the decorative. A rosewood sofa against the wall, surmounted by an engraving from Kaulbach; a neatly drawn carpet, faded, but little worn, and sprigged with a floral figure; a chimney-piece of black marble, veined with yellow, garnished with an empire clock and antiquated lamps; half a dozen large mirrors, with very narrow frames; and an immense glazed screen representing, in the livid tints of early worsted-work, a ruined temple overhanging a river—these were some of the more obvious of Miss Daintry's treasures. Her sister-in-law was a votary of the newer school, and had made sacrifices to have everything in black and gilt; but she could not fail to see that Lucretia had some very good pieces. It was a wonder how she made them last, for Lucretia had never been supposed to know much about the keeping of a house, and no one would have thought of asking her how she treated the marble floor of her vestibule, or what measures she took in the spring with regard to her curtains. Her work in life lay outside. She took an interest in questions and institutions, sat on committees, and had views on Female Suffrage—a movement which she strongly opposed. She even wrote letters sometimes to the *Transcript*, not "chatty" and jocular, and signed with a fancy name, but "over" her initials, as the phrase was—every one recognised them—and bearing on some important topic. She was not, however, in the faintest degree slipshod or dishevelled, like some of the ladies of the newspaper and the forum; she had no ink on her fingers, and she wore her bonnet as scientifically poised as the dome of the State House. When you rang at her door-bell you were never kept waiting, and when you entered her dwelling you were not greeted with those culinary odours which, pervading halls and parlours, had in certain other cases been described as the right smell in the wrong place. If Mrs Daintry was made to wait some time before her hostess appeared, there was nothing extraordinary in this, for none of her friends came down directly, and she never did herself. To come down directly would have seemed to her to betray a frivolous eagerness for the social act. The delay, moreover, not only gave her, as I have said, opportunity to turn over her errand afresh, but enabled her to say to herself, as she had often said before, that though Lucretia had no taste, she had some very good things, and to wonder both how she had kept them so well, and how she had originally got them. Mrs Daintry knew that they proceeded from her mother and her aunts, who had been supposed to distribute among the children of the second generation the accumulations of the old house in Federal Street, where many Daintrys had been born in the early part of the century. Of course she knew nothing of the principles on which the distribution had been made, but all she could say was that Lucretia had evidently been first in the field. There was apparently no limit to what had come to her. Mrs Daintry was not obliged to look, to assure herself that there was another clock in the back parlour—which would seem to indicate that all the clocks had fallen to Lucretia. She knew of four other timepieces in other parts of the house, for of course in former years she had often been upstairs; it was only in comparatively recent times that she had renounced that practice. There had been a period when she ascended to the second story as a matter of course, without asking leave. On seeing that her sister-in-law was in neither of the parlours, she mounted and talked with Lucretia at the door of her bedroom, if it happened to be closed. And there had been another season when she stood at the foot of

the staircase, and, lifting her voice, inquired of Miss Daintry
—who called down with some shrillness in return—whether
she might climb, while the maidservant, wandering away with
a vague cachinnation, left her to her own devices. But both of
these phases belonged to the past. Lucretia never came into
her bedroom to-day, nor did she presume to penetrate into
Lucretia's; so that she did not know for a long time whether
she had renewed her chintz nor whether she had hung in that
bower the large photograph of Florimond, presented by Mrs
Daintry herself to his aunt, which had been placed in neither
of the parlours. Mrs Daintry would have given a good deal to
know whether this memento had been honoured with a place
in her sister-in-law's "chamber"—it was by this name, on
each side, that these ladies designated their sleeping-apart-
ment; but she could not bring herself to ask directly, for it
would be embarrassing to learn—what was possible—that
Lucretia had not paid the highest respect to Florimond's
portrait. The point was cleared up by its being revealed to her
accidentally that the photograph—an expensive and very
artistic one, taken in Paris—had been relegated to the spare-
room, or guest-chamber. Miss Daintry was very hospitable,
and constantly had friends of her own sex staying with her.
They were very apt to be young women in their twenties; and
one of them had remarked to Mrs Daintry that her son's
portrait—he must be wonderfully handsome—was the first
thing she saw when she woke up in the morning. Certainly
Florimond was handsome; but his mother had a lurking
suspicion that, in spite of his beauty, his aunt was not fond of
him. She doubtless thought he ought to come back and settle
down in Boston; he was the first of the Daintrys who had had
so much in common with Paris. Mrs Daintry knew as a fact
that, twenty-eight years before, Lucretia, whose opinions even
at that period were already wonderfully formed, had not
approved of the romantic name which, in a moment of par-
donable weakness, she had conferred upon her rosy babe. The

spinster (she had been as much of a spinster at twenty as she was to-day) had accused her of making a fool of the child. Every one was reading old ballads in Boston then, and Mrs Daintry had found the name in a ballad. It doubled any anxiety she might feel with regard to her present business to think that, as certain foreign newspapers which her son sent her used to say about ambassadors, Florimond was perhaps not a *persona grata* to his aunt. She reflected, however, that if his fault were in his absenting himself, there was nothing that would remedy it so effectively as his coming home. She reflected, too, that if she and Lucretia no longer took liberties with each other, there was still something a little indiscreet in her purpose this morning. But it fortified and consoled her for everything to remember, as she sat looking at the empire clock, which was a very handsome one, that her husband at least had been disinterested.

Miss Daintry found her visitor in this attitude, and thought it was an expression of impatience; which led her to explain that she had been on the roof of her house with a man who had come to see about repairing it. She had walked all over it, and peeped over the cornice, and not been in the least dizzy; and had come to the conclusion that one ought to know a great deal more about one's roof than was usual.

"I am sure you have never been over yours," she said to her sister-in-law.

Mrs Daintry confessed with some embarrassment that she had not, and felt, as she did so, that she was superficial and slothful. It annoyed her to reflect that while she supposed, in her new house, she had thought of everything, she had not thought of this important feature. There was no one like Lucretia for giving one such reminders.

"I will send Florimond up when he comes," she said; "he will tell me all about it."

"Do you suppose he knows about roofs, except tumble-down ones, in his little pictures? I am afraid it will make him

giddy." This had been Miss Daintry's rejoinder, and the tone
of it was not altogether reassuring. She was nearly fifty years
old; she had a plain, fresh, delightful face, and in whatever
part of the world she might have been met, an attentive
observer of American life would not have had the least difficulty in guessing what phase of it she represented. She represented the various and enlightened activities which cast their
rapid shuttle—in the comings and goings of eager workers—
from one side to the other of Boston Common. She had in an
eminent degree the physiognomy, the accent, the costume, the
conscience, and the little eyeglass, of her native place. She had
never sacrificed to the graces, but she inspired unlimited confidence. Moreover, if she was thoroughly in sympathy with
the New England capital, she reserved her liberty; she had a
great charity, but she was independent and witty; and if she
was as earnest as other people, she was not quite so serious.
Her voice was a little masculine; and it had been said of her
that she didn't care in the least how she looked. This was far
from true, for she would not for the world have looked better
than she thought was right for so plain a woman.

Mrs Daintry was fond of calculating consequences; but she
was not a coward, and she arrived at her business as soon as
possible.

"You know that Florimond sails on the 20th of this month.
He will get home by the 1st of December."

"Oh yes, my dear, I know it; everybody is talking about it.
I have heard it thirty times. That's where Boston is so small,"
Lucretia Daintry remarked.

"Well, it's big enough for me," said her sister-in-law.
"And of course people notice his coming back; it shows that
everything that has been said is false, and that he really does
like us."

"He likes his mother, I hope; about the rest I don't know
that it matters."

"Well, it certainly will be pleasant to have him," said Mrs

Daintry, who was not content with her companion's tone, and wished to extract from her some recognition of the importance of Florimond's advent. "It will prove how unjust so much of the talk has been."

"My dear woman, I don't know anything about the talk. We make too much fuss about everything. Florimond was an infant when I last saw him."

This was open to the interpretation that too much fuss had been made about Florimond—an idea that accorded ill with the project that had kept Mrs Daintry waiting a quarter of an hour while her hostess walked about on the roof. But Miss Daintry continued, and in a moment gave her sister-in-law the best opportunity she could have hoped for. "I don't suppose he will bring with him either salvation or the other thing; and if he has decided to winter among the bears, it will matter much more to him than to any one else. But I shall be very glad to see him if he behaves himself; and I needn't tell you that if there is anything I can do for him——" and Miss Daintry, tightening her lips together a little, paused, suiting her action to the idea that professions were usually humbug.

"There is indeed something you can do for him," her sister-in-law hastened to respond; "or something you can do for me, at least," she added, more discreetly.

"Call it for both of you. What is it?" and Miss Daintry put on her eyeglass.

"I know you like to do kindnesses, when they are *real* ones; and you almost always have some one staying with you for the winter."

Miss Daintry stared. "Do you want to put him to live with me?"

"No, indeed! Do you think I could part with him? It's another person—a lady!"

"A lady! Is he going to bring a woman with him?"

"My dear Lucretia, you won't wait. I want to make it as pleasant for him as possible. In that case he may stay longer.

He has promised three months; but I should so like to keep him till the summer. It would make me very happy."

"Well, my dear, keep him, then, if you can."

"But I can't, unless I am helped."

"And you want me to help you? Tell me what I must do. Should you wish me to make love to him?"

Mrs Daintry's hesitation at this point was almost as great as if she had found herself obliged to say yes. She was well aware that what she had come to suggest was very delicate; but it seemed to her at the present moment more delicate than ever. Still, her cause was good, because it was the cause of maternal devotion. "What I should like you to do would be to ask Rachel Torrance to spend the winter with you."

Miss Daintry had not sat so much on committees without getting used to queer proposals, and she had long since ceased to waste time in expressing a vain surprise. Her method was Socratic; she usually entangled her interlocutor in a net of questions.

"Ah, do you want *her* to make love to him?"

"No, I don't want any love at all. In such a matter as that I want Florimond to be perfectly free. But Rachel is such an attractive girl; she is so artistic and so bright."

"I don't doubt it; but I can't invite all the attractive girls in the country. Why don't you ask her yourself?"

"It would be too marked. And then Florimond might not like her in the same house; he would have too much of her. Besides, she is no relation of mine, you know; the cousinship —such as it is, it is not very close—is on your side. I have reason to believe she would like to come; she knows so little of Boston, and admires it so much. It is astonishing how little idea the New York people have. She would be different from any one here, and that would make a pleasant change for Florimond. She was in Europe so much when she was young. She speaks French perfectly, and Italian, I think, too; and she was brought up in a kind of artistic way. Her father never did anything; but even when he hadn't bread to give his children, he always arranged to have a studio, and they gave musical parties. That's the way Rachel was brought up. But they tell me that it hasn't in the least spoiled her; it has only made her very familiar with life."

"Familiar with rubbish!" Miss Daintry ejaculated.

"My dear Lucretia, I assure you she is a very good girl, or I never would have proposed such a plan as this. She paints very well herself, and tries to sell her pictures. They are dreadfully poor—I don't mean the pictures, but Mrs Torrance and the rest—and they live in Brooklyn, in some second-rate boarding-house. With that, Rachel has everything about her that would enable her to appreciate Boston. Of course it would be a real kindness, because there would be one less to pay for at the boarding-house. You haven't a son, so you can't understand how a mother feels. I want to prepare everything, to have everything pleasantly arranged. I want to deprive him of every pretext for going away before the summer; because in August—I don't know whether I have told you—I have a kind of idea of going back with him myself. I am so afraid he will miss the artistic side. I don't mind saying that to you, Lucretia, for I have heard you say yourself that you thought it had been left out here. Florimond might go and see Rachel Torrance every day if he liked; of course, being his cousin, and calling her Rachel, it couldn't attract any particular attention. I shouldn't much care if it did," Mrs Daintry went on, borrowing a certain bravado that in calmer moments was eminently foreign to her nature from the impunity with which she had hitherto proceeded. Her project, as she heard herself unfold it, seemed to hang together so well that she felt something of the intoxication of success. "I shouldn't care if it did," she repeated, "so long as Florimond had a little of the conversation that he is accustomed to, and I was not in perpetual fear of his starting off."

Miss Daintry had listened attentively while her sister-in-law spoke, with eager softness, passing from point to point with a *crescendo* of lucidity, like a woman who had thought it all out and had the consciousness of many reasons on her side. There had been momentary pauses, of which Lucretia had not taken advantage, so that Mrs Daintry rested at last in the enjoyment of a security that was almost complete and that her companion's first question was not of a nature to dispel.

"It's so long since I have seen her. Is she pretty?" Miss Daintry inquired.

"She is decidedly striking; she has magnificent hair!" her visitor answered, almost with enthusiasm.

"Do you want Florimond to marry her?"

This, somehow, was less pertinent. "Ah, no, my dear," Mrs Daintry rejoined, very judicially. "That is not the kind of education—the kind of *milieu*—one would wish for the wife of one's son." She knew, moreover, that her sister-in-law knew her opinion about the marriage of young people. It was a sacrament more high and holy than any words could express, the propriety and timeliness of which lay deep in the hearts of the contracting parties, below all interference from parents and friends; it was an inspiration from above, and she would no more have thought of laying a train to marry her son than she would have thought of breaking open his letters. More relevant even than this, however, was the fact that she did not believe he would wish to make a wife of a girl from a slipshod family in Brooklyn, however little he might care to lose sight of the artistic side. It will be observed that she gave Florimond the credit of being a very discriminating young man; and she indeed discriminated for him in cases in which she would not have presumed to discriminate for herself.

"My dear Susan, you are simply the most immoral woman in Boston!" These were the words of which, after a moment, her sister-in-law delivered herself.

Mrs Daintry turned a little pale. "Don't you think it would be right?" she asked quickly.

"To sacrifice the poor girl to Florimond's amusement? What has she done that you should wish to play her such a trick?" Miss Daintry did not look shocked: she never looked shocked, for even when she was annoyed she was never frightened; but after a moment she broke into a loud, uncompromising laugh—a laugh which her sister-in-law knew of old and regarded as a peculiarly dangerous form of criticism.

"I don't see why she should be sacrificed. She would have a lovely time if she were to come on. She would consider it the greatest kindness to be asked."

"To be asked to come and amuse Florimond."

Mrs Daintry hesitated a moment. "I don't see why she should object to that. Florimond is certainly not beneath a person's notice. Why, Lucretia, you speak as if there were something disagreeable about Florimond."

"My dear Susan," said Miss Daintry, "I am willing to believe that he is the first young man of his time; but, all the same, it isn't a thing to do."

"Well, I have thought of it in every possible way, and I haven't seen any harm in it. It isn't as if she were giving up anything to come."

"You have thought of it too much, perhaps. Stop thinking for a while. I should have imagined you were more scrupulous."

Mrs Daintry was silent a moment; she took her sister-in-law's asperity very meekly, for she felt that if she had been wrong in what she proposed she deserved a severe judgment. But why was she wrong? She clasped her hands in her lap and rested her eyes with extreme seriousness upon Lucretia's little *pince-nez*, inviting her to judge her, and too much interested in having the question of her culpability settled to care whether or no she were hurt. "It is very hard to know what is right," she said presently. "Of course it is only a plan; I wondered how it would strike you."

"You had better leave Florimond alone," Miss Daintry

answered. "I don't see why you should spread so many carpets for him. Let him shift for himself. If he doesn't like
Boston, Boston can spare him."

"You are not nice about him; no, you are not, Lucretia!"
Mrs Daintry cried, with a slight tremor in her voice.

"Of course I am not as nice as you—he is not my son; but
I am trying to be nice about Rachel Torrance."

"I am sure she would like him—she would delight in
him!" Mrs Daintry broke out.

"That's just what I'm afraid of; I couldn't stand that."

"Well, Lucretia, I am not convinced," Mrs Daintry said,
rising, with perceptible coldness. "It is very hard to be sure
one is not unjust. Of course I shall not expect you to send for
her; but I shall think of her with a good deal of compassion,
all winter, in that dingy place in Brooklyn. And if you have
some one else with you—and I am sure you will, because you
always do, unless you remain alone on purpose this year, to
put me in the wrong—if you have some one else I shall keep
saying to myself: 'Well, after all, it might have been Rachel!'"

Miss Daintry gave another of her loud laughs at the idea
that she might remain alone "on purpose." "I shall have a
visitor, but it will be some one who will not amuse Florimond
in the least. If he wants to go away, it won't be for anything in
this house that he will stay."

"I really don't see why you should hate him," said poor
Mrs Daintry.

"Where do you find that? On the contrary, I appreciate
him very highly. That's just why I think it very possible that
a girl like Rachel Torrance—an odd, uninstructed girl, who
hasn't had great advantages—may fall in love with him and
break her heart."

Mrs Daintry's clear eyes expanded. "Is *that* what you are
afraid of?"

"Do you suppose my solicitude is for Florimond? An
accident of that sort—if she were to show him her heels at

the end—might perhaps do him good. But I am thinking of the girl, since you say you don't want him to marry her."

"It was not for that that I suggested what I did. I don't want him to marry any one—I have no plans for that," Mrs Daintry said, as if she were resenting an imputation.

"Rachel Torrance least of all!" And Miss Daintry indulged still again in that hilarity, so personal to herself, which sometimes made the subject look so little jocular to others. "My dear Susan, I don't blame you," she said; "for I suppose mothers are necessarily unscrupulous. But that is why the rest of us should hold them in check."

"It's merely an assumption, that she would fall in love with him," Mrs Daintry continued, with a certain majesty; "there is nothing to prove it, and I am not bound to take it for granted."

"In other words, you don't care if she should! Precisely; that, I suppose, is your *rôle*. I am glad I haven't any children; it is very sophisticating. For so good a woman, you are very bad. Yes, you *are* good, Susan; and you *are* bad."

"I don't know that I pretend to be particularly good," Susan remarked, with the warmth of one who had known something of the burden of such a reputation, as she moved toward the door.

"You have a conscience, and it will wake up," her companion returned. "It will come over you in the watches of the night that your idea was—as I have said—immoral."

Mrs Daintry paused in the hall, and stood there looking at Lucretia. It was just possible that she was being laughed at, for Lucretia's deepest mirth was sometimes silent—that is, one heard the laughter several days later. Suddenly she coloured to the roots of her hair, as if the conviction of her error had come over her. Was it possible she had been corrupted by an affection in itself so pure? "I only want to do right," she said softly. "I would rather he should never come home than that I should go too far."

She was turning away, but her sister-in-law held her a moment and kissed her. "You are a delightful woman, but I won't ask Rachel Torrance!" This was the understanding on which they separated.

III

MISS DAINTRY, after her visitor had left her, recognised that she had been a little brutal; for Susan's proposition did not really strike her as so heinous. Her eagerness to protect the poor girl in Brooklyn was not a very positive quantity, inasmuch as she had an impression that this young lady was on the whole very well able to take care of herself. What her talk with Mrs Daintry had really expressed was the lukewarmness of her sentiment with regard to Florimond. She had no wish to help his mother lay carpets for him, as she said. Rightly or wrongly, she had a conviction that he was selfish, that he was spoiled, that he was conceited; and she thought Lucretia Daintry meant for better things than the service of sugaring for the young man's lips the pill of a long-deferred visit to Boston. It was quite indifferent to her that he should be conscious, in that city, of unsatisfied needs. At bottom, she had never forgiven him for having sought another way of salvation. Moreover, she had a strong sense of humour, and it amused her more than a little that her sister-in-law—of all women in Boston—should have come to her on that particular errand. It completed the irony of the situation that one should frighten Mrs Daintry—just a little—about what she had undertaken; and more than once that day Lucretia had, with a smile, the vision of Susan's countenance as she remarked to her that she was immoral. In reality, and speaking seriously, she did not consider Mrs Daintry's inspiration unpardonable; what was very positive was simply that she had no wish to invite Rachel

Torrance for the benefit of her nephew. She was by no means
sure that she should like the girl for her own sake, and it was
still less apparent that she should like her for that of Florimond. With all this, however, Miss Daintry had a high love of
justice; she revised her social accounts from time to time to
see that she had not cheated any one. She thought over her
interview with Mrs Daintry the next day, and it occurred to
her that she had been a little unfair. But she scarcely knew
what to do to repair her mistake, by which Rachel Torrance
also had suffered, perhaps; for after all, if it had not been
wicked of her sister-in-law to ask such a favour, it had at least
been cool; and the penance that presented itself to Lucretia
Daintry did not take the form of despatching a letter to
Brooklyn. An accident came to her help, and four days after
the conversation I have narrated she wrote her a note which
explains itself and which I will presently transcribe. Meanwhile
Mrs Daintry, on her side, had held an examination of her
heart; and though she did not think she had been very civilly
treated, the result of her reflections was to give her a fit of
remorse. Lucretia was right: she had been anything but
scrupulous; she had skirted the edge of an abyss. Questions
of conduct had long been familiar to her; and the cardinal rule
of life in her eyes was, that before one did anything which
involved in any degree the happiness or the interest of another, one should take one's motives out of the closet in
which they are usually laid away and give them a thorough
airing. This operation, undertaken before her visit to Lucretia,
had been cursory and superficial; for now that she repeated it,
she discovered among the recesses of her spirit a number of
nut-like scruples which she was astonished to think she should
have overlooked. She had really been very wicked, and there
was no doubt about *her* proper penance. It consisted of a letter
to her sister-in-law, in which she completely disavowed her
little project, attributing it to momentary intermission of her
reason. She saw it would never do, and she was quite ashamed

of herself. She did not exactly thank Miss Daintry for the manner in which she had admonished her, but she spoke as one saved from a great danger, and assured her relative of Mount Vernon Place that she should not soon again expose herself. This letter crossed with Miss Daintry's missive, which ran as follows:—

"My Dear Susan—I have been thinking over our conversation of last Tuesday, and I am afraid I went rather too far in my condemnation of your idea with regard to Rachel Torrance. If I expressed myself in a manner to wound your feelings, I can assure you of my great regret. Nothing could have been further from my thoughts than the belief that you are wanting in delicacy. I know very well that you were prompted by the highest sense of duty. It is possible, however, I think, that your sense of duty to poor Florimond is a little too high. You think of him too much as that famous dragon of antiquity—wasn't it in Crete, or somewhere?—to whom young virgins had to be sacrificed. It may relieve your mind, however, to hear that this particular virgin will probably, during the coming winter, be provided for. Yesterday, at Doll's, where I had gone in to look at the new pictures (there is a striking Appleton Brown), I met Pauline Mesh, whom I had not seen for ages, and had half an hour's talk with her. She seems to me to have come out very much this winter, and to have altogether a higher tone. In short, she is much enlarged, and seems to want to take an interest in something. Of course you will say: Has she not her children? But, somehow, they don't seem to fill her life. You must remember that they are very small as yet to fill anything. Anyway, she mentioned to me her great disappointment in having had to give up her sister, who was to have come on from Baltimore to spend the greater part of the winter. Rosalie is very pretty, and Pauline expected to give a lot of Germans, and make things generally pleasant. I shouldn't wonder if she thought something might

happen that would make Rosalie a fixture in our city. She
would have liked this immensely; for, whatever Pauline's
faults may be, she has plenty of family feeling. But her sister
has suddenly got engaged in Baltimore (I believe it's much
easier than here), so that the visit has fallen through. Pauline
seemed to be quite in despair, for she had made all sorts of
beautifications in one of her rooms, on purpose for Rosalie;
and not only had she wasted her labour (you know how she
goes into those things, whatever we may think, sometimes, of
her taste), but she spoke as if it would make a great difference
in her winter; said she should suffer a great deal from loneliness. She says Boston is no place for a married woman, standing on her own merits; she can't have any sort of time unless
she hitches herself to some attractive girl who will help her to
pull the social car. You know that isn't what every one says,
and how much talk there has been the last two or three winters
about the frisky young matrons. Well, however that may be,
I don't pretend to know much about it, not being in the
married set. Pauline spoke as if she were really quite high and
dry, and I felt so sorry for her that it suddenly occurred to me
to say something about Rachel Torrance. I remembered that
she is related to Donald Mesh in about the same degree as she
is to me—a degree nearer, therefore, than to Florimond.
Pauline didn't seem to think much of the relationship—it's so
remote; but when I told her that Rachel (strange as it might
appear) would probably be thankful for a season in Boston,
and might be a good substitute for Rosalie, why she quite
jumped at the idea. She has never seen her, but she knows who
she is—fortunately, for I could never begin to explain. She
seems to think such a girl will be quite a novelty in this place.
I don't suppose Pauline can do her any particular harm, from
what you tell me of Miss Torrance; and, on the other hand, I
don't know that she could injure Pauline. She is certainly very
kind (Pauline, of course), and I have no doubt she will
immediately write to Brooklyn, and that Rachel will come on.

Florimond won't, of course, see as much of her as if she were staying with me, and I don't know that he will particularly care about Pauline Mesh, who, you know, is intensely American; but they will go out a great deal, and he will meet them (if he takes the trouble), and I have no doubt that Rachel will take the edge off the east wind for him. At any rate I have perhaps done her a good turn. I must confess to you—and it won't surprise you—that I was thinking of her, and not of him, when I spoke to Pauline. Therefore I don't feel that I have taken a risk, but I don't much care if I have. I have my views, but I never worry. I recommend you not to do so either—for you go, I know, from one extreme to the other. I have told you my little story; it was on my mind. Aren't you glad to see the lovely snow?—Ever affectionately yours,

L. D.

"*P.S.*—The more I think of it, the more convinced I am that you *will* worry now about the danger for Rachel. Why did I drop the poison into your mind? Of course I didn't say a word about you or Florimond."

This epistle reached Mrs Daintry, as I have intimated, about an hour after her letter to her sister-in-law had been posted; but it is characteristic of her that she did not for a moment regret having made a retractation rather humble in form, and which proved after all, scarcely to have been needed. The delight of having done that duty carried her over the sense of having given herself away. Her sister-in-law spoke from knowledge when she wrote that phrase about Susan's now beginning to worry from the opposite point of view. Her conscience, like the good Homer, might sometimes nod; but when it woke, it woke with a start; and for many a day afterward its vigilance was feverish. For the moment her emotions were mingled. She thought Lucretia very strange, and that *she* was scarcely in a position to talk about one's going from one extreme to the other. It was good news to her that Rachel

Torrance would probably be on the ground after all, and she was delighted that on Lucretia the responsibility of such a fact should rest. This responsibility, even after her revulsion, as we know, she regarded as grave; she exhaled an almost voluptuous sigh when she thought of having herself escaped from it. What she did not quite understand was Lucretia's apology, and her having, even if Florimond's happiness were not her motive, taken almost the very step which three days before she had so severely criticised. This was puzzling, for Lucretia was usually so consistent. But all the same Mrs Daintry did not repent of her own penance; on the contrary, she took more and more comfort in it. If, with that, Rachel Torrance should be really useful, it would be delightful.

IV

FLORIMOND DAINTRY had stayed at home for three days after his arrival; he had sat close to the fire, in his slippers, every now and then casting a glance over his shoulders at the hard white world which seemed to glare at him from the other side of the window-panes. He was very much afraid of the cold, and he was not in a hurry to go out and meet it. He had met it, on disembarking in New York, in the shape of a wave of frozen air, which had travelled from some remote point in the West (he was told), on purpose, apparently, to smite him in the face. That portion of his organism tingled yet with it, though the gasping, bewildered look which sat upon his features during the first few hours had quite left it. I am afraid it will be thought he was a young man of small courage; and on a point so delicate I do not hold myself obliged to pronounce. It is only fair to add that it was delightful to him to be with his mother and that they easily spent three days in talking. Moreover he had the company of Joanna and her children,

who, after a little delay, occasioned apparently by their waiting to see whether he would not first come to them, had
arrived in a body and had spent several hours. As regards the
majority of them, they had repeated this visit several times in
the three days, Joanna being obliged to remain at home with
the two younger ones. There were four older ones, and their
grandmother's house was open to them as a second nursery.
The first day, their Uncle Florimond thought them charming;
and, as he had brought a French toy for each, it is probable
that this impression was mutual. The second day, their little
ruddy bodies and woollen clothes seemed to him to have a
positive odour of the cold—it was disagreeable to him, and he
spoke to his mother about their "wintry smell." The third day
they had become very familiar; they called him "Florry;" and
he had made up his mind that, to let them loose in that way on
his mother, Joanna must be rather wanting in delicacy—not
mentioning this deficiency, however, as yet, for he saw that his
mother was not prepared for it. She evidently thought it
proper, or at least it seemed inevitable, that either she should
be round at Joanna's or the children should be round in Newbury Street; for "Joanna's" evidently represented primarily
the sound of small, loud voices, and the hard breathing that
signalised the intervals of romps. Florimond was rather disappointed in his sister, seeing her after a long separation; he
remarked to his mother that she seemed completely sub-
merged. As Mrs Daintry spent most of her time under the
waves with her daughter, she had grown to regard this element as sufficiently favourable to life, and was rather surprised
when Florimond said to her that he was sorry to see she and
his sister appeared to have been converted into a pair of
bonnes d'enfants. Afterward, however, she perceived what he
meant; she was not aware, until he called her attention to it,
that the little Merrimans took up an enormous place in the
intellectual economy of two households. "You ought to
remember that they exist for you, and not you for them,"

Florimond said to her in a tone of friendly admonition; and he remarked on another occasion that the perpetual presence of children was a great injury to conversation—it kept it down so much; and that in Boston they seemed to be present even when they were absent, inasmuch as most of the talk was about them. Mrs Daintry did not stop to ask herself what her son knew of Boston, leaving it years before, as a boy, and not having so much as looked out of the window since his return; she was taken up mainly with noting certain little habits of speech which he evidently had formed, and in wondering how they would strike his fellow-citizens. He was very definite and trenchant; he evidently knew perfectly what he thought; and though his manner was not defiant—he had, perhaps, even too many of the forms of politeness, as if sometimes, for mysterious reasons, he were playing upon you—the tone in which he uttered his opinions did not appear exactly to give you the choice. And then apparently he had a great many; there was a moment when Mrs Daintry vaguely foresaw that the little house in Newbury Street would be more crowded with Florimond's views than it had ever been with Joanna's children. She hoped very much people would like him, and she hardly could see why they should fail to find him agreeable. To herself he was sweeter than any grandchild; he was as kind as if he had been a devoted parent. Florimond had but a small acquaintance with his brother-in-law; but after he had been at home forty-eight hours he found that he bore Arthur Merriman a grudge, and was ready to think rather ill of him— having a theory that he ought to have held up Joanna and interposed to save her mother. Arthur Merriman was a young and brilliant commission-merchant, who had not married Joanna Daintry for the sake of Florimond, and, doing an active business all day in East Boston, had a perfectly good conscience in leaving his children's mother and grandmother to establish their terms of intercourse.

Florimond, however, did not particularly wonder why his

brother-in-law had not been round to bid him welcome. It was for Mrs Daintry that this anxiety was reserved; and what made it worse was her uncertainty as to whether she should be justified in mentioning the subject to Joanna. It might wound Joanna to suggest to her that her husband was derelict—especially if she did not think so, and she certainly gave her mother no opening; and on the other hand Florimond might have ground for complaint if Arthur should continue not to notice him. Mrs Daintry earnestly desired that nothing of this sort should happen, and took refuge in the hope that Florimond would have adopted the foreign theory of visiting, in accordance with which the newcomer was to present himself first. Meanwhile the young man, who had looked upon a meeting with his brother-in-law as a necessity rather than a privilege, was simply conscious of a reprieve; and up in Clarendon Street, as Mrs Daintry said, it never occurred to Arthur Merriman to take this social step, nor to his wife to propose it to him. Mrs Merriman simply took for granted that her brother would be round early some morning to see the children. A day or two later the couple dined at her mother's, and that virtually settled the question. It is true that Mrs Daintry, in later days, occasionally recalled the fact that, after all, Joanna's husband never had called upon Florimond; and she even wondered why Florimond, who sometimes said bitter things, had not made more of it. The matter came back at moments when, under the pressure of circumstances which, it must be confessed, were rare, she found herself giving assent to an axiom that sometimes reached her ears. This axiom, it must be added, did not justify her in the particular case I have mentioned, for the full purport of it was that the queerness of Bostonians was collective, not individual.

There was no doubt, however, that it was Florimond's place to call first upon his aunt, and this was a duty of which she could not hesitate to remind him. By the time he took his way across the long expanse of the new land and up the

charming hill which constitutes, as it were, the speaking face
of Boston, the temperature either had relaxed, or he had got
used, even in his mother's hot little house, to his native air. He
breathed the bright cold sunshine with pleasure; he raised his
eyes to the arching blueness, and thought he had never seen a
dome so magnificently painted. He turned his head this way
and that, as he walked (now that he had recovered his legs, he
foresaw that he should walk a good deal), and freely indulged
his most valued organ, the organ that had won him such
reputation as he already enjoyed. In the little artistic circle in
which he moved in Paris, Florimond Daintry was thought to
have a great deal of eye. His power of rendering was questioned, his execution had been called pretentious and feeble;
but a conviction had somehow been diffused that he saw
things with extraordinary intensity. No one could tell better
than he what to paint, and what not to paint, even though his
interpretation were sometimes rather too sketchy. It will have
been guessed that he was an impressionist; and it must be
admitted that this was the character in which he proceeded on
his visit to Miss Daintry. He was constantly shutting one eye,
to see the better with the other, making a little telescope by
curving one of his hands together, waving these members in
the air with vague pictorial gestures, pointing at things which,
when people turned to follow his direction, seemed to mock
the vulgar vision by eluding it. I do not mean that he practised
these devices as he walked along Beacon Street, into which he
had crossed shortly after leaving his mother's house; but now
that he had broken the ice he acted quite in the spirit of the
reply he had made to a friend in Paris, shortly before his
departure, who asked him why he was going back to America
—"I am going to see how it looks." He was of course very
conscious of his eye; and his effort to cultivate it was both
intuitive and deliberate. He spoke of it freely, as he might
have done of a valuable watch or a horse. He was always
trying to get the visual impression; asking himself, with

regard to such and such an object or a place, of what its
"character" would consist. There is no doubt he really saw
with great intensity; and the reader will probably feel that he
was welcome to this ambiguous privilege. It was not important for him that things should be beautiful; what he sought to
discover was their identity—the signs by which he should
know them. He began this inquiry as soon as he stepped into
Newbury Street from his mother's door, and he was destined
to continue it for the first few weeks of his stay in Boston. As
time went on, his attention relaxed; for one couldn't do more
than see, as he said to his mother and another person; and he
had seen. Then the novelty wore off—the novelty which is
often so absurdly great in the eyes of the American who
returns to his native land after a few years spent in the foreign
element—an effect to be accounted for only on the supposition
that in the secret parts of his mind he recognises the aspect of
life in Europe as, through long heredity, the more familiar;
so that superficially, having no interest to oppose it, it quickly
supplants the domestic type, which, upon his return, becomes
supreme, but with its credit in many cases appreciably and
permanently diminished. Florimond painted a few things
while he was in America, though he had told his mother he
had come home to rest; but when, several months later, in
Paris, he showed his "notes," as he called them, to a friend,
the young Frenchman asked him if Massachusetts were really
so much like Andalusia.

There was certainly nothing Andalusian in the prospect as
Florimond traversed the artificial bosom of the Back Bay. He
had made his way promptly into Beacon Street, and he greatly
admired that vista. The long straight avenue lay airing its
newness in the frosty day, and all its individual façades, with
their neat, sharp ornaments, seemed to have been scoured,
with a kind of friction, by the hard, salutary light. Their brilliant browns and drabs, their rosy surfaces of brick, made a
variety of fresh, violent tones, such as Florimond liked to

memorise, and the large clear windows of their curved fronts faced each other, across the street, like candid, inevitable eyes. There was something almost terrible in the windows; Florimond had forgotten how vast and clean they were, and how, in their sculptured frames, the New England air seemed, like a zealous housewife, to polish and preserve them. A great many ladies were looking out, and groups of children, in the drawing-rooms, were flattening their noses against the transparent plate. Here and there, behind it, the back of a statuette or the symmetry of a painted vase, erect on a pedestal, presented itself to the street, and enabled the passer to construct, more or less, the room within—its frescoed ceilings, its new silk sofas, its untarnished fixtures. This continuity of glass constituted a kind of exposure, within and without, and gave the street the appearance of an enormous corridor, in which the public and the private were familiar and intermingled. But it was all very cheerful and commodious, and seemed to speak of diffused wealth, of intimate family life, of comfort constantly renewed. All sorts of things in the region of the temperature had happened during the few days that Florimond had been in the country. The cold wave had spent itself, a snowstorm had come and gone, and the air, after this temporary relaxation, had renewed its keenness. The snow, which had fallen in but moderate abundance, was heaped along the side of the pavement; it formed a radiant cornice on the house-tops and crowned the windows with a plain white cap. It deepened the colour of everything else, made all surfaces look ruddy, and at a distance sent into the air a thin, delicate mist —a vaporous blur—which occasionally softened an edge. The upper part of Beacon Street seemed to Florimond charming— the long, wide, sunny slope, the uneven line of the older houses, the contrasted, differing, bulging fronts, the painted bricks, the tidy facings, the immaculate doors, the burnished silver plates, the denuded twigs of the far extent of the Common, on the other side; and to crown the eminence and complete the picture, high in the air, poised in the right place, over everything that clustered below, the most felicitous object in Boston—the gilded dome of the State House. It was in the shadow of this monument, as we know, that Miss Daintry lived; and Florimond, who was always lucky, had the good fortune to find her at home.

V

IT may seem that I have assumed on the part of the reader too great a curiosity about the impressions of this young man, who was not very remarkable, and who has not even the recommendation of being the hero of our perhaps too descriptive tale. The reader will already have discovered that a hero fails us here; but if I go on at all risks to say a few words about Florimond, he will perhaps understand the better why this part has not been filled. Miss Daintry's nephew was not very original; it was his own illusion that he had in a considerable degree the value of rareness. Even this youthful conceit was not rare, for it was not of heroic proportions, and was liable to lapses and discouragements. He was a fair, slim, civil young man, and you would never have guessed from his appearance that he was an impressionist. He was neat and sleek and quite anti-Bohemian, and in spite of his looking about him as he walked, his figure was much more in harmony with the Boston landscape than he supposed. He was a little vain, a little affected, a little pretentious, a little good-looking, a little amusing, a little spoiled, and at times a little tiresome. If he was disagreeable, however, it was also only a little; he did not carry anything to a very high pitch; he was accomplished, industrious, successful—all in the minor degree. He was fond of his mother and fond of himself; he also liked the people who liked him. Such people could belong only to the class of good listeners, for Florimond, with the least encouragement (he was very susceptible to that), would chatter by the hour. As he was very observant, and knew a great many stories, his talk was often entertaining, especially to women, many of whom thought him wonderfully sympathetic. It may be added that he was still very young and fluid, and neither his defects nor his virtues had a great consistency. He was fond of the society of women, and had an idea that he knew a great deal about that element of humanity. He believed himself to know everything about art, and almost everything about life, and he expressed himself as much as possible in the phrases that are current in studios. He spoke French very well, and it had rubbed off on his English.

His aunt listened to him attentively, with her nippers on her nose. She had been a little restless at first, and, to relieve herself, had vaguely punched the sofa-cushion which lay beside her—a gesture that her friends always recognised; they knew it to express a particular emotion. Florimond, whose egotism was candid and confiding, talked for an hour about himself—about what he had done, and what he intended to do, what he had said and what had been said to him; about his habits, tastes, achievements, peculiarities, which were apparently so numerous; about the decorations of his studio in Paris; about the character of the French, the works of Zola, the theory of art for art, the American type, the "stupidity" of his mother's new house—though of course it had some things that were knowing—the pronunciation of Joanna's children, the effect of the commission-business on Arthur Merriman's conversation, the effect of everything on his mother, Mrs Daintry, and the effect of Mrs Daintry on her son Florimond. The young man had an epithet which he constantly introduced to express disapproval; when he spoke of the architecture of his mother's house, over which she had taken great pains (she remembered the gabled fronts of Nuremberg), he said that a certain effect had been dreadfully missed, that the character of the doorway

was simply "crass." He expressed, however, a lively sense of
the bright cleanness of American interiors. "Oh, as for that,"
he said, "the place is kept—it's kept;" and, to give an image
of this idea, he put his gathered fingers to his lips an instant,
seemed to kiss them or blow upon them, and then opened
them into the air. Miss Daintry had never encountered this
gesture before; she had heard it described by travelled persons; but to see her own nephew in the very act of it led her to
administer another thump to the sofa-cushion. She finally got
this article under control, and sat more quiet, with her hands
clasped upon it, while her visitor continued to discourse. In
pursuance of his character as an impressionist, he gave her a
great many impressions; but it seemed to her that as he talked,
he simply exposed himself—exposed his egotism, his little
pretensions. Lucretia Daintry, as we know, had a love of
justice, and though her opinions were apt to be very positive,
her charity was great and her judgments were not harsh; moreover, there was in her composition not a drop of acrimony.
Nevertheless, she was, as the phrase is, rather hard on poor
little Florimond; and to explain her severity we are bound to
assume that in the past he had in some way offended her.
To-day, at any rate, it seemed to her that he patronised his
maiden-aunt. He scarcely asked about her health, but took for
granted on her part an unlimited interest in his own sensations.
It came over her afresh that his mother had been absurd in
thinking that the usual resources of Boston would not have
sufficed to maintain him; and she smiled a little grimly at the
idea that a special provision should have been made. This idea
presently melted into another, over which she was free to
regale herself only after her nephew had departed. For the
moment she contented herself with saying to him, when a
pause in his young eloquence gave her a chance—"You will
have a great many people to go and see. You pay the penalty
of being a Bostonian; you have several hundred cousins. One
pays for everything."

Florimond lifted his eyebrows. "I pay for that every day of my life. Have I got to go and see them all?"

"All—every one," said his aunt, who in reality did not hold this obligation in the least sacred.

"And to say something agreeable to them all?" the young man went on.

"Oh no, that is not necessary," Miss Daintry rejoined, with more exactness. "There are one or two, however, who always appreciate a pretty speech." She added in an instant, "Do you remember Mrs Mesh?"

"Mrs Mesh?" Florimond apparently did not remember.

"The wife of Donald Mesh; your grandfathers were first cousins. I don't mean her grandfather, but her husband's. If you don't remember her, I suppose he married her after you went away."

"I remember Donald; but I never knew he was a relation. He was single then, I think."

"Well, he's double now," said Miss Daintry; "he's triple, I may say, for there are two ladies in the house."

"If you mean he's a polygamist—are there Mormons even here?" Florimond, leaning back in his chair, with his elbow on the arm, and twisting with his gloved fingers the point of a small fair moustache, did not appear to have been arrested by this account of Mr Mesh's household; for he almost immediately asked, in a large, detached way—"Are there any nice women here?"

"It depends on what you mean by nice women; there are some very sharp ones."

"Oh, I don't like sharp ones," Florimond remarked, in a tone which made his aunt long to throw her sofa-cushion at his head. "Are there any pretty ones?"

She looked at him a moment, hesitating. "Rachel Torrance is pretty, in a strange, unusual way—black hair and blue eyes, a serpentine figure, old coins in her tresses; that sort of thing."

"I have seen a good deal of that sort of thing," said Florimond, abstractedly.

"That I know nothing about. I mention Pauline Mesh's as one of the houses that you ought to go to, and where I know you are expected."

"I remember now that my mother has said something about that. But who is the woman with coins in her hair?— what has she to do with Pauline Mesh?"

"Rachel is staying with her; she came from New York a week ago, and I believe she means to spend the winter. She isn't a woman, she's a girl."

"My mother didn't speak of her," said Florimond; "but I don't think she would recommend me a girl with a serpentine figure."

"Very likely not," Miss Daintry answered, dryly. "Rachel Torrance is a far-away cousin of Donald Mesh, and consequently of mine and of yours. She's an artist, like yourself; she paints flowers on little panels and *plaques.*"

"Like myself?—I never painted a *plaque* in my life!" exclaimed Florimond, staring.

"Well, she's a model also; you can paint her if you like; she has often been painted, I believe."

Florimond had begun to caress the other tip of his moustache. "I don't care for women who have been painted before. I like to find them out. Besides, I want to rest this winter."

His aunt was disappointed; she wished to put him into relation with Rachel Torrance, and his indifference was an obstacle. The meeting was sure to take place sooner or later, but she would have him glad to precipitate it, and, above all, to quicken her nephew's susceptibilities. "Take care you are not found out yourself!" she exclaimed, tossing away her sofa-cushion and getting up.

Florimond did not see what she meant, and he accordingly bore her no rancour; but when, before he took his leave, he said to her, rather irrelevantly, that if he should find himself in the mood during his stay in Boston, he should like to do her portrait—she had such a delightful face—she almost thought the speech a deliberate impertinence. "Do you mean that you have discovered me—that no one has suspected it before?" she inquired with a laugh, and a little flush in the countenance that he was so good as to appreciate.

Florimond replied, with perfect coolness and good-nature, that he didn't know about this, but that he was sure no one had seen her in just the way he saw her; and he waved his hand in the air with strange circular motions, as if to evoke before him the image of a canvas, with a figure just rubbed in. He repeated this gesture, or something very like it, by way of farewell, when he quitted his aunt, and she thought him insufferably patronising.

This is why she wished him, without loss of time, to make the acquaintance of Rachel Torrance, whose treatment of his pretensions she thought would be salutary. It may now be communicated to the reader—after a delay proportionate to the momentousness of the fact—that this had been the idea which suddenly flowered in her brain, as she sat face to face with her irritating young visitor. It had vaguely shaped itself after her meeting with that strange girl from Brooklyn, whom Mrs Mesh, all gratitude—for she liked strangeness—promptly brought to see her; and her present impression of her nephew rapidly completed it. She had not expected to take an interest in Rachel Torrance, and could not see why, through a freak of Susan's, she should have been called upon to think so much about her; but, to her surprise, she perceived that Mrs Daintry's proposed victim was not the usual forward girl. She perceived at the same time that it had been ridiculous to think of Rachel as a victim—to suppose that she was in danger of vainly fixing her affections upon Florimond. She was much more likely to triumph than to suffer; and if her visit to Boston were to produce bitter fruits, it would not be she who should taste them. She had a striking, oriental head, a beautiful smile, a manner of dressing which carried out her exotic type, and a great deal of experience and wit. She evidently knew the world, as one knows it when one has to live by its help. If she had an aim in life, she would draw her bow well above the tender breast of Florimond Daintry. With all this, she certainly was an honest, obliging girl, and had a sense of humour which was a fortunate obstacle to her falling into a pose. Her coins and amulets and seamless garments were, for her, a part of the general joke of one's looking like a Circassian or a Smyrniote—an accident for which nature was responsible; and it may be said of her that she took herself much less seriously than other people took her. This was a defect for which Lucretia Daintry had a great kindness; especially as she quickly saw that Rachel was not of an insipid paste, as even triumphant coquettes sometimes are. In spite of her poverty and the opportunities her beauty must have brought her, she had not yet seen fit to marry—which was a proof that she was clever as well as disinterested. It looks dreadfully cold-blooded as I write it here, but the notion that this capable creature might administer poetic justice to Florimond gave a measurable satisfaction to Miss Daintry. He was in distinct need of a snub, for down in Newbury Street his mother was perpetually swinging the censer; and no young nature could stand that sort of thing—least of all such a nature as Florimond's. She said to herself that such a "putting in his place" as he might receive from Rachel Torrance would probably be a permanent correction. She wished his good, as she wished the good of every one; and that desire was at the bottom of her vision. She knew perfectly what she should like: she should like him to fall in love with Rachel, as he probably would, and to have no doubt of her feeling immensely honoured. She should like Rachel to encourage him just enough—just so far as she might, without being false. A little would do, for Florimond would always take his success for granted. To this point did the study of her nephew's moral regeneration bring the

excellent woman who a few days before had accused his mother
of a lack of morality. His mother was thinking only of his
pleasure; *she* was thinking of his immortal spirit. She should
like Rachel to tell him at the end that he was a presumptuous
little boy, and that since it was his business to render "impressions," he might see what he could do with that of having
been jilted. This extraordinary flight of fancy on Miss Daintry's part was caused in some degree by the high spirits which
sprang from her conviction, after she met the young lady,
that Mrs Mesh's companion was not in danger; for even when
she wrote to her sister-in-law in the manner the reader knows,
her conscience was not wholly at rest. There was still a risk,
and she knew not why she should take risks for Florimond.
Now, however, she was prepared to be perfectly happy when
she should hear that the young man was constantly in
Arlington Street; and at the end of a little month she enjoyed
this felicity.

VI

MRS MESH sat on one side of the fire, and Florimond on the
other; he had by this time acquired the privilege of a customary seat. He had taken a general view of Boston. It was like a
first introduction, for before his going to live in Paris he had
been too young to judge; and the result of this survey was the
conviction that there was nothing better than Mrs Mesh's
drawing-room. She was one of the few persons whom one
was certain to find at home after five o'clock; and the place
itself was agreeable to Florimond, who was very fastidious
about furniture and decorations. He was willing to concede
that Mrs Mesh (the relationship had not yet seemed close
enough to justify him in calling her Pauline) knew a great deal
about such matters; though it was clear that she was indebted
for some of her illumination to Rachel Torrance, who had

induced her to make several changes. These two ladies, between them, represented a great fund of taste; with a difference that was a result of Rachel's knowing clearly beforehand what she liked (Florimond called her, at least, by her baptismal name), and Mrs Mesh's only knowing it after a succession of experiments, of transposings and drapings, all more or less ingenious and expensive. If Florimond liked Mrs Mesh's drawing-room better than any other corner of Boston, he also had his preference in regard to its phases and hours. It was most charming in the winter twilight, by the glow of the fire, before the lamps had been brought in. The ruddy flicker played over many objects, making them look more mysterious than Florimond had supposed anything could look in Boston, and, among others, upon Rachel Torrance, who, when she moved about the room in a desultory way (never so much *enfoncée*, as Florimond said, in a chair as Mrs Mesh was) certainly attracted and detained the eye. The young man from his corner (he was almost as much *enfoncé* as Mrs Mesh) used to watch her; and he could easily see what his aunt had meant by saying she had a serpentine figure. She was slim and flexible, she took attitudes which would have been awkward in other women, but which her charming pliancy made natural. She reminded him of a celebrated actress in Paris who was the ideal of tortuous thinness. Miss Torrance used often to seat herself for a short time at the piano; and though she never had been taught this art (she played only by ear), her musical feeling was such that she charmed the twilight hour. Mrs Mesh sat on one side of the fire, as I have said, and Florimond on the other; the two might have been found in this relation—listening, face to face—almost any day in the week. Mrs Mesh raved about her new friend, as they said in Boston—I mean about Rachel Torrance, not about Florimond Daintry. She had at last got hold of a mind that understood her own (Mrs Mesh's mind contained depths of mystery), and she sacrificed herself, generally, to throw her companion into relief. Her sacrifice was rewarded, for the girl was universally liked and admired; she was a new type altogether; she was the lioness of the winter. Florimond had an opportunity to see his native town in one of its fits of enthusiasm. He had heard of the infatuations of Boston, literary and social; of its capacity for giving itself with intensity to a temporary topic; and he was now conscious, on all sides, of the breath of New England discussion. Some one had said to him—or had said to some one, who repeated it—that there was no place like Boston for taking up with such seriousness a second-rate spinster from Brooklyn. But Florimond himself made no criticism; for, as we know, he speedily fell under the charm of Rachel Torrance's personality. He was perpetually talking with Mrs Mesh about it; and when Mrs Mesh herself descanted on the subject, he listened with the utmost attention. At first, on his return, he rather feared the want of topics; he foresaw that he should miss the talk of the studios, of the theatres, of the boulevard, of a little circle of "naturalists" (in literature and art) to which he belonged, without sharing all its views. But he presently perceived that Boston, too, had its actualities, and that it even had this in common with Paris—that it gave its attention most willingly to a female celebrity. If he had had any hope of being himself the lion of the winter, it had been dissipated by the spectacle of his cousin's success. He saw that while she was there he could only be a subject of secondary reference. He bore her no grudge for this. I must hasten to declare that from the pettiness of this particular jealousy poor Florimond was quite exempt. Moreover, he was swept along by the general chorus; and he perceived that when one changes one's sky, one inevitably changes, more or less, one's standard. Rachel Torrance was neither an actress, nor a singer, nor a beauty, nor one of the ladies who were chronicled in the *Figaro*, nor the author of a successful book, nor a person of the great world; she had neither a future, nor a past, nor a position, nor even a husband, to make her identity more solid; she was a simple American girl, of the class that lived in *pensions* (a class of which Florimond had ever entertained a theoretic horror); and yet she had profited to the degree of which our young man was witness, by those treasures of sympathy constantly in reserve in the American public (as has already been intimated) for the youthful-feminine. If Florimond was struck with all this, it may be imagined whether or not his mother thought she had been clever when it occurred to her (before any one else) that Rachel would be a resource for the term of hibernation. She had forgotten all her scruples and hesitations; she only knew she had seen very far. She was proud of her prescience, she was even amused with it; and for the moment she held her head rather high. No one knew of it but Lucretia —for she had never confided it to Joanna, of whom she would have been more afraid in such a connection even than of her sister-in-law; but Mr and Mrs Merriman perceived an unusual lightness in her step, a fitful sparkle in her eye. It was of course easy for them to make up their mind that she was exhilarated to this degree by the presence of her son; especially as he seemed to be getting on beautifully in Boston.

"She stays out longer every day; she is scarcely ever home to tea," Mrs Mesh remarked, looking up at the clock on the chimney-piece.

Florimond could not fail to know to whom she alluded, for it has been intimated that between these two there was much conversation about Rachel Torrance. "It's funny, the way the girls run about alone here," he said, in the amused, contemplative tone in which he frequently expressed himself on the subject of American life. "Rachel stays out after dark, and no one thinks any the worse of her."

"Oh, well, she's old enough," Mrs Mesh rejoined, with a little sigh, which seemed to suggest that Rachel's age was really affecting. Her eyes had been opened by Florimond to many of the peculiarities of the society that surrounded her; and though she had spent only as many months in Europe as her visitor had spent years, she now sometimes spoke as if she thought the manners of Boston more odd even than he could pretend to do. She was very quick at picking up an idea, and there was nothing she desired more than to have the last on every subject. This winter, from her two new friends, Florimond and Rachel, she had extracted a great many that were new to her; the only trouble was that, coming from different sources, they sometimes contradicted each other. Many of them, however, were very vivifying; they added a new zest to that prospect of life which had always, in winter, the denuded bushes, the solid pond, the plank-covered walks, the exaggerated bridge, the patriotic statues, the dry, hard texture, of the Public Garden for its foreground, and for its middle distance the pale, frozen twigs, stiff in the windy sky that whistled over the Common, the domestic dome of the State House, familiar in the untinted air, and the competitive spires of a liberal faith. Mrs Mesh had an active imagination, and plenty of time on her hands. Her two children were young, and they slept a good deal; she had explained to Florimond, who observed that she was a great deal less in the nursery than his sister, that she pretended only to give her attention to their waking hours. "I have people for the rest of the time," she said; and the rest of the time was considerable; so that there were very few obstacles to her cultivation of ideas. There was one in her mind now, and I may as well impart it to the reader without delay. She was not quite so delighted with Rachel Torrance as she had been a month ago; it seemed to her that the young lady took up—socially speaking—too much room in the house; and she wondered how long she intended to remain, and whether it would be possible, without a direct request, to induce her to take her way back to Brooklyn. This last was the conception with which she was at present engaged; she was at moments much pressed by it, and she had thoughts of taking Florimond Daintry into her confidence. This, however, she determined not to do, lest he should regard it as a sign that she was jealous of her companion. I know not whether she was, but this I know—that Mrs Mesh was a woman of a high ideal and would not for the world have appeared so. If she was jealous, this would imply that she thought Florimond was in love with Rachel; and she could only object to that on the ground of being in love with him herself. She was not in love with him, and had no intention of being; of this the reader, possibly alarmed, may definitely rest assured. Moreover, she did not think him in love with Rachel; as to her reason for this reserve, I need not, perhaps, be absolutely outspoken. She was not jealous, she would have said; she was only oppressed —she was a little over-ridden. Rachel pervaded her house, pervaded her life, pervaded Boston; every one thought it necessary to talk to her about Rachel, to rave about her in the Boston manner, which seemed to Mrs Mesh, in spite of the Puritan tradition, very much more unbridled than that of Baltimore. They thought it would give her pleasure; but by this time she knew everything about Rachel. The girl had proved rather more of a figure than she expected; and though she could not be called pretentious, she had the air, in staying with Pauline Mesh, of conferring rather more of a favour than she received. This was absurd for a person who was, after all, though not in her first youth, only a girl, and who, as Mrs Mesh was sure from her biography—for Rachel had related every item—had never before had such unrestricted access to the fleshpots. The fleshpots were full, under Donald Mesh's roof, and his wife could easily believe that the poor girl would not be in a hurry to return to her boarding-house in Brooklyn. For that matter there were lots of people in Boston who would be delighted that she should come to them. It was doubtless an inconsistency on Mrs Mesh's part that if she was overdone with the praises of Rachel Torrance which fell from every lip, she should not herself have forborne to broach the topic. But I have sufficiently intimated that it had a perverse fascination for her; it is true she did not speak of Rachel only to praise her. Florimond, in truth, was a little weary of the young lady's name; he had plenty of topics of his own, and he had his own opinion about Rachel Torrance. He did not take up Mrs Mesh's remark as to her being old enough.

"You must wait till she comes in. Please ring for tea," said Mrs Mesh, after a pause. She had noticed that Florimond was comparing his watch with her clock; it occurred to her that he might be going.

"Oh, I always wait, you know; I like to see her when she has been anywhere. She tells one all about it, and describes everything so well."

Mrs Mesh looked at him a moment. "She sees a great deal more in things than I am usually able to discover. She sees the most extraordinary things in Boston."

"Well, so do I," said Florimond, placidly.

"Well, I don't, I must say!" She asked him to ring again; and then, with a slight irritation, accused him of not ringing hard enough; but before he could repeat the operation she left her chair and went herself to the bell. After this she stood before the fire a moment, gazing into it; then suggested to Florimond that he should put on a log.

"Is it necessary—when your servant is coming in a moment?" the young man asked, unexpectedly, without moving. In an instant, however, he rose; and then he explained that this was only his little joke.

"Servants are too stupid," said Mrs Mesh. "But I spoil you. What would your mother say?" She watched him while he placed the log. She was plump, and she was not tall; but she was a very pretty woman. She had round brown eyes, which looked as if she had been crying a little—she had nothing in life to cry about; and dark, wavy hair, which here and there, in short, crisp tendrils, escaped artfully from the form in which it was dressed. When she smiled, she showed very pretty teeth; and the combination of her touching eyes and her parted lips was at such moments almost bewitching. She was accustomed to express herself in humorous superlatives, in pictorial circumlocutions; and had acquired in Boston the rudiments of a social dialect which, to be heard in perfection, should be heard on the lips of a native. Mrs Mesh had picked it up; but it must be confessed that she used it without originality. It was an accident that on this occasion she had not expressed her wish for her tea by saying that she should like a pint or two of that Chinese fluid.

"My mother believes I can't be spoiled," said Florimond, giving a little push with his toe to the stick that he had placed in the embers; after which he sank back into his chair, while Mrs Mesh resumed possession of her own. "I am ever fresh —ever pure."

"You are ever conceited. I don't see what you find so extraordinary in Boston," Mrs Mesh added, reverting to his remark of a moment before.

"Oh, everything! the ways of the people, their ideas, their peculiar *cachet*. The very expression of their faces amuses me."

"Most of them have no expression at all."

"Oh, you are used to it," Florimond said. "You have become one of themselves; you have ceased to notice."

"I am more of a stranger than you; I was born beneath other skies. Is it possible that you don't know yet that I am a native of Baltimore? 'Maryland, my Maryland!'"

"Have they got so much expression in Maryland? No, I thank you; no tea. Is it possible," Florimond went on, with the familiarity of pretended irritation, "is it possible that you haven't noticed yet that I never take it? *Boisson fade, écœurante*, as Balzac calls it."

"Ah, well, if you don't take it on account of Balzac!" said Mrs Mesh. "I never saw a man who had such fantastic reasons. Where, by the way, is the volume of that depraved old author you promised to bring me?"

"When do you think he flourished? You call everything old, in this country, that isn't in the morning paper. I haven't brought you the volume, because I don't want to bring you presents," Florimond said; "I want you to love me for myself, as they say in Paris."

"Don't quote what they say in Paris! Don't profane this innocent bower with those fearful words!" Mrs Mesh rejoined, with a jocose intention. "Dear lady, your son is not everything we could wish!" she added in the same mock-dramatic tone, as the curtain of the door was lifted, and Mrs Daintry rather timidly advanced. Mrs Daintry had come to satisfy a curiosity, after all quite legitimate; she could no longer resist the impulse to ascertain for herself, so far as she might, how Rachel Torrance and Florimond were getting on. She had had no definite expectation of finding Florimond at Mrs Mesh's; but she supposed that at this hour of the afternoon—it was already dark, and the ice, in many parts of Beacon Street, had a polish which gleamed through the dusk—she should find Rachel. "Your son has lived too long in far-off lands; he has dwelt among outworn things," Mrs Mesh went on, as she conducted her visitor to a chair. "Dear lady, you are not as Balzac was; do you start at the mention of his name?—therefore you will have some tea in a little painted cup."

Mrs Daintry was not bewildered, though it may occur to the reader that she might have been; she was only a little disappointed. She had hoped she might have occasion to talk about Florimond; but the young man's presence was a denial of this privilege. "I am afraid Rachel is not at home," she remarked. "I am afraid she will think I have not been very attentive."

"She will be in in a moment; we are waiting for her," Florimond said. "It's impossible she should think any harm of you. I have told her too much good."

"Ah, Mrs Daintry, don't build too much on what he has told her! He's a false and faithless man!" Pauline Mesh interposed; while the good lady from Newbury Street, smiling at this adjuration, but looking a little grave, turned from one of her companions to the other. Florimond had relapsed into his chair by the fireplace; he sat contemplating the embers, and fingering the tip of his moustache. Mrs Daintry imbibed her tea, and told how often she had slipped coming down the hill. These expedients helped her to wear a quiet face; but in reality she was nervous, and she felt rather foolish. It came over her that she was rather dishonest; she had presented herself at Mrs Mesh's in the capacity of a spy. The reader already knows she was subject to sudden revulsions of feeling. There is an adage about repenting at leisure; but Mrs Daintry always repented in a hurry. There was something in the air—something impalpable, magnetic—that told her she had better not have come; and even while she conversed with Mrs Mesh she wondered what this mystic element could be. Of course she had been greatly preoccupied, these last weeks; for it had seemed to her that her plan with regard to Rachel Torrance was succeeding only too well. Florimond had frankly accepted her in the spirit in which she had been offered, and it was very plain that she was helping him to pass his winter. He was constantly at the house—Mrs Daintry could not tell exactly how often; but she knew very well that in Boston, if one saw anything of a person, one saw a good deal. At first he used to speak of it; for two or three weeks he had talked a good deal about Rachel Torrance. More lately, his allusions had become few; yet to the best of Mrs Daintry's belief his step was often in Arlington Street. This aroused her suspicions, and at times it troubled her conscience; there were moments when she wondered whether, in arranging a genial winter for Florimond, she had also prepared a season of torment for herself. Was he in love with the girl, or had he already discovered that the girl was in love with him? The delicacy of either situation would account for his silence. Mrs Daintry said to herself that it would be a grim joke if she should prove to have plotted only too well. It was her sister-in-law's warning in especial that haunted her imagination, and she scarcely knew, at times, whether more to hope that Florimond might have been smitten, or to pray that Rachel might remain indifferent. It was impossible for Mrs Daintry to shake off the sense of responsibility; she could not shut her eyes to the fact that she had been the prime mover. It was all very well to say that the situation, as it stood, was of Lucretia's making; the thing never would have come into Lucretia's head if she had not laid it before her. Unfortunately, with the quiet life she led, she had very little chance to observe; she went out so little, that she was reduced to guessing what the manner of the two young persons might be to each other when they met in society, and she should have thought herself wanting in delicacy if she had sought to be intimate with Rachel Torrance. Now that her plan was in operation, she could make no attempt to foster it, to acknowledge it in the face of Heaven. Fortunately, Rachel had so many attentions, that there was no fear of her missing those of Newbury Street. She had dined there once, in the first days of her sojourn, without Pauline and Donald, who had declined, and with Joanna and Joanna's husband for all "company." Mrs Daintry had noticed nothing particular then, save that Arthur Merriman talked rather more than usual—though he was always a free talker—and had bantered Rachel rather more familiarly than was perhaps necessary (considering that *he*, after all, was not her cousin) on her ignorance of Boston, and her thinking that Pauline Mesh could tell her anything about it. On this occasion Florimond talked very little; of course he could not say much when Arthur was in such extraordinary spirits. She knew by this time all that Florimond thought of his brother-in-law, and she herself had to confess that she liked Arthur better in his jaded hours, even though then he was a little cynical. Mrs Daintry had been perhaps a little disappointed in Rachel, whom she saw for the first time in several years. The girl was less peculiar than she remembered her being, savoured less of the old studio, the musical parties, the creditors waiting at the door. However, people in

Boston found her unusual, and Mrs Daintry reflected, with a twinge at her depravity, that perhaps she had expected something too dishevelled. At any rate, several weeks had elapsed since then, and there had been plenty of time for Miss Torrance to attach herself to Florimond. It was less than ever Mrs Daintry's wish that he should (even in this case) ask her to be his wife. It seemed to her less than ever the way her son should marry—because he had got entangled with a girl in consequence of his mother's rashness. It occurred to her, of course, that she might warn the young man; but when it came to the point she could not bring herself to speak. She had never discussed the question of love with him, and she didn't know what ideas he might have brought with him from Paris. It was too delicate; it might put notions into his head. He might say something strange and French, which she shouldn't like; and then perhaps she should feel bound to warn Rachel herself—a complication from which she absolutely shrank. It was part of her embarrassment now, as she sat in Mrs Mesh's drawing-room, that she should probably spoil Florimond's entertainment for this afternoon, and that such a crossing of his inclination would make him the more dangerous. He had told her that he was waiting for Rachel to come in; and at the same time, in view of the lateness of the hour and her being on foot, when she herself should take her leave he would be bound in decency to accompany her. As for remaining after Rachel should come in, that was an indiscretion which scarcely seemed to her possible. Mrs Daintry was an American mother, and she knew what the elder generation owes to the younger. If Florimond had come there to call on a young lady, he didn't, as they used to say, want any mothers round. She glanced covertly at her son, to try and find some comfort in his countenance; for her perplexity was heavy. But she was struck only with his looking very handsome, as he lounged there in the firelight, and with his being very much at home. This did not lighten her burden, and she expressed all the

weight of it—in the midst of Mrs Mesh's flights of comparison
—in an irrelevant little sigh. At such a time her only comfort could be the thought that at all events she had not betrayed herself to Lucretia. She had scarcely exchanged a
word with Lucretia about Rachel since that young lady's
arrival; and she had observed in silence that Miss Daintry
now had a guest in the person of a young woman who had
lately opened a kindergarten. This reticence might surely pass
for natural.

Rachel came in before long, but even then Mrs Daintry
ventured to stay a little. The visitor from Brooklyn embraced
Mrs Mesh, who told her that, prodigal as she was, there was
no fatted calf for her return; she must content herself with
cold tea. Nothing could be more charming than her manner,
which was full of native archness; and it seemed to Mrs
Daintry that she directed her pleasantries at Florimond with a
grace that was intended to be irresistible. The relation between
them was a relation of "chaff," and consisted, on one side and
the other, in alternations of attack and defence. Mrs Daintry
reflected that she should not wish her son to have a wife who
should be perpetually turning him into a joke; for it seemed
to her, perhaps, that Rachel Torrance put in her thrusts rather
faster than Florimond could parry them. She was evidently
rather wanting in the faculty of reverence, and Florimond
panted a little. They presently went into an adjoining room,
where the lamplight was brighter; Rachel wished to show the
young man an old painted fan, which she had brought back
from the repairer's. They remained there ten minutes. Mrs
Daintry, as she sat with Mrs Mesh, heard their voices much
intermingled. She wished very much to confide herself a little
to Pauline—to ask her whether she thought Rachel was in
love with Florimond. But she had a foreboding that this
would not be safe; Pauline was capable of repeating her
question to the others, of calling out to Rachel to come back
and answer it. She contented herself, therefore, with asking her

hostess about the little Meshes, and regaling her with anecdotes of Joanna's progeny.

"Don't you ever have your little ones with you at this hour?" she inquired. "You know this is what Longfellow calls the children's hour."

Mrs Mesh hesitated a moment. "Well, you know, one can't have everything at once. I have my social duties now; I have my guests. I have Miss Torrance—you see she is not a person one can overlook."

"I suppose not," said poor Mrs Daintry, remembering how little she herself had overlooked her.

"Have you done brandishing that superannuated relic?" Mrs Mesh asked of Rachel and Florimond, as they returned to the fireside. "I should as soon think of fanning myself with the fire-shovel!"

"He has broken my heart," Rachel said. "He tells me it is not a Watteau."

"Do you believe everything he tells you, my dear? His word is the word of the betrayer."

"Well, I know Watteau didn't paint fans," Florimond remarked, "any more than Michael Angelo."

"I suppose you think he painted ceilings," said Rachel Torrance. "I have painted a great many myself."

"A great many ceilings? I should like to see that!" Florimond exclaimed.

Rachel Torrance, with her usual promptness, adopted this fantasy. "Yes, I have decorated half the churches in Brooklyn; you know how many there are."

"If you mean fans, I wish men carried them," the young man went on; "I should like to have one *de votre façon.*"

"You're cool enough as you are; I should be sorry to give you anything that would make you cooler!"

This retort, which may not strike the reader by its originality, was pregnant enough for Mrs Daintry; it seemed to her to denote that the situation was critical; and she proposed to retire. Florimond walked home with her; but it was only as they reached their door that she ventured to say to him what had been on her tongue's end since they left Arlington Street.

"Florimond, I want to ask you something. I think it is important, and you mustn't be surprised. Are you in love with Rachel Torrance?"

Florimond stared, in the light of the street-lamp. The collar of his overcoat was turned up; he stamped a little as he stood still; the breath of the February evening pervaded the empty vistas of the "new land." "In love with Rachel Torrance? *Jamais de la vie!* What put that into your head?"

"Seeing you with her, that way, this evening. You know you are very attentive."

"How do you mean, attentive?"

"You go there very often. Isn't it almost every day?"

Florimond hesitated, and, in spite of the frigid dusk, his mother could see that there was irritation in his eye. "Where else can I go, in this precious place? It's the pleasantest house here."

"Yes, I suppose it's very pleasant," Mrs Daintry murmured. "But I would rather have you return to Paris than go there too often," she added, with sudden energy.

"How do you mean, too often? *Qu'est-ce qui vous prend, ma mère?*" said Florimond.

"Is Rachel—Rachel in love with *you?*" she inquired solemnly. She felt that this question, though her heart beat as she uttered it, should not be mitigated by a circumlocution.

"Good heavens! mother, fancy talking about love in this temperature!" Florimond exclaimed. "Let one at least get into the house."

Mrs Daintry followed him reluctantly; for she always had a feeling that if anything disagreeable were to be done one should not make it less drastic by selecting agreeable conditions. In the drawing-room, before the fire, she returned to her inquiry. "My son, you have not answered me about Rachel."

"Is she in love with me? Why, very possibly!"

"Are you serious, Florimond?"

"Why shouldn't I be? I have seen the way women go off."

Mrs Daintry was silent a moment. "Florimond, is it true?" she said presently.

"Is what true? I don't see where you want to come out."

"Is it true that that girl has fixed her affections——" and Mrs Daintry's voice dropped.

"Upon me, *ma mère*? I don't say it's true, but I say it's possible. You ask me, and I can only answer you. I am not swaggering, I am simply giving you decent satisfaction. You wouldn't have me think it impossible that a woman should fall in love with me? You know what women are, and how there is nothing, in that way, too queer for them to do."

Mrs Daintry, in spite of the knowledge of her sex that she might be supposed to possess, was not prepared to rank herself on the side of this axiom. "I wished to warn you," she simply said; "do be very careful."

"Yes, I'll be careful; but I can't give up the house."

"There are other houses, Florimond."

"Yes, but there is a special charm there."

"I would rather you should return to Paris than do any harm."

"Oh, I shan't do any harm; don't worry, *ma mère*," said Florimond.

It was a relief to Mrs Daintry to have spoken, and she endeavoured not to worry. It was doubtless this effort that, for the rest of the winter, gave her a somewhat rigid, anxious look. People who met her in Beacon Street missed something from her face. It was her usual confidence in the clearness of human duty; and some of her friends explained the change by saying that she was disappointed about Florimond—she was afraid he was not particularly liked.

VII

BY the first of March this young man had received a good many optical impressions, and had noted in water-colours several characteristic winter effects. He had perambulated Boston in every direction, he had even extended his researches to the suburbs; and if his eye had been curious, his eye was now almost satisfied. He perceived that even amid the simple civilisation of New England there was material for the naturalist; and in Washington Street of a winter's afternoon, it came home to him that it was a fortunate thing the impressionist was not exclusively preoccupied with the beautiful. He became familiar with the slushy streets, crowded with thronging pedestrians and obstructed horse-cars, bordered with strange, promiscuous shops, which seemed at once violent and indifferent, overhung with snowbanks from the house-tops; the avalanche that detached itself at intervals, fell with an enormous thud amid the dense processions of women, made for a moment a clear space, splashed with whiter snow, on the pavement, and contributed to the gaiety of the Puritan capital. Supreme in the thoroughfare was the rigid groove of the railway, where oblong receptacles, of fabulous capacity, governed by familiar citizens, jolted and jingled eternally, close on each other's rear, absorbing and emitting innumerable specimens of a single type. The road on either side, buried in mounds of pulverised, mud-coloured ice, was ploughed across by labouring vehicles, and traversed periodically by the sisterhood of "shoppers," laden with satchels and parcels, and protected by a round-backed policeman. Florimond looked at the shops, saw the women disgorged, surging, ebbing, dodged the avalanches, squeezed in and out of the horse-cars, made himself, on their little platforms, where flatness was enforced, as perpendicular as possible. The horses steamed in the sunny air, the conductor punched the tickets and poked the passengers, some of whom were under and some above, and all alike stabled in trampled straw. They were precipitated, collectively, by stoppages and starts; the tight, silent interior stuffed itself more and more, and the whole machine heaved and reeled in its interrupted course. Florimond had forgotten the look of many things, the details of American publicity; in some cases, indeed, he only pretended to himself that he had forgotten them, because it helped to entertain him. The houses—a bristling, jagged line of talls and shorts, a particoloured surface, expressively commercial—were spotted with staring signs, with labels and pictures, with advertisements familiar, colloquial, vulgar; the air was traversed with the tangle of the telegraph, with festoons of bunting, with banners not of war, with inexplicable loops and ropes; the shops, many of them enormous, had heterogeneous fronts, with queer juxtapositions in the articles that peopled them, an incompleteness of array, the stamp of the latest modern ugliness. They had pendant stuffs in the doorways, and flapping tickets outside. Every fifty yards there was a "candy store;" in the intervals was the painted panel of a chiropodist, representing him in his professional attitude. Behind the plates of glass, in the hot interiors, behind the counters, were pale, familiar, delicate, tired faces of women, with polished hair and glazed complexions. Florimond knew their voices; he knew how women would speak when their hair was "treated," as they said in the studios, like that. But the women that passed through the streets were the main spectacle. Florimond had forgotten their extraordinary numerosity, and the impression that they produced of a deluge of petticoats. He could see that they were perfectly at home on the road; they had an air of possession, of perpetual equipment, a look, in the eyes, of always meeting the gaze of crowds, always seeing people pass, noting things in shop-windows, and being on the watch at crossings; many of them evidently passed most of their time in these conditions, and Florimond wondered what sort of *intérieurs* they could have. He felt at moments that he was in a city of women, in a country of women. The same impression came to him *dans le monde*, as he used to say, for he made the most incongruous application of his little French phrases to Boston. The talk, the social life, were so completely in the hands of the ladies, the masculine note was so subordinate, that on certain occasions he could have believed himself (putting the brightness aside) in a country stricken by a war, where the men had all gone to the army, or in a seaport half depopulated by the absence of its vessels. This idea had intermissions; for instance, when he walked out to Cambridge. In this little excursion he often indulged; he used to go and see one of his college-mates, who was now a tutor at Harvard. He stretched away across the long, mean bridge that spans the mouth of the Charles—a mile of wooden piles, supporting a brick pavement, a roadway deep in mire, and a rough timber fence, over which the pedestrian enjoys a view of the frozen bay, the backs of many new houses, and a big brown marsh. The horse-cars bore him company, relieved here of the press of the streets, though not of their internal congestion, and constituting the principal feature of the wide, blank avenue, where the puddles lay large across the bounding rails. He followed their direction through a middle region, in which the small wooden houses had an air of tent-like impermanence, and the February mornings, splendid and indiscreet, stared into bare windows and seemed to make civilisation transparent. Further, the suburb remained wooden, but grew neat, and the painted houses looked out on the car-track with an expression almost of superiority. At Harvard, the buildings were square and fresh; they stood in a yard planted with slender elms, which the winter had reduced to spindles; the town stretched away from the horizontal palings of the collegiate precinct, low, flat and immense, with vague, featureless

spaces and the air of a clean encampment. Florimond remembered that when the summer came in, the whole place was
transformed. It was pervaded by verdure and dust, the slender
elms became profuse, arching over the unpaved streets, the
green shutters bowed themselves before the windows, the
flowers and creeping-plants bloomed in the small gardens, and
on the piazzas, in the gaps of dropped awnings, light dresses
arrested the eye. At night, in the warm darkness—for Cambridge is not festooned with lamps—the bosom of nature
would seem to palpitate, there would be a smell of earth and
vegetation—a smell more primitive than the odour of Europe
—and the air would vibrate with the sound of insects. All this
was in reserve, if one would have patience, especially from
March to June; but for the present the seat of the University
struck our poor little critical Florimond as rather hard and
bare. As the winter went on, and the days grew longer, he
knew that Mrs Daintry often believed him to be in Arlington
Street when he was walking out to see his friend the tutor, who
had once spent a winter in Paris and never tired of talking
about it. It is to be feared that he did not undeceive her so
punctually as he might; for, in the first place, he was at Mrs
Mesh's very often; in the second, he failed to understand how
worried his mother was; and in the third, the idea that he
should be thought to have the peace of mind of a brilliant girl
in his keeping was not disagreeable to him.

One day his Aunt Lucretia found him in Arlington Street;
it occurred to her about the middle of the winter that, considering she liked Rachel Torrance so much, she had not been
to see her very often. She had little time for such indulgences;
but she caught a moment in its flight, and was told at Mrs
Mesh's door that this lady had not yet come in, but that her
companion was accessible. Florimond was in his customary
chair by the chimney-corner (his aunt perhaps did not know
quite how customary it was), and Rachel, at the piano, was
regaling him with a composition of Schubert. Florimond, up

to this time, had not become very intimate with his aunt, who had not, as it were, given him the key of her house, and in whom he detected a certain want of interest in his affairs. He had a limited sympathy with people who were interested only in their own, and perceived that Miss Daintry belonged to this preoccupied and ungraceful class. It seemed to him that it would have been more becoming in her to feign at least a certain attention to the professional and social prospects of the most promising of her nephews. If there was one thing that Florimond disliked more than another, it was an eager self-absorption; and he could not see that it was any better for people to impose their personality upon committees and charities than upon general society. He would have modified this judgment of his kinswoman, with whom he had dined but once, if he could have guessed with what anxiety she watched for the symptoms of that salutary change which she expected to see wrought in him by the fascinating independence of Rachel Torrance. If she had dared, she would have prompted the girl a little; she would have confided to her this secret desire. But the matter was delicate; and Miss Daintry was shrewd enough to see that everything must be spontaneous. When she paused at the threshold of Mrs Mesh's drawing-room, looking from one of her young companions to the other, she felt a slight pang, for she feared they were getting on too well. Rachel was pouring sweet music into the young man's ears, and turning to look at him over her shoulder while she played; and he, with his head tipped back and his eyes on the ceiling, hummed an accompaniment which occasionally became an articulate remark. Harmonious intimacy was stamped upon the scene, and poor Miss Daintry was not struck with its being in any degree salutary. She was not reassured when, after ten minutes, Florimond took his departure; she could see that he was irritated by the presence of a third person; and this was a proof that Rachel had not yet begun to do her duty by him. It is possible that when the two ladies were left together, her disappointment would have led her to betray her views, had not Rachel almost immediately said to her: "My dear cousin, I am so glad you have come; I might not have seen you again. I go away in three days."

"Go away? Where do you go to?"

"Back to Brooklyn," said Rachel, smiling sweetly.

"Why on earth—I thought you had come here to stay for six months?"

"Oh, you know, six months would be a terrible visit for these good people; and of course no time was fixed. That would have been very absurd. I have been here an immense time already. It was to be as things should go."

"And haven't they gone well?"

"Oh yes, they have gone beautifully."

"Then why in the world do you leave?"

"Well, you know, I have duties at home. My mother coughs a good deal, and they write me dismal letters."

"They are ridiculous, selfish people. You are going home because your mother coughs? I don't believe a word of it!" Miss Daintry cried. "You have some other reason. Something has happened here; it has become disagreeable. Be so good as to tell me the whole story."

Rachel answered that there was not any story to tell, and that her reason consisted entirely of conscientious scruples as to absenting herself so long from her domestic circle. Miss Daintry esteemed conscientious scruples when they were well placed, but she thought poorly on the present occasion of those of Mrs Mesh's visitor; they interfered so much with her own sense of fitness. "Has Florimond been making love to you?" she suddenly inquired. "You mustn't mind that—beyond boxing his ears."

Her question appeared to amuse Miss Torrance exceedingly; and the girl, a little inarticulate with her mirth, answered very positively that the young man had done her no such honour.

"I am very sorry to hear it," said Lucretia; "I was in hopes he would give you a chance to take him down. He needs it very much. He's dreadfully puffed up."

"He's an amusing little man!"

Miss Daintry put on her nippers. "Don't tell me it's you that are in love!"

"Oh, dear no! I like big, serious men; not small Frenchified gentlemen, like Florimond. Excuse me if he's your nephew, but you began it. Though I am fond of art," the girl added, "I don't think I am fond of artists."

"Do you call Florimond an artist?"

Rachel Torrance hesitated a little, smiling. "Yes, when he poses for Pauline Mesh."

This rejoinder for a moment left Miss Daintry in visible perplexity; then a sudden light seemed to come to her. She flushed a little; what she found was more than she was looking for. She thought of many things quickly, and among others she thought that she had accomplished rather more than she intended. "Have you quarrelled with Pauline?" she said presently.

"No, but she is tired of me."

"Everything has not gone well, then, and you *have* another reason for going home than your mother's cough?"

"Yes, if you must know, Pauline wants me to go. I didn't feel free to tell you that; but since you guess it——" said Rachel, with her rancourless smile.

"Has she asked you to decamp?"

"Oh, dear no! for what do you take us? But she absents herself from the house; she stays away all day. I have to play to Florimond to console him."

"So you *have* been fighting about him?" Miss Daintry remarked, perversely.

"Ah, my dear cousin, what have you got in your head? Fighting about sixpence! if you knew how Florimond bores me! I play to him to keep him silent. I have heard everything he has to say, fifty times over!"

Miss Daintry sank back in her chair; she was completely out of her reckoning. "I think he might have made love to you a little!" she exclaimed, incoherently.

"So do I! but he didn't—not a crumb. He is afraid of me —thank heaven!"

"It isn't for you he comes, then?" Miss Daintry appeared to cling to her theory.

"No, my dear cousin, it isn't!"

"Just now, as he sat there, one could easily have supposed it. He didn't at all like my interruption."

"That was because he was waiting for Pauline to come in. He will wait that way an hour. You may imagine whether he likes me for boring her so that, as I tell you, she can't stay in the house. I am out myself as much as possible. But there are days when I drop with fatigue; then I must rest. I can assure you that it's fortunate that I go so soon."

"Is Pauline in love with him?" Miss Daintry asked, gravely.

"Not a grain. She is the best little woman in the world."

"Except for being a goose. Why, then, does she object to your company—after being so enchanted with you?"

"Because even the best little woman in the world must object to something. She has everything in life, and nothing to complain of. Her children sleep all day, and her cook is a jewel. Her husband adores her, and she is perfectly satisfied with Mr Mesh. I act on her nerves, and I think she believes I regard her as rather silly to care so much for Florimond. Excuse me again!"

"You contradict yourself. She *does* care for him, then?"

"Oh, as she would care for a new *coupé!* She likes to have a young man of her own—fresh from Paris—quite to herself. She has everything else—why shouldn't she have that? She thinks your nephew very original, and he thinks her what she is—the prettiest woman in Boston. They have an idea that they are making a 'celebrated friendship'—like Horace Walpole and Madame du Deffand. They sit there face to face—

they are as innocent as the shovel and tongs. But, all the same, I am in the way, and Pauline is provoked that I am not jealous."

Miss Daintry got up with energy. "She's a vain, hollow, silly little creature, and you are quite right to go away; you are worthy of better company. Only you will not go back to Brooklyn, in spite of your mother's cough; you will come straight to Mount Vernon Place."

Rachel hesitated to agree to this. She appeared to think it was her duty to quit Boston altogether; and she gave as a reason that she had already refused other invitations. But Miss Daintry had a better reason than this—a reason that glowed in her indignant breast. It was she who had been the cause of the girl's being drawn into this sorry adventure; it was she who should charge herself with the reparation. The conversation I have related took place on a Tuesday; and it was settled that on the Friday Miss Torrance should take up her abode for the rest of the winter under her Cousin Lucretia's roof. This lady left the house without having seen Mrs Mesh.

On Thursday she had a visit from her sister-in-law, the motive of which was not long in appearing. All winter Mrs Daintry had managed to keep silent on the subject of her doubts and fears. Discretion and dignity recommended this course; and the topic was a painful one to discuss with Lucretia, for the bruises of their primary interview still occasionally throbbed. But at the first sign of alleviation the excellent woman overflowed, and she lost no time in announcing to Lucretia, as a heaven-sent piece of news, that Rachel had been called away by the illness of poor Mrs Torrance and was to leave Boston from one day to the other. Florimond had given her this information the evening before, and it had made her so happy that she couldn't help coming to let Lucretia know that they were safe. Lucretia listened to her announcement in silence, fixing her eyes on her sister-in-law with an expression that the latter thought singular; but when Mrs

Daintry, expanding still further, went on to say that she had spent a winter of misery, that the harm the two together (she and Lucretia) might have done was never out of her mind, for Florimond's assiduity in Arlington Street had become notorious, and she had been told that the most cruel things were said—when Mrs Daintry, expressing herself to this effect, added that from the present moment she breathed, the danger was over, the sky was clear, and her conscience might take a holiday—her hostess broke into the most prolonged, the most characteristic and most bewildering fit of laughter in which she had ever known her to indulge. They were safe, Mrs Daintry had said? For Lucretia this was true, now, of herself, at least; she was secure from the dangers of her irritation; her sense of the whole affair had turned to hilarious music. The contrast that rose before her between her visitor's anxieties and the real position of the parties, her quick vision of poor Susan's dismay in case *that* reality should meet her eyes, among the fragments of her squandered scruples—these things smote the chords of mirth in Miss Daintry's spirit, and seemed to her in their high comicality to offer a sufficient reason for everything that had happened. The picture of her sister-in-law sitting all winter with her hands clasped and her eyes fixed on the wrong object was an image that would abide with her always; and it would render her an inestimable service—it would cure her of the tendency to worry. As may be imagined, it was eminently open to Mrs Daintry to ask her what on earth she was laughing at; and there was a colour in the cheek of Florimond's mother that brought her back to propriety. She suddenly kissed this lady very tenderly—to the latter's great surprise, there having been no kissing since her visit in November—and told her that she would reveal to her some day, later, the cause of so much merriment. She added that Miss Torrance was leaving Arlington Street, yes; but only to go as far as Mount Vernon Place. She was engaged to spend three months in that very house. Mrs Daintry's countenance at this fell several inches, and her joy appeared completely to desert her. She gave her sister-in-law a glance of ineffable reproach, and in a moment she exclaimed: "Then nothing is gained! it will all go on here!"

"Nothing will go on here. If you mean that Florimond will pursue the young lady into this mountain fastness, you may simply be quiet. He is not fond enough of me to wear out my threshold."

"Are you very sure?" Mrs Daintry murmured, dubiously.

"I know what I say. Hasn't he told you he hates me?"

Mrs Daintry coloured again, and hesitated. "I don't know how you think we talk," she said.

"Well, he does, and he will leave us alone."

Mrs Daintry sprang up with an elasticity that was comical. "That's all I ask!" she exclaimed.

"I believe you hate me too!" Lucretia said, laughing; but at any risk she kissed her sister-in-law again before they separated.

Three weeks later Mrs Daintry paid her another visit; and this time she looked very serious. "It's very strange. I don't know what to think. But perhaps you know it already?" This was her *entrée en matière*, as the French say. "Rachel's leaving Arlington Street has made no difference. He goes there as much as ever. I see no change at all. Lucretia, I have not the peace that I thought had come," said poor Mrs Daintry, whose voice had failed, below her breath.

"Do you mean that he goes to see Pauline Mesh?"

"I am afraid so, every day."

"Well, my dear, what's the harm?" Miss Daintry asked. "He can't hurt *her* by not marrying her."

Mrs Daintry stared; she was amazed at her sister-in-law's tone. "But it makes one suppose that all winter, for so many weeks, it has been for *her* that he has gone!" And the image of the *tête-à-tête* in which she had found them immersed that day, rose again before her; she could interpret it now.

"You wanted some one; why may not Pauline have served?"

Mrs Daintry was silent, with the same expanded eyes. "Lucretia, it is not right!"

"My dear Susan, you are touching," Lucretia said.

Mrs Daintry went on, without heeding her. "It appears that people are talking about it; they have noticed it for ever so long. Joanna never hears anything, or she would have told me. The children are too much. I have been the last to know."

"I knew it a month ago," said Miss Daintry, smiling.

"And you never told me?"

"I knew that you wanted to detain him. Pauline will detain him a year."

Mrs Daintry gathered herself together. "Not a day, not an hour, that I can help! He shall go, if I have to take him."

"My dear Susan," murmured her sister-in-law on the threshold. Miss Daintry scarcely knew what to say; she was almost frightened at the rigidity of her face.

"My dear Lucretia, it is not right!" This ejaculation she solemnly repeated, and she took her departure as if she were decided upon action.

She had found so little sympathy in her sister-in-law that she made no answer to a note Miss Daintry wrote her that evening, to remark that she was really unjust to Pauline, who was silly, vain, and flattered by the development of her ability to monopolise an impressionist, but a perfectly innocent little woman and incapable of a serious flirtation. Miss Daintry had been careful to add to these last words no comment that could possibly shock Florimond's mother. Mrs Daintry announced, about the 10th of April, that she had made up her mind she needed a change, and had determined to go abroad for the summer; and she looked so tired that people could see there was reason in it. Her summer began early; she embarked on the 20th of the month, accompanied by Florimond. Miss Daintry, who had not been obliged to dismiss the young lady of the kindergarten to make room for Rachel Torrance, never knew what had passed between the mother and the son, and she was disappointed at Mrs Mesh's coolness in the face of this catastrophe. She disapproved of her flirtation with Florimond, and yet she was vexed at Pauline's pert resignation; it proved her to be so superficial. She disposed of everything with her absurd little phrases, which were half slang and half quotation. Mrs Daintry was a native of Salem, and this gave Pauline, as a Baltimorean and a descendant of the Cavaliers, an obvious opportunity. Rachel repeated her words to Miss Daintry, for she had spoken to Rachel of Florimond's departure, the day after he embarked. "Oh yes, he's in the midst of the foam, the cruel, crawling foam! I 'kind of' miss him, afternoons; he was so useful round the fire. It's his mother that charmed him away; she's a most uncanny old party. I don't care for Salem witches, anyway; she has worked on him with philters and spells!" Lucretia was obliged to recognise a grain of truth in this last assertion; she felt that her sister-in-law must indeed have worked upon Florimond, and she smiled to think that the conscientious Susan should have descended, in the last resort, to an artifice, to a pretext. She had probably persuaded him she was out of patience with Joanna's children.

THE PATH OF DUTY

I AM glad I said to you the other night at Doubleton, inquiring —too inquiring—compatriot, that I wouldn't undertake to tell you the story (about Ambrose Tester), but would write it out for you; inasmuch as, thinking it over since I came back to town, I see that it may really be made interesting. It *is* a story, with a regular development, and for telling it I have the advantage that I happened to know about it from the first, and was more or less in the confidence of every one concerned. Then it will amuse me to write it, and I shall do so as carefully and as cleverly as possible. The first winter days in London are not madly gay, so that I have plenty of time, and if the fog is brown outside, the fire is red within. I like the quiet of this season; the glowing chimney-corner, in the midst of the December mirk, makes me think, as I sit by it, of all sorts of things. The idea that is almost always uppermost is the bigness and strangeness of this London world. Long as I have lived here—the sixteenth anniversary of my marriage is only ten days off—there is still a kind of novelty and excitement in it. It is a great pull, as they say here, to have remained sensitive— to have kept one's own point of view. I mean it's more entertaining—it makes you see a thousand things (not that they are all very charming). But the pleasure of observation does not in the least depend on the beauty of what one observes. You see innumerable little dramas; in fact almost everything has acts and scenes, like a comedy. Very often it is a comedy with tears. There have been a good many of them, I am afraid, in the case I am speaking of. It is because this history of Sir Ambrose Tester and Lady Vandeleur struck me, when you asked me about the relations of the parties, as having that kind of progression, that when I was on the point of responding I checked myself, thinking it a pity to tell you a little when I might tell you all. I scarcely know what made you ask, inasmuch as I had said nothing to excite your curiosity. Whatever you suspected you suspected on your own hook, as they say. You had simply noticed the pair together that evening at Doubleton. If you suspected anything in particular, it is a proof that you are rather sharp, because they are very careful about the way they behave in public. At least they think they are; the result, perhaps, doesn't necessarily follow. If I have been in their confidence you may say that I make a strange use of my privilege in serving them up to feed the prejudices of an opinionated American. You think English society very wicked, and my little story will probably not correct the impression. Though, after all, I don't see why it should minister to it; for what I said to you (it was all I did say) remains the truth. They are treading together the path of duty. You would be quite right about its being base in me to betray them. It is very true that they have ceased to confide in me; even Joscelind has said nothing to me for more than a year. That is doubtless a sign that the situation is more serious than before, all round—too serious to be talked about. It is also true that you are remarkably discreet, and that even if you were not it would not make much difference, inasmuch as if you were to repeat my revelations in America no one would know whom you were talking about. But, all the same, I should be base; and, therefore, after I have written out my reminiscences for your delectation, I shall simply keep them for my own. You must content yourself with the explanation I have already given you of Sir Ambrose Tester and Lady Vandeleur: they are following—hand in hand, as it were—the path of duty. This will not prevent me from telling everything; on the contrary, don't you see?

I

His brilliant prospects dated from the death of his brother, who had no children, had indeed steadily refused to marry. When I say brilliant prospects, I mean the vision of the baronetcy, one of the oldest in England, of a charming seventeenth-century house, with its park, in Dorsetshire, and a property worth some twenty thousand a year. Such a collection of items is still dazzling to me, even after what you would call, I suppose, a familiarity with British grandeur. My husband isn't a baronet (or we probably shouldn't be in London in December), and he is far, alas, from having twenty thousand a year. The full enjoyment of these luxuries, on Ambrose Tester's part, was dependent naturally on the death of his father, who was still very much to the fore at the time I first knew the young man. The proof of it is the way he kept nagging at his sons, as the younger used to say, on the question of taking a wife. The nagging had been of no avail, as I have mentioned, with regard to Francis, the elder, whose affections were centred (his brother himself told me) on the wine-cup and the faro-table. He was not a person to admire or imitate, and as the heir to an honourable name and a fine estate was very unsatisfactory indeed. It had been possible in those days to put him into the army, but it was not possible to keep him there, and he was still a very young man when it became plain that any parental dream of a "career" for Frank Tester was exceedingly vain. Old Sir Edmund had thought matrimony would perhaps correct him, but a sterner process than this was needed, and it came to him one day at Monaco—he was most of the time abroad—after an illness so short that none of the family arrived in time. He was reformed altogether, he was utterly abolished. The second son, stepping into his shoes, was such an improvement that it was impossible there should be much simulation of mourning. You have seen him, you know what he is, there is very little mystery about him. As I am not going to show this composition to you, there is no harm in my writing here that he is—or, at any rate, he was—a remarkably attractive man. I don't say this because he made love to me, but precisely because he didn't. He was always in love with some one else—generally with Lady Vandeleur. You may say that in England that usually doesn't prevent; but Mr Tester, though he had almost no intermissions, didn't, as a general thing, have duplicates. He was not provided with a second loved object, "understudying," as they say, the part. It was his practice to keep me accurately informed of the state of his affections—a matter about which he was never in the least vague. When he was in love he knew it and rejoiced in it, and when by a miracle he was not he greatly regretted it. He expatiated to me on the charms of other persons, and this interested me much more than if he had attempted to direct the conversation to my own, as regards which I had no illusions. He has told me some singular things, and I think I may say that for a considerable period my most valued knowledge of English society was extracted from this genial youth. I suppose he usually found me a woman of good counsel, for certain it is that he has appealed to me for the light of wisdom in very extraordinary predicaments. In his earlier years he was perpetually in hot water; he tumbled into scrapes as children tumble into puddles. He invited them, he invented them; and when he came to tell you how his trouble had come about (and he always told the whole truth) it was difficult to believe that a man should have been so idiotic.

And yet he was not an idiot; he was supposed to be very clever, and certainly is very quick and amusing. He was only reckless, and extraordinarily natural, as natural as if he had been an Irishman. In fact, of all the Englishmen that I have known he is the most Irish in temperament (though he has

got over it comparatively of late). I used to tell him that it was
a great inconvenience that he didn't speak with a brogue,
because then we should be forewarned and know with whom
we were dealing. He replied that, by analogy, if he were Irish
enough to have a brogue he would probably be English;
which seemed to me an answer wonderfully in character. Like
most young Britons of his class he went to America, to see the
great country, before he was twenty, and he took a letter to my
father, who had occasion, à propos of some pickle, of course,
to render him a considerable service. This led to his coming to
see me—I had already been living here three or four years—
on his return; and that, in the course of time, led to our
becoming fast friends, without, as I tell you, the smallest
philandering on either side. But I mustn't protest too much;
I shall excite your suspicion. "If he has made love to so many
women, why shouldn't he have made love to you?"—some
inquiry of that sort you will be likely to make. I have answered
it already, "Simply on account of those very engagements."
He couldn't make love to every one, and with me it wouldn't
have done him the least good. It was a more amiable weakness
than his brother's, and he has always behaved very well. How
well he behaved on a very important occasion is precisely the
subject of my story.

He was supposed to have embraced the diplomatic career,
had been secretary of legation at some German capital; but
after his brother's death he came home and looked out for a
seat in Parliament. He found it with no great trouble, and has
kept it ever since. No one would have the heart to turn him
out, he is so good-looking. It's a great thing to be represented
by one of the handsomest men in England, it creates such a
favourable association of ideas. Any one would be amazed to
discover that the borough he sits for, and the name of which
I am always forgetting, is not a very pretty place. I have never
seen it, and have no idea that it isn't, and I am sure he will
survive every revolution. The people must feel that if they

shouldn't keep him some monster would be returned. You remember his appearance, how tall, and fair, and strong he is, and always laughing, yet without looking silly. He is exactly the young man girls in America figure to themselves—in the place of the hero—when they read English novels and wish to imagine something very aristocratic and Saxon. A "bright Bostonian" who met him once at my house, exclaimed as soon as he had gone out of the room, "At last, at last, I behold it, the moustache of Roland Tremayne!"

"Of Roland Tremayne?"

"Don't you remember in *A Lawless Love*, how often it's mentioned, and how glorious and golden it was? Well, I have never seen it till now, but now I *have* seen it!"

If you hadn't seen Ambrose Tester, the best description I could give of him would be to say that he looked like Roland Tremayne. I don't know whether that hero was a "strong Liberal," but this is what Sir Ambrose is supposed to be. (He succeeded his father two years ago, but I shall come to that.) He is not exactly what I should call thoughtful, but he is interested, or thinks he is, in a lot of things that I don't understand, and that one sees and skips in the newspapers—volunteering, and redistribution, and sanitation, and the representation of minors—minorities—what is it? When I said just now that he is always laughing, I ought to have explained that I didn't mean when he is talking to Lady Vandeleur. She makes him serious, makes him almost solemn; by which I don't mean that she bores him. Far from it; but when he is in her company he is thoughtful; he pulls his golden moustache, and Roland Tremayne looks as if his vision were turned in, and he were meditating on her words. He doesn't say much himself; it is she—she used to be so silent—who does the talking. She has plenty to say to him; she describes to him the charms that she discovers in the path of duty. He seldom speaks in the House, I believe, but when he does it's off-hand, and amusing, and sensible, and every one likes it. He will never be

a great statesman, but he will add to the softness of Dorsetshire, and remain, in short, a very gallant, pleasant, prosperous, typical English gentleman, with a name, a fortune, a
perfect appearance, a devoted, bewildered little wife, a great
many reminiscences, a great many friends (including Lady
Vandeleur and myself), and, strange to say, with all these
advantages, something that faintly resembles a conscience.

II

F IVE years ago he told me his father insisted on his marrying
—would not hear of his putting it off any longer. Sir Edmund
had been harping on this string ever since he came back from
Germany, had made it both a general and a particular request,
not only urging him to matrimony in the abstract, but pushing
him into the arms of every young woman in the country.
Ambrose had promised, procrastinated, temporised; but at
last he was at the end of his evasions, and his poor father had
taken the tone of supplication. "He thinks immensely of the
name, of the place, and all that, and he has got it into his head
that if I don't marry before he dies I won't marry after." So
much I remember Ambrose Tester said to me. "It's a fixed
idea; he has got it on the brain. He wants to see me married
with his eyes, and he wants to take his grandson in his arms.
Not without that will he be satisfied that the whole thing will
go straight. He thinks he is nearing his end, but he isn't—he
will live to see a hundred, don't you think so?—and he has
made me a solemn appeal to put an end to what he calls his
suspense. He has an idea some one will get hold of me—some
woman I can't marry. As if I were not old enough to take care
of myself!"

"Perhaps he is afraid of me," I suggested, facetiously.

"No, it isn't you," said my visitor, betraying by his tone

that it was some one, though he didn't say whom. "That's all rot, of course; one marries sooner or later, and I shall do like every one else. If I marry before I die it's as good as if I marry before he dies, isn't it? I should be delighted to have the governor at my wedding, but it isn't necessary for the legality, is it?"

I asked him what he wished me to do, and how I could help him. He knew already my peculiar views, that I was trying to get husbands for all the girls of my acquaintance and to prevent the men from taking wives. The sight of an unmarried woman afflicted me, and yet when my male friends changed their state I took it as a personal offence. He let me know that, so far as he was concerned, I must prepare myself for this injury, for he had given his father his word that another twelvemonth should not see him a bachelor. The old man had given him *carte blanche*, he made no condition beyond exacting that the lady should have youth and health. Ambrose Tester, at any rate, had taken a vow, and now he was going seriously to look about him. I said to him that what must be must be, and that there were plenty of charming girls about the land, among whom he could suit himself easily enough. There was no better match in England, I said, and he would only have to make his choice. That, however, is not what I thought, for my real reflections were summed up in the silent exclamation, "What a pity Lady Vandeleur isn't a widow!" I hadn't the smallest doubt that if she were he would marry her on the spot; and after he had gone I wondered considerably what *she* thought of this turn in his affairs. If it was disappointing to me, how little it must be to *her* taste! Sir Edmund had not been so much out of the way in fearing there might be obstacles to his son's taking the step he desired. Margaret Vandeleur was an obstacle—I knew it as well as if Mr Tester had told me.

I don't mean there was anything in their relation he might not freely have alluded to, for Lady Vandeleur, in spite of her beauty and her tiresome husband, was not a woman who could be accused of an indiscretion. Her husband was a pedant about trifles—the shape of his hat-brim, the *pose* of his coachman, and cared for nothing else; but she was as nearly a saint as one may be when one has rubbed shoulders for ten years with the best society in Europe. It is a characteristic of that society that even its saints are suspected, and I go too far in saying that little pin-pricks were not administered, in considerable numbers, to her reputation. But she didn't feel them, for, still more than Ambrose Tester, she was a person to whose happiness a good conscience was necessary. I should almost say that for her happiness it was sufficient, and, at any rate, it was only those who didn't know her that pretended to speak of her lightly. If one had the honour of her acquaintance one might have thought her rather shut up to her beauty and her grandeur, but one couldn't but feel there was something in her composition that would keep her from vulgar aberrations. Her husband was such a feeble type that she must have felt doubly she had been put upon her honour. To deceive such a man as that was to make him more ridiculous than he was already, and from such a result a woman bearing his name may very well have shrunk. Perhaps it would have been worse for Lord Vandeleur, who had every pretension of his order and none of its amiability, if he had been a better or, at least, a cleverer man. When a woman behaves so well she is not obliged to be careful, and there is no need of consulting appearances when one is one's self an appearance. Lady Vandeleur accepted Ambrose Tester's attentions, and heaven knows they were frequent; but she had such an air of perfect equilibrium that one couldn't see her, in imagination, bend responsive. Incense was incense, but one saw her sitting quite serene among the fumes. That honour of her acquaintance of which I just now spoke it had been given me to enjoy; that is to say, I met her a dozen times in the season in a hot crowd, and we smiled sweetly and murmured a vague question or two, without hearing, or even trying to hear, each other's answer. If I knew that Ambrose Tester was perpetually in and out of her house and always arranging with her that they should go to the same places, I doubt whether she, on her side, knew how often he came to see me. I don't think he would have let her know, and am conscious, in saying this, that it indicated an advanced state of intimacy (with her, I mean).

I also doubt very much whether he asked her to look about, on his behalf, for a future Lady Tester. This request he was so good as to make of me; but I told him I would have nothing to do with the matter. If Joscelind is unhappy, I am thankful to say the responsibility is not mine. I have found English husbands for two or three American girls, but providing English wives is a different affair. I know the sort of men that will suit women, but one would have to be very clever to know the sort of women that will suit men. I told Ambrose Tester that he must look out for himself, but, in spite of his promise, I had very little belief that he would do anything of the sort. I thought it probable that the old baronet would pass away without seeing a new generation come in; though when I intimated as much to Mr Tester, he made answer in substance (it was not quite so crudely said) that his father, old as he was, would hold on till his bidding was done, and if it should not be done he would hold on out of spite. "Oh, he will tire me out": that I remember Ambrose Tester did say. I had done him injustice, for six months later he told me he was engaged. It had all come about very suddenly. From one day to the other the right young woman had been found. I forget who had found her; some aunt or cousin, I think; it had not been the young man himself. But when she was found, he rose to the occasion; he took her up seriously, he approved of her thoroughly, and I am not sure that he didn't fall a little in love with her, ridiculous (excuse my London tone) as this accident may appear. He told me that his father was delighted, and I knew afterwards that he had good reason to be. It was not till some weeks later that I saw the girl; but meanwhile I had received the pleasantest impression of her, and this impression came—must have come—mainly from what her intended told me. That proves that he spoke with some positiveness, spoke as if he really believed he was doing a good thing. I had it on my tongue's end to ask him how Lady Vandeleur liked her, but I fortunately checked this vulgar inquiry. He liked her, evidently, as I say; every one liked her, and when I knew her I liked her better even than the others. I like her to-day more than ever; it is fair you should know that, in reading this account of her situation. It doubtless colours my picture, gives a point to my sense of the strangeness of my little story.

Joscelind Bernardstone came of a military race, and had been brought up in camps—by which I don't mean she was one of those objectionable young women who are known as garrison-hacks. She was in the flower of her freshness, and had been kept in the tent, receiving, as an only daughter, the most "particular" education from the excellent Lady Emily (General Bernardstone married a daughter of Lord Clanduffy), who looks like a pink-faced rabbit, and is (after Joscelind) one of the nicest women I know. When I met them in a country-house, a few weeks after the marriage was "arranged," as they say here, Joscelind won my affections by saying to me, with her timid directness (the speech made me feel sixty years old), that she must thank me for having been so kind to Mr Tester. You saw her at Doubleton, and you will remember that, though she has no regular beauty, many a prettier woman would be very glad to look like her. She is as fresh as a new-laid egg, as light as a feather, as strong as a mail-phaeton. She is perfectly mild, yet she is clever enough to be sharp if she would. I don't know that clever women are necessarily thought ill-natured, but it is usually taken for granted that amiable women are very limited. Lady Tester is a refutation of the theory, which must have been invented by a vixenish woman who was *not* clever. She has an adoration for her husband, which absorbs her without in the least making her silly, unless indeed it is silly to be modest, as in this brutal world I sometimes believe. Her modesty is so great that being unhappy has hitherto presented itself to her as a form of egotism—that egotism which she has too much delicacy to cultivate. She is by no means sure that, if being married to her beautiful baronet is not the ideal state she dreamed it, the weak point of the affair is not simply in her own presumption. It doesn't express her condition, at present, to say that she is unhappy or disappointed, or that she has a sense of injury. All this is latent; meanwhile, what is obvious is that she is bewildered—she simply doesn't understand, and her perplexity, to me, is unspeakably touching. She looks about her for some explanation, some light. She fixes her eyes on mine sometimes, and on those of other people, with a kind of searching dumbness, as if there were some chance that I—that they—may explain, may tell her what it is that has happened to her. I can explain very well—but not to her—only to you!

III

It was a brilliant match for Miss Bernardstone, who had no fortune at all, and all her friends were of the opinion that she had done very well. After Easter she was in London with her people, and I saw a good deal of them—in fact, I rather cultivated them. They might perhaps even have thought me a little patronising, if they had been given to thinking that sort of thing. But they were not; that is not in their line. English people are very apt to attribute motives—some of them attribute much worse ones than we poor simpletons in America recognise, than we have even heard of. But that is only some of them; others don't, but take everything literally and genially. That was the case with the Bernardstones; you could be sure that on their way home, after dining with you, they wouldn't ask each other how in the world any one could call you pretty, or say that many people *did* believe, all the same, that you had poisoned your grandfather.

Lady Emily was exceedingly gratified at her daughter's engagement; of course she was very quiet about it, she didn't clap her hands or drag in Mr Tester's name; but it was easy to see that she felt a kind of maternal peace, an abiding satisfaction. The young man behaved as well as possible, was constantly seen with Joscelind, and smiled down at her in the kindest, most protecting way. They looked beautiful together —you would have said it was a duty for people whose colour matched so well to marry. Of course he was immensely taken up, and didn't come very often to see me; but he came sometimes, and when he sat there he had a look which I didn't understand at first. Presently I saw what it expressed; in my drawing-room he was off duty, he had no longer to sit up and play a part; he would lean back and rest and draw a long breath, and forget that the day of his execution was fixed. There was to be no indecent haste about the marriage; it was not to take place till after the session, at the end of August. It puzzled me and rather distressed me that his heart shouldn't be a little more in the matter; it seemed strange to be engaged to so charming a girl and yet go through with it as if it were simply a social duty. If one hadn't been in love with her at first, one ought to have been at the end of a week or two. If Ambrose Tester was not (and to me he didn't pretend to be), he carried it off, as I have said, better than I should have expected. He was a gentleman, and he behaved like a gentleman—with the added punctilio, I think, of being sorry for his betrothed. But it was difficult to see what, in the long run, he could expect to make of such a position. If a man marries an ugly, unattractive woman for reasons of state, the thing is comparatively simple; it is understood between them, and he need have no remorse at not offering her a sentiment of which there has been no question. But when he picks out a charming creature to gratify his father and *les convenances*, it is not so easy to be happy in not being able to care for her. It seemed to me that it would have been much better for Ambrose Tester to bestow himself upon a girl who might have given him an excuse for tepidity. His wife should have been healthy but stupid, prolific but morose. Did he expect to continue not to be in love with Joscelind, or to conceal from her the mechanical nature of his attentions? It was difficult to see how he could wish to do the one or succeed in doing the other. Did he expect such a girl as that would be happy if he didn't love her? and did he think himself capable of being happy if it should turn out that she was miserable? If she shouldn't be miserable—that is, if she should be indifferent, and, as they say, console herself, would he like that any better?

I asked myself all these questions and I should have liked to ask them of Mr Tester; but I didn't, for after all he couldn't have answered them. Poor young man! he didn't pry into things as I do; he was not analytic, like us Americans, as they say in reviews. He thought he was behaving remarkably well, and so he was—for a man; that was the strange part of it. It had been proper that in spite of his reluctance he should take a wife, and he had dutifully set about it. As a good thing is better for being well done, he had taken the best one he could possibly find. He was enchanted with—with his young lady, you might ask? Not in the least; with himself; that is the sort of person a man is! Their virtues are more dangerous than their vices, and heaven preserve you when they want to keep a promise! It is never a promise to *you*, you will notice. A man will sacrifice a woman to live as a gentleman should, and then ask for your sympathy—for *him!* And I don't speak of the bad ones, but of the good. They, after all, are the worst. Ambrose Tester, as I say, didn't go into these details, but, synthetic as he might be, was conscious that his position was false. He felt that sooner or later, and rather sooner than later, he would have to make it true—a process that couldn't pos-

sibly be agreeable. He would really have to make up his mind
to care for his wife or not to care for her. What would Lady
Vandeleur say to one alternative, and what would little Joscelind say to the other? That is what it was to have a pertinacious
father and to be an accommodating son. With me it was easy
for Ambrose Tester to be superficial, for, as I tell you, if I
didn't wish to engage him, I didn't wish to disengage him, and
I didn't insist. Lady Vandeleur insisted, I was afraid; to be
with her was, of course, very complicated; even more than
Miss Bernardstone she must have made him feel that his position was false. I must add that he once mentioned to me that
she had told him he ought to marry. At any rate it is an immense thing to be a pleasant fellow. Our young fellow was so
universally pleasant that, of course, his *fiancée* came in for her
share. So did Lady Emily, suffused with hope, which made her
pinker than ever; she told me he sent flowers even to her. One
day in the Park, I was riding early; the Row was almost
empty. I came up behind a lady and gentleman who were
walking their horses, close to each other, side by side. In a
moment I recognised her, but not before seeing that nothing
could have been more benevolent than the way Ambrose
Tester was bending over his future wife. If he struck me as a
lover at that moment, of course he struck her so. But that isn't
the way they ride to-day.

IV

ONE day, about the end of June, he came in to see me when
I had two or three other visitors; you know that even at that
season I am almost always at home from six to seven. He had
not been three minutes in the room before I saw that he was
different—different from what he had been the last time, and
I guessed that something had happened in relation to his
marriage. My visitors didn't, unfortunately, and they stayed

and stayed until I was afraid he would have to go away without telling me what, I was sure, he had come for. But he sat them out; I think that, by exception, they didn't find him pleasant. After we were alone he abused them a little, and then he said, "Have you heard about Vandeleur? He's very ill. She's awfully anxious." I hadn't heard, and I told him so, asking a question or two; then my inquiries ceased, my breath almost failed me, for I had become aware of something very strange. The way he looked at me when he told me his news was a full confession—a confession so full that I had needed a moment to take it in. He was not too strong a man to be taken by surprise—not so strong but that in the presence of an unexpected occasion his first movement was to look about for a little help. I venture to call it help, the sort of thing he came to me for on that summer afternoon. It is always help when a woman who is not an idiot lets an embarrassed man take up her time. If he too is not an idiot, that doesn't diminish the service; on the contrary his superiority to the average helps him to profit. Ambrose Tester had said to me more than once, in the past, that he was capable of telling me things, because I was an American, that he wouldn't confide to his own people. He had proved it before this, as I have hinted, and I must say that being an American, with him, was sometimes a questionable honour. I don't know whether he thinks us more discreet and more sympathetic (if he keeps up the system: he has abandoned it with me), or only more insensible, more proof against shocks; but it is certain that, like some other Englishmen I have known, he has appeared, in delicate cases, to think I would take a comprehensive view. When I have inquired into the grounds of this discrimination in our favour, he has contented himself with saying, in the British-cursory manner, "Oh, I don't know; you are different!" I remember he remarked once that our impressions were fresher. And I am sure that now it was because of my nationality, in addition to other merits, that he treated me to the confession I have just alluded to. At least I don't suppose he would have gone about saying to people in general, "Her husband will probably die, you know; then why shouldn't I marry Lady Vandeleur?"

That was the question which his whole expression and manner asked of me, and of which, after a moment, I decided to take no notice. Why shouldn't he? There was an excellent reason why he shouldn't. It would just kill Joscelind Bernardstone; that was why he shouldn't! The idea that he should be ready to do it frightened me, and, independent as he might think my point of view, I had no desire to discuss such abominations. It struck me as an abomination at this very first moment, and I have never wavered in my judgment of it. I am always glad when I can take the measure of a thing as soon as I see it; it's a blessing to *feel* what we think, without balancing and comparing. It's a great rest, too, and a great luxury. That, as I say, was the case with the feeling excited in me by this happy idea of Ambrose Tester's. Cruel and wanton I thought it then, cruel and wanton I thought it later, when it was pressed upon me. I knew there were many other people that didn't agree with me, and I can only hope for them that their conviction was as quick and positive as mine; it all depends upon the way a thing strikes one. But I will add to this another remark. I thought I was right then, and I still think I was right; but it strikes me as a pity that I should have wished so much to be right. Why couldn't I be content to be wrong? to renounce my influence (since I appeared to possess the mystic article), and let my young friend do as he liked? As you observed the situation at Doubleton, shouldn't you say it was of a nature to make one wonder whether, after all, one did render a service to the younger lady?

At all events, as I say, I gave no sign to Ambrose Tester that I understood him, that I guessed what he wished to come to. He got no satisfaction out of me that day; it is very true that he made up for it later. I expressed regret at Lord Vandeleur's illness, inquired into its nature and origin, hoped it wouldn't prove as grave as might be feared, said I would call at the house and ask about him, commiserated discreetly her ladyship, and, in short, gave my young man no chance whatever. He knew that I had guessed his *arrière-pensée*, but he let me off for the moment, for which I was thankful; either because he was still ashamed of it, or because he supposed I was reserving myself for the catastrophe—should it occur. Well, my dear, it did occur, at the end of ten days. Mr Tester came to see me twice in that interval, each time to tell me that poor Vandeleur was worse; he had some internal inflammation which, in nine cases out of ten, is fatal. His wife was all devotion; she was with him night and day. I had the news from other sources as well; I leave you to imagine whether in London, at the height of the season, such a situation could fail to be considerably discussed. To the discussion as yet, however, I contributed little, and with Ambrose Tester nothing at all. I was still on my guard. I never admitted for a moment that it was possible there should be any change in his plans. By this time, I think, he had quite ceased to be ashamed of his idea, he was in a state almost of exultation about it; but he was very angry with me for not giving him an opening.

As I look back upon the matter now, there is something almost amusing in the way we watched each other—he thinking that I evaded his question only to torment him (he believed me, or pretended to believe me, capable of this sort of perversity), and I determined not to lose ground by betraying an insight into his state of mind which he might twist into an expression of sympathy. I wished to leave my sympathy where I had placed it, with Lady Emily and her daughter, of whom I continued, bumping against them at parties, to have some observation. They gave no signal of alarm; of course it would have been premature. The girl, I am sure, had no idea of the existence of a rival. How they had kept her in the dark I don't know; but it was easy to see she was too much in love to suspect or to criticise. With Lady Emily it was different; she was a woman of charity, but she touched the world at too many points not to feel its vibrations. However, the dear little lady planted herself firmly; to the eye she was still enough. It was not from Ambrose Tester that I first heard of Lord Vandeleur's death; it was announced, with a quarter of a column of "padding," in the *Times*. I have always known the *Times* was a wonderful journal, but this never came home to me so much as when it produced a quarter of a column about Lord Vandeleur. It was a triumph of word-spinning. If he had carried out his vocation, if he had been a tailor or a hatter (that's how I see him), there might have been something to say about him. But he missed his vocation, he missed everything but posthumous honours. I was so sure Ambrose Tester would come in that afternoon, and so sure he knew I should expect him, that I threw over an engagement on purpose. But he didn't come in, nor the next day, nor the next. There were two possible explanations of his absence. One was that he was giving all his time to consoling Lady Vandeleur; the other was that he was giving it all, as a blind, to Joscelind Bernardstone. Both proved incorrect, for when he at last turned up he told me he had been for a week in the country, at his father's. Sir Edmund also had been unwell; but he had pulled through better than poor Lord Vandeleur. I wondered at first whether his son had been talking over with him the question of a change of base; but guessed in a moment that he had not suffered this alarm. I don't think that Ambrose would have spared him if he had thought it necessary to give him warning; but he probably held that his father would have no ground for complaint so long as he should marry some one; would have no right to remonstrate if he simply transferred his contract. Lady Vandeleur had had two children (whom she had lost), and might, therefore, have others whom she shouldn't lose; that would have been a reply to nice discriminations on Sir Edmund's part.

V

In reality what the young man had been doing was thinking
it over beneath his ancestral oaks and beeches. His countenance showed this—showed it more than Miss Bernardstone
could have liked. He looked like a man who was crossed, not
like a man who was happy, in love. I was no more disposed
than before to help him out with his plot, but at the end of
ten minutes we were articulately discussing it. When I say *we*
were, I mean he was; for I sat before him quite mute, at first,
and amazed at the clearness with which, before his conscience,
he had argued his case. He had persuaded himself that it was
quite a simple matter to throw over poor Joscelind and keep
himself free for the expiration of Lady Vandeleur's term of
mourning. The deliberations of an impulsive man sometimes
land him in strange countries. Ambrose Tester confided his
plan to me as a tremendous secret. He professed to wish
immensely to know how it appeared to me, and whether my
woman's wit couldn't discover for him some loophole big
enough round, some honourable way of not keeping faith.
Yet at the same time he seemed not to foresee that I should,
of necessity, be simply horrified. Disconcerted and perplexed
(a little), that he was prepared to find me; but if I had refused,
as yet, to come to his assistance, he appeared to suppose it was
only because of the real difficulty of suggesting to him that
perfect pretext of which he was in want. He evidently counted
upon me, however, for some illuminating proposal, and I
think he would have liked to say to me, "You have always
pretended to be a great friend of mine"—I hadn't; the pretension was all on his side—"and now is your chance to show
it. Go to Joscelind and make her feel (women have a hundred
ways of doing that sort of thing) that through Vandeleur's

death the change in my situation is complete. If she is the girl I take her for, she will know what to do in the premises."

I was not prepared to oblige him to this degree, and I lost no time in telling him so, after my first surprise at seeing how definite his purpose had become. His contention, after all, was very simple. He had been in love with Lady Vandeleur for years, and was now more in love with her than ever. There had been no appearance of her being, within a calculable period, liberated by the death of her husband. This nobleman was—he didn't say what just then (it was too soon)—but he was only forty years old, and in such health and preservation as to make such a contingency infinitely remote. Under these circumstances, Ambrose had been driven, for the most worldly reasons—he was ashamed of them, pah!—into an engagement with a girl he didn't love, and didn't pretend to love. Suddenly the unexpected occurred; the woman he did love had become accessible to him, and all the relations of things were altered. Why shouldn't he alter too?—why shouldn't Miss Bernardstone alter, Lady Emily alter, and every one alter? It would be *wrong* in him to marry Joscelind in so changed a world—a moment's consideration would certainly assure me of that. He could no longer carry out his part of the bargain, and the transaction must stop before it went any further. If Joscelind knew, she would be the first to recognise this, and the thing for her now was to know.

"Go and tell her, then, if you are so sure of it," I said. "I wonder you have put it off so many days."

He looked at me with a melancholy eye. "Of course I know it's beastly awkward."

It was beastly awkward certainly; there I could quite agree with him, and this was the only sympathy he extracted from me. It was impossible to be less helpful, less merciful, to an embarrassed young man than I was on that occasion. But other occasions followed very quickly, on which Mr Tester renewed his appeal with greater eloquence. He assured me that it was torture to be with his intended, and every hour that he didn't break off committed him more deeply and more fatally. I repeated only once my previous question—asked him only once why then he didn't tell her he had changed his mind. The inquiry was idle, was even unkind, for my young man was in a very tight place. He didn't tell her, simply because he couldn't, in spite of the anguish of feeling that his chance to right himself was rapidly passing away. When I asked him if Joscelind appeared to have guessed nothing he broke out, "How in the world can she guess when I am so kind to her? I am so sorry for her, poor little wretch, that I can't help being nice to her. And from the moment I am nice to her she thinks it's all right."

I could see perfectly what he meant by that, and I liked him more for this little generosity than I disliked him for his nefarious scheme. In fact, I didn't dislike him at all when I saw what an influence my judgment would have on him. I very soon gave him the full benefit of it. I had thought over his case with all the advantages of his own presentation of it, and it was impossible for me to see how he could decently get rid of the girl. That, as I have said, had been my original opinion, and quickened reflection only confirmed it. As I have also said, I hadn't in the least recommended him to become engaged; but once he had done so I recommended him to abide by it. It was all very well being in love with Lady Vandeleur; he might be in love with her, but he hadn't promised to marry her. It was all very well not being in love with Miss Bernardstone; but, as it happened, he had promised to marry her, and in my country a gentleman was supposed to keep such promises. If it was a question of keeping them only so long as was convenient where would any of us be? I assure you I became very eloquent and moral—yes, moral, I maintain the word, in spite of your perhaps thinking (as you are very capable of doing) that I ought to have advised him in just the opposite sense. It was not a question of love, but of marriage, for he had never promised to love poor Joscelind. It was useless his saying it was dreadful to marry without love; he knew that he thought it, and the people he lived with thought it, nothing of the kind. Half his friends had married on those terms. "Yes, and a pretty sight their private life presented!" That might be, but it was the first time I had ever heard him say it. A fortnight before he had been quite ready to do like the others. I knew what I thought, and I suppose I expressed it with some clearness, for my arguments made him still more uncomfortable, unable as he was either to accept them or to act in contempt of them. Why he should have cared so much for my opinion is a mystery I can't elucidate; to understand my little story you must simply swallow it. That he did care is proved by the exasperation with which he suddenly broke out, "Well, then, as I understand you, what you recommend me is to marry Miss Bernardstone, and carry on an intrigue with Lady Vandeleur!"

He knew perfectly that I recommended nothing of the sort, and he must have been very angry to indulge in this *boutade*. He told me that other people didn't think as I did—that every one was of the opinion that between a woman he didn't love and a woman he had adored for years it was a plain moral duty not to hesitate. "Don't hesitate then!" I exclaimed; but I didn't get rid of him with this, for he returned to the charge more than once (he came to me so often that I thought he must neglect both his other alternatives), and let me know again that the voice of society was quite against my view. You will doubtless be surprised at such an intimation that he had taken "society" into his confidence, and wonder whether he went about asking people whether they thought he might back out. I can't tell you exactly, but I know that for some weeks his dilemma was a great deal talked about. His friends perceived he was at the parting of the roads, and many of them had no difficulty in saying which one *they* would take. Some observers thought he ought to do nothing, to leave

things as they were. Others took very high ground and discoursed upon the sanctity of love and the wickedness of really
deceiving the girl, as that would be what it would amount to
(if he should lead her to the altar). Some held that it was too
late to escape, others maintained that it is never too late. Some
thought Miss Bernardstone very much to be pitied; some
reserved their compassion for Ambrose Tester; others, still,
lavished it upon Lady Vandeleur. The prevailing opinion, I
think, was that he ought to obey the promptings of his heart
—London cares so much for the heart! Or is it that London is
simply ferocious, and always prefers the spectacle that is more
entertaining? As it would prolong the drama for the young
man to throw over Miss Bernardstone, there was a considerable readiness to see the poor girl sacrificed. She was like a
Christian maiden in the Roman arena. That is what Ambrose
Tester meant by telling me that public opinion was on his
side. I don't think he chattered about his quandary, but people,
knowing his situation, guessed what was going on in his
mind, and he, on his side, guessed what they said. London
discussions might as well go on in the whispering-gallery of
St Paul's.

I could, of course, do only one thing—I could but re-
affirm my conviction that the Roman attitude, as I may call it,
was cruel, was falsely sentimental. This naturally didn't help
him as he wished to be helped—didn't remove the obstacle to
his marrying in a year or two Lady Vandeleur. Yet he continued to look to me for inspiration—I must say it at the cost
of making him appear a very feeble-minded gentleman. There
was a moment when I thought him capable of an oblique
movement, of temporising with a view to escape. If he succeeded in postponing his marriage long enough, the Bernardstones would throw *him* over, and I suspect that for a day he
entertained the idea of fixing this responsibility on them. But
he was too honest and too generous to do so for longer, and
his destiny was staring him in the face when an accident gave

him a momentary relief. General Bernardstone died, after an illness as sudden and short as that which had carried off Lord Vandeleur; his wife and daughter were plunged into mourning and immediately retired into the country. A week later we heard that the girl's marriage would be put off for several months—partly on account of her mourning and partly because her mother, whose only companion she had now become, could not bear to part with her at the time originally fixed and actually so near. People of course looked at each other—said it was the beginning of the end, a "dodge" of Ambrose Tester's. I wonder they didn't accuse him of poisoning the poor old general. I know to a certainty that he had nothing to do with the delay, that the proposal came from Lady Emily, who, in her bereavement, wished, very naturally, to keep a few months longer the child she was going to lose for ever. It must be said, in justice to her prospective son-in-law, that he was capable either of resigning himself or of frankly (with however many blushes) telling Joscelind he couldn't keep his agreement, but was not capable of trying to wriggle out of his difficulty. The plan of simply telling Joscelind he couldn't—this was the one he had fixed upon as the best, and this was the one of which I remarked to him that it had a defect which should be counted against its advantages. The defect was that it would kill Joscelind on the spot.

I think he believed me, and his believing me made this unexpected respite very welcome to him. There was no knowing what might happen in the interval, and he passed a large part of it in looking for an issue. And yet, at the same time, he kept up the usual forms with the girl whom in his heart he had renounced. I was told more than once (for I had lost sight of the pair during the summer and autumn) that these forms were at times very casual, that he neglected Miss Bernardstone most flagrantly, and had quite resumed his old intimacy with Lady Vandeleur. I don't exactly know what was meant by this, for she spent the first three months of her widowhood in complete seclusion, in her own old house in Norfolk, where he certainly was not staying with her. I believe he stayed some time, for the partridge-shooting, at a place a few miles off. It came to my ears that if Miss Bernardstone didn't take the hint it was because she was determined to stick to him through thick and thin. She never offered to let him off, and I was sure she never would; but I was equally sure that, strange as it may appear, he had not ceased to be nice to her. I have never exactly understood why he didn't hate her, and I am convinced that he was not a comedian in his conduct to her—he was only a good fellow. I have spoken of the satisfaction that Sir Edmund took in his daughter-in-law that was to be; he delighted in looking at her, longed for her when she was out of his sight, and had her, with her mother, staying with him in the country for weeks together. If Ambrose was not so constantly at her side as he might have been, this deficiency was covered by his father's devotion to her, by her appearance of being already one of the family. Mr Tester was away as he might be away if they were already married.

VI

In October I met him at Doubleton; we spent three days there together. He was enjoying his respite, as he didn't scruple to tell me, and he talked to me a great deal—as usual—about Lady Vandeleur. He didn't mention Joscelind, except by implication, in this assurance of how much he valued his weeks of grace.

"Do you mean to say that, under the circumstances, Lady Vandeleur is willing to marry you?"

I made this inquiry more expressively, doubtless, than before; for when we had talked of the matter then he had naturally spoken of her consent as a simple contingency. It was contingent upon the lapse of the first months of her bereavement; it was not a question he could begin to press a few days after her husband's death.

"Not immediately, of course, but if I wait I think so." That, I remember, was his answer.

"If you wait till you get rid of that poor girl, of course."

"She knows nothing about that—it's none of her business."

"Do you mean to say she doesn't know you are engaged?"

"How should she know it, how should she believe it, when she sees how I love her?" the young man exclaimed; but he admitted afterwards that he had not deceived her, and that she rendered full justice to the motives that had determined him. He thought he could answer for it that she would marry him some day or other.

"Then she is a very cruel woman," I said, "and I should like, if you please, to hear no more about her." He protested against this, and, a month later, brought her up again, for a purpose. The purpose, you will see, was a very strange one. I had then come back to town; it was the early part of December. I supposed he was hunting, with his own hounds; but he appeared one afternoon in my drawing-room and told me I should do him a great favour if I would go and see Lady Vandeleur.

"Go and see her? where do you mean, in Norfolk?"

"She has come up to London—didn't you know it? She has a lot of business. She will be kept here till Christmas; I wish you would go."

"Why should I go?" I asked. "Won't you be kept here till Christmas too, and isn't that company enough for her?"

"Upon my word, you are cruel," he said, "and it's a great shame of you, when a man is trying to do his duty and is behaving like a saint."

"Is that what you call saintly, spending all your time with Lady Vandeleur? I will tell you whom I think a saint, if you would like to know."

"You needn't tell me, I know it better than you. I haven't a word to say against her; only she is stupid and hasn't any perceptions. If I am stopping a bit in London you don't understand why; it's as if you hadn't any perceptions either! If I am here for a few days I know what I am about."

"Why should I understand?" I asked—not very candidly, because I should have been glad to. "It's your own affair, you know what you are about, as you say, and of course you have counted the cost."

"What cost do you mean? It's a pretty cost, I can tell you." And then he tried to explain—if I would only enter into it, and not be so suspicious. He was in London for the express purpose of breaking off.

"Breaking off what—your engagement?"

"No, no, damn my engagement—the other thing. My acquaintance, my relations——"

"Your intimacy with Lady Van——?" It was not very gentle, but I believe I burst out laughing. "If this is the way you break off, pray, what would you do to keep up?"

He flushed, and looked both foolish and angry, for of course it was not very difficult to see my point. But he was—in a very clumsy manner of his own—trying to cultivate a good conscience, and he was getting no credit for it. "I suppose I may be allowed to look at her! It's a matter we have to talk over. One doesn't drop such a friend in half an hour."

"One doesn't drop her at all, unless one has the strength to make a sacrifice."

"It's easy for you to talk of sacrifice. You don't know what she is!" my visitor cried.

"I think I know what she is not. She is not a friend, as you call her, if she encourages you in the wrong, if she doesn't help you. No, I have no patience with her," I declared; "I don't like her, and I won't go to see her!"

Mr Tester looked at me a moment, as if he were too vexed to trust himself to speak. He had to make an effort not to say something rude. That effort, however, he was capable of making, and though he held his hat as if he were going to walk out of the house, he ended by staying, by putting it down again, by leaning his head, with his elbows on his knees, in his hands, and groaning out that he had never heard of anything so impossible, and that he was the most wretched man in England. I was very sorry for him, and of course I told him so; but privately I didn't think he stood up to his duty as he ought. I said to him, however, that if he would give me his word of honour that he would not abandon Miss Bernardstone, there was no trouble I wouldn't take to be of use to him. I didn't think Lady Vandeleur was behaving well. He must allow me to repeat that; but if going to see her would give him any pleasure (of course there was no question of pleasure for *her*) I would go fifty times. I couldn't imagine how it would help him, but I would do it, as I would do anything else he asked me. He didn't give me his word of honour, but he said quietly, "*I* shall go straight; you needn't be afraid;" and as he spoke there was honour enough in his face. This left an opening, of course, for another catastrophe. There might be further postponements, and poor Lady Emily, indignant for the first time in her life, might declare that her daughter's situation had become intolerable, and that they withdrew from the engagement. But this was too odious a chance, and I accepted Mr Tester's assurance. He told me that the good I could do by going to see Lady Vandeleur was that it would cheer her up, in that dreary, big house in Upper Brook Street, where she was absolutely alone, with horrible overalls on the furniture, and newspapers—actually newspapers—on the mirrors. She was seeing no one, there was no one to see; but he knew she would see me. I asked him if she knew, then, he was to speak to me of coming, and whether I might allude to him, whether it was not too delicate. I shall never forget his answer to this, nor the tone in which he made it, blushing a little and looking away. "Allude to me? Rather!" It was not the most fatuous speech I had ever heard; it had the effect of being the most modest; and it gave me an odd idea, and especially a new one, of the condition in which, at any time, one might be destined to find Lady Vandeleur. If she, too, were engaged in a struggle with her conscience (in this light they were an edifying pair!) it had perhaps changed her considerably, made her more approachable; and I reflected, ingeniously, that it probably had a humanising effect upon her. Ambrose Tester didn't go away after I had told him that I would comply with his request. He lingered, fidgeting with his stick and gloves, and I perceived that he had more to tell me, and that the real reason why he wished me to go and see Lady Vandeleur was not that she had newspapers on her mirrors. He came out with it at last, for that "Rather!" of his (with the way I took it) had broken the ice.

"You say you don't think she behaves well" (he naturally wished to defend her). "But I daresay you don't understand her position. Perhaps you wouldn't behave any better in her place."

"It's very good of you to imagine me there!" I remarked, laughing.

"It's awkward for me to say. One doesn't want to dot one's i's to that extent."

"She would be delighted to marry you. That's not such a mystery."

"Well, she likes me awfully," Mr Tester said, looking like a handsome child. "It's not all on one side, it's on both. That's the difficulty."

"You mean she won't let you go?—she holds you fast?"

But the poor fellow had, in delicacy, said enough, and at this he jumped up. He stood there a moment, smoothing his hat; then he broke out again. "Please do this. Let her know—make her feel. You can bring it in, you know." And here he paused, embarrassed.

"What can I bring in, Mr Tester? That's the difficulty, as you say."

"What you told me the other day. You know. What you have told me before."

"What I have told you . . . ?"

"That it would put an end to Joscelind! If you can't work round to it, what's the good of being—you?" And with this tribute to my powers he took his departure.

VII

I T was all very well of him to be so flattering, but I really didn't see myself talking in that manner to Lady Vandeleur. I wondered why he didn't give her this information himself, and what particular value it could have as coming from me. Then I said to myself that of course he *had* mentioned to her the truth I had impressed upon him (and which by this time he had evidently taken home), but that to enable it to produce its full effect upon Lady Vandeleur the further testimony of a witness more independent was required. There was nothing for me but to go and see her, and I went the next day, fully conscious that to execute Mr Tester's commission I should have either to find myself very brave or to find her strangely confidential; and fully prepared, also, not to be admitted. But she received me, and the house in Upper Brook Street was as dismal as Ambrose Tester had represented it. The December fog (the afternoon was very dusky) seemed to pervade the muffled rooms, and her ladyship's pink lamp-light to waste itself in the brown atmosphere. He had mentioned to me that the heir to the title (a cousin of her husband), who had left her unmolested for several months, was now taking possession of everything, so that what kept her in town was the business of her "turning out," and certain formalities connected with her dower. This was very ample, and the large provision made for her included the London house. She was very gracious on this occasion, but she certainly had remarkably little to say. Still, she was different, or, at any rate (having taken that hint), I saw her differently. I saw, indeed, that I had never quite done her justice, that I had exaggerated her stiffness, attributed to her a kind of conscious grandeur which was in reality much more an accident of her appearance, of her figure, than a quality of her character. Her appearance is as grand as you know, and on the day I speak of, in her simplified mourning, under those vaguely-gleaming *lambris*, she looked as beautiful as a great white lily. She is very simple and good-natured; she will never make an advance, but she will always respond to one, and I saw, that evening, that the way to get on with her was to treat her as if she were not too imposing. I saw also that, with her nun-like robes and languid eyes, she was a woman who might be immensely in love. All the same, we hadn't much to say to each other. She remarked that it was very kind of me to come, that she wondered how I could endure London at that season, that she had taken a drive and found the Park too dreadful, that she would ring for some more tea if I didn't like what she had given me. Our conversation wandered, stumbling a little, among these platitudes, but no allusion was made on either side to Ambrose Tester. Nevertheless, as I have said, she was different, though it was not till I got home that I phrased to myself what I had detected.

Then, recalling her white face, and the deeper, stranger expression of her beautiful eyes, I entertained myself with the idea that she was under the influence of "suppressed exaltation." The more I thought of her the more she appeared to me not natural; wound up, as it were, to a calmness beneath which there was a deal of agitation. This would have been nonsense if I had not, two days afterwards, received a note from her which struck me as an absolutely "exalted" production. Not superficially, of course; to the casual eye it

would have been perfectly commonplace. But this was precisely its peculiarity, that Lady Vandeleur should have written
me a note which had no apparent point save that she should
like to see me again, a desire for which she did succeed in
assigning a reason. She reminded me that she was paying no
calls, and she hoped I wouldn't stand on ceremony, but come
in very soon again, she had enjoyed my visit so much. We had
not been on note-writing terms, and there was nothing in that
visit to alter our relations; moreover, six months before, she
would not have dreamed of addressing me in that way. I was
doubly convinced, therefore, that she was passing through a
crisis—that she was not in her normal equilibrium. Mr Tester
had not reappeared since the occasion I have described at
length, and I thought it possible he had been capable of the
bravery of leaving town. I had, however, no fear of meeting
him in Upper Brook Street; for, according to my theory of his
relations with Lady Vandeleur he regularly spent his evenings
with her, it being clear to me that they must dine together.
I could answer her note only by going to see her the next day,
when I found abundant confirmation of that idea about the
crisis. I must confess to you in advance that I have never
really understood her behaviour—never understood why she
should have taken to me so suddenly—with whatever reserves,
and however much by implication merely—into her confidence. All I can say is that this is an accident to which one is
exposed with English people, who, in my opinion, and contrary to common report, are the most demonstrative, the most
expansive, the most gushing in the world. I think she felt
rather isolated at this moment, and she had never had many
intimates of her own sex. That sex, as a general thing, disapproved of her proceedings during the last few months, held
that she was making Joscelind Bernardstone suffer too cruelly.
She possibly felt the weight of this censure, and at all events
was not above wishing some one to know that, whatever
injury had fallen upon the girl to whom Mr Tester had so

stupidly engaged himself, had not, so far as she was concerned, been wantonly inflicted. I was there, I was more or less aware of her situation, and I would do as well as any one else.

She seemed really glad to see me, but she was very nervous. Nevertheless, nearly half an hour elapsed, and I was still wondering whether she had sent for me only to discuss the question of how a London house whose appointments had the stamp of a debased period (it had been thought very handsome in 1850) could be "done up" without being made æsthetic. I forget what satisfaction I gave her on this point; I was asking myself how I could work round in the manner prescribed by Joscelind's intended. At the last, however, to my extreme surprise, Lady Vandeleur herself relieved me of this effort.

"I think you know Mr Tester rather well," she remarked abruptly, irrelevantly, and with a face more conscious of the bearings of things than any I had ever seen her wear. On my confessing to such an acquaintance, she mentioned that Mr Tester (who had been in London a few days—perhaps I had seen him) had left town and wouldn't come back for several weeks. This, for the moment, seemed to be all she had to communicate; but she sat looking at me from the corner of her sofa as if she wished me to profit in some way by the opportunity she had given me. Did she want help from outside, this proud, inscrutable woman, and was she reduced to throwing out signals of distress? Did she wish to be protected against herself—applauded for such efforts as she had already made? I didn't rush forward, I was not precipitate, for I felt that now, surely, I should be able at my convenience to execute my commission. What concerned me was not to prevent Lady Vandeleur's marrying Mr Tester, but to prevent Mr Tester's marrying her. In a few moments—with the same irrelevance—she announced to me that he wished to, and asked whether I didn't know it. I saw that this was my chance, and instantly with extreme energy, I exclaimed—

"Ah, for heaven's sake, don't listen to him! It would kill Miss Bernardstone!"

The tone of my voice made her colour a little, and she repeated, "Miss Bernardstone?"

"The girl he is engaged to—or has been—don't you know? Excuse me, I thought every one knew."

"Of course I know he is dreadfully entangled. He was fairly hunted down." Lady Vandeleur was silent a moment, and then she added, with a strange smile, "Fancy, in such a situation, his wanting to marry me!"

"Fancy!" I replied. I was so struck with the oddity of her telling me her secrets that for the moment my indignation did not come to a head—my indignation, I mean, at her accusing poor Lady Emily (and even the girl herself) of having "trapped" our friend. Later I said to myself that I supposed she was within her literal right in abusing her rival, if she was trying sincerely to give him up. "I don't know anything about his having been hunted down," I said; "but this I do know, Lady Vandeleur, I assure you, that if he should throw Joscelind over she would simply go out like that!" And I snapped my fingers.

Lady Vandeleur listened to this serenely enough; she tried at least to take the air of a woman who has no need of new arguments. "Do you know her very well?" she asked, as if she had been struck by my calling Miss Bernardstone by her Christian name.

"Well enough to like her very much." I was going to say "to pity her;" but I thought better of it.

"She must be a person of very little spirit. If a man were to jilt me, I don't think I should go out!" cried her ladyship, with a laugh.

"Nothing is more probable than that she has not your courage or your wisdom. She may be weak, but she is passionately in love with him."

I looked straight into Lady Vandeleur's eyes as I said this, and I was conscious that it was a tolerably good description of my hostess.

"Do you think she would really die?" she asked in a moment.

"Die as if one should stab her with a knife. Some people don't believe in broken hearts," I continued. "I didn't till I knew Joscelind Bernardstone; then I felt that she had one that wouldn't be proof."

"One ought to live—one ought always to live," said Lady Vandeleur; "and always to hold up one's head."

"Ah, I suppose that one oughtn't to feel at all, if one wishes to be a great success."

"What do you call a great success?" she asked.

"Never having occasion to be pitied."

"Being pitied? That must be odious!" she said; and I saw that though she might wish for admiration, she would never wish for sympathy. Then, in a moment, she added that men, in her opinion, were very base—a remark that was deep, but not, I think, very honest; that is, in so far as the purpose of it had been to give me the idea that Ambrose Tester had done nothing but press her, and she had done nothing but resist. They were very odd, the discrepancies in the statements of each of this pair; but it must be said for Lady Vandeleur that now that she had made up her mind (as I believed she had) to sacrifice herself, she really persuaded herself that she had not had a moment of weakness. She quite unbosomed herself, and I fairly assisted at her crisis. It appears that she had a conscience—very much so, and even a high ideal of duty. She represented herself as moving heaven and earth to keep Ambrose Tester up to the mark, and you would never have guessed from what she told me that she had entertained, ever so faintly, the idea of marrying him. I am sure this was a dreadful perversion, but I forgave it on the score of that exaltation of which I have spoken. The things she said, and the way she said them, come back to me, and I thought that if she

looked as handsome as that when she preached virtue to Mr
Tester, it was no wonder he liked the sermon to be going on
perpetually.

"I daresay you know what old friends we are; but that
doesn't make any difference, does it? Nothing would induce
me to marry him—I haven't the smallest intention of marrying
again. It is not a time for me to think of marrying, before his
lordship has been dead six months. The girl is nothing to me;
I know nothing about her, and I don't wish to know; but I
should be very, very sorry if she were unhappy. He is the best
friend I ever had, but I don't see that that's any reason I
should marry him, do you?" Lady Vandeleur appealed to me,
but without waiting for my answers, asking advice in spite
of herself, and then remembering it was beneath her dignity
to appear to be in need of it. "I have told him that if he doesn't
act properly I shall never speak to him again. She's a charming
girl, every one says, and I have no doubt she will make him
perfectly happy. Men don't feel things like women, I think,
and if they are coddled and flattered they forget the rest.
I have no doubt she is very sufficient for all that. For me, at
any rate, once I see a thing in a certain way, I must abide by
that. I think people are so dreadful—they do such horrible
things. They don't seem to think what one's duty may be.
I don't know whether you think much about that, but really
one must at times, don't you think so? Every one is so selfish,
and then, when they have never made an effort or a sacrifice
themselves, they come to you and talk such a lot of hypocrisy.
I know so much better than any one else whether I should
marry or not. But I don't mind telling you that I don't see
why I should. I am not in such a bad position—with my
liberty and a decent maintenance."

In this manner she rambled on, gravely and communi-
catively, contradicting herself at times; not talking fast (she
never did), but dropping one simple sentence, with an interval, after the other, with a certain richness of voice which

always was part of the charm of her presence. She wished to be convinced against herself, and it was a comfort to her to hear herself argue. I was quite willing to be part of the audience, though I had to confine myself to very superficial remarks; for when I had said the event I feared would kill Miss Bernardstone I had said everything that was open to me. I had nothing to do with Lady Vandeleur's marrying, apart from that. I probably disappointed her. She had caught a glimpse of the moral beauty of self-sacrifice, of a certain ideal of conduct (I imagine it was rather new to her), and would have been glad to elicit from me, as a person of some experience of life, an assurance that such joys are not unsubstantial. I had no wish to wind her up to a spiritual ecstasy from which she would inevitably descend again, and I let her deliver herself according to her humour, without attempting to answer for it that she would find renunciation the road to bliss. I believed that if she should give up Mr Tester she would suffer accordingly; but I didn't think that a reason for not giving him up. Before I left her she said to me that nothing would induce her to do anything that she didn't think right. "It would be no pleasure to me, don't you see? I should be always thinking that another way would have been better. Nothing would induce me—nothing, nothing!"

VIII

SHE protested too much, perhaps, but the event seemed to show that she was in earnest. I have described these two first visits of mine in some detail, but they were not the only ones I paid her. I saw her several times again, before she left town, and we became intimate, as London intimacies are measured. She ceased to protest (to my relief, for it made me nervous), she was very gentle, and gracious, and reasonable, and there

was something in the way she looked and spoke that told me
that for the present she found renunciation its own reward.
So far, my scepticism was put to shame; her spiritual ecstasy
maintained itself. If I could have foreseen then that it would
maintain itself till the present hour I should have felt that Lady
Vandeleur's moral nature is finer indeed than mine. I heard
from her that Mr Tester remained at his father's, and that Lady
Emily and her daughter were also there. The day for the
wedding had been fixed, and the preparations were going
rapidly forward. Meanwhile—she didn't tell me, but I gathered
it from things she dropped—she was in almost daily correspondence with the young man. I thought this a strange
concomitant of his bridal arrangements; but apparently, henceforth, they were bent on convincing each other that the torch
of virtue lighted their steps, and they couldn't convince each
other too much. She intimated to me that she had now effectually persuaded him (always by letter) that he would fail
terribly if he should try to found his happiness on an injury
done to another, and that of course she could never be happy
(in a union with him) with the sight of his wretchedness before
her. That a good deal of correspondence should be required to
elucidate this is perhaps after all not remarkable. One day,
when I was sitting with her (it was just before she left town),
she suddenly burst into tears. Before we parted I said to her
that there were several women in London I liked very much—
that was common enough—but for her I had a positive
respect, and that was rare. My respect continues still, and it
sometimes makes me furious.

About the middle of January Ambrose Tester reappeared
in town. He told me he came to bid me good-bye. He was
going to be beheaded. It was no use saying that old relations
would be the same after a man was married; they would be
different, everything would be different. I had wanted him to
marry, and now I should see how I liked it. He didn't mention
that I had also wanted him not to marry, and I was sure that if

Lady Vandeleur had become his wife she would have been a much greater impediment to our harmless friendship than Joscelind Bernardstone would ever be. It took me but a short time to observe that he was in very much the same condition as Lady Vandeleur. He was finding how sweet it is to renounce, hand in hand with one we love. Upon him, too, the peace of the Lord had descended. He spoke of his father's delight at the nuptials being so near at hand; at the festivities that would take place in Dorsetshire when he should bring home his bride. The only allusion he made to what we had talked of the last time we were together was to exclaim suddenly, "How can I tell you how easy she has made it? She is so sweet, so noble! She really is a perfect creature!" I took for granted that he was talking of his future wife, but in a moment, as we were at cross-purposes, perceived that he meant Lady Vandeleur. This seemed to me really ominous—it stuck in my mind after he had left me. I was half tempted to write him a note, to say, "There is, after all, perhaps, something worse than your jilting Miss Bernardstone; and that is the danger that your rupture with Lady Vandeleur may become more of a bond than your marrying her would have been. For heaven's sake, let your sacrifice *be* a sacrifice; keep it in its proper place!"

Of course I didn't write; even the slight responsibility I had already incurred began to frighten me, and I never saw Mr Tester again till he was the husband of Joscelind Bernardstone. They have now been married some four years; they have two children, the elder of whom is, as he should be, a boy. Sir Edmund waited till his grandson had made good his place in the world, and then, feeling it was safe, he quietly, genially, surrendered his trust. He died, holding the hand of his daughter-in-law, and giving it doubtless a pressure which was an injunction to be brave. I don't know what he thought of the success of his plan for his son; but perhaps, after all, he saw nothing amiss, for Joscelind is the last woman in the world to have troubled him with her sorrows. From him, no doubt, she successfully concealed that bewilderment on which I have touched. You see I speak of her sorrows as if they were a matter of common recognition; certain it is that any one who meets her must see that she doesn't pass her life in joy. Lady Vandeleur, as you know, has never married again; she is still the most beautiful widow in England. She enjoys the esteem of every one, as well as the approbation of her conscience, for every one knows the sacrifice she made, knows that she was even more in love with Sir Ambrose than he was with her. She goes out again, of course, as of old, and she constantly meets the baronet and his wife. She is supposed to be even "very nice" to Lady Tester, and she certainly treats her with exceeding civility. But you know (or perhaps you don't know) all the deadly things that, in London, may lie beneath that method. I don't in the least mean that Lady Vandeleur has any deadly intentions; she is a very good woman, and I am sure that in her heart she thinks she lets poor Joscelind off very easily. But the result of the whole situation is that Joscelind is in dreadful fear of her, for how can she help seeing that she has a very peculiar power over her husband? There couldn't have been a better occasion for observing the three together (if together it may be called, when Lady Tester is so completely outside) than those two days of ours at Doubleton. That's a house where they have met more than once before; I think she and Sir Ambrose like it. By "she" I mean, as he used to mean, Lady Vandeleur. You saw how Lady Tester was absolutely white with uneasiness. What can she do when she meets everywhere the implication that if two people in our time have distinguished themselves for their virtue, it is her husband and Lady Vandeleur? It is my impression that this pair are exceedingly happy. His marriage *has* made a difference, and I see him much less frequently and less intimately. But when I meet him I notice in him a kind of emanation of quiet bliss. Yes, they are certainly in felicity, they have trod the clouds together, they have soared into the blue, and they wear in their faces the glory of those altitudes. They encourage, they cheer, inspire, sustain each other; remind each other that they have chosen the better part. Of course they have to meet for this purpose, and their interviews are filled, I am sure, with its sanctity. He holds up his head, as a man may who on a very critical occasion behaved like a perfect gentleman. It is only poor Joscelind that droops. Haven't I explained to you now why she doesn't understand?

MRS TEMPERLY

I

"WHY, Cousin Raymond, how can you suppose? Why, she's only sixteen!"

"She told me she was seventeen," said the young man, as if it made a great difference.

"Well, only *just!*" Mrs Temperly replied, in the tone of graceful, reasonable concession.

"Well, that's a very good age for me. I'm very young."

"You are old enough to know better," the lady remarked, in her soft, pleasant voice, which always drew the sting from a reproach, and enabled you to swallow it as you would a cooked plum, without the stone. "Why, she hasn't finished her education!"

"That's just what I mean," said her interlocutor. "It would finish it beautifully for her to marry me."

"Have you finished yours, my dear?" Mrs Temperly inquired. "The way you young people talk about marrying!" she exclaimed, looking at the itinerant functionary with the long wand who touched into a flame the tall gas-lamp on the other side of the Fifth Avenue. The pair were standing, in the recess of a window, in one of the big public rooms of an immense hotel, and the October day was turning to dusk.

"Well, would you have us leave it to the old?" Raymond asked. "That's just what I think—she would be such a help to me," he continued. "I want to go back to Paris to study more. I have come home too soon. I don't know half enough; they know more here than I thought. So it would be perfectly easy, and we should all be together."

"Well, my dear, when you do come back to Paris we will

talk about it," said Mrs Temperly, turning away from the window.

"I should like it better, Cousin Maria, if you trusted me a little more," Raymond sighed, observing that she was not really giving her thoughts to what he said. She irritated him somehow; she was so full of her impending departure, of her arrangements, her last duties and memoranda. She was not exactly important, any more than she was humble; she was too conciliatory for the one and too positive for the other. But she bustled quietly and gave one the sense of being "up to" everything; the successive steps of her enterprise were in advance perfectly clear to her, and he could see that her imagination (conventional as she was she had plenty of that faculty) had already taken up its abode on one of those fine *premiers* which she had never seen, but which by instinct she seemed to know all about, in the very best part of the quarter of the Champs Elysées. If she ruffled him envy had perhaps something to do with it: she was to set sail on the morrow for the city of his affection and he was to stop in New York, where the fact that he was but half pleased did not alter the fact that he had his studio on his hands and that it was a bad one (though perhaps as good as any use he should put it to), which no one would be in a hurry to relieve him of.

It was easy for him to talk to Mrs Temperly in that airy way about going back, but he couldn't go back unless the old gentleman gave him the means. He had already given him a great many things in the past, and with the others coming on (Marian's marriage-outfit, within three months, had cost literally thousands), Raymond had not at present the face to ask for more. He must sell some pictures first, and to sell them he must first paint them. It was his misfortune that he saw what he wanted to do so much better than he could do it. But he must really try and please himself—an effort that appeared more possible now that the idea of following Dora across the ocean had become an incentive. In spite of secret aspirations and even intentions, however, it was not encouraging to feel that he made really no impression at all on Cousin Maria. This certitude was so far from agreeable to him that he almost found it in him to drop the endearing title by which he had hitherto addressed her. It was only that, after all, her husband had been distantly related to his mother. It was not as a cousin that he was interested in Dora, but as something very much more intimate. I know not whether it occurred to him that Mrs Temperly herself would never give his displeasure the benefit of dropping the affectionate form. She might shut her door to him altogether, but he would always be her kinsman and her dear. She was much addicted to these little embellishments of human intercourse—the friendly apostrophe and even the caressing hand—and there was something homely and cosy, a rustic, motherly *bonhomie*, in her use of them. She was as lavish of them as she was really careful in the selection of her friends.

She stood there with her hand in her pocket, as if she were feeling for something; her little plain, pleasant face was presented to him with a musing smile, and he vaguely wondered whether she were fumbling for a piece of money to buy him off from wishing to marry her daughter. Such an idea would be quite in keeping with the disguised levity with which she treated his state of mind. If her levity was wrapped up in the air of tender solicitude for everything that related to the feelings of her child, that only made her failure to appreciate his suit more deliberate. She struck him almost as impertinent (at the same time that he knew this was never her intention) as she looked up at him—her tiny proportions always made her throw back her head and set something dancing in her cap —and inquired whether he had noticed if she gave two keys, tied together by a blue ribbon, to Susan Winkle, when that faithful but flurried domestic met them in the lobby. She was thinking only of questions of luggage, and the fact that he wished to marry Dora was the smallest incident in their getting off.

"I think you ask me that only to change the subject," he said. "I don't believe that ever in your life you have been unconscious of what you have done with your keys."

"Not often, but you make me nervous," she answered, with her patient, honest smile.

"Oh, Cousin Maria!" the young man exclaimed, ambiguously, while Mrs Temperly looked humanely at some totally uninteresting people who came straggling into the great hot, frescoed, velvety drawing-room, where it was as easy to see you were in an hotel as it was to see that, if you were, you were in one of the very best. Mrs Temperly, since her husband's death, had passed much of her life at hotels, where she flattered herself that she preserved the tone of domestic life free from every taint and promoted the refined development of her children; but she selected them as well as she selected her friends. Somehow they became better from the very fact of her being there, and her children were smuggled in and out in the most extraordinary way; one never met them racing and whooping, as one did hundreds of others, in the lobbies. Her frequentation of hotels, where she paid enormous bills, was part of her expensive but practical way of living, and also of her theory that, from one week to another, she was going to Europe for a series of years as soon as she had wound up certain complicated affairs which had devolved upon her at her husband's death. If these affairs had dragged on it was owing to their inherent troublesomeness and implied no doubt of her capacity to bring them to a solution and to administer the very considerable fortune that Mr Temperly had left. She used, in a superior, unprejudiced way, every convenience that the civilisation of her time offered her, and would have lived without hesitation in a lighthouse if this had contributed to her general scheme. She was now, in the interest of this scheme, preparing to use Europe, which she had not yet visited and with none of

whose foreign tongues she was acquainted. This time she was
certainly embarking.

She took no notice of the discredit which her young friend
appeared to throw on the idea that she had nerves, and betrayed no suspicion that he believed her to have them in about
the same degree as a sound, productive Alderney cow. She
only moved toward one of the numerous doors of the room,
as if to remind him of all she had still to do before night. They
passed together into the long, wide corridor of the hotel—a
vista of soft carpet, numbered doors, wandering women and
perpetual gaslight—and approached the staircase by which
she must ascend again to her domestic duties. She counted
over, serenely, for his enlightenment, those that were still to
be performed; but he could see that everything would be
finished by nine o'clock—the time she had fixed in advance.
The heavy luggage was then to go to the steamer; she herself
was to be on board, with the children and the smaller things,
at eleven o'clock the next morning. They had thirty pieces,
but this was less than they had when they came from California five years before. She wouldn't have done that again.
It was true that at that time she had had Mr Temperly to help:
he had died, Raymond remembered, six months after the
settlement in New York. But, on the other hand, she knew
more now. It was one of Mrs Temperly's amiable qualities
that she admitted herself so candidly to be still susceptible of
development. She never professed to be in possession of all the
knowledge requisite for her career; not only did she let her
friends know that she was always learning, but she appealed
to them to instruct her, in a manner which was in itself an
example.

When Raymond said to her that he took for granted she
would let him come down to the steamer for a last good-bye,
she not only consented graciously but added that he was free
to call again at the hotel in the evening, if he had nothing
better to do. He must come between nine and ten; she expected

several other friends—those who wished to see the last of
them, yet didn't care to come to the ship. Then he would see
all of them—she meant all of themselves, Dora and Effie and
Tishy, and even Mademoiselle Bourde. She spoke exactly as
if he had never approached her on the subject of Dora and as
if Tishy, who was ten years of age, and Mademoiselle Bourde,
who was the French governess and forty, were objects of no
less an interest to him. He felt what a long pull he should have
ever to get round her, and the sting of this knowledge was in
his consciousness that Dora was really in her mother's hands.
In Mrs Temperly's composition there was not a hint of the
bully; but none the less she held her children—she would hold
them for ever. It was not simply by tenderness; but what it
was by she knew best herself. Raymond appreciated the privilege of seeing Dora again that evening as well as on the
morrow; yet he was so vexed with her mother that his vexa-
tion betrayed him into something that almost savoured of
violence—a fact which I am ashamed to have to chronicle, as
Mrs Temperly's own urbanity deprived such breaches of every
excuse. It may perhaps serve partly as an excuse for Raymond
Bestwick that he was in love, or at least that he thought he
was. Before she parted from him at the foot of the staircase he
said to her, "And of course, if things go as you like over
there, Dora will marry some foreign prince."

She gave no sign of resenting this speech, but she looked at
him for the first time as if she were hesitating, as if it were not
instantly clear to her what to say. It appeared to him, on his
side, for a moment, that there was something strange in her
hesitation, that abruptly, by an inspiration, she was almost
making up her mind to reply that Dora's marriage to a prince
was, considering Dora's peculiarities (he knew that her
mother deemed her peculiar, and so did he, but that was
precisely why he wished to marry her), so little probable that,
after all, once such a union was out of the question, *he* might
be no worse than another plain man. These, however, were

not the words that fell from Mrs Temperly's lips. Her embarrassment vanished in her clear smile. "Do you know what Mr Temperly used to say? He used to say that Dora was the pattern of an old maid—she would never make a choice."

"I hope—because that would have been too foolish—that he didn't say she wouldn't have a chance."

"Oh, a chance! what do you call by that fine name?" Cousin Maria exclaimed, laughing, as she ascended the stair.

II

WHEN he came back, after dinner, she was again in one of the public rooms; she explained that a lot of the things for the ship were spread out in her own parlours: there was no space to sit down. Raymond was highly gratified by this fact; it offered an opportunity for strolling away a little with Dora, especially as, after he had been there ten minutes, other people began to come in. They were entertained by the rest, by Effie and Tishy, who was allowed to sit up a little, and by Mademoiselle Bourde, who besought every visitor to indicate her a remedy that was *really* effective against the sea—some charm, some philter, some potion or spell. "Never mind, ma'm'selle, I've got a remedy," said Cousin Maria, with her cheerful decision, each time; but the French instructress always began afresh.

As the young man was about to be parted for an indefinite period from the girl whom he was ready to swear that he adored, it is clear that he ought to have been equally ready to swear that she was the fairest of her species. In point of fact, however, it was no less vivid to him than it had been before that he loved Dora Temperly for qualities which had nothing to do with straightness of nose or pinkness of complexion. Her figure was straight, and so was her character, but her nose was not, and Philistines and other vulgar people would have

committed themselves, without a blush on their own flat
faces, to the assertion that she was decidedly plain. In his
artistic imagination he had analogies for her, drawn from
legend and literature; he was perfectly aware that she struck
many persons as silent, shy and angular, while his own version
of her peculiarities was that she was like a figure on the
predella of an early Italian painting or a mediæval maiden
wandering about a lonely castle, with her lover gone to the
Crusades. To his sense, Dora had but one defect—her admiration for her mother was too undiscriminating. An ardent
young man may well be slightly vexed when he finds that a
young lady will probably never care for him so much as she
cares for her parent; and Raymond Bestwick had this added
ground for chagrin, that Dora had—if she chose to take it—
so good a pretext for discriminating. For she had nothing
whatever in common with the others; she was not of the same
stuff as Mrs Temperly and Effie and Tishy.

She was original and generous and uncalculating, besides
being full of perception and taste in regard to the things *he*
cared about. She knew nothing of conventional signs or esti-
mates, but understood everything that might be said to her
from an artistic point of view. She was formed to live in a
studio, and not in a stiff drawing-room, amid upholstery horribly new; and moreover her eyes and her voice were both
charming. It was only a pity she was so gentle; that is, he liked
it for himself, but he deplored it for her mother. He considered that he had virtually given that lady his word that he
would not make love to her; but his spirits had risen since his
visit of three or four hours before. It seemed to him, after
thinking things over more intently, that a way would be
opened for him to return to Paris. It was not probable that in
the interval Dora would be married off to a prince; for in the
first place the foolish race of princes would be sure not to
appreciate her, and in the second she would not, in this
matter, simply do her mother's bidding—her gentleness

would not go so far as that. She might remain single by the maternal decree, but she would not take a husband who was disagreeable to her. In this reasoning Raymond was obliged to shut his eyes very tight to the danger that some particular prince might not be disagreeable to her, as well as to the attraction proceeding from what her mother might announce that she would "do." He was perfectly aware that it was in Cousin Maria's power, and would probably be in her pleasure, to settle a handsome marriage-fee upon each of her daughters. He was equally certain that this had nothing to do with the nature of his own interest in the eldest, both because it was clear that Mrs Temperly would do very little for *him*, and because he didn't care how little she did.

Effie and Tishy sat in the circle, on the edge of rather high chairs, while Mademoiselle Bourde surveyed in them with complacency the results of her own superiority. Tishy was a child, but Effie was fifteen, and they were both very nice little girls, arrayed in fresh travelling dresses and deriving a quaintness from the fact that Tishy was already armed, for foreign adventures, with a smart new reticule, from which she could not be induced to part, and that Effie had her finger in her "place" in a fat red volume of *Murray*. Raymond knew that in a general way their mother would not have allowed them to appear in the drawing-room with these adjuncts, but something was to be allowed to the fever of anticipation. They were both pretty, with delicate features and blue eyes, and would grow up into worldly, conventional young ladies, just as Dora had not done. They looked at Mademoiselle Bourde for approval whenever they spoke, and, in addressing their mother alternately with that accomplished woman, kept their two languages neatly distinct.

Raymond had but a vague idea of who the people were who had come to bid Cousin Maria farewell, and he had no wish for a sharper one, though she introduced him, very definitely, to the whole group. She might make light of him in

her secret soul, but she would never put herself in the wrong
by omitting the smallest form. Fortunately, however, he was
not obliged to like all her forms, and he foresaw the day when
she would abandon this particular one. She was not so well
made up in advance about Paris but that it would be in reserve
for her to detest the period when she had thought it proper to
"introduce all round." Raymond detested it already, and tried
to make Dora understand that he wished her to take a walk
with him in the corridors. There was a gentleman with a curl
on his forehead who especially displeased him; he made
childish jokes, at which the others laughed all at once, as if
they had rehearsed for it—jokes à la portée of Effie and Tishy
and mainly about them. These two joined in the merriment, as
if they followed perfectly, as indeed they might, and gave a
small sigh afterward, with a little factitious air. Dora remained
grave, almost sad; it was when she was different, in this way,
that he felt how much he liked her. He hated, in general, a
large ring of people who had drawn up chairs in the public
room of an hotel: some one was sure to undertake to be funny.

He succeeded at last in drawing Dora away; he endeavoured
to give the movement a casual air. There was nothing peculiar, after all, in their walking a little in the passage; a dozen
other persons were doing the same. The girl had the air of not
suspecting in the least that he could have anything particular
to say to her—of responding to his appeal simply out of her
general gentleness. It was not in her companion's interest that
her mind should be such a blank; nevertheless his conviction
that in spite of the ministrations of Mademoiselle Bourde she
was not falsely ingenuous made him repeat to himself that
he would still make her his own. They took several turns in
the hall, during which it might still have appeared to Dora
Temperly that her cousin Raymond had nothing particular
to say to her. He remarked several times that he should certainly turn up in Paris in the spring; but when once she had
replied that she was very glad that subject seemed exhausted.

The young man cared little, however; it was not a question now of making any declaration: he only wanted to be with her. Suddenly, when they were at the end of the corridor furthest removed from the room they had left, he said to her: "Your mother is very strange. Why has she got such an idea about Paris?"

"How do you mean, such an idea?" He had stopped, making the girl stand there before him.

"Well, she thinks so much of it without having ever seen it, or really knowing anything. She appears to have planned out such a great life there."

"She thinks it's the best place," Dora rejoined, with the dim smile that always charmed our young man.

"The best place for what?"

"Well, to learn French." The girl continued to smile.

"Do you mean for her? She'll never learn it; she can't."

"No; for us. And other things."

"You know it already. And *you* know other things," said Raymond.

"She wants us to know them better—better than any girls know them."

"I don't know what things you mean," exclaimed the young man, rather impatiently.

"Well, we shall see," Dora returned, laughing.

He said nothing for a minute, at the end of which he resumed: "I hope you won't be offended if I say that it seems curious your mother should have such aspirations—such Napoleonic plans. I mean being just a quiet little lady from California, who has never seen any of the kind of thing that she has in her head."

"That's just why she wants to see it, I suppose; and I don't know why her being from California should prevent. At any rate she wants us to have the best. Isn't the best taste in Paris?"

"Yes; and the worst." It made him gloomy when she defended the old lady, and to change the subject he asked:

"Aren't you sorry, this last night, to leave your own country for such an indefinite time?"

It didn't cheer him up that the girl should answer: "Oh, I would go anywhere with mother!"

"And with *her?*" Raymond demanded, sarcastically, as Mademoiselle Bourde came in sight, emerging from the drawing-room. She approached them; they met her in a moment, and she informed Dora that Mrs Temperly wished her to come back and play a part of that composition of Saint-Saens—the last one she had been learning—for Mr and Mrs Parminter: they wanted to judge whether their daughter could manage it.

"I don't believe she can," said Dora, smiling; but she was moving away to comply when her companion detained her a moment.

"Are you going to bid me good-bye?"

"Won't you come back to the drawing-room?"

"I think not; I don't like it."

"And to mamma—you'll say nothing?" the girl went on.

"Oh, we have made our farewell; we had a special interview this afternoon."

"And you won't come to the ship in the morning?"

Raymond hesitated a moment. "Will Mr and Mrs Parminter be there?"

"Oh, surely they will!" Mademoiselle Bourde declared, surveying the young couple with a certain tactful serenity, but standing very close to them, as if it might be her duty to interpose.

"Well then, I won't come."

"Well, good-bye then," said the girl gently, holding out her hand.

"Good-bye, Dora." He took it, while she smiled at him, but he said nothing more—he was so annoyed at the way Mademoiselle Bourde watched them. He only looked at Dora; she seemed to him beautiful.

"My dear child—that poor Madame Parminter," the governess murmured.

"I shall come over very soon," said Raymond, as his companion turned away.

"That will be charming." And she left him quickly, without looking back.

Mademoiselle Bourde lingered—he didn't know why, unless it was to make him feel, with her smooth, finished French assurance, which had the manner of extreme benignity, that she was following him up. He sometimes wondered whether she copied Mrs Temperly or whether Mrs Temperly tried to copy her. Presently she said, slowly rubbing her hands and smiling at him:

"You will have plenty of time. We shall be long in Paris."

"Perhaps you will be disappointed," Raymond suggested.

"How can we be—unless *you* disappoint us?" asked the governess, sweetly.

He left her without ceremony: the imitation was probably on the part of Cousin Maria.

III

"ONLY just ourselves," her note had said; and he arrived, in his natural impatience, a few moments before the hour. He remembered his Cousin Maria's habitual punctuality, but when he entered the splendid *salon* in the quarter of the Parc Monceau—it was there that he had found her established—he saw that he should have it, for a little, to himself. This was pleasing, for he should be able to look round—there were admirable things to look at. Even to-day Raymond Bestwick was not sure that he had learned to paint, but he had no doubt of his judgment of the work of others, and a single glance

showed him that Mrs Temperly had "known enough" to
select, for the adornment of her walls, half a dozen immensely
valuable specimens of contemporary French art. Her choice
of other objects had been equally enlightened, and he remembered what Dora had said to him five years before—that
her mother wished them to have the best. Evidently, now
they had got it; if five years was a long time for him to
have delayed (with his original plan of getting off so soon) to
come to Paris, it was a very short one for Cousin Maria
to have taken to arrive at the highest good.

Rather to his surprise the first person to come in was
Effie, now so complete a young lady, and such a very pretty
girl, that he scarcely would have known her. She was fair, she
was graceful, she was lovely, and as she entered the room,
blushing and smiling, with a little floating motion which suggested that she was in a liquid element, she brushed down the
ribbons of a delicate Parisian *toilette de jeune fille*. She
appeared to expect that he would be surprised, and as if to
justify herself for being the first she said, "Mamma told me to
come; she knows you are here; she said I was not to wait."
More than once, while they conversed, during the next few
moments, before any one else arrived, she repeated that she
was acting by her mamma's directions. Raymond perceived
that she had not only the costume but several other of the
attributes of a *jeune fille*. They talked, I say, but with a certain
difficulty, for Effie asked him no questions, and this made him
feel a little stiff about thrusting information upon her. Then
she was so pretty, so exquisite, that this by itself disconcerted
him. It seemed to him almost that she had falsified a prophecy,
instead of bringing one to pass. He had foretold that she
would be like this; the only difference was that she was so
much more like it. She made no inquiries about his arrival, his
people in America, his plans; and they exchanged vague
remarks about the pictures, quite as if they had met for the
first time.

When Cousin Maria came in Effie was standing in front of the fire fastening a bracelet, and he was at a distance gazing in silence at a portrait of his hostess by Bastien-Lepage. One of his apprehensions had been that Cousin Maria would allude ironically to the difference there had been between his threat (because it had been really almost a threat) of following them speedily to Paris and what had in fact occurred; but he saw in a moment how superficial this calculation had been. Besides, when had Cousin Maria ever been ironical? She treated him as if she had seen him last week (which did not preclude kindness), and only expressed her regret at having missed his visit the day before, in consequence of which she had immediately written to him to come and dine. He might have come from round the corner, instead of from New York and across the wintry ocean. This was a part of her "cosiness," her friendly, motherly optimism, of which, even of old, the habit had been never to recognise nor allude to disagreeable things; so that to-day, in the midst of so much that was not disagreeable, the custom would of course be immensely confirmed.

Raymond was perfectly aware that it was not a pleasure, even for her, that, for several years past, things should have gone so ill in New York with his family and himself. His father's embarrassments, of which Marian's silly husband had been the cause and which had terminated in general ruin and humiliation, to say nothing of the old man's "stroke" and the necessity, arising from it, for a renunciation on his own part of all present thoughts of leaving home again and even for a partial relinquishment of present work, the old man requiring so much of his personal attention—all this constituted an episode which could not fail to look sordid and dreary in the light of Mrs Temperly's high success. The odour of success was in the warm, slightly heavy air, which seemed distilled from rare old fabrics, from brocades and tapestries, from the deep, mingled tones of the pictures, the subdued radiance of cabinets and old porcelain and the jars of winter roses standing

in soft circles of lamp-light. Raymond felt himself in the
presence of an effect in regard to which he remained in ignorance of the cause—a mystery that required a key. Cousin
Maria's success was unexplained so long as she simply stood
there with her little familiar, comforting, upward gaze, talking
in coaxing cadences, with exactly the same manner she had
brought ten years ago from California, to a tall, bald, bending,
smiling young man, evidently a foreigner, who had just come
in and whose name Raymond had not caught from the lips of
the *maître d'hôtel*. Was he just one of themselves—was he
there for Effie, or perhaps even for Dora? The unexplained
must preponderate till Dora came in; he found he counted
upon her, even though in her letters (it was true that for the
last couple of years they had come but at long intervals) she
had told him so little about their life. She never spoke of
people; she talked of the books she read, of the music she had
heard or was studying (a whole page sometimes about the last
concert at the Conservatoire), the new pictures and the
manner of the different artists.

When she entered the room three or four minutes after the
arrival of the young foreigner, with whom her mother conversed in just the accents Raymond had last heard at the hotel
in the Fifth Avenue (he was obliged to admit that she gave
herself no airs; it was clear that her success had not gone in the
least to her head); when Dora at last appeared she was accompanied by Mademoiselle Bourde. The presence of this lady—
he didn't know she was still in the house—Raymond took as a
sign that they were really dining *en famille*, so that the young
man was either an actual or a prospective intimate. Dora
shook hands first with her cousin, but he watched the manner
of her greeting with the other visitor and saw that it indicated
extreme friendliness—on the part of the latter. If there was a
charming flush in her cheek as he took her hand, that was the
remainder of the colour that had risen there as she came
toward Raymond. It will be seen that our young man still

had an eye for the element of fascination, as he used to regard it, in this quiet, dimly-shining maiden.

He saw that Effie was the only one who had changed (Tishy remained yet to be judged), except that Dora really looked older, quite as much older as the number of years had given her a right to: there was as little difference in her as there was in her mother. Not that she was like her mother, but she was perfectly like herself. Her meeting with Raymond was bright, but very still; their phrases were awkward and commonplace, and the thing was mainly a contact of looks—conscious, embarrassed, indirect, but brightening every moment with old familiarities. Her mother appeared to pay no attention, and neither, to do her justice, did Mademoiselle Bourde, who, after an exchange of expressive salutations with Raymond, began to scrutinise Effie with little admiring gestures and smiles. She surveyed her from head to foot; she pulled a ribbon straight; she was evidently a flattering governess. Cousin Maria explained to Cousin Raymond that they were waiting for one more friend—a very dear lady. "But she lives near, and when people live near they are always late—haven't you noticed that?"

"Your hotel is far away, I know, and yet you were the first," Dora said, smiling to Raymond.

"Oh, even if it were round the corner I should be the first—to come to *you!*" the young man answered, speaking loud and clear, so that his words might serve as a notification to Cousin Maria that his sentiments were unchanged.

"You are more French than the French," Dora returned.

"You say that as if you didn't like them: I hope you don't," said Raymond, still with intentions in regard to his hostess.

"We like them more and more, the more we see of them," this lady interposed; but gently, impersonally, and with an air of not wishing to put Raymond in the wrong.

"*Mais j'espère bien!*" cried Mademoiselle Bourde, holding up her head and opening her eyes very wide. "Such friendships

as we form, and, I may say, as we inspire! *Je m'en rapporte
à Effie,*" the governess continued.

"We have received immense kindness; we have established
relations that are so pleasant for us, Cousin Raymond. We
have the *entrée* of so many charming homes," Mrs Temperly
remarked.

"But ours is the most charming of all; that I will say,"
exclaimed Mademoiselle Bourde. "Isn't it so, Effie?"

"Oh yes, I think it is; especially when we are expecting the
Marquise," Effie responded. Then she added, "But here she
comes now; I hear her carriage in the court."

The Marquise too was just one of themselves; she was a
part of their charming home.

"She *is* such a love!" said Mrs Temperly to the foreign
gentleman, with an irrepressible movement of benevolence.

To which Raymond heard the gentleman reply that, Ah,
she was the most distinguished woman in France.

"Do you know Madame de Brives?" Effie asked of Raymond, while they were waiting for her to come in.

She came in at that moment, and the girl turned away
quickly without an answer.

"How in the world should I know her?" That was the
answer he would have been tempted to give. He felt very
much out of Cousin Maria's circle. The foreign gentleman
fingered his moustache and looked at him sidewise. The
Marquise was a very pretty woman, fair and slender, of middle
age, with a smile, a complexion, a diamond necklace, of great
splendour, and a charming manner. Her greeting to her
friends was sweet and familiar, and was accompanied with
much kissing of a sisterly, motherly, daughterly kind; and yet
with this expression of simple, almost homely sentiment
there was something in her that astonished and dazzled. She
might very well have been, as the foreign young man said, the
most distinguished woman in France. Dora had not rushed
forward to meet her with nearly so much *empressement* as

Effie, and this gave him a chance to ask the former who she
was. The girl replied that she was her mother's most intimate
friend: to which he rejoined that that was not a description;
what he wanted to know was her title to this exalted position.

"Why, can't you see it? She is beautiful and she is good."

"I see that she is beautiful; but how can I see that she is
good?"

"Good to mamma, I mean, and to Effie and Tishy."

"And isn't she good to you?"

"Oh, I don't know her so well. But I delight to look at
her."

"Certainly, that must be a great pleasure," said Raymond.
He enjoyed it during dinner, which was now served, though
his enjoyment was diminished by his not finding himself next
to Dora. They sat at a small round table and he had at his
right his Cousin Maria, whom he had taken in. On his left was
Madame de Brives, who had the foreign gentleman for a
neighbour. Then came Effie and Mademoiselle Bourde, and
Dora was on the other side of her mother. Raymond regarded
this as marked—a symbol of the fact that Cousin Maria would
continue to separate them. He remained in ignorance of the
other gentleman's identity, and remembered how he had pro-
phesied at the hotel in New York that his hostess would give
up introducing people. It was a friendly, easy little family
repast, as she had said it would be, with just a marquise and a
secretary of embassy—Raymond ended by guessing that the
stranger was a secretary of embassy—thrown in. So far from
interfering with the family tone Madame de Brives directly
contributed to it. She eminently justified the affection in which
she was held in the house; she was in the highest degree
sociable and sympathetic, and at the same time witty (there
was no insipidity in Madame de Brives), and was the cause of
Raymond's making the reflection—as he had made it often in
his earlier years—that an agreeable Frenchwoman is a triumph
of civilisation. This did not prevent him from giving the

Marquise no more than half of his attention; the rest was dedicated to Dora, who, on her side, though in common with Effie and Mademoiselle Bourde she bent a frequent, interested gaze on the splendid French lady, very often met our young man's eyes with mute, vague but, to his sense, none the less valuable intimations. It was as if she knew what was going on in his mind (it is true that he scarcely knew it himself), and might be trusted to clear things up at some convenient hour.

Madame de Brives talked across Raymond, in excellent English, to Cousin Maria, but this did not prevent her from being gracious, even encouraging, to the young man, who was a little afraid of her and thought her a delightful creature. She asked him more questions about himself than any of them had done. Her conversation with Mrs Temperly was of an intimate, domestic order, and full of social, personal allusions, which Raymond was unable to follow. It appeared to be concerned considerably with the private affairs of the old French *noblesse*, into whose councils—to judge by the tone of the Marquise—Cousin Maria had been admitted by acclamation. Every now and then Madame de Brives broke into French, and it was in this tongue that she uttered an apostrophe to her hostess: "Oh, you, *ma toute-bonne*, you who have the genius of good sense!" And she appealed to Raymond to know if his Cousin Maria had not the genius of good sense—the wisdom of the ages. The old lady did not defend herself from the compliment; she let it pass, with her motherly, tolerant smile; nor did Raymond attempt to defend her, for he felt the justice of his neighbour's description: Cousin Maria's good sense was incontestable, magnificent. She took an affectionate, indulgent view of most of the persons mentioned, and yet her tone was far from being vapid or vague. Madame de Brives usually remarked that they were coming very soon again to see her, she did them so much good. "The freshness of your judgment —the freshness of your judgment!" she repeated, with a kind of glee, and she narrated that Eléonore (a personage unknown to Raymond) had said that she was a woman of Plutarch. Mrs Temperly talked a great deal about the health of their friends; she seemed to keep the record of the influenzas and neuralgias of a numerous and susceptible circle. He did not find it in him quite to agree—the Marquise dropping the statement into his ear at a moment when their hostess was making some inquiry of Mademoiselle Bourde—that she was a nature absolutely marvellous; but he could easily see that to world-worn Parisians her quiet charities of speech and manner, with something quaint and rustic in their form, might be restorative and salutary. She allowed for everything, yet she was so good, and indeed Madame de Brives summed this up before they left the table in saying to her, "Oh, you, my dear, your success, more than any other that has ever taken place, has been a *succès de bonté*." Raymond was greatly amused at this idea of Cousin Maria's *succès de bonté:* it seemed to him delightfully Parisian.

Before dinner was over she inquired of him how he had got on "in his profession" since they last met, and he was too proud, or so he thought, to tell her anything but the simple truth, that he had not got on very well. If he was to ask her again for Dora it would be just as he was, an honourable but not particularly successful man, making no show of lures and bribes. "I am not a remarkably good painter," he said. "I judge myself perfectly. And then I have been handicapped at home. I have had a great many serious bothers and worries."

"Ah, we were so sorry to hear about your dear father."

The tone of these words was kind and sincere; still Raymond thought that in this case her *bonté* might have gone a little further. At any rate this was the only allusion that she made to his bothers and worries. Indeed, she always passed over such things lightly; she was an optimist for others as well as for herself, which doubtless had a great deal to do (Raymond indulged in the reflection) with the headway she made in a society tired of its own pessimism.

After dinner, when they went into the drawing-room, the

young man noted with complacency that this apartment, vast
in itself, communicated with two or three others into which it
would be easy to pass without attracting attention, the doors
being replaced by old tapestries, looped up and offering no
barrier. With pictures and curiosities all over the place, there
were plenty of pretexts for wandering away. He lost no time
in asking Dora whether her mother would send Mademoiselle
Bourde after them if she were to go with him into one of the
other rooms, the same way she had done—didn't she remember?—that last night in New York, at the hotel. Dora didn't
admit that she remembered (she was too loyal to her mother
for that, and Raymond foresaw that this loyalty would be a
source of irritation to him again, as it had been in the past),
but he perceived, all the same, that she had not forgotten. She
raised no difficulty, and a few moments later, while they stood
in an adjacent *salon* (he had stopped to admire a bust of Effie,
wonderfully living, slim and juvenile, the work of one of the
sculptors who are the pride of contemporary French art), he
said to her, looking about him, "How has she done it so fast?"

"Done what, Raymond?"

"Why, done everything. Collected all these wonderful
things; become intimate with Madame de Brives and every
one else; organised her life—the life of all of you—so bril-
liantly."

"I have never seen mamma in a hurry," Dora replied.

"Perhaps she will be, now that I have come," Raymond
suggested, laughing.

The girl hesitated a moment. "Yes, she was, to invite you
—the moment she knew you were here."

"She has been most kind, and I talk like a brute. But I am
liable to do worse—I give you notice. She won't like it any
more than she did before, if she thinks I want to make up to
you."

"Don't, Raymond—don't!" the girl exclaimed, gently,
but with a look of sudden pain.

"Don't what, Dora?—don't make up to you?"

"Don't begin to talk of those things. There is no need. We can go on being friends."

"I will do exactly as you prescribe, and heaven forbid I should annoy you. But would you mind answering me a question? It is very particular, very intimate." He stopped, and she only looked at him, saying nothing. So he went on: "Is it an idea of your mother's that you should marry—some person here?" He gave her a chance to reply, but still she was silent, and he continued: "Do you mind telling me this? Could it ever be an idea of your own?"

"Do you mean some Frenchman?"

Raymond smiled. "Some protégé of Madame de Brives."

Then the girl simply gave a slow, sad head-shake which struck him as the sweetest, proudest, most suggestive thing in the world. "Well, well, that's all right," he remarked, cheerfully, and looked again a while at the bust, which he thought extraordinarily clever. "And haven't *you* been done by one of these great fellows?"

"Oh dear no; only mamma and Effie. But Tishy is going to be, in a month or two. The next time you come you must see her. She remembers you vividly."

"And I remember her that last night, with her reticule. Is she always pretty?"

Dora hesitated a moment. "She is a very sweet little creature, but she is not so pretty as Effie."

"And have none of them wished to do you—none of the painters?"

"Oh, it's not a question of me. I only wish them to let me alone."

"For me it would be a question of you, if you would sit for me. But I daresay your mother wouldn't allow that."

"No, I think not," said Dora, smiling.

She smiled, but her companion looked grave. However,

not to pursue the subject, he asked, abruptly, "Who is this Madame de Brives?"

"If you lived in Paris you would know. She is very celebrated."

"Celebrated for what?"

"For everything."

"And is she good—is she genuine?" Raymond asked. Then, seeing something in the girl's face, he added: "I told you I should be brutal again. Has she undertaken to make a great marriage for Effie?"

"I don't know what she has undertaken," said Dora, impatiently.

"And then for Tishy, when Effie has been disposed of?"

"Poor little Tishy!" the girl continued, rather inscrutably.

"And can she do nothing for you?" the young man inquired.

Her answer surprised him—after a moment. "She has kindly offered to exert herself, but it's no use."

"Well, that's good. And who is it the young man comes for —the secretary of embassy?"

"Oh, he comes for all of us," said Dora, laughing.

"I suppose your mother would prefer a preference," Raymond suggested.

To this she replied, irrelevantly, that she thought they had better go back; but as Raymond took no notice of the recommendation she mentioned that the secretary was no one in particular. At this moment Effie, looking very rosy and happy, pushed through the *portière* with the news that her sister must come and bid good-bye to the Marquise. She was taking her to the Duchess's—didn't Dora remember? To the *bal blanc*—the *sauterie de jeunes filles*.

"I thought we should be called," said Raymond, as he followed Effie; and he remarked that perhaps Madame de Brives would find something suitable at the Duchess's.

"I don't know. Mamma would be very particular," the girl

rejoined; and this was said simply, sympathetically, without the least appearance of deflection from that loyalty which Raymond deplored.

IV

"You must come to us on the 17th; we expect to have a few people and some good music," Cousin Maria said to him before he quitted the house; and he wondered whether, the 17th being still ten days off, this might not be an intimation that they could abstain from his society until then. He chose, at any rate, not to take it as such, and called several times in the interval, late in the afternoon, when the ladies would be sure to have come in.

They were always there, and Cousin Maria's welcome was, for each occasion, maternal, though when he took leave she made no allusion to future meetings—to his coming again; but there were always other visitors as well, collected at tea round the great fire of logs, in the friendly, brilliant drawing-room where the luxurious was no enemy to the casual and Mrs Temperly's manner of dispensing hospitality recalled to our young man somehow certain memories of his youthful time: visits in New England, at old homesteads flanked with elms, where a talkative, democratic, delightful farmer's wife pressed upon her company rustic viands in which she herself had had a hand. Cousin Maria enjoyed the services of a distinguished *chef*, and delicious *petits fours* were served with her tea; but Raymond had a sense that to complete the impression hot home-made gingerbread should have been produced.

The atmosphere was suffused with the presence of Madame de Brives. She was either there or she was just coming or she was just gone; her name, her voice, her example and encouragement were in the air. Other ladies came and went—sometimes accompanied by gentlemen who looked worn out, had

waxed moustaches and knew how to talk—and they were
sometimes designated in the same manner as Madame de
Brives; but she remained the Marquise *par excellence,* the
incarnation of brilliancy and renown. The conversation moved
among simple but civilised topics, was not dull and, considering that it consisted largely of personalities, was not ill-
natured. Least of all was it scandalous, for the girls were
always there, Cousin Maria not having thought it in the least
necessary, in order to put herself in accord with French
traditions, to relegate her daughters to the middle distance.
They occupied a considerable part of the foreground, in the
prettiest, most modest, most becoming attitudes.

It was Cousin Maria's theory of her own behaviour that she
did in Paris simply as she had always done; and though this
would not have been a complete account of the matter Raymond could not fail to notice the good sense and good taste
with which she laid down her lines and the quiet *bonhomie* of
the authority with which she caused the tone of the American
home to be respected. Scandal stayed outside, not simply
because Effie and Tishy were there, but because, even if
Cousin Maria had received alone, she never would have
received evil-speakers. Indeed, for Raymond, who had been
accustomed to think that in a general way he knew pretty well
what the French capital was, this was a strange, fresh Paris
altogether, destitute of the salt that seasoned it for most
palates, and yet not insipid nor innutritive. He marvelled at
Cousin Maria's air, in such a city, of knowing, of recognising
nothing bad: all the more that it represented an actual state of
mind. He used to wonder sometimes what she would do and
how she would feel if some day, in consequence of researches
made by the Marquise in the *grand monde,* she should find
herself in possession of a son-in-law formed according to
one of the types of which *he* had impressions. However,
it was not credible that Madame de Brives would play her
a trick. There were moments when Raymond almost wished

she might—to see how Cousin Maria would handle the gentleman.

Dora was almost always taken up by visitors, and he had scarcely any direct conversation with her. She was there, and he was glad she was there, and she knew he was glad (he knew that), but this was almost all the communion he had with her. She was mild, exquisitely mild—this was the term he mentally applied to her now—and it amply sufficed him, with the conviction he had that she was not stupid. She attended to the tea (for Mademoiselle Bourde was not always free), she handed the *petits fours*, she rang the bell when people went out; and it was in connection with these offices that the idea came to him once—he was rather ashamed of it afterward—that she was the Cinderella of the house, the domestic drudge, the one for whom there was no career, as it was useless for the Marquise to take up her case. He was ashamed of this fancy, I say, and yet it came back to him; he was even surprised that it had not occurred to him before. Her sisters were neither ugly nor proud (Tishy, indeed, was almost touchingly delicate and timid, with exceedingly pretty points, yet with a little appealing, oldwomanish look, as if, small—very small—as she was, she was afraid she shouldn't grow any more); but her mother, like the mother in the fairy-tale, was a *femme forte*. Madame de Brives could do nothing for Dora, not absolutely because she was too plain, but because she would never lend herself, and that came to the same thing. Her mother accepted her as recalcitrant, but Cousin Maria's attitude, at the best, could only be resignation. She would respect her child's preferences, she would never put on the screw; but this would not make her love the child any more. So Raymond interpreted certain signs, which at the same time he felt to be very slight, while the conversation in Mrs Temperly's *salon* (this was its preponderant tendency) rambled among questions of bric-à-brac, of where Tishy's portrait should be placed when it was finished, and the current prices of old Gobelins.

Ces dames were not in the least above the discussion of prices.

On the 17th it was easy to see that more lamps than usual had been lighted. They streamed through all the windows of the charming hotel and mingled with the radiance of the carriage-lanterns, which followed each other slowly, in couples, in a close, long rank, into the fine sonorous court, where the high stepping of valuable horses was sharp on the stones, and up to the ruddy portico. The night was wet, not with a downpour, but with showers interspaced by starry patches, which only added to the glitter of the handsome, clean Parisian surfaces. The *sergents de ville* were about the place, and seemed to make the occasion important and official. These night aspects of Paris in the *beaux quartiers* had always for Raymond a particularly festive association, and as he passed from his cab under the wide permanent tin canopy, painted in stripes like an awning, which protected the low steps, it seemed to him odder than ever that all this established prosperity should be Cousin Maria's.

If the thought of how well she did it bore him company from the threshold, it deepened to admiration by the time he had been half an hour in the place. She stood near the entrance with her two elder daughters, distributing the most familiar, most encouraging smiles, together with hand-shakes which were in themselves a whole system of hospitality. If her party was grand Cousin Maria was not; she indulged in no assumption of stateliness and no attempt at graduated welcomes. It seemed to Raymond that it was only because it would have taken too much time that she didn't kiss every one. Effie looked lovely and just a little frightened, which was exactly what she ought to have done; and he noticed that among the arriving guests those who were not intimate (which he could not tell from Mrs Temperly's manner, but could from their own) recognised her as a daughter much more quickly than they recognised Dora, who hung back disinterestedly, as if not to challenge their discernment, while the current passed her, keeping her little sister in position on its brink meanwhile by the tenderest small gesture.

"May I talk with you a little, later?" he asked of Dora, with only a few seconds for the question, as people were pressing behind him. She answered evasively that there would be very little talk—they would all have to listen—it was very serious; and the next moment he had received a programme from the hand of a monumental yet gracious personage who stood beyond and who had a silver chain round his neck.

The place was arranged for music, and how well arranged he saw later, when every one was seated, spaciously, luxuriously, without pushing or overpeeping, and the finest talents in Paris performed selections at which the best taste had presided. The singers and players were all stars of the first magnitude. Raymond was fond of music and he wondered whose taste it had been. He made up his mind it was Dora's—it was only she who could have conceived a combination so exquisite; and he said to himself: "How they all pull together! She is not in it, she is not of it, and yet she too works for the common end." And by "all" he meant also Mademoiselle Bourde and the Marquise. This impression made him feel rather hopeless, as if, *en fin de compte,* Cousin Maria were too large an adversary. Great as was the pleasure of being present on an occasion so admirably organised, of sitting there in a beautiful room, in a still, attentive, brilliant company, with all the questions of temperature, space, light and decoration solved to the gratification of every sense, and listening to the best artists doing their best—happily constituted as our young man was to enjoy such a privilege as this, the total effect was depressing: it made him feel as if the gods were not on his side.

"And does she do it so well without a man? There must be so many details a woman can't tackle," he said to himself; for even counting in the Marquise and Mademoiselle Bourde this only made a multiplication of petticoats. Then it came over him that she *was* a man as well as a woman—the masculine element was included in her nature. He was sure that she bought her horses without being cheated, and very few men could do that. She had the American national quality—she had "faculty" in a supreme degree. "Faculty—faculty," the voices of the quartette of singers seemed to repeat, in the quick movement of a composition they rendered beautifully, while they swelled and went faster, till the thing became a joyous chant of praise, a glorification of Cousin Maria's practical genius.

During the intermission, in the middle of the concert, people changed places more or less and circulated, so that, walking about at this time, he came upon the Marquise, who, in her sympathetic, demonstrative way, appeared to be on the point of clasping her hostess in her arms. "Décidément, ma bonne, il n'y a que vous! C'est une perfection——" he heard her say. To which, gratified but unelated, Cousin Maria replied, according to her simple, sociable wont: "Well, it *does* seem quite a successful occasion. If it will only keep on to the end!"

Raymond, wandering far, found himself in a world that was mainly quite new to him, and explained his ignorance of it by reflecting that the people were probably celebrated: so many of them had decorations and stars and a quiet of manner that could only be accounted for by renown. There were plenty of Americans with no badge but a certain fine negativeness, and *they* were quiet for a reason which by this time had become very familiar to Raymond: he had heard it so often mentioned that his country-people were supremely "adaptable." He tried to get hold of Dora, but he saw that her mother had arranged things beautifully to keep her occupied with other people; so at least he interpreted the fact—after all very natural—that she had half a dozen fluttered young girls on her mind, whom she was providing with programmes, seats, ices, occasional murmured remarks and general support and protection. When the concert was over she supplied them with further entertainment in the form of several young men who had pliable backs and flashing breastpins and whom she inarticulately introduced to them, which gave her still more to do, as after this serious step she had to stay and watch all parties. It was strange to Raymond to see her transformed by her mother into a precocious duenna. Him she introduced to no young girl, and he knew not whether to regard this as cold neglect or as high consideration. If he had liked he might have taken it as a sweet intimation that she knew he couldn't care for any girl but her.

On the whole he was glad, because it left him free—free to get hold of her mother, which by this time he had boldly determined to do. The conception was high, inasmuch as Cousin Maria's attention was obviously required by the ambassadors and other grandees who had flocked to do her homage. Nevertheless, while supper was going on (he wanted none, and neither apparently did she), he collared her, as he phrased it to himself, in just the right place—on the threshold of the conservatory. She was flanked on either side with a foreigner of distinction, but he didn't care for her foreigners now. Besides, a conservatory was meant only for couples; it was a sign of her comprehensive sociability that she should have been rambling among the palms and orchids with a double escort. Her friends would wish to quit her but would not wish to appear to give way to each other; and Raymond felt that he was relieving them both (though he didn't care) when he asked her to be so good as to give him a few minutes' conversation. He made her go back with him into the con-servatory: it was the only thing he had ever made her do, or probably ever would. She began to talk about the great Gregorini—how it had been too sweet of her to repeat one of her songs, when it had really been understood in advance that repetitions were not expected. Raymond had no interest at present in the great Gregorini. He asked Cousin Maria

vehemently if she remembered telling him in New York—
that night at the hotel, five years before—that when he should
have followed them to Paris he would be free to address her
on the subject of Dora. She had given him a promise that she
would listen to him in this case, and now he must keep her up
to the mark. It was impossible to see her alone, but, at whatever inconvenience to herself, he must insist on her giving
him his opportunity.

"About Dora, Cousin Raymond?" she asked, blandly and
kindly—almost as if she didn't exactly know who Dora
was.

"Surely you haven't forgotten what passed between us the
evening before you left America. I was in love with her then
and I have been in love with her ever since. I told you so then,
and you stopped me off, but you gave me leave to make
another appeal to you in the future. I make it now—this is the
only way I have—and I think you ought to listen to it. Five
years have passed, and I love her more than ever. I have
behaved like a saint in the interval: I haven't attempted to
practise upon her without your knowledge."

"I am so glad; but she would have let me know," said
Cousin Maria, looking round the conservatory as if to see if
the plants were all there.

"No doubt. I don't know what you do to her. But I trust
that to-day your opposition falls—in face of the proof that we
have given you of mutual fidelity."

"Fidelity?" Cousin Maria repeated, smiling.

"Surely—unless you mean to imply that Dora has given
me up. I have reason to believe that she hasn't."

"I think she will like better to remain just as she is."

"Just as she is?"

"I mean, not to make a choice," Cousin Maria went on,
smiling.

Raymond hesitated a moment. "Do you mean that you
have tried to make her make one?"

At this the good lady broke into a laugh. "My dear Raymond, how little you must think I know my child!"

"Perhaps, if you haven't tried to make her you have tried to prevent her. Haven't you told her I am unsuccessful, I am poor?"

She stopped him, laying her hand with unaffected solicitude on his arm. "*Are* you poor, my dear? I should be so sorry!"

"Never mind; I can support a wife," said the young man.

"It wouldn't matter, because I am happy to say that Dora has something of her own," Cousin Maria went on, with her imperturbable candour. "Her father thought that was the best way to arrange it. I had quite forgotten my opposition, as you call it; that was so long ago. Why, she was only a little girl. Wasn't that the ground I took? Well, dear, she's older now, and you can say anything to her you like. But I do think she wants to stay——" And she looked up at him, cheerily.

"Wants to stay?"

"With Effie and Tishy."

"Ah, Cousin Maria," the young man exclaimed, "you are modest about yourself!"

"Well, we are all together. Now is that all? I *must* see if there is enough champagne. Certainly—you can say to her what you like. But twenty years hence she will be just as she is to-day; that's how I see her."

"Lord, what is it you do to her?" Raymond groaned, as he accompanied his hostess back to the crowded rooms.

He knew exactly what she would have replied if she had been a Frenchwoman; she would have said to him, triumphantly, overwhelmingly: "Que voulez-vous? Elle adore sa mère!" She was, however, only a Californian, unacquainted with the language of epigram, and her answer consisted simply of the words: "I am sorry you have ideas that make you unhappy. I guess you are the only person here who hasn't enjoyed himself to-night."

Raymond repeated to himself, gloomily, for the rest of the

evening, "Elle adore sa mère—elle adore sa mère!" He remained very late, and when but twenty people were left and he had observed that the Marquise, passing her hand into Mrs Temperly's arm, led her aside as if for some important confabulation (some new light doubtless on what might be hoped for Effie), he persuaded Dora to let the rest of the guests depart in peace (apparently her mother had told her to look out for them to the very last), and come with him into some quiet corner. They found an empty sofa in the outlasting lamp-light, and there the girl sat down with him. Evidently she knew what he was going to say, or rather she thought she did; for in fact, after a little, after he had told her that he had spoken to her mother and she had told him he might speak to *her*, he said things that she could not very well have expected.

"Is it true that you wish to remain with Effie and Tishy? That's what your mother calls it when she means that you will give me up."

"How can I give you up?" the girl demanded. "Why can't we go on being friends, as I asked you the evening you dined here?"

"What do you mean by friends?"

"Well, not making everything impossible."

"You didn't think anything impossible of old," Raymond rejoined, bitterly. "I thought you liked me then, and I have even thought so since."

"I like you more than I like any one. I like you so much that it's my principal happiness."

"Then why are there impossibilities?"

"Oh, some day I'll tell you!" said Dora, with a quick sigh. "Perhaps after Tishy is married. And meanwhile, are you not going to remain in Paris, at any rate? Isn't your work here? You are not here for me only. You can come to the house often. That's what I mean by our being friends."

Her companion sat looking at her with a gloomy stare, as if he were trying to make up the deficiencies in her logic.

"After Tishy is married? I don't see what that has to do with it. Tishy is little more than a baby; she may not be married for ten years."

"That is very true."

"And you dispose of the interval by a simple 'meanwhile'? My dear Dora, your talk is strange," Raymond continued, with his voice passionately lowered. "And I may come to the house—often? How often do you mean—in ten years? Five times—or even twenty?" He saw that her eyes were filling with tears, but he went on: "It has been coming over me little by little (I notice things very much if I have a reason), and now I think I understand your mother's system."

"Don't say anything against my mother," the girl broke in, beseechingly.

"I shall not say anything unjust. That is if I am unjust you must tell me. This is my idea, and your speaking of Tishy's marriage confirms it. To begin with she has had immense plans for you all; she wanted each of you to be a princess or a duchess—I mean a good one. But she has had to give *you* up."

"No one has asked for me," said Dora, with unexpected honesty.

"I don't believe it. Dozens of fellows have asked for you, and you have shaken your head in that divine way (divine for me, I mean) in which you shook it the other night."

"My mother has never said an unkind word to me in her life," the girl declared, in answer to this.

"I never said she had, and I don't know why you take the precaution of telling me so. But whatever you tell me or don't tell me," Raymond pursued, "there is one thing I see very well—that so long as you won't marry a duke Cousin Maria has found means to prevent you from marrying till your sisters have made rare alliances."

"Has found means?" Dora repeated, as if she really wondered what was in his thought.

"Of course I mean only through your affection for her.
How she works that, you know best yourself."

"It's delightful to have a mother of whom every one is so
fond," said Dora, smiling.

"She is a most remarkable woman. Don't think for a
moment that I don't appreciate her. You don't want to quarrel
with her, and I daresay you are right."

"Why, Raymond, of course I'm right!"

"It proves you are not madly in love with me. It seems to
me that for you *I* would have quarrelled——"

"Raymond, Raymond!" she interrupted, with the tears
again rising.

He sat looking at her, and then he said, "Well, when they
are married?"

"I don't know the future—I don't know what may
happen."

"You mean that Tishy is so small—she doesn't grow—and
will therefore be difficult? Yes, she *is* small." There was bitterness in his heart, but he laughed at his own words. "However,
Effie ought to go off easily," he went on, as Dora said nothing.
"I really wonder that, with the Marquise and all, she hasn't
gone off yet. This thing, to-night, ought to do a great deal
for her."

Dora listened to him with a fascinated gaze; it was as if he
expressed things for her and relieved her spirit by making
them clear and coherent. Her eyes managed, each time, to be
dry again, and now a somewhat wan, ironical smile moved her
lips. "Mamma knows what she wants—she knows what she
will take. And she will take only that."

"Precisely—something tremendous. And she is willing to
wait, eh? Well, Effie is very young, and she's charming. But
she won't be charming if she has an ugly appendage in the
shape of a poor unsuccessful American artist (not even a good
one), whose father went bankrupt, for a brother-in-law. That
won't smooth the way, of course; and if a prince is to come

into the family, the family must be kept tidy to receive him."
Dora got up quickly, as if she could bear his lucidity no
longer, but he kept close to her as she walked away. "And she
can sacrifice you like that, without a scruple, without a pang?"

"I might have escaped—if I would marry," the girl
replied.

"Do you call that escaping? She has succeeded with you,
but is it a part of what the Marquise calls her *succès de bonté?*"

"Nothing that you can say (and it's far worse than the
reality) can prevent her being delightful."

"Yes, that's your loyalty, and I could shoot you for it!" he
exclaimed, making her pause on the threshold of the adjoining
room. "So you think it will take about ten years, considering
Tishy's size—or want of size?" He himself again was the only
one to laugh at this. "Your mother is closeted, as much as
she can be closeted now, with Madame de Brives, and perhaps
this time they are really settling something."

"I have thought that before and nothing has come.
Mamma wants something so good; not only every advantage
and every grandeur, but every virtue under heaven, and every
guarantee. Oh, she wouldn't expose them!"

"I see; that's where her goodness comes in and where the
Marquise is impressed." He took Dora's hand; he felt that he
must go, for she exasperated him with her irony that stopped
short and her patience that wouldn't stop. "You simply propose that I should wait?" he said, as he held her hand.

"It seems to me that you might, if *I* can." Then the girl
remarked, "Now that you are here, it's far better."

There was a sweetness in this which made him, after
glancing about a moment, raise her hand to his lips. He went
away without taking leave of Cousin Maria, who was still out
of sight, her conference with the Marquise apparently not
having terminated. This looked (he reflected as he passed out)
as if something might come of it. However, before he went
home he fell again into a gloomy forecast. The weather had

changed, the stars were all out, and he walked the empty streets for an hour. Tishy's perverse refusal to grow and Cousin Maria's conscientious exactions promised him a terrible probation. And in those intolerable years what further interference, what meddlesome, effective pressure, might not make itself felt? It may be added that Tishy is decidedly a dwarf and his probation is not yet over.

LOUISA PALLANT

I

NEVER say you know the last word about any human heart!
I was once treated to a revelation which startled and touched
me, in the nature of a person with whom I had been acquainted
(well, as I supposed) for years, whose character I had had good
reasons, heaven knows, to appreciate and in regard to whom
I flattered myself that I had nothing more to learn.

It was on the terrace of the Kursaal at Homburg, nearly ten
years ago, one lovely night toward the end of July. I had come
to the place that day from Frankfort, with vague intentions,
and was mainly occupied in waiting for my young nephew,
the only son of my sister, who had been intrusted to my care
by a very fond mother for the summer (I was expected to
show him Europe—only the very best of it), and was on his
way from Paris to join me. The excellent band discoursed
music not too abstruse, and the air was filled besides with the
murmur of different languages, the smoke of many cigars,
the creak on the gravel of the gardens of strolling shoes and
the thick tinkle of beer-glasses. There were a hundred people
walking about, there were some in clusters at little tables and
many on benches and rows of chairs, watching the others as if
they had paid for the privilege and were rather disappointed.
I was among these last; I sat by myself, smoking my cigar and
thinking of nothing very particular while families and couples
passed and repassed me.

I scarcely know how long I had sat there when I became
aware of a recognition which made my meditations definite.
It was on my own part, and the object of it was a lady who
moved to and fro, unconscious of my observation, with a

young girl at her side. I had not seen her for ten years, and what first struck me was the fact not that she was Mrs Henry Pallant but that the girl who was with her was remarkably pretty—or rather first of all that every one who passed her turned round to look at her. This led me to look at the young lady myself, and her charming face diverted my attention for some time from that of her companion. The latter, moreover, though it was night, wore a thin, light veil which made her features vague. The couple walked and walked, slowly, but though they were very quiet and decorous, and also very well dressed, they seemed to have no friends. Every one looked at them but no one spoke; they appeared even to talk very little to each other. Moreover they bore with extreme composure and as if they were thoroughly used to it the attention they excited. I am afraid it occurred to me to take for granted that they were not altogether honourable and that if they had been the elder lady would have covered the younger up a little more from the public stare and not have been so ashamed to exhibit her own face. Perhaps this question came into my mind too easily just then—in view of my prospective mentorship to my nephew. If I was to show him only the best of Europe I should have to be very careful about the people he should meet—especially the ladies—and the relations he should form. I suspected him of knowing very little of life and I was rather uneasy about my responsibilities. Was I completely relieved and reassured when I perceived that I simply had Louisa Pallant before me and that the girl was her daughter Linda, whom I had known as a child—Linda grown up into a regular beauty?

The question is delicate and the proof that I was not very sure is perhaps that I forbore to speak to the ladies immediately. I watched them awhile—I wondered what they would do. No great harm, assuredly; but I was anxious to see if they were really isolated. Homburg is a great resort of the English —the London season takes up its tale there toward the first of August—and I had an idea that in such a company as that

Louisa would naturally know people. It was my impression
that she "cultivated" the English, that she had been much in
London and would be likely to have views in regard to a
permanent settlement there. This supposition was quickened
by the sight of Linda's beauty, for I knew there is no country
in which a handsome person is more appreciated. You will see
that I took time, and I confess that as I finished my cigar I
thought it all over. There was no good reason in fact why I
should have rushed into Mrs Pallant's arms. She had not
treated me well and we had never really made it up. Somehow
even the circumstance that (after the first soreness) I was glad
to have lost her had never put us quite right with each other;
nor, for herself, had it made her less ashamed of her heartless
behaviour that poor Pallant after all turned out no great catch.
I had forgiven her; I had not felt that it was anything but an
escape not to have married a girl who had it in her to take
back her given word and break a fellow's heart, for mere fleshpots—or the shallow promise, as it pitifully proved, of fleshpots; moreover we had met since then, on the occasion of my
former visit to Europe; we had looked each other in the eyes,
we had pretended to be free friends and had talked of the
wickedness of the world as composedly as if we were the only
just, the only pure. I knew then what she had given out—that
I had driven her off by my insane jealousy before she ever
thought of Henry Pallant, before she had ever seen him. This
had not been then and it could not be to-day a ground of real
reunion, especially if you add to it that she knew perfectly
what I thought of her. It is my belief that it does not often
minister to friendship that your friend shall know your real
opinion, for he knows it mainly when it is unfavourable, and
this is especially the case when (if the solecism may pass) he is
a woman. I had not followed Mrs Pallant's fortunes; the years
elapsed, for me, in my own country, whereas she led her life,
which I vaguely believed to be difficult after her husband's
death—virtually that of a bankrupt—in foreign lands. I heard

of her from time to time; always as "established" somewhere,
but on each occasion in a different place. She drifted from
country to country, and if she had been of a hard composition
at the beginning it could never occur to me that her struggle
with society, as it might be called, would have softened the
paste. Whenever I heard a woman spoken of as "horribly
worldly" I thought immediately of the object of my early
passion. I imagined she had debts, and when I now at last
made up my mind to recall myself to her it was present to me
that she might ask me to lend her money. More than anything
else, at this time of day, I was sorry for her, so that such an
idea did not operate as a deterrent.

She pretended afterwards that she had not noticed me—
expressing great surprise and wishing to know where I had
dropped from; but I think the corner of her eye had taken me
in and she was waiting to see what I would do. She had ended
by sitting down with her girl on the same row of chairs with
myself, and after a little, on the seat next to her becoming
vacant, I went and stood before her. She looked up at me a
moment, staring, as if she could not imagine who I was or
what I wanted; then, smiling and extending her hands, she
broke out, "Ah, my dear old friend—what a delight!" If she
had waited to see what I would do, in order to choose her own
line, she at least carried out this line with the utmost grace.
She was cordial, friendly, artless, interested, and indeed I am
sure she was very glad to see me. I may as well say immediately, however, that she gave neither then nor later any sign
of a disposition to borrow money. She had none too much—
that I learned—but for the moment she seemed able to pay her
way. I took the empty chair and we remained talking for an
hour. After a while she made me sit on the other side of her,
next to her daughter, whom she wished to know me—to love
me—as one of their oldest friends. "It goes back, back, back,
doesn't it?" said Mrs Pallant; "and of course she remembers
you as a child." Linda smiled very sweetly and indefinitely,

and I saw she remembered me not at all. When her mother intimated that they had often talked about me she failed to take it up, though she looked extremely nice. Looking nice was her strong point; she was prettier even than her mother had been. She was such a little lady that she made me ashamed of having doubted, however vaguely and for a moment, of her position in the scale of propriety. Her appearance seemed to say that if she had no acquaintances, it was because she did not want to—because there was nobody there who struck her as attractive: there was not the slightest difficulty about her choosing her friends. Linda Pallant, young as she was, and fresh and fair and charming and gentle and sufficiently shy, looked somehow exclusive—as if the dust of the common world had never been meant to settle upon her. She was simpler than her mother and was evidently not a young woman of professions—except in so far as she was committed to an interest in you by her bright, pure, intelligent smile. A girl who had such a lovely way of showing her teeth could never pass for heartless.

As I sat between the pair I felt that I had been taken possession of and that for better or worse my stay at Homburg would be intimately associated with theirs. We gave each other a great deal of news and expressed unlimited interest in each other's history since our last meeting. I know not what Mrs Pallant kept back, but for myself I was frank enough. She let me see at any rate that her life had been a good deal what I supposed, though the terms she used to describe it were less crude than those of my thought. She confessed that they had drifted and that they were drifting still. Her narrative rambled and got what is vulgarly called somewhat mixed, as I thought Linda perceived while she sat watching the passers in a manner which betrayed no consciousness of their attention, without coming to her mother's aid. Once or twice Mrs Pallant made me feel like a cross-questioner, which I had no intention of being. I took it that if the girl never put in a word it was

LOUISA PALLANT

because she had perfect confidence in her mother's ability to come out straight. It was suggested to me, I scarcely knew how, that this confidence between the two ladies went to a great length; that their union of thought, their system of reciprocal divination, was remarkable, and that they probably seldom needed to resort to the clumsy and in some cases dangerous expedient of putting their ideas into words. I suppose I made this reflection not all at once—it was not wholly the result of that first meeting. I was with them constantly for the next several days and my impressions had time to clarify.

I do remember however that it was on this first evening that Archie's name came up. She attributed her own stay at Homburg to no refined nor exalted motive—did not say that she was there because she always came or because a high medical authority had ordered her to drink the waters; she frankly admitted that the reason of her visit had been simply that she did not know where else to turn. But she appeared to assume that my behaviour rested on higher grounds and even that it required explanation, the place being frivolous and modern—devoid of that interest of antiquity which I used to value. "Don't you remember—ever so long ago—that you wouldn't look at anything in Europe that was not a thousand years old? Well, as we advance in life I suppose we don't think that's quite such a charm." And when I told her that I had come to Homburg because it was as good a place as another to wait for my nephew, she exclaimed: "Your nephew —what nephew? He must have come up of late." I answered that he was a youth named Archer Pringle and very modern indeed; he was coming of age in a few months and was in Europe for the first time. My last news of him had been from Paris and I was expecting to hear from him from one day to the other. His father was dead, and though a selfish bachelor, little versed in the care of children, I was considerably counted on by his mother to see that he did not smoke too much nor fall off an Alp.

Mrs Pallant immediately guessed that his mother was my sister Charlotte, whom she spoke of familiarly, though I knew she had seen her but once or twice. Then in a moment it came to her which of the Pringles Charlotte had married; she remembered the family perfectly, in the old New York days—"that disgustingly rich lot." She said it was very nice having the boy come out that way to my care; to which I replied that it was very nice for him. She declared that she meant for me —I ought to have had children; there was something so parental about me and I would have brought them up so well. She could make an allusion like that—to all that might have been and had not been—without a gleam of guilt in her eye; and I foresaw that before I left the place I should have confided to her that though I detested her and was very glad we had fallen out, yet our old relations had left me no heart for marrying another woman. If I was a maundering old bachelor to-day it was no one's fault but hers. She asked me what I meant to do with my nephew and I said it was much more a question of what he would do with me. She inquired whether he were a nice young man and had brothers and sisters and any particular profession. I told her that I had really seen but little of him; I believed him to be six feet high and of tolerable parts. He was an only son, but there was a little sister at home, a delicate, unsuccessful child, demanding all the mother's care.

"So that makes your responsibility greater, as it were, about the boy, doesn't it?" said Mrs Pallant.

"Greater? I'm sure I don't know."

"Why, if the girl's life is uncertain he may be, some moment, all the mother has. So that being in your hands——"

"Oh, I shall keep him alive, I suppose, if you mean that," I rejoined.

"Well, *we* won't kill him, shall we, Linda?" Mrs Pallant went on, with a laugh.

"I don't know—perhaps we shall!" said the girl, smiling.

II

I CALLED on them the next day at their lodgings, the modesty
of which was enhanced by a hundred pretty feminine devices
—flowers and photographs and portable knick-knacks and a
hired piano and morsels of old brocade flung over angular
sofas. I asked them to drive; I met them again at the Kursaal;
I arranged that we should dine together, after the Homburg
fashion, at the same *table d'hôte;* and during several days this
revived familiar intercourse continued, imitating intimacy if
it did not quite achieve it. I liked it, for my companions passed
my time for me and the conditions of our life were soothing—
the feeling of summer and shade and music and leisure, in the
German gardens and woods, where we strolled and sat and
gossiped; to which may be added a kind of sociable sense that
among people whose challenge to the curiosity was mainly not
irresistible we kept quite to ourselves. We were on the footing
of old friends who, with regard to each other, still had discoveries to make. We knew each other's nature but we did not
know each other's experience; so that when Mrs Pallant
related to me what she had been "up to" (as I called it) for so
many years, the former knowledge attached a hundred inter-
pretative footnotes (as if I had been editing an author who
presented difficulties) to the interesting page. There was
nothing new to me in the fact that I did not esteem her, but
there was a sort of refreshment in finding that this was not
necessary at Homburg and that I could like her in spite of it.
She seemed to me, in the oddest way, both improved and
degenerate, as if in her nature the two processes had gone on
together. She was battered and world-worn and, spiritually
speaking, vulgarised; something fresh had rubbed off her (it
even included the vivacity of her early desire to do the best
thing for herself), and something very stale had rubbed on.

On the other hand she betrayed a scepticism, and that was rather becoming, as it quenched the eagerness of her prime, which had taken a form so unfortunate for me. She had grown weary and indifferent, and as she struck me as having seen more of the evil of the world than of the good, that was a gain; in other words the cynicism that had formed itself in her nature had a softer surface than some of her old ambitions. And then I had to recognise that her devotion to her daughter had been a kind of religion; she had done the very best possible for Linda.

Linda was curious—Linda was interesting; I have seen girls I liked better (charming as she was), but I have never seen one who for the time I was with her (the impression passed, somehow, when she was out of sight) occupied me more. I can best describe the sort of attention that she excited by saying that she struck one above all things as a final product —just as some plant or fruit does, some waxen orchid or some perfect peach. More than any girl I ever saw she was the result of a process of calculation; a process patiently educative; a pressure exerted in order that she should reach a high point. This high point had been the star of her mother's heaven (it hung before her so definitely), and had been the source of the only light—in default of a better—that shone upon the poor lady's path. It stood her in stead of every other religion. The very most and the very best—that was what the girl had been led on to achieve; I mean, of course (for no real miracle had been wrought), the most and the best that she was capable of. She was as pretty, as graceful, as intelligent, as well-bred, as well-informed, as well-dressed, as it would have been possible for her to be; her music, her singing, her German, her French, her English, her step, her tone, her glance, her manner, and everything in her person and movement, from the shade and twist of her hair to the way you saw her finger-nails were pink when she raised her hand, had been carried so far that one found one's self accepting them as a kind of standard. I

regarded her as a model, and yet it was a part of her perfection
that she had none of the stiffness of a pattern. If she held the
observation it was because one wondered where and when she
would break down; but she never did, either in her French
accent or in her *rôle* of educated angel.

After Archie had come the ladies were manifestly a great
resource to him, and all the world knows that a party of four
is more convenient than a party of three. My nephew kept me
waiting a week, with a placidity all his own; but this same
placidity was an element of success in our personal relations—
so long, that is, as I did not lose my temper with it. I did not,
for the most part, because my young man's unsurprised
acceptance of the most various forms of good fortune had
more than anything else the effect of amusing me. I had seen
little of him for the last three or four years. I knew not what
his impeding majority would have made of him (he did not
look himself in the least as if the wind were rising), and I
watched him with a solicitude which usually ended in a joke.
He was a tall, fresh-coloured youth, with a candid circular
countenance and a love of cigarettes, horses and boats which
had not been sacrificed to more transcendent studies. He was
refreshingly natural, in a supercivilised age, and I soon made
up my mind that the formula of his character was a certain
simplifying serenity. After that I had time to meditate on the
line which divides the serene from the inane and simplification
from death. Archie was not clever—that theory it was not
possible to maintain, though Mrs Pallant tried it once or
twice; but on the other hand it seemed to me that his want of
wit was a good defensive weapon. It was not the sort of
density that would let him in, but the sort that would keep
him out. By which I don't mean that he had shortsighted
suspicions, but on the contrary that imagination would never
be needed to save him, because she would never put him in
danger. In short he was a well-grown, well-washed, muscular
young American, whose extreme good-nature might have

made him pass for conceited. If he looked pleased with himself it was only because he was pleased with life (as well he might be, with the money he was on the point of stepping into), and his big healthy, independent person was an inevitable part of that. I am bound to add that he was accommodating—for which I was grateful. His own habits were active, but he did not insist on my adopting them and he made noteworthy sacrifices for the sake of my society. When I say for the sake of mine I must of course remember that mine and that of Mrs Pallant and Linda were now very much the same thing. He was willing to sit and smoke for hours under the trees or, regulating his long legs to the pace of his three companions, stroll through the nearer woods of the charming little hill-range of the Taunus to those rustic *Wirthschaften* where coffee might be drunk under a trellis.

Mrs Pallant took a great interest in him; she talked a great deal about him and thought him a delightful specimen, as a young gentleman of his period and country. She even asked me the sort of "figure" that his fortune might really amount to and expressed the most hungry envy when I told her what I supposed it to be. While we talked together Archie, on his side, could not do less than converse with Linda, nor to tell the truth did he manifest the least inclination for any different exercise. They strolled away together while their elders rested; two or three times, in the evening, when the ballroom of the Kursaal was lighted and dance-music played, they whirled over the smooth floor in a waltz that made me remember. Whether it had the same effect on Mrs Pallant I know not, for she held her peace. We had on certain occasions our moments, almost our half-hours, of unembarrassed silence while our young companions disported themselves. But if at other times her inquiries and comments were numerous on the subject of my ingenuous kinsman this might very well have passed for a courteous recognition of the frequent admiration that I expressed for Linda—an admiration to which I noticed that she was apt to give but a small direct response. I was struck with something anomalous in her way of taking my remarks about her daughter—they produced so little of a maternal flutter. Her detachment, her air of having no fatuous illusions and not being blinded by prejudice seemed to me at times to amount to an affectation. Either she answered me with a vague, slightly impatient sigh and changed the subject, or else she said before doing so: "Oh yes, yes, she's a very brilliant creature. She ought to be; God knows what I have done for her!"

The reader will have perceived that I am fond of looking at the explanations of things, and in regard to this I had my theory that she was disappointed in the girl. What had been her particular disappointment? As she could not possibly have wished her prettier or more pleasing it could only be that Linda had not made a successful use of her gifts. Had she expected her to capture a prince the day after she left the schoolroom? After all there was plenty of time for this, as Linda was only two and twenty. It did not occur to me to wonder whether the source of her mother's tepidity was that the young lady had not turned out so nice a nature as she had hoped, because in the first place Linda struck me as perfectly innocent and in the second I was not paid, as the French say, for thinking that Louisa Pallant would much mind whether she were or not. The last hypothesis I should have resorted to was that of private despair at bad moral symptoms. And in relation to Linda's nature I had before me the daily spectacle of her manner with my nephew. It was as charming as it could be, without the smallest indication of a desire to lead him on. She was as familiar as a cousin, but as a distant one—a cousin who had been brought up to observe degrees. She was so much cleverer than Archie that she could not help laughing at him, but she did not laugh enough to exclude variety, being well aware, no doubt, that a woman's cleverness most shines in contrast with a man's stupidity when she pretends to take that stupidity for wisdom. Linda Pallant moreover was not a chatterbox; as she knew the value of many things she knew the value of intervals. There were a good many in the conversation of these young persons; my nephew's own speech, to say nothing of his thought, being not exempt from periods of repose; so that I sometimes wondered how their association was kept at that pitch of friendliness of which it certainly bore the stamp.

It was friendly enough, evidently, when Archie sat near her —near enough for low murmurs, if they had risen to his lips— and watched her with interested eyes and with liberty not to try too hard to make himself agreeable. She was always doing something—finishing a flower in a piece of tapestry, cutting the leaves of a magazine, sewing a button on her glove (she carried a little work-bag in her pocket and was a person of the daintiest habits), or plying her pencil in a sketchbook which she rested on her knee. When we were indoors, at her mother's house, she had always the resource of her piano, of which she was of course a perfect mistress. These avocations enabled her to bear such close inspection with composure (I ended by rebuking Archie for it—I told him he stared at the poor girl too much), and she sought further relief in smiling all over the place. When my young man's eyes shone at her those of Miss Pallant addressed themselves brightly to the trees and clouds and other surrounding objects, including her mother and me. Sometimes she broke out into a sudden embarrassed, happy, pointless laugh. When she wandered away from us she looked back at us in a manner which said that it was not for long—that she was with us still in spirit. If I was pleased with her it was for a good reason: it was many a day since any pretty girl had had the air of taking me so much into account. Sometimes, when they were so far away as not to disturb us, she read aloud a little to Mr Archie. I don't know where she got her books—I never provided them, and certainly he did not. He was no reader and I daresay he went to sleep.

III

I REMEMBER well the first time—it was at the end of about ten days of this—that Mrs Pallant remarked to me: "My dear friend, you are quite amazing! You behave for all the world as if you were perfectly ready to accept certain consequences." She nodded in the direction of our young companions, but I nevertheless put her at the pains of saying what consequences she meant. "What consequences?" she repeated. "Why, the consequences that ensued when you and I first became acquainted."

I hesitated a moment and then, looking her in the eyes, I said, "Do you mean that she would throw him over?"

"You are not kind, you are not generous," she replied, colouring quickly. "I am giving you a warning."

"You mean that my boy may fall in love with her?"

"Certainly. It looks even as if the harm might be already done."

"Then your warning is too late," I said, smiling. "But why do you call it a harm?"

"Haven't you any sense of responsibility?" she asked. "Is that what his mother sent him out to you for—that you should find him a wife—let him put his head into a noose the day after his arrival?"

"Heaven forbid I should do anything of the kind! I know moreover that his mother doesn't want him to marry young. She thinks it's a mistake and that at that age a man never really chooses. He doesn't choose till he has lived awhile—till he has looked about and compared."

"And what do you think yourself?"

"I should like to say I consider that love itself, however young, is a sufficient choice. But my being a bachelor at this time of day would contradict me too much."

"Well then, you're too primitive. You ought to leave this place to-morrow."

"So as not to see Archie tumble in?"

"You ought to fish him out now and take him with you."

"Do you think he is in very far?" I inquired.

"If I were his mother I know what I should think. I can put myself in her place—I am not narrow—I know perfectly well how she must regard such a question."

"And don't you know that in America that's not thought important—the way the mother regards it?"

Mrs Pallant was silent a moment, as if I partly mystified and partly vexed her. "Well, we are not in America; we happen to be here."

"No; my poor sister is up to her neck in New York."

"I am almost capable of writing to her to come out," said Mrs Pallant.

"You *are* warning me," I exclaimed, "but I hardly know of what. It seems to me that my responsibility would begin only at the moment when it should appear that your daughter herself was in danger."

"Oh, you needn't mind that; I'll take care of her."

"If you think she is in danger already I'll take him away to-morrow," I went on.

"It would be the best thing you could do."

"I don't know. I should be very sorry to act on a false alarm. I am very well here; I like the place and the life and your society. Besides, it doesn't strike me that—on her side—there is anything."

She looked at me with an expression that I had never seen in her face, and if I had puzzled her she repaid me in kind. "You are very annoying; you don't deserve what I would do for you."

What she would do for me she did not tell me that day, but we took up the subject again. I said to her that I did not really

see why we should assume that a girl like Linda—brilliant
enough to make one of the greatest matches—would fall into
my nephew's arms. Might I inquire whether her mother had
won a confession from her—whether she had stammered out
her secret? Mrs Pallant answered that they did not need to tell
each other such things—they had not lived together twenty
years in such intimacy for nothing. To this I rejoined that I
had guessed as much but that there might be an exception for
a great occasion like the present. If Linda had shown nothing
it was a sign that for her the occasion was not great; and I
mentioned that Archie had not once spoken to me of the
young lady, save to remark casually and rather patronisingly,
after his first encounter with her, that she was a regular little
flower. (The little flower was nearly three years older than
himself.) Apart from this he had not alluded to her and had
taken up no allusion of mine. Mrs Pallant informed me again
(for which I was prepared) that I was quite too primitive; and
then she said: "We needn't discuss the matter if you don't
wish to, but I happen to know—how I obtained my knowledge is not important—that the moment Mr Pringle should
propose to my daughter she would gobble him down. Surely
it's a detail worth mentioning to you."

"Very good. I will sound him. I will look into the matter
to-night."

"Don't, don't; you will spoil everything!" she murmured,
in a peculiar tone of discouragement. "Take him off—that's
the only thing."

I did not at all like the idea of taking him off; it seemed too
summary, unnecessarily violent, even if presented to him on
specious grounds; and, moreover, as I had told Mrs Pallant,
I really had no wish to move. I did not consider it a part of
my bargain with my sister that, with my middle-aged habits,
I should duck and dodge about Europe. So I said: "Should
you really object to the boy so much as a son-in-law? After
all he's a good fellow and a gentleman."

"My poor friend, you are too superficial—too frivolous," Mrs Pallant rejoined, with considerable bitterness.

There was a vibration of contempt in this which nettled me, so that I exclaimed, "Possibly; but it seems odd that a lesson in consistency should come from you."

I had no retort from her; but at last she said, quietly: "I think Linda and I had better go away. We have been here a month—that's enough."

"Dear me, that will be a bore!" I ejaculated; and for the rest of the evening, until we separated (our conversation had taken place after dinner, at the Kursaal), she remained almost silent, with a subdued, injured air. This, somehow, did not soothe me, as it ought to have done, for it was too absurd that Louisa Pallant, of all women, should propose to put me in the wrong. If ever a woman had been in the wrong herself——! Archie and I usually attended the ladies back to their own door—they lived in a street of minor accommodation, at a certain distance from the Rooms—and we parted for the night late, on the big cobble-stones, in the little sleeping German town, under the closed windows of which, suggesting stuffy interiors, our English farewells sounded gay. On this occasion however they were not gay, for the difficulty that had come up, for me, with Mrs Pallant appeared to have extended by a mysterious sympathy to the young couple. They too were rather conscious and dumb.

As I walked back to our hotel with my nephew I passed my hand into his arm and asked him, by no roundabout approach to the question, whether he were in serious peril of love.

"I don't know, I don't know—really, uncle, I don't know!" —this was all the satisfaction I could extract from the youth, who had not the smallest vein of introspection. He might not know, but before we reached the inn (we had a few more words on the subject), it seemed to me that I did. His mind was not made to contain many objects at once, but Linda Pallant for the moment certainly constituted its principal furniture. She pervaded his consciousness, she solicited his curiosity, she associated herself, in a manner as yet undefined and unformulated, with his future. I could see that she was the first intensely agreeable impression of his life. I did not betray to him, however, how much I saw, and I slept not particularly well, for thinking that, after all, it had been none of my business to provide him with intensely agreeable impressions. To find him a wife was the last thing that his mother had expected of me or that I had expected of myself. Moreover it was quite my opinion that he himself was too young to be a judge of wives. Mrs Pallant was right and I had been strangely superficial in regarding her, with her beautiful daughter, as a "resource." There were other resources and one of them would be most decidedly to go away. What did I know after all about the girl except that I was very glad to have escaped from marrying her mother? That mother, it was true, was a singular person, and it was strange that her conscience should have begun to fidget before my own did and that she was more anxious on my nephew's behalf than I was. The ways of women were mysterious and it was not a novelty to me that one never knew where one would find them. As I have not hesitated in this narrative to reveal the irritable side of my own nature I will confess that I even wondered whether Mrs Pallant's solicitude had not been a deeper artifice. Was it not possibly a plan of her own for making sure of my young man —though I did not quite see the logic of it? If she regarded him, as she might in view of his large fortune, as a great catch, might she not have arranged this little comedy, in their personal interest, with the girl?

That possibility at any rate only made it a happier thought that I should carry the boy away to visit other cities. There were many assuredly much more worthy of his attention than Homburg. In the course of the morning (it was after our early luncheon) I walked round to Mrs Pallant's, to let her know that this truth had come over me with force; and while I did so I again felt the unlikelihood of the part attributed by my fears and by the mother's own, if they were real, to Linda. Certainly if she was such a girl as these fears represented her she would fly at higher game. It was with an eye to high game, Mrs Pallant had frankly admitted to me, that she had been trained, and such an education, to say nothing of such a subject, justified a hope of greater returns. A young American who could give her nothing but pocket-money was a very moderate prize, and if she were prepared to marry for ambition (there was no such hardness in her face or tone, but then there never is), her mark would be at the least an English duke. I was received at Mrs Pallant's lodgings with the announcement that she had left Homburg with her daughter half an hour before. The good woman who had entertained the pair professed to know nothing of their movements beyond the fact that they had gone to Frankfort, where however it was her belief that they did not intend to remain. They were evidently travelling beyond. Sudden? Oh yes, tremendously sudden. They must have spent the night in packing, they had so many things and such pretty ones; and their poor maid all the morning had scarcely had time to swallow her coffee. But they evidently were ladies accustomed to come and go. It did not matter: with such rooms as hers she never wanted; there was a new family coming in at three o'clock.

IV

THIS piece of strategy left me staring and I confess it made me rather angry. My only consolation was that Archie, when I told him, looked as blank as myself and that the trick touched him more nearly, for I was not in love with Louisa. We agreed that we required an explanation and we pretended to expect one the next day in the shape of a letter satisfactory even to the

point of being apologetic. When I say "we" pretended I
mean that I did, for my suspicion that he knew (through an
arrangement with Linda) what had become of our friends
lasted only a moment. If his resentment was less than my own
his surprise was equally great. I had been willing to bolt, but I
felt rather slighted by the facility with which Mrs Pallant had
shown that she could part with us. Archie was not angry,
because in the first place he was good-natured and in the
second it was evidently not definite to him that he had been
encouraged, having, I think, no very particular idea of what
constituted encouragement. He was fresh from the wonderful
country in which between the ingenuous young there may be
so little question of "intentions." He was but dimly conscious
of his own and would have had no opinion as to whether he
had been provoked or jilted. I had no wish to exasperate him,
but when at the end of three days more we were still without
news of our late companions I remarked that it was very
simple; it was plain they were just hiding from us; they
thought us dangerous; they wished to avoid entanglements.
They had found us too attentive and wished not to raise false
hopes. He appeared to accept this explanation and even had
the air (so at least I judged from his asking me no questions)
of thinking that the matter might be delicate for myself. The
poor youth was altogether much mystified, and I smiled at the
image in his mind of Mrs Pallant fleeing from his uncle's
importunities.

We decided to leave Homburg, but if we did not pursue her
it was not simply that we were ignorant of where she was.
I could have found that out with a little trouble, but I was
deterred by the reflection that this would be her own reasoning. She was dishonest and her departure was a provocation—
I am afraid that it was in that stupid conviction that I made
out a little independent itinerary with Archie. I even said to
myself that we should learn where they were quite soon
enough and that our patience—even my young man's—would

be longer than theirs. Therefore I uttered a small private cry of triumph when three weeks later (we happened to be at Interlaken) he told me that he had received a note from Miss Pallant. His manner of telling me was to inquire whether there were any particular reasons why we should longer delay our projected visit to the Italian lakes; was not the fear of the hot weather, which was moreover in summer our native temperature, at an end, as it was already the middle of September? I answered that we would start on the morrow if he liked, and then, pleased apparently that I was so easy to deal with, he revealed his little secret. He showed me the letter, which was a graceful, natural document—it covered with a few flowing strokes but a single page of notepaper—not at all compromising to the young lady. If however it was almost the apology I had looked for (save that that should have come from the mother), it was not ostensibly in the least an invitation. It mentioned casually (the mention was mainly in the date) that they were on the Lago Maggiore, at Baveno; but it consisted mainly of the expression of a regret that they had to leave us at Homburg without giving notice. Linda did not say under what necessity they had found themselves; she only hoped we had not judged them too harshly and would accept "these few hasty words" as a substitute for the omitted good-bye. She also hoped we were passing our time in an interesting manner and having the same lovely weather that prevailed south of the Alps; and she remained very sincerely, with the kindest remembrances to me.

The note contained no message from her mother and it was open to me to suppose, as I should judge, either that Mrs Pallant had not known she was writing or that they wished to make us think she had not known. The letter might pass as a common civility of the girl's to a person with whom she had been on very familiar terms. It was however as something more than this that my nephew took it; at least so I was warranted in inferring from the very distinct nature of his determination to go to Baveno. I saw it was useless to drag him another way; he had money in his own pocket and was quite capable of giving me the slip. Yet—such are the sweet incongruities of youth—when I asked him if he had been thinking of Linda Pallant ever since they left us in the lurch he replied, "Oh dear no; why should I?" This fib was accompanied by an exorbitant blush. Since he must obey the young lady's call I must also go and see where it would take him, and one splendid morning we started over the Simplon in a post-chaise.

I represented to him successfully that it would be in much better taste for us to alight at Stresa, which as every one knows is a resort of tourists, also on the shore of the major lake, at about a mile's distance from Baveno. If we stayed at the latter place we should have to inhabit the same hotel as our friends, and this would be indiscreet, considering our peculiar relations with them. Nothing would be easier than to go and come between the two points, especially by the water, which would give Archie a chance for unlimited paddling. His face lighted up at the vision of a pair of oars; he pretended to take my plea for discretion very seriously and I could see that he immediately began to calculate opportunities for being afloat with Linda. Our post-chaise (I had insisted on easy stages and we were three days on the way) deposited us at Stresa toward the middle of the afternoon, and it was within an amazingly short time that I found myself in a small boat with my nephew, who pulled us over to Baveno with vigorous strokes. I remember the sweetness of the whole impression (I had had it before, but to my companion it was new and he thought it as pretty as the opera); the enchanting beauty of the place and hour, the stillness of the air and water, with the romantic, fantastic Borromean Islands in the midst of them. We disembarked at the steps at the garden-foot of the hotel, and somehow it seemed a perfectly natural part of the lovely situation that I should immediately become conscious

Mrs Pallant and her daughter were sitting there—on the terrace—quietly watching us. They had all the air of expecting us and I think we looked for it in them. I had not even asked Archie if he had answered Linda's note; that was between themselves and in the way of supervision I had done enough in coming with him.

There is no doubt there was something very odd in our meeting with our friends—at least as between Louisa and me. I was too much taken up with that part of it to notice very much what was the manner of the encounter of the young people. I have sufficiently indicated that I could not get it out of my head that Mrs Pallant was "up to" something, and I am afraid she saw in my face that this suspicion had been the motive of my journey. I had come there to find her out. The knowledge of my purpose could not help her to make me very welcome, and that is why I say we met in strange conditions. However, on this occasion we observed all forms and the admirable scene gave us plenty to talk about. I made no reference before Linda to the retreat from Homburg. She looked even prettier than she had done on the eve of that manœuvre and gave no sign of an awkward consciousness. She struck me so, afresh, as a charming, clever girl that I was puzzled afresh to know why we should get—or should have got—into a tangle about her. People had to want to complicate a situation to do it on so simple a pretext as that Linda was admirable. So she was, and why should not the consequences be equally so? One of them, on the spot, was that at the end of a very short time Archie proposed to her to take a turn with him in his boat, which awaited us at the foot of the steps. She looked at her mother with a smiling "May I, mamma?" and Mrs Pallant answered, "Certainly, darling, if you are not afraid." At this —I scarcely knew why—I burst out laughing; it seemed so droll to me somehow that timidity should be imputed to this competent young lady. She gave me a quick, slightly sharp look as she turned away with my nephew; it appeared to

challenge me a little—to say, "Pray what is the matter with
you?" It was the first expression of the kind I had ever seen in
her face. Mrs Pallant's eyes, on the other hand, were not
turned to mine; after we had been left there together she sat
silent, not heeding me, looking at the lake and mountains—at
the snowy crests which wore the flush of evening. She seemed
not even to watch our young companions as they got into
their boat and pushed off. For some minutes I respected her
reverie; I walked slowly up and down the terrace and lighted
a cigar, as she had always permitted me to do at Homburg.
I noticed that she had an expression of weariness which I had
never seen before; her delicate, agreeable face was pale; I made
out that there were new lines of fatigue, almost of age, in it.
At last I stopped in front of her and asked her, since she looked
so sad, if she had any bad news.

"The only bad news was when I learned—through your
nephew's note to Linda—that you were coming to us."

"Ah, then he wrote?" I exclaimed.

"Certainly he wrote."

"You take it all harder than I do," I remarked, sitting down
beside her. And then I added, smiling, "Have you written to
his mother?"

She slowly turned her face to me and rested her eyes on
mine. "Take care, take care, or you'll insult me," she said,
with an air of patience before the inevitable.

"Never, never! Unless you think I do so if I ask you if you
knew when Linda wrote."

She hesitated a moment. "Yes; she showed me her letter.
She wouldn't have done anything else. I let it go because I
didn't know what it was best to do. I am afraid to oppose her,
to her face."

"Afraid, my dear friend, with that girl?"

"That girl? Much you know about her! It didn't follow
that you would come—I didn't think it need follow."

"I am like you," I said—"I am afraid of my nephew. I

don't venture to oppose him to his face. The only thing I could do under the circumstances was to come with him."

"I see; I'm glad you have done it," said Mrs Pallant, thoughtfully.

"Oh, I was conscientious about that! But I have no authority; I can't order him nor forbid him—I can use no force. Look at the way he is pulling that boat and see if you can fancy me."

"You could tell him she's a bad, hard girl, who would poison any good man's life!" my companion suddenly broke out, with a kind of passion.

"Dear Mrs Pallant, what do you mean?" I murmured, staring.

She bent her face into her hands, covering it over with them, and remained so for a minute; then she went on, in a different manner, as if she had not heard my question: "I hoped you were too disgusted with us, after the way we left you planted."

"It was disconcerting, assuredly, and it might have served if Linda hadn't written. That patched it up," I said, laughing. But my laughter was hollow, for I had been exceedingly impressed with her little explosion of a moment before. "Do you really mean she is bad?" I added.

Mrs Pallant made no immediate answer to this; she only said that it did not matter after all whether the crisis should come a few weeks sooner or a few weeks later, since it was destined to come at the first opening. Linda had marked my young man—and when Linda had marked a thing!

"Bless my soul—how very grim! Do you mean she's in love with him?" I demanded, incredulous.

"It's enough if she makes him think she is—though even that isn't essential."

"If she makes him think so? Dearest lady, what do you mean? I have observed her, I have watched her, and after all what has she done? She has been nice to him, but it would have been much more marked if she hadn't. She has really shown him nothing but the common friendliness of a bright, good-natured girl. Her note was nothing; he showed it to me."

"I don't think you have heard every word that she has said to him," Mrs Pallant rejoined, with a persistence that struck me as unnatural.

"No more have you, I take it!" I exclaimed. She evidently meant more than she said, and this impression chilled me, made me really uncomfortable.

"No, but I know my own daughter. She's a very rare young woman."

"You have a singular tone about her," I responded—"such a tone as I think I have never heard on a mother's lips. I have observed it before, but never so accentuated."

At this Mrs Pallant got up; she stood there an instant, looking down at me. "You make my reparation—my expiation—difficult!" And leaving me rather startled, she began to move along the terrace.

I overtook her presently and repeated her words. "Your reparation—your expiation? What on earth do you mean by that?"

"You know perfectly what I mean—it is too magnanimous of you to pretend you don't."

"Well, at any rate I don't see what good it does me or what it makes up to me for that you should abuse your daughter."

"Oh, I don't care; I shall save him!" she exclaimed, as we went, with a kind of perverse cheerfulness. At the same moment two ladies, apparently English, came toward us (scattered groups had been sitting there and the inmates of the hotel were moving to and fro), and I observed the immediate charming transition (it seemed to me to show such years of social practice), by which, as they greeted us, she exchanged her excited, almost fevered expression for an air of recognition and pleasure. They stopped to speak to her and she asked with eagerness whether their mother were better.

I strolled on and she presently rejoined me; after which she said impatiently, "Come away from this—come down into the garden." We descended into the garden, strolled through it and paused on the border of the lake.

V

THE charm of the evening had deepened, the stillness was like a solemn expression on a beautiful face and the whole air of the place divine. In the fading light my nephew's boat was too far out to be perceived. I looked for it a little and then, as I gave it up, I remarked that from such an excursion as that, on such a lake, at such an hour, a young man and a young woman of ordinary sensibility could only come back doubly pledged to each other. To this observation Mrs Pallant's answer was, superficially at least, irrelevant; she said after a pause:

"With you, my dear sir, one has certainly to dot one's 'i's.' Haven't you discovered, and didn't I tell you at Homburg, that we are miserably poor?"

"Isn't 'miserably' rather too much, when you are living at an expensive hotel?"

"They take us *en pension*, for ever so little a day. I have been knocking about Europe long enough to learn there are certain ways of doing things. Besides, don't speak of hotels; we have spent half our life in them and Linda told me only last night that she hoped never to put her foot into one again. She thinks that when she comes to such a place as this it's the least that she should find a villa of her own."

"Well, her companion there is perfectly competent to give her one. Don't think I have the least desire to push them into each other's arms; I only ask to wash my hands of them. But I should like to know why you want, as you said just now, to save him. When you speak as if your daughter were a monster I take it that you are not serious."

She was facing me there in the twilight, and to let me know that she was more serious perhaps than she had ever been in her life she had only to look at me awhile without protestation. "It's Linda's standard. God knows I myself could get on! She is ambitious, luxurious, determined to have what she wants, more than any one I have ever seen. Of course it's open to you to tell me that it's my fault, that I was so before her and have made her so. But does that make me like it any better?"

"Dear Mrs Pallant, you are most extraordinary," I stammered, infinitely surprised and not a little pained.

"Oh yes, you have made up your mind about me; you see me in a certain way and you don't like the trouble of changing. *Votre siège est fait.* But you will have to change—if you have any generosity!" Her eyes shone in the summer dusk and she looked remarkably handsome.

"Is this a part of the reparation, of the expiation?" I inquired. "I don't see what you ever did to Archie."

"It's enough that he belongs to you. But it isn't for you that I do it; it's for myself," she went on.

"Doubtless you have your own reasons, which I can't penetrate. But can't you sacrifice something else?—must you sacrifice your child?"

"She's my punishment and she's my stigma!" cried Louisa Pallant, with veritable exaltation.

"It seems to me rather that you are hers."

"Hers? What does *she* know of such things?—what can she ever feel? She's cased in steel; she has a heart of marble. It's true—it's true. She appals me!"

I laid my hand upon the poor lady's; I uttered, with the intention of checking and soothing her, the first incoherent words that came into my head and I drew her toward a bench which I perceived a few yards away. She dropped upon it; I placed myself near her and besought her to consider well what she was saying. She owed me nothing and I wished no one injured, no one denounced or exposed for my sake.

"For your sake? Oh, I am not thinking of you!" she answered; and indeed the next moment I thought my words rather fatuous. "It's a satisfaction to my own conscience—for I have one, little as you think I have a right to speak of it. I have been punished by my sin itself. I have been hideously worldly, I have thought only of that, and I have taught her to be so—to do the same. That's the only instruction I have ever given her, and she has learned the lesson so well that now that I see it printed there in all her nature I am horrified at my work. For years we have lived that way; we have thought of nothing else. She has learned it so well that she has gone far beyond me. I say I am horrified, because she is horrible."

"My poor extravagant friend," I pleaded, "isn't it still more so to hear a mother say such things?"

"Why so, if they are abominably true? Besides, I don't care what I say, if I save him."

"Do you expect me to repeat to him——?"

"Not in the least," she broke in; "I will do it myself." At this I uttered some strong inarticulate protest, and she went on with a sort of simplicity: "I was very glad at first, but it would have been better if we hadn't met."

"I don't agree to that, for you interest me immensely."

"I don't care for that—if I can interest him."

"You must remember then that your charges are strangely vague, considering how violent they are. Never had a girl a more innocent appearance. You know how I have admired it."

"You know nothing about her. I do, for she is the work of my hand!" Mrs Pallant declared, with a bitter laugh. "I have watched her for years and little by little, for the last two or three, it has come over me. There is not a tender spot in her whole composition. To arrive at a brilliant social position, if it were necessary, she would see me drown in this lake without lifting a finger, she would stand there and see it—she would push me in—and never feel a pang. That's my young lady! To climb up to the top and be splendid and envied there—to

do it at any cost or by any meanness and cruelty, is the only
thing she has a heart for. She would lie for it, she would steal
for it, she would kill for it!" My companion brought out these
words with a tremendous low distinctness and an air of sincerity that was really solemn. I watched her pale face and
glowing eyes; she held me in a kind of stupor, but her strange,
almost vindictive earnestness imposed itself. I found myself
believing her, pitying her more than I pitied the girl. It was as
if she had been bottled up for longer than she could bear,
suffering more and more from the ferment of her knowledge.
It relieved her to warn and denounce and expose. "God has
let me see it in time, in his mercy," she continued; "but his
ways are strange, that he has let me see it in my daughter. It is
myself that he has let me see, myself as I was for years. But
she's worse—she is, I assure you; she's worse than I ever
intended or dreamed." Her hands were clasped tightly together in her lap; her low voice quavered and her breath came
short; she looked up at the faint stars with religious perversity.

"Have you ever spoken to her as you speak to me?" I
asked. "Have you ever admonished her, reproached her?"

"Reproached her? How can I? when all she would have to
say would be, 'You—*you*—you base one—who made me!'"

"Then why do you want to play her a trick?"

"I'm not bound to tell you and you wouldn't understand
if I did. I should play that boy a far worse trick if I were to
hold my tongue."

"If he loves her he won't believe a word you say."

"Very possibly, but I shall have done my duty."

"And shall you say to him simply what you have said to
me?"

"Never mind what I shall say to him. It will be something
that will perhaps affect him, if I lose no time."

"If you are so bent on gaining time," I said, "why did you
let her go out in the boat with him?"

"Let her? how could I prevent it?"

"But she asked your permission."

"That's a part of all the comedy!"

We were silent a moment, after which I resumed: "Then she doesn't know you hate her?"

"I don't know what she knows. She has depths and depths, and all of them bad. Besides, I don't hate her in the least; I pity her simply, for what I have made of her. But I pity still more the man who may find himself married to her."

"There's not much danger of there being any such person, at the rate you go on."

"Oh, perfectly; she'll marry some one. She'll marry a title as well as a fortune."

"It's a pity my nephew hasn't a title," I murmured, smiling.

She hesitated a moment. "I see you think I want that and that I am acting a part. God forgive you! Your suspicion is perfectly natural: how can any one tell, with people like us?"

The way she uttered these last words brought tears to my eyes. I laid my hand on her arm, holding her awhile, and we looked at each other through the dusk. "You couldn't do more if he were my son," I said at last.

"Oh, if he had been your son he would have kept out of it! I like him for himself; he's simple and honest—he needs affection."

"He would have an admirable, a devoted, mother-in-law," I went on.

Mrs Pallant gave a little impatient sigh and replied that she was not joking. We sat there some time longer, while I thought over what she had said to me and she apparently did the same. I confess that even close at her side, with the echo of her passionate, broken voice still in the air, some queer ideas came into my head. Was the comedy on *her* side and not on the girl's, and was she posturing as a magnanimous woman at poor Linda's expense? Was she determined, in spite of the young lady's preference, to keep her daughter for a grander personage than a young American whose dollars were not numerous enough (numerous as they were) to make up for his want of high relationships, and had she brought forth these cruel imputations to help her to her end? If she was prepared really to denounce the girl to Archie she would have to go very far to overcome the suspicion he would be sure to feel at so unnatural a proceeding. Was she prepared to go far enough? The answer to these doubts was simply the way I had been touched—it came back to me the next moment—when she used the words, "people like us." The effect of them was poignant. She made herself humble indeed and I felt in a manner ashamed, on my own side, that I saw her in the dust. She said to me at last that I must wait no longer; I must go away before the young people came back. They were staying very long, too long; all the more reason that she should deal with Archie that evening. I must drive back to Stresa or, if I liked, I could go on foot: it was not far—for a man. She disposed of me freely, she was so full of her purpose; and after we had quitted the garden and returned to the terrace of the hotel she seemed almost to push me to leave her—I felt her find hands, quivering a little, on my shoulders. I was ready to do what she liked: she affected me painfully and I wanted to get away from her. Before I went I asked her why Linda should regard my young man as such a *parti;* it did not square after all with her account of the girl's fierce ambitions. By that picture it would seem that a reigning prince was the least she would look at.

"Oh, she has reflected well; she has regarded the question in every light," said Mrs Pallant. "If she has made up her mind it is because she sees what she can do."

"Do you mean that she has talked it over with you?"

"Lord! for what do you take us? We don't talk over things to-day. We know each other's point of view and we only have to act. We can take reasons, which are awkward things, for granted."

"But in this case she certainly doesn't know your point of view, poor thing."

"No—that's because I haven't played fair. Of course she couldn't expect I would cheat. There ought to be honour among thieves. But it was open to her to do the same."

"How do you mean, to do the same?"

"She might have fallen in love with a poor man; then I should have been done."

"A rich one is better; he can do more," I replied, with conviction.

"So you would have reason to know if you had led the life that we have! Never to have had really enough—I mean to do just the few simple things we have wanted; never to have had the sinews of war, I suppose you would call them—the funds for a campaign; to have felt every day and every hour the hard, monotonous pinch and found the question of dollars and cents (and so horridly few of them) mixed up with every experience, with every impulse—that *does* make one mercenary, it does make money seem a good beyond all others, and it's quite natural it should. That is why Linda is of the opinion that a fortune is always a fortune. She knows all about that of your nephew, how it's invested, how it may be expected to increase, exactly on what sort of footing it would enable her to live. She has decided that it's enough, and enough is as good as a feast. She thinks she could lead him by the nose, and I daresay she could. She will make him live here: she has not the least intention of settling in America. I think she has views upon London, because in England he can hunt and shoot, and that will make him let her alone."

"It strikes me that he would like that very much," I interposed; "that's not at all a bad programme, even from Archie's point of view."

"It's no use of talking about princes," Mrs Pallant pursued, as if she had not heard me. "Yes, they are most of them more in want of money even than we are. Therefore a title is out of the question, and we recognised that at an early stage. Your nephew is exactly the sort of young man we had constructed in advance—he was made on purpose. Dear Linda was her mother's own daughter when she recognised him on the spot! It's enough of a title to-day to be an American—with the way they have come up. It does as well as anything and it's a great simplification. If you don't believe me go to London and see."

She had come with me out to the road. I had said I would walk back to Stresa and we stood there in the complete evening. As I took her hand, bidding her good-night, I exclaimed, "Poor Linda—poor Linda!"

"Oh, she'll live to do better," said Mrs Pallant.

"How can she do better, since you have described this as perfection?"

She hesitated a moment. "I mean better for Mr Pringle."

I still had her hand—I remained looking at her. "How came it that you could throw me over—such a woman as you?"

"Ah, my friend, if I hadn't thrown you over I couldn't do this for you?" And disengaging herself she turned away quickly and went back to the hotel.

VI

I DON'T know whether she blushed as she made this avowal, which was a retraction of a former denial and the real truth, as I permitted myself to believe; but I did, while I took my way to Stresa—it is a walk of half an hour—in the darkness. The new and singular character in which she had appeared to me produced an effect of excitement which would have made it impossible for me to sit still in a carriage. This same agitation kept me up late after I had reached my hotel; as I knew that I should not sleep it was useless to go to bed. Long, however, as I deferred this ceremony Archie had not turned up when the lights in the hotel began to be put out. I felt even slightly nervous about him and wondered whether he had had an accident on the lake. I reflected that in this case—if he had not brought his companion back to Baveno—Mrs Pallant would already have sent after me. It was foolish moreover to suppose that anything could have happened to him after putting off from Baveno by water to rejoin me, for the evening was absolutely windless and more than sufficiently clear and the lake as calm as glass. Besides I had unlimited confidence in his power to take care of himself in circumstances much more difficult. I went to my room at last; his own was at some distance, the people of the hotel not having been able—it was the height of the autumn season—to place us together. Before I went to bed I had occasion to ring for a servant, and then I learned by a chance inquiry that my nephew had returned an hour before and had gone straight to his own apartment. I had not supposed he could come in without my seeing him—I was wandering about the saloons and terraces—and it had not occurred to me to knock at his door. I had half a mind to do so then—I had such a curiosity as to how I should find him; but I checked myself, for evidently he had not wished to see me. This did not diminish my curiosity, and I slept even less than I had expected. His dodging me that way (for if he had not perceived me downstairs he might have looked for me in my room) was a sign that Mrs Pallant's interview with him had really come off. What had she said to him? What strong measures had she taken? The impression of almost morbid eagerness of purpose that she had given me suggested possibilities that I was afraid to think of. She had spoken of these things as we parted there as something she would do for me; but I had made the mental comment, as I walked away from her, that she had not done it yet. It would not really be done till Archie had backed out. Perhaps it was done by this time; his avoiding me seemed almost a proof. That was what I thought of most of the night. I spent a considerable part of it at my window, looking out at the sleeping mountains. *Had* he backed out?—was he making up his mind to back out? There was a strange contradiction in it; there were in fact more contradictions than ever. I believed what Mrs Pallant had told me about Linda, and yet that other idea made me ashamed of my nephew. I was sorry for the girl; I regretted her loss of a great chance, if loss it was to be; and yet I hoped that the manner in which her mother had betrayed her (there was no other word) to her lover had been thoroughgoing. It would need very radical measures on Mrs Pallant's part to excuse Archie. For him too I was sorry, if she had made an impression on him—the impression she desired. Once or twice I was on the point of going in to condole with him, in my dressing-gown; I was sure he too had jumped up from his bed and was looking out of his window at the everlasting hills.

I am bound to say that he showed few symptoms when we met in the morning and breakfasted together. Youth is strange; it has resources that experience seems only to take away from us. One of these is simply (in the given case) to do nothing—to say nothing. As we grow older and cleverer we think that is too simple, too crude; we dissimulate more elaborately, but with an effect much less baffling. My young man looked not in the least as if he had lain awake or had something on his mind; and when I asked him what he had done after my premature departure (I explained this by saying I had been tired of waiting for him—I was weary with my journey and wanted to go to bed), he replied: "Oh, nothing in particular. I hung about the place; I like it better than this. We had an awfully jolly time on the water. *I* wasn't in the least tired." I did not worry him with questions; it seemed to me indelicate to try to probe his secret. The only indication he gave was on my saying after breakfast that I should go over again to see our friends and my appearing to take for granted that he would be glad to accompany me. Then he remarked that he would stop at Stresa—he had paid them such a tremendous visit; also he had some letters to write. There was a freshness in his scruples about the length of his visits, and I knew something about his correspondence, which consisted entirely of twenty pages every week from his mother. But he satisfied my curiosity so little that it was really this sentiment that carried me back to Baveno. This time I ordered a conveyance, and as I got into it he stood watching me in the porch of the hotel with his hands in his pockets. Then it was for the first time that I saw in this young man's face the expression of a person slightly dazed, slightly foolish even, to whom something disagreeable has happened. Our eyes met as I observed him, and I was on the point of saying, "You had really better come with me," when he turned away. He went into the house as if he wished to escape from my call. I said to myself that Mrs Pallant had warned him off but that it would not take much to bring him back.

The servant to whom I spoke at Baveno told me that my friends were in a certain summer-house in the garden, to which he led the way. The place had an empty air; most of the inmates of the hotel were dispersed on the lake, on the hills, in picnics, excursions, visits to the Borromean Islands. My guide was so far right as that Linda was in the summer-house, but she was there alone. On finding this to be the case I stopped short, rather awkwardly, for I had a sudden sense of being an unmasked hypocrite—a conspirator against her security and honour. But there was no awkwardness about Linda Pallant; she looked up with a little cry of pleasure from the book she was reading and held out her hand with the most engaging frankness. I felt as if I had no right to touch her hand and I pretended not to see it. But this gave no chill to her pretty manner; she moved a roll of tapestry off the bench, so that I might sit down, and praised the place as a delightful shady corner. She had never been fresher, fairer, kinder; she made her mother's damning talk about her seem a hideous dream. She told me Mrs Pallant was coming to join her; she had remained indoors to write a letter. One could not write out there, though it was so nice in other respects: the table was too rickety. They too then had pretexts between them in the way of letters: I judged this to be a token that the situation was tense. It was the only one however that Linda gave: like Archie she was young enough to carry it off. She had been used to seeing us always together and she made no comment on my having come over without him. I waited in vain for her to say something about it; this would only be natural—it was almost unfriendly to omit it. At last I observed that my nephew was very unsociable that morning; I had expected him to join me but he had left me to come alone.

"I am very glad," she answered. "You can tell him that if you like."

"If I tell him that he will come immediately."

"Then don't tell him; I don't want him to come. He stayed too long last night," Linda went on, "and kept me out on the water till the most dreadful hours. That isn't done here, you know, and every one was shocked when we came back—or rather when we didn't come back. I begged him to bring me in, but he wouldn't. When we did return—I almost had to take the oars myself—I felt as if every one had been sitting up to time us, to stare at us. It was very embarrassing."

These words made an impression upon me; and as I have treated the reader to most of the reflections—some of them perhaps rather morbid—in which I indulged on the subject of this young lady and her mother I may as well complete the record and let him know that I now wondered whether Linda —candid and accomplished maiden—had conceived the fine idea of strengthening her hold of Archie by attempting to prove that he had "compromised" her. "Ah, no doubt that was the reason he had a bad conscience last evening!" I exclaimed. "When he came back to Stresa he sneaked off to his room; he wouldn't look me in the face."

"Mamma was so vexed that she took him apart and gave

him a scolding," the girl went on. "And to punish *me* she sent me straight to bed. She has very old-fashioned ideas—haven't you, mamma?" she added, looking over my head at Mrs Pallant, who had just come in behind me.

I forget what answer Mrs Pallant made to Linda's appeal; she stood there with two letters, sealed and addressed, in her hand. She greeted me gaily and then asked her daughter if she had any postage-stamps. Linda consulted a somewhat shabby pocket-book and confessed that she was destitute; whereupon her mother gave her the letters, with the request that she would go into the hotel, buy the proper stamps at the office, carefully affix them and put the letters into the box. She was to pay for the stamps, not have them put on the bill—a preference for which Mrs Pallant gave her reasons. I had bought some at Stresa that morning and I was on the point of offering them, when, apparently having guessed my intention, the elder lady silenced me with a look. Linda told her she had no money and she fumbled in her pocket for a franc. When she had found it and the girl had taken it Linda kissed her before going off with the letters.

"Darling mother, you haven't any too many of them, have you?" she murmured; and she gave me, sidelong, as she left us, the prettiest half comical, half pitiful smile.

"She's amazing—she's amazing," said Mrs Pallant, as we looked at each other.

"Does she know what you have done?"

"She knows I have done something and she is making up her mind what it is—or she will in the course of the next twenty-four hours, if your nephew doesn't come back. I think I can promise you he won't."

"And won't she ask you?"

"Never!"

"Shall you not tell her? Can you sit down together in this summer-house, this divine day, with such a dreadful thing as that between you?"

"Don't you remember what I told you about our relations
—that everything was implied between us and nothing
expressed? The ideas we have had in common—our perpetual
worldliness, our always looking out for chances—are not the
sort of thing that can be uttered gracefully between persons
who like to keep up forms, as we both do: so that if we
understood each other it was enough. We shall understand
each other now, as we have always done, and nothing will be
changed, because there has always been something between us
that couldn't be talked about."

"Certainly, she is amazing—she is amazing," I repeated;
"but so are you." And then I asked her what she had said to
my boy.

She seemed surprised. "Hasn't he told you?"

"No, and he never will."

"I am glad of that," she said, simply.

"But I am not sure he won't come back. He didn't this
morning, but he had already half a mind to."

"That's your imagination," said Mrs. Pallant, decisively.
"If you knew what I told him you would be sure."

"And you won't let me know?"

"Never, my near friend."

"And did he believe you?"

"Time will show; but I think so."

"And how did you make it plausible to him that you should
take so unnatural a course?"

For a moment she said nothing, only looking at me. Then
at last—"I told him the truth."

"The truth?" I repeated.

"Take him away—take him away!" she broke out. "That's
why I got rid of Linda, to tell you that you mustn't stay—you
must leave Stresa to-morrow. This time it's you that must do
it; I can't fly from you again—it costs too much!" And she
smiled strangely.

"Don't be afraid; don't be afraid. We will leave to-morrow;

I want to go myself." I took her hand in farewell, and while I held it I said, "The way you put it, about Linda, was very bad?"

"It was horrible."

I turned away—I felt indeed that I wanted to leave the neighbourhood. She kept me from going to the hotel, as I might meet Linda coming back, which I was far from wishing to do, and showed me another way into the road. Then she turned round to meet her daughter and spend the rest of the morning in the summer-house with her, looking at the bright blue lake and the snowy crests of the Alps. When I reached Stresa again I found that Archie had gone off to Milan (to see the cathedral, the servant said), leaving a message for me to the effect that, as he should not be back for a day or two (though there were numerous trains), he had taken a small portmanteau with him. The next day I got a telegram from him notifying me that he had determined to go on to Venice and requesting me to forward the rest of his luggage. "Please don't come after me," this missive added; "I want to be alone; I shall do no harm." That sounded pathetic to me, in the light of what I knew, and I was glad to leave the poor boy to his own devices. He proceeded to Venice and I recrossed the Alps. For several weeks after this I expected to discover that he had rejoined Mrs Pallant; but when we met in Paris, in November, I saw that he had nothing to hide from me, except indeed the secret of what that lady had told him. This he concealed from me then and has concealed ever since. He returned to America before Christmas and then I felt that the crisis had passed. I have never seen my old friend since. About a year after the time to which my story refers, Linda married, in London, a young Englishman, the possessor of a large fortune, a fortune acquired by his father in some useful industry. Mrs Gimingham's photographs (such is her present name) may be obtained from the principal stationers. I am convinced her mother was sincere. My nephew has not changed his state yet, and now even my sister is beginning, for the first time, to desire it. I related to her as soon as I saw her the substance of the story I have written here, and (such is the inconsequence of women) nothing can exceed her reprobation of Louisa Pallant.

THE ASPERN PAPERS

I

I HAD taken Mrs Prest into my confidence; in truth without her I should have made but little advance, for the fruitful idea in the whole business dropped from her friendly lips. It was she who invented the short cut, who severed the Gordian knot. It is not supposed to be the nature of women to rise as a general thing to the largest and most liberal view—I mean of a practical scheme; but it has struck me that they sometimes throw off a bold conception—such as a man would not have risen to—with singular serenity. "Simply ask them to take you in on the footing of a lodger"—I don't think that unaided I should have risen to that. I was beating about the bush, trying to be ingenious, wondering by what combination of arts I might become an acquaintance, when she offered this happy suggestion that the way to become an acquaintance was first to become an inmate. Her actual knowledge of the Misses Bordereau was scarcely larger than mine, and indeed I had brought with me from England some definite facts which were new to her. Their name had been mixed up ages before with one of the greatest names of the century, and they lived now in Venice in obscurity, on very small means, unvisited, un-approachable, in a dilapidated old palace on an out-of-the-way canal: this was the substance of my friend's impression of them. She herself had been established in Venice for fifteen years and had done a great deal of good there; but the circle of her benevolence did not include the two shy, mysterious and, as it was somehow supposed, scarcely respectable Americans (they were believed to have lost in their long exile all national quality, besides having had, as their name implied, some

275

French strain in their origin), who asked no favours and desired no attention. In the early years of her residence she had made an attempt to see them, but this had been successful only as regards the little one, as Mrs Prest called the niece; though in reality, as I afterwards learned, she was considerably the bigger of the two. She had heard Miss Bordereau was ill and had a suspicion that she was in want; and she had gone to the house to offer assistance, so that if there were suffering (and American suffering), she should at least not have it on her conscience. The "little one" received her in the great cold, tarnished Venetian sala, the central hall of the house, paved with marble and roofed with dim cross-beams, and did not even ask her to sit down. This was not encouraging for me, who wished to sit so fast, and I remarked as much to Mrs Prest. She however replied with profundity, "Ah, but there's all the difference: I went to confer a favour and you will go to ask one. If they are proud you will be on the right side." And she offered to show me their house to begin with—to row me thither in her gondola. I let her know that I had already been to look at it half a dozen times; but I accepted her invitation, for it charmed me to hover about the place. I had made my way to it the day after my arrival in Venice (it had been described to me in advance by the friend in England to whom I owed definite information as to their possession of the papers), and I had besieged it with my eyes while I considered my plan of campaign. Jeffrey Aspern had never been in it that I knew of; but some note of his voice seemed to abide there by a roundabout implication, a faint reverberation.

Mrs Prest knew nothing about the papers, but she was interested in my curiosity, as she was always interested in the joys and sorrows of her friends. As we went, however, in her gondola, gliding there under the sociable hood with the bright Venetian picture framed on either side by the movable window, I could see that she was amused by my infatuation, the way my interest in the papers had become a fixed idea.

"One would think you expected to find in them the answer to the riddle of the universe," she said; and I denied the impeachment only by replying that if I had to choose between that precious solution and a bundle of Jeffrey Aspern's letters I knew indeed which would appear to me the greater boon. She pretended to make light of his genius and I took no pains to defend him. One doesn't defend one's god: one's god is in himself a defence. Besides, to-day, after his long comparative obscuration, he hangs high in the heaven of our literature, for all the world to see; he is a part of the light by which we walk. The most I said was that he was no doubt not a woman's poet: to which she rejoined aptly enough that he had been at least Miss Bordereau's. The strange thing had been for me to discover in England that she was still alive: it was as if I had been told Mrs Siddons was, or Queen Caroline, or the famous Lady Hamilton, for it seemed to me that she belonged to a generation as extinct. "Why, she must be tremendously old —at least a hundred," I had said; but on coming to consider dates I saw that it was not strictly necessary that she should have exceeded by very much the common span. None the less she was very far advanced in life and her relations with Jeffrey Aspern had occurred in her early womanhood. "That is her excuse," said Mrs Prest, half sententiously and yet also somewhat as if she were ashamed of making a speech so little in the real tone of Venice. As if a woman needed an excuse for having loved the divine poet! He had been not only one of the most brilliant minds of his day (and in those years, when the century was young, there were, as every one knows, many), but one of the most genial men and one of the handsomest.

The niece, according to Mrs Prest, was not so old, and she risked the conjecture that she was only a grand-niece. This was possible; I had nothing but my share in the very limited knowledge of my English fellow-worshipper John Cumnor, who had never seen the couple. The world, as I say, had recognised Jeffrey Aspern, but Cumnor and I had recognised him most. The multitude, to-day, flocked to his temple, but of that temple he and I regarded ourselves as the ministers. We held, justly, as I think, that we had done more for his memory than any one else, and we had done it by opening lights into his life. He had nothing to fear from us because he had nothing to fear from the truth, which alone at such a distance of time we could be interested in establishing. His early death had been the only dark spot in his life, unless the papers in Miss Bordereau's hands should perversely bring out others. There had been an impression about 1825 that he had "treated her badly," just as there had been an impression that he had "served," as the London populace says, several other ladies in the same way. Each of these cases Cumnor and I had been able to investigate, and we had never failed to acquit him conscientiously of shabby behaviour. I judged him perhaps more indulgently than my friend; certainly, at any rate, it appeared to me that no man could have walked straighter in the given circumstances. These were almost always awkward. Half the women of his time, to speak liberally, had flung themselves at his head, and out of this pernicious fashion many complications, some of them grave, had not failed to arise. He was not a woman's poet, as I had said to Mrs Prest, in the modern phase of his reputation; but the situation had been different when the man's own voice was mingled with his song. That voice, by every testimony, was one of the sweetest ever heard. "Orpheus and the Mænads!" was the exclamation that rose to my lips when I first turned over his correspondence. Almost all the Mænads were unreasonable and many of them insupportable; it struck me in short that he was kinder, more considerate than, in his place (if I could imagine myself in such a place!) I should have been.

It was certainly strange beyond all strangeness, and I shall not take up space with attempting to explain it, that whereas in all these other lines of research we had to deal with phantoms and dust, the mere echoes of echoes, the one living

source of information that had lingered on into our time had
been unheeded by us. Every one of Aspern's contemporaries
had, according to our belief, passed away; we had not been
able to look into a single pair of eyes into which his had looked
or to feel a transmitted contact in any aged hand that his had
touched. Most dead of all did poor Miss Bordereau appear,
and yet she alone had survived. We exhausted in the course of
months our wonder that we had not found her out sooner,
and the substance of our explanation was that she had kept so
quiet. The poor lady on the whole had had reason for doing
so. But it was a revelation to us that it was possible to keep so
quiet as that in the latter half of the nineteenth century—the
age of newspapers and telegrams and photographs and inter-
viewers. And she had taken no great trouble about it either:
she had not hidden herself away in an undiscoverable hole; she
had boldly settled down in a city of exhibition. The only
secret of her safety that we could perceive was that Venice
contained so many curiosities that were greater than she. And
then accident had somehow favoured her, as was shown for
example in the fact that Mrs Prest had never happened to
mention her to me, thought I had spent three weeks in Venice
—under her nose, as it were—five years before. Mrs Prest had
not mentioned this much to any one; she appeared almost to
have forgotten she was there. Of course she had not the
responsibilities of an editor. It was no explanation of the old
woman's having eluded us to say that she lived abroad, for our
researches had again and again taken us (not only by correspondence but by personal inquiry) to France, to Germany, to
Italy, in which countries, not counting his important stay in
England, so many of the too few years of Aspern's career
were spent. We were glad to think at least that in all our pub-
lishings (some people consider I believe that we have overdone them), we had only touched in passing and in the most
discreet manner on Miss Bordereau's connection. Oddly
enough, even if we had had the material (and we often

wondered what had become of it), it would have been the most difficult episode to handle.

The gondola stopped, the old palace was there; it was a house of the class which in Venice carries even in extreme dilapidation the dignified name. "How charming! It's gray and pink!" my companion exclaimed; and that is the most comprehensive description of it. It was not particularly old, only two or three centuries; and it had an air not so much of decay as of quiet discouragement, as if it had rather missed its career. But its wide front, with a stone balcony from end to end of the *piano nobile* or most important floor, was architectural enough, with the aid of various pilasters and arches; and the stucco with which in the intervals it had long ago been endued was rosy in the April afternoon. It overlooked a clean, melancholy, unfrequented canal, which had a narrow *riva* or convenient footway on either side. "I don't know why—there are no brick gables," said Mrs Prest, "but this corner has seemed to me before more Dutch than Italian, more like Amsterdam than like Venice. It's perversely clean, for reasons of its own; and though you can pass on foot scarcely any one ever thinks of doing so. It has the air of a Protestant Sunday. Perhaps the people are afraid of the Misses Bordereau. I daresay they have the reputation of witches."

I forget what answer I made to this—I was given up to two other reflections. The first of these was that if the old lady lived in such a big, imposing house she could not be in any sort of misery and therefore would not be tempted by a chance to let a couple of rooms. I expressed this idea to Mrs Prest, who gave me a very logical reply. "If she didn't live in a big house how could it be a question of her having rooms to spare? If she were not amply lodged herself you would lack ground to approach her. Besides, a big house here, and especially in this *quartier perdu*, proves nothing at all: it is perfectly compatible with a state of penury. Dilapidated old palazzi, if you will go out of the way for them, are to be had for five shillings a year. And as for the people who live in them—no, until you have explored Venice socially as much as I have you can form no idea of their domestic desolation. They live on nothing, for they have nothing to live on." The other idea that had come into my head was connected with a high blank wall which appeared to confine an expanse of ground on one side of the house. Blank I call it, but it was figured over with the patches that please a painter, repaired breaches, crumblings of plaster, extrusions of brick that had turned pink with time; and a few thin trees, with the poles of certain rickety trellises, were visible over the top. The place was a garden and apparently it belonged to the house. It suddenly occurred to me that if it did belong to the house I had my pretext.

I sat looking out on all this with Mrs Prest (it was covered with the golden glow of Venice) from the shade of our *felze*, and she asked me if I would go in then, while she waited for me, or come back another time. At first I could not decide—it was doubtless very weak of me. I wanted still to think I *might* get a footing, and I was afraid to meet failure, for it would leave me, as I remarked to my companion, without another arrow for my bow. "Why not another?" she inquired, as I sat there hesitating and thinking it over; and she wished to know why even now and before taking the trouble of becoming an inmate (which might be wretchedly uncomfortable after all, even if it succeeded), I had not the resource of simply offering them a sum of money down. In that way I might obtain the documents without bad nights.

"Dearest lady," I exclaimed, "excuse the impatience of my tone when I suggest that you must have forgotten the very fact (surely I communicated it to you) which pushed me to throw myself upon your ingenuity. The old woman won't have the documents spoken of; they are personal, delicate, intimate, and she hasn't modern notions, God bless her! If I should sound that note first I should certainly spoil the game.

I can arrive at the papers only by putting her off her guard, and I can put her off her guard only by ingratiating diplomatic practices. Hypocrisy, duplicity are my only chance. I am sorry for it, but for Jeffrey Aspern's sake I would do worse still. First I must take tea with her; then tackle the main job." And I told over what had happened to John Cumnor when he wrote to her. No notice whatever had been taken of his first letter, and the second had been answered very sharply, in six lines, by the niece. "Miss Bordereau requested her to say that she could not imagine what he meant by troubling them. They had none of Mr Aspern's papers, and if they had should never think of showing them to any one on any account whatever. She didn't know what he was talking about and begged he would let her alone." I certainly did not want to be met that way.

"Well," said Mrs Prest, after a moment, provokingly, "perhaps after all they haven't any of his things. If they deny it flat how are you sure?"

"John Cumnor is sure, and it would take me long to tell you how his conviction, or his very strong presumption—strong enough to stand against the old lady's not unnatural fib—has built itself up. Besides, he makes much of the internal evidence of the niece's letter."

"The internal evidence?"

"Her calling him 'Mr Aspern.'"

"I don't see what that proves."

"It proves familiarity, and familiarity implies the possession of mementoes, of relics. I can't tell you how that 'Mr' touches me—how it bridges over the gulf of time and brings our hero near to me—nor what an edge it gives to my desire to see Juliana. You don't say 'Mr' Shakespeare."

"Would I, any more, if I had a box full of his letters?"

"Yes, if he had been your lover and some one wanted them!" And I added that John Cumnor was so convinced, and so all the more convinced by Miss Bordereau's tone, that he would have come himself to Venice on the business were it not that for him there was the obstacle that it would be difficult to disprove his identity with the person who had written to them, which the old ladies would be sure to suspect in spite of dissimulation and a change of name. If they were to ask him point-blank if he were not their correspondent it would be too awkward for him to lie; whereas I was fortunately not tied in that way. I was a fresh hand and could say no without lying.

"But you will have to change your name," said Mrs Prest. "Juliana lives out of the world as much as it is possible to live, but none the less she has probably heard of Mr Aspern's editors; she perhaps possesses what you have published."

"I have thought of that," I returned; and I drew out of my pocket-book a visiting-card, neatly engraved with a name that was not my own.

"You are very extravagant; you might have written it," said my companion.

"This looks more genuine."

"Certainly, you are prepared to go far! But it will be awkward about your letters; they won't come to you in that mask."

"My banker will take them in and I will go every day to fetch them. It will give me a little walk."

"Shall you only depend upon that?" asked Mrs Prest. "Aren't you coming to see me?"

"Oh, you will have left Venice, for the hot months, long before there are any results. I am prepared to roast all summer —as well as hereafter, perhaps you'll say! Meanwhile, John Cumnor will bombard me with letters addressed, in my feigned name, to the care of the *padrona*."

"She will recognise his hand," my companion suggested.

"On the envelope he can disguise it."

"Well, you're a precious pair! Doesn't it occur to you that

even if you are able to say you are not Mr Cumnor in person they may still suspect you of being his emissary?"

"Certainly, and I see only one way to parry that."

"And what may that be?"

I hesitated a moment. "To make love to the niece."

"Ah," cried Mrs Prest, "wait till you see her!"

II

"I MUST work the garden—I must work the garden," I said to myself, five minutes later, as I waited, upstairs, in the long, dusky sala, where the bare scagliola floor gleamed vaguely in a chink of the closed shutters. The place was impressive but it looked cold and cautious. Mrs Prest had floated away, giving me a rendezvous at the end of half an hour by some neighbouring watersteps; and I had been let into the house, after pulling the rusty bell-wire, by a little red-headed, white-faced maid-servant, who was very young and not ugly and wore clicking pattens and a shawl in the fashion of a hood. She had not contented herself with opening the door from above by the usual arrangement of a creaking pulley, though she had looked down at me first from an upper window, dropping the inevitable challenge which in Italy precedes the hospitable act. As a general thing I was irritated by this survival of mediæval manners, though as I liked the old I suppose I ought to have liked it; but I was so determined to be genial that I took my false card out of my pocket and held it up to her, smiling as if it were a magic token. It had the effect of one indeed, for it brought her, as I say, all the way down. I begged her to hand it to her mistress, having first written on it in Italian the words, "Could you very kindly see a gentleman, an American, for a moment?" The little maid was not hostile, and I reflected that even that was perhaps something gained.

She coloured, she smiled and looked both frightened and pleased. I could see that my arrival was a great affair, that visits were rare in that house, and that she was a person who would have liked a sociable place. When she pushed forward the heavy door behind me I felt that I had a foot in the citadel. She pattered across the damp, stony lower hall and I followed her up the high staircase—stonier still, as it seemed—without an invitation. I think she had meant I should wait for her below, but such was not my idea, and I took up my station in the sala. She flitted, at the far end of it, into impenetrable regions, and I looked at the place with my heart beating as I had known it to do in the dentist's parlour. It was gloomy and stately, but it owed its character almost entirely to its noble shape and to the fine architectural doors—as high as the doors of houses—which, leading into the various rooms, repeated themselves on either side at intervals. They were surmounted with old faded painted escutcheons, and here and there, in the spaces between them, brown pictures, which I perceived to be bad, in battered frames, were suspended. With the exception of several straw-bottomed chairs with their backs to the wall, the grand obscure vista contained nothing else to minister to effect. It was evidently never used save as a passage, and little even as that. I may add that by the time the door opened again through which the maid-servant had escaped, my eyes had grown used to the want of light.

I had not meant by my private ejaculation that I must myself cultivate the soil of the tangled enclosure which lay beneath the windows, but the lady who came toward me from the distance over the hard, shining floor might have supposed as much from the way in which, as I went rapidly to meet her, I exclaimed, taking care to speak Italian: "The garden, the garden—do me the pleasure to tell me if it's yours!"

She stopped short, looking at me with wonder; and then, "Nothing here is mine," she answered in English, coldly and sadly.

"Oh, you are English; how delightful!" I remarked, ingenuously. "But surely the garden belongs to the house?"

"Yes, but the house doesn't belong to me." She was a long, lean, pale person, habited apparently in a dull-coloured dressing-gown, and she spoke with a kind of mild literalness. She did not ask me to sit down, any more than years before (if she were the niece) she had asked Mrs Prest, and we stood face to face in the empty pompous hall.

"Well then, would you kindly tell me to whom I must address myself? I'm afraid you'll think me odiously intrusive, but you know I *must* have a garden—upon my honour I must!"

Her face was not young, but it was simple; it was not fresh, but it was mild. She had large eyes which were not bright, and a great deal of hair which was not "dressed," and long fine hands which were—possibly—not clean. She clasped these members almost convulsively as, with a confused, alarmed look, she broke out, "Oh, don't take it away from us; we like it ourselves!"

"You have the use of it then?"

"Oh yes. If it wasn't for that!" And she gave a shy, melancholy smile.

"Isn't it a luxury, precisely? That's why, intending to be in Venice some weeks, possibly all summer, and having some literary work, some reading and writing to do, so that I must be quiet, and yet if possible a great deal in the open air—that's why I have felt that a garden is really indispensable. I appeal to your own experience," I went on, smiling. "Now can't I look at yours?"

"I don't know; I don't understand," the poor woman murmured, planted there and letting her embarrassed eyes wander all over my strangeness.

"I mean only from one of those windows—such grand ones as you have here—if you will let me open the shutters." And I walked toward the back of the house. When I had advanced half-way I stopped and waited, as if I took it for granted she would accompany me. I had been of necessity very abrupt, but I strove at the same time to give her the impression of extreme courtesy. "I have been looking at furnished rooms all over the place, and it seems impossible to find any with a garden attached. Naturally in a place like Venice gardens are rare. It's absurd if you like, for a man, but I can't live without flowers."

"There are none to speak of down there." She came nearer to me, as if, though she mistrusted me, I had drawn her by an invisible thread. I went on again, and she continued as she followed me: "We have a few, but they are very common. It costs too much to cultivate them; one has to have a man."

"Why shouldn't I be the man?" I asked. "I'll work without wages; or rather I'll put in a gardener. You shall have the sweetest flowers in Venice."

She protested at this, with a queer little sigh which might also have been a gush of rapture at the picture I presented. Then she observed, "We don't know you—we don't know you."

"You know me as much as I know you; that is much more, because you know my name. And if you are English I am almost a countryman."

"We are not English," said my companion, watching me helplessly while I threw open the shutters of one of the divisions of the wide high window.

"You speak the language so beautifully: might I ask what you are?" Seen from above the garden was certainly shabby; but I perceived at a glance that it had great capabilities. She made no rejoinder, she was so lost in staring at me, and I exclaimed, "You don't mean to say you are also by chance American?"

"I don't know; we used to be."

"Used to be? Surely you haven't changed?"

"It's so many years ago—we are nothing."

"So many years that you have been living here? Well, I don't wonder at that; it's a grand old house. I suppose you all use the garden," I went on, "but I assure you I shouldn't be in your way. I would be very quiet and stay in one corner."

"We all use it?" she repeated after me, vaguely, not coming close to the window but looking at my shoes. She appeared to think me capable of throwing her out.

"I mean all your family, as many as you are."

"There is only one other; she is very old—she never goes down."

"Only one other, in all this great house!" I feigned to be not only amazed but almost scandalised. "Dear lady, you must have space then to spare!"

"To spare?" she repeated, in the same dazed way.

"Why, you surely don't live (two quiet women—I see *you* are quiet, at any rate) in fifty rooms!" Then with a burst of hope and cheer I demanded: "Couldn't you let me two or three? That would set me up!"

I had now struck the note that translated my purpose and I need not reproduce the whole of the tune I played. I ended by making my interlocutress believe that I was an honourable person, though of course I did not even attempt to persuade her that I was not an eccentric one. I repeated that I had studies to pursue; that I wanted quiet; that I delighted in a garden and had vainly sought one up and down the city; that I would undertake that before another month was over the dear old house should be smothered in flowers. I think it was the flowers that won my suit, for I afterwards found that Miss Tita (for such the name of this high tremulous spinster proved somewhat incongruously to be) had an insatiable appetite for them. When I speak of my suit as won I mean that before I left her she had promised that she would refer the question to her aunt. I inquired who her aunt might be and she answered, "Why, Miss Bordereau!" with an air of surprise, as if I might have been expected to know. There were contradictions like this in Tita Bordereau which, as I observed later, contributed to make her an odd and affecting person. It was the study of the two ladies to live so that the world should not touch them, and yet they had never altogether accepted the idea that it never heard of them. In Tita at any rate a grateful susceptibility to human contact had not died out, and contact of a limited order there would be if I should come to live in the house.

"We have never done anything of the sort; we have never had a lodger or any kind of inmate." So much as this she made a point of saying to me. "We are very poor, we live very badly. The rooms are very bare—that you might take; they have nothing in them. I don't know how you would sleep, how you would eat."

"With your permission, I could easily put in a bed and a few tables and chairs. *C'est la moindre des choses* and the affair of an hour or two. I know a little man from whom I can hire what I should want for a few months, for a trifle, and my gondolier can bring the things round in his boat. Of course in this great house you must have a second kitchen, and my servant, who is a wonderfully handy fellow" (this personage was an evocation of the moment), "can easily cook me a chop there. My tastes and habits are of the simplest; I live on flowers!" And then I ventured to add that if they were very poor it was all the more reason they should let their rooms. They were bad economists—I had never heard of such a waste of material.

I saw in a moment that the good lady had never before been spoken to in that way, with a kind of humorous firmness which did not exclude sympathy but was on the contrary founded on it. She might easily have told me that my sympathy was impertinent, but this by good fortune did not occur to her. I left her with the understanding that she would consider the matter with her aunt and that I might come back the next day for their decision.

"The aunt will refuse; she will think the whole proceeding

very *louche!*" Mrs Prest declared shortly after this, when I had resumed my place in her gondola. She had put the idea into my head and now (so little are women to be counted on) she appeared to take a despondent view of it. Her pessimism provoked me and I pretended to have the best hopes; I went so far as to say that I had a distinct presentiment that I should succeed. Upon this Mrs Prest broke out, "Oh, I see what's in your head! You fancy you have made such an impression in a quarter of an hour that she is dying for you to come and can be depended upon to bring the old one round. If you do get in you'll count it as a triumph."

I did count it as a triumph, but only for the editor (in the last analysis), not for the man, who had not the tradition of personal conquest. When I went back on the morrow the little maid-servant conducted me straight through the long sala (it opened there as before in perfect perspective and was lighter now, which I thought a good omen) into the apartment from which the recipient of my former visit had emerged on that occasion. It was a large shabby parlour, with a fine old painted ceiling and a strange figure sitting alone at one of the windows. They come back to me now almost with the palpitation they caused, the successive feelings that accompanied my consciousness that as the door of the room closed behind me I was really face to face with the Juliana of some of Aspern's most exquisite and most renowned lyrics. I grew used to her afterwards, though never completely; but as she sat there before me my heart beat as fast as if the miracle of resurrection had taken place for my benefit. Her presence seemed somehow to contain his, and I felt nearer to him at that first moment of seeing her than I ever had been before or ever have been since. Yes, I remember my emotions in their order, even including a curious little tremor that took me when I saw that the niece was not there. With her, the day before, I had become sufficiently familiar, but it almost exceeded my courage (much as I had longed for the event) to be left alone with such a terrible relic as the aunt. She was too strange, too literally resurgent. Then came a check, with the perception that we were not really face to face, inasmuch as she had over her eyes a horrible green shade which, for her, served almost as a mask. I believed for the instant that she had put it on expressly, so that from underneath it she might scrutinise me without being scrutinised herself. At the same time it increased the presumption that there was a ghastly death's-head lurking behind it. The divine Juliana as a grinning skull —the vision hung there until it passed. Then it came to me that she *was* tremendously old—so old that death might take her at any moment, before I had time to get what I wanted from her. The next thought was a correction to that; it lighted up the situation. She would die next week, she would die to-morrow—then I could seize her papers. Meanwhile she sat there neither moving nor speaking. She was very small and shrunken, bent forward, with her hands in her lap. She was dressed in black and her head was wrapped in a piece of old black lace which showed no hair.

My emotion keeping me silent she spoke first, and the remark she made was exactly the most unexpected.

III

"Our house is very far from the centre, but the little canal is very *comme il faut.*"

"It's the sweetest corner of Venice and I can imagine nothing more charming," I hastened to reply. The old lady's voice was very thin and weak, but it had an agreeable, cultivated murmur and there was wonder in the thought that that individual note had been in Jeffrey Aspern's ear.

"Please to sit down there. I hear very well," she said quietly, as if perhaps I had been shouting at her; and the chair she pointed to was at a certain distance. I took possession of it, telling her that I was perfectly aware that I had intruded, that I had not been properly introduced and could only throw myself upon her indulgence. Perhaps the other lady, the one I had had the honour of seeing the day before, would have explained to her about the garden. That was literally what had given me courage to take a step so unconventional. I had fallen in love at sight with the whole place (she herself probably was so used to it that she did not know the impression it was capable of making on a stranger), and I had felt it was really a case to risk something. Was her own kindness in receiving me a sign that I was not wholly out in my calculation? It would render me extremely happy to think so. I could give her my word of honour that I was a most respectable, inoffensive person and that as an inmate they would be barely conscious of my existence. I would conform to any regulations, any restrictions if they would only let me enjoy the garden. Moreover I should be delighted to give her references, guarantees; they would be of the very best, both in Venice and in England as well as in America.

She listened to me in perfect stillness and I felt that she was looking at me with great attention, though I could see only the lower part of her bleached and shrivelled face. Independently of the refining process of old age it had a delicacy which once must have been great. She had been very fair, she had had a wonderful complexion. She was silent a little after I had ceased speaking; then she inquired, "If you are so fond of a garden why don't you go to *terra firma*, where there are so many far better than this?"

"Oh, it's the combination!" I answered, smiling; and then, with rather a flight of fancy, "It's the idea of a garden in the middle of the sea."

"It's not in the middle of the sea; you can't see the water."

I stared a moment, wondering whether she wished to

convict me of fraud. "Can't see the water? Why, dear madam, I can come up to the very gate in my boat."

She appeared inconsequent, for she said vaguely in reply to this, "Yes, if you have got a boat. I haven't any; it's many years since I have been in one of the gondolas." She uttered these words as if the gondolas were a curious far-away craft which she knew only by hearsay.

"Let me assure you of the pleasure with which I would put mine at your service!" I exclaimed. I had scarcely said this however before I became aware that the speech was in questionable taste and might also do me the injury of making me appear too eager, too possessed of a hidden motive. But the old woman remained impenetrable and her attitude bothered me by suggesting that she had a fuller vision of me than I had of her. She gave me no thanks for my somewhat extravagant offer but remarked that the lady I had seen the day before was her niece; she would presently come in. She had asked her to stay away a little on purpose, because she herself wished to see me at first alone. She relapsed into silence and I asked myself why she had judged this necessary and what was coming yet; also whether I might venture on some judicious remark in praise of her companion. I went so far as to say that I should be delighted to see her again: she had been so very courteous to me, considering how odd she must have thought me—a declaration which drew from Miss Bordereau another of her whimsical speeches.

"She has very good manners; I bred her up myself!" I was on the point of saying that that accounted for the easy grace of the niece, but I arrested myself in time, and the next moment the old woman went on: "I don't care who you may be—I don't want to know; it signifies very little to-day." This had all the air of being a formula of dismissal, as if her next words would be that I might take myself off now that she had had the amusement of looking on the face of such a monster of indiscretion. Therefore I was all the more surprised when she

added, with her soft, venerable quaver, "You may have as
many rooms as you like—if you will pay a good deal of
money."

I hesitated but for a single instant, long enough to ask
myself what she meant in particular by this condition. First it
struck me that she must have really a large sum in her mind;
then I reasoned quickly that her idea of a large sum would
probably not correspond to my own. My deliberation, I think,
was not so visible as to diminish the promptitude with which I
replied, "I will pay with pleasure and of course in advance
whatever you may think it proper to ask me."

"Well then, a thousand francs a month," she rejoined
instantly, while her baffling green shade continued to cover
her attitude.

The figure, as they say, was startling and my logic had been
at fault. The sum she had mentioned was, by the Venetian
measure of such matters, exceedingly large; there was many an
old palace in an out-of-the-way corner that I might on such
terms have enjoyed by the year. But so far as my small means
allowed I was prepared to spend money, and my decision was
quickly taken. I would pay her with a smiling face what she
asked, but in that case I would give myself the compensation
of extracting the papers from her for nothing. Moreover if she
had asked five times as much I should have risen to the occasion; so odious would it have appeared to me to stand chaffer-
ing with Aspern's Juliana. It was queer enough to have a
question of money with her at all. I assured her that her views
perfectly met my own and that on the morrow I should have
the pleasure of putting three months' rent into her hand. She
received this announcement with serenity and with no apparent sense that after all it would be becoming of her to say that
I ought to see the rooms first. This did not occur to her and
indeed her serenity was mainly what I wanted. Our little
bargain was just concluded when the door opened and the
younger lady appeared on the threshold. As soon as Miss

Bordereau saw her niece she cried out almost gaily, "He will give three thousand—three thousand to-morrow!"

Miss Tita stood still, with her patient eyes turning from one of us to the other; then she inquired, scarcely above her breath, "Do you mean francs?"

"Did you mean francs or dollars?" the old woman asked of me at this.

"I think francs were what you said," I answered, smiling.

"That is very good," said Miss Tita, as if she had become conscious that her own question might have looked over-reaching.

"What do *you* know? You are ignorant," Miss Bordereau remarked; not with acerbity but with a strange, soft coldness.

"Yes, of money—certainly of money!" Miss Tita hastened to exclaim.

"I am sure you have your own branches of knowledge," I took the liberty of saying, genially. There was something painful to me, somehow, in the turn the conversation had taken, in the discussion of the rent.

"She had a very good education when she was young. I looked into that myself," said Miss Bordereau. Then she added, "But she has learned nothing since."

"I have always been with you," Miss Tita rejoined very mildly, and evidently with no intention of making an epigram.

"Yes, but for that!" her aunt declared, with more satirical force. She evidently meant that but for this her niece would never have got on at all; the point of the observation however being lost on Miss Tita, though she blushed at hearing her history revealed to a stranger. Miss Bordereau went on, addressing herself to me: "And what time will you come to-morrow with the money?"

"The sooner the better. If it suits you I will come at noon."

"I am always here but I have my hours," said the old woman, as if her convenience were not to be taken for granted.

"You mean the times when you receive?"

"I never receive. But I will see you at noon, when you come with the money."

"Very good, I shall be punctual;" and I added, "May I shake hands with you, on our contract?" I thought there ought to be some little form, it would make me really feel easier, for I foresaw that there would be no other. Besides, though Miss Bordereau could not to-day be called personally attractive and there was something even in her wasted antiquity that bade one stand at one's distance, I felt an irresistible desire to hold in my own for a moment the hand that Jeffrey Aspern had pressed.

For a minute she made no answer and I saw that my proposal failed to meet with her approbation. She indulged in no movement of withdrawal, which I half expected; she only said coldly, "I belong to a time when that was not the custom."

I felt rather snubbed but I exclaimed good-humouredly to Miss Tita, "Oh, you will do as well!" I shook hands with her while she replied, with a small flutter, "Yes, yes, to show it's all arranged!"

"Shall you bring the money in gold?" Miss Bordereau demanded, as I was turning to the door.

I looked at her a moment. "Aren't you a little afraid, after all, of keeping such a sum as that in the house?" It was not that I was annoyed at her avidity but I was really struck with the disparity between such a treasure and such scanty means of guarding it.

"Whom should I be afraid of if I am not afraid of you?" she asked with her shrunken grimness.

"Ah well," said I, laughing, "I shall be in point of fact a protector and I will bring gold if you prefer."

"Thank you," the old woman returned with dignity and with an inclination of her head which evidently signified that I might depart. I passed out of the room, reflecting that it would not be easy to circumvent her. As I stood in the sala again I saw that Miss Tita had followed me and I supposed that as her aunt had neglected to suggest that I should take a look at my quarters it was her purpose to repair the omission. But she made no such suggestion; she only stood there with a dim, though not a languid smile, and with an effect of irresponsible, incompetent youth which was almost comically at variance with the faded facts of her person. She was not infirm, like her aunt, but she struck me as still more helpless, because her inefficiency was spiritual, which was not the case with Miss Bordereau's. I waited to see if she would offer to show me the rest of the house, but I did not precipitate the question, inasmuch as my plan was from this moment to spend as much of my time as possible in her society. I only observed at the end of a minute:

"I have had better fortune than I hoped. It was very kind of her to see me. Perhaps you said a good word for me."

"It was the idea of the money," said Miss Tita.

"And did you suggest that?"

"I told her that you would perhaps give a good deal."

"What made you think that?"

"I told her I thought you were rich."

"And what put that idea into your head?"

"I don't know; the way you talked."

"Dear me, I must talk differently now," I declared. "I'm sorry to say it's not the case."

"Well," said Miss Tita, "I think that in Venice the *forestieri*, in general, often give a great deal for something that after all isn't much." She appeared to make this remark with a comforting intention, to wish to remind me that if I had been extravagant I was not really foolishly singular. We walked together along the sala, and as I took its magnificent measure I said to her that I was afraid it would not form a part of my *quartiere*. Were my rooms by chance to be among those that opened into it? "Not if you go above, on the second floor," she answered with a little startled air, as if she had rather taken for granted I would know my proper place.

"And I infer that that's where your aunt would like me to be."

"She said your apartments ought to be very distinct."

"That certainly would be best." And I listened with respect while she told me that up above I was free to take whatever I liked; that there was another staircase, but only from the floor on which we stood, and that to pass from it to the garden-story or to come up to my lodging I should have in effect to cross the great hall. This was an immense point gained; I foresaw that it would constitute my whole leverage in my relations with the two ladies. When I asked Miss Tita how I was to manage at present to find my way up she replied with an access of that sociable shyness which constantly marked her manner.

"Perhaps you can't. I don't see—unless I should go with you." She evidently had not thought of this before.

We ascended to the upper floor and visited a long succession of empty rooms. The best of them looked over the garden; some of the others had a view of the blue lagoon, above the opposite rough-tiled housetops. They were all dusty and even a little disfigured with long neglect, but I saw that by spending a few hundred francs I should be able to convert three or four of them into a convenient habitation. My experiment was turning out costly, yet now that I had all but taken possession I ceased to allow this to trouble me. I mentioned to my companion a few of the things that I should put in, but she replied rather more precipitately than usual that I might do exactly what I liked; she seemed to wish to notify me that the Misses Bordereau would take no overt interest in my proceedings. I guessed that her aunt had instructed her to adopt this tone, and I may as well say now that I came afterwards to distinguish perfectly (as I believed) between the speeches she made on her own responsibility and those the old lady imposed upon her. She took no notice of the unswept condition of the rooms and indulged in no explanations nor apologies. I said to myself that this was a sign that Juliana and her niece (disenchanting idea!) were untidy persons, with a low Italian standard; but I afterwards recognised that a lodger who had forced an entrance had no *locus standi* as a critic. We looked out of a good many windows, for there was nothing within the rooms to look at, and still I wanted to linger. I asked her what several different objects in the prospect might be, but in no case did she appear to know. She was evidently not familiar with the view—it was as if she had not looked at it for years—and I presently saw that she was too preoccupied with something else to pretend to care for it. Suddenly she said—the remark was not suggested:

"I don't know whether it will make any difference to you, but the money is for me."

"The money?"

"The money you are going to bring."

"Why, you'll make me wish to stay here two or three years." I spoke as benevolently as possible, though it had begun to act on my nerves that with these women so associated with Aspern the pecuniary question should constantly come back.

"That would be very good for me," she replied, smiling.

"You put me on my honour!"

She looked as if she failed to understand this, but went on: "She wants me to have more. She thinks she is going to die."

"Ah, not soon, I hope!" I exclaimed, with genuine feeling. I had perfectly considered the possibility that she would destroy her papers on the day she should feel her end really approach. I believed that she would cling to them till then and I think I had an idea that she read Aspern's letters over every night or at least pressed them to her withered lips. I would have given a good deal to have a glimpse of the latter spectacle. I asked Miss Tita if the old lady were seriously ill and she replied that she was only very tired—she had lived so very, very long. That was what she said herself—she wanted to die for a change. Besides, all her friends were dead long ago; either they ought to have remained or she ought to have gone. That was another thing her aunt often said—she was not at all content.

"But people don't die when they like, do they?" Miss Tita inquired. I took the liberty of asking why, if there was actually enough money to maintain both of them, there would not be more than enough in case of her being left alone. She considered this difficult problem a moment and then she said, "Oh, well, you know, she takes care of me. She thinks that when I'm alone I shall be a great fool, I shall not know how to manage."

"I should have supposed rather that you took care of her. I'm afraid she is very proud."

"Why, have you discovered that already?" Miss Tita cried, with the glimmer of an illumination in her face.

"I was shut up with her there for a considerable time, and she struck me, she interested me extremely. It didn't take me long to make my discovery. She won't have much to say to me while I'm here."

"No, I don't think she will," my companion averred.

"Do you suppose she has some suspicion of me?"

Miss Tita's honest eyes gave me no sign that I had touched a mark. "I shouldn't think so—letting you in after all so easily."

"Oh, so easily! she has covered her risk. But where is it that one could take an advantage of her?"

"I oughtn't to tell you if I knew, ought I?" And Miss Tita added, before I had time to reply to this, smiling dolefully, "Do you think we have any weak points?"

"That's exactly what I'm asking. You would only have to mention them for me to respect them religiously."

She looked at me, at this, with that air of timid but candid and even gratified curiosity with which she had confronted me from the first; and then she said, "There is nothing to tell. We are terribly quiet. I don't know how the days pass. We have no life."

"I wish I might think that I should bring you a little."

"Oh, we know what we want," she went on. "It's all right."

There were various things I desired to ask her: how in the world they did live; whether they had any friends or visitors, any relations in America or in other countries. But I judged such an inquiry would be premature; I must leave it to a later chance. "Well, don't *you* be proud," I contented myself with saying. "Don't hide from me altogether."

"Oh, I must stay with my aunt," she returned, without looking at me. And at the same moment, abruptly, without any ceremony of parting, she quitted me and disappeared, leaving me to make my own way downstairs. I remained a while longer, wandering about the bright desert (the sun was pouring in) of the old house, thinking the situation over on the spot. Not even the pattering little *serva* came to look after me and I reflected that after all this treatment showed confidence.

IV

PERHAPS it did, but all the same, six weeks later, towards the middle of June, the moment when Mrs Prest undertook her annual migration, I had made no measureable advance. I was obliged to confess to her that I had no results to speak of. My first step had been unexpectedly rapid, but there was no appearance that it would be followed by a second. I was a thousand miles from taking tea with my hostesses—that privilege of which, as I reminded Mrs Prest, we both had had a vision. She reproached me with wanting boldness and I answered that even to be bold you must have an opportunity: you may push on through a breach but you can't batter down a dead wall. She answered that the breach I had already made was big enough to admit an army and accused me of wasting precious hours in whimpering in her salon when I ought to have been carrying on the struggle in the field. It is true that I went to see her very often, on the theory that it would console me (I freely expressed my discouragement) for my want of success on my own premises. But I began to perceive that it did not console me to be perpetually chaffed for my scruples, especially when I was really so vigilant; and I was rather glad when my derisive friend closed her house for the summer. She had expected to gather amusement from the drama of my intercourse with the Misses Bordereau and she was disappointed that the intercourse, and consequently the drama, had not come off. "They'll lead you on to your ruin," she said before she left Venice. "They'll get all your money without showing you a scrap." I think I settled down to my business with more concentration after she had gone away.

It was a fact that up to that time I had not, save on a single brief occasion, had even a moment's contact with my queer hostesses. The exception had occurred when I carried them according to my promise the terrible three thousand francs. Then I found Miss Tita waiting for me in the hall, and she took the money from my hand so that I did not see her aunt. The old lady had promised to receive me, but she apparently thought nothing of breaking that vow. The money was contained in a bag of chamois leather, of respectable dimensions, which my banker had given me, and Miss Tita had to make a big fist to receive it. This she did with extreme solemnity, though I tried to treat the affair a little as a joke. It was in no jocular strain, yet it was with simplicity, that she inquired, weighing the money in her two palms: "Don't you think it's too much?" To which I replied that that would depend upon the amount of pleasure I should get for it. Hereupon she turned away from me quickly, as she had done the day before, murmuring in a tone different from any she had used hitherto: "Oh, pleasure, pleasure—there's no pleasure in this house!"

After this, for a long time, I never saw her, and I wondered that the common chances of the day should not have helped us to meet. It could only be evident that she was immensely on her guard against them; and in addition to this the house was so big that for each other we were lost in it. I used to look out for her hopefully as I crossed the sala in my comings and goings, but I was not rewarded with a glimpse of the tail of her dress. It was as if she never peeped out of her aunt's apartment. I used to wonder what she did there week after week and year after year. I had never encountered such a violent *parti pris* of seclusion; it was more than keeping quiet—it was like hunted creatures feigning death. The two ladies appeared to have no visitors whatever and no sort of contact with the world. I judged at least that people could not have come to the house and that Miss Tita could not have gone out without my having some observation of it. I did what I disliked myself for doing (reflecting that it was only once in a way): I questioned my servant about their habits and let him divine that I should be interested in any information he could pick up. But he picked up amazingly little for a knowing Venetian: it must be added that where there is a perpetual fast there are very few crumbs on the floor. His cleverness in other ways was sufficient if it was not quite all that I had attributed to him on the occasion of my first interview with Miss Tita. He had helped my gondolier to bring me round a boat-load of furniture; and when these articles had been carried to the top of the palace and distributed according to our associated wisdom he organised my household with such promptitude as was consistent with the fact that it was composed exclusively of himself. He made me in short as comfortable as I could be with my indifferent prospects. I should have been glad if he had fallen

in love with Miss Bordereau's maid or, failing this, had taken
her in aversion; either event might have brought about some
kind of catastrophe and a catastrophe might have led to some
parley. It was my idea that she would have been sociable, and
I myself on various occasions saw her flit to and fro on
domestic errands, so that I was sure she was accessible. But
I tasted of no gossip from that fountain, and I afterwards
learned that Pasquale's affections were fixed upon an object
that made him heedless of other women. This was a young
lady with a powdered face, a yellow cotton gown and much
leisure, who used often to come to see him. She practised, at
her convenience, the art of a stringer of beads (these ornaments are made in Venice, in profusion; she had her pocket
full of them and I used to find them on the floor of my apartment), and kept an eye on the maiden in the house. It was not
for me of course to make the domestics tattle, and I never said
a word to Miss Bordereau's cook.

It seemed to me a proof of the old lady's determination to
have nothing to do with me that she should never have sent
me a receipt for my three months' rent. For some days I
looked out for it and then, when I had given it up, I wasted a
good deal of time in wondering what her reason had been for
neglecting so indispensable and familiar a form. At first I was
tempted to send her a reminder, after which I relinquished the
idea (against my judgment as to what was right in the particular case), on the general ground of wishing to keep quiet. If
Miss Bordereau suspected me of ulterior aims, she would
suspect me less if I should be businesslike, and yet I consented
not to be so. It was possible she intended her omission as an
impertinence, a visible irony, to show how she could overreach people who attempted to overreach her. On that hypothesis it was well to let her see that one did not notice her little
tricks. The real reading of the matter, I afterwards perceived,
was simply the poor old woman's desire to emphasise the fact
that I was in the enjoyment of a favour as rigidly limited as it

had been liberally bestowed. She had given me part of her house and now she would not give me even a morsel of paper with her name on it. Let me say that even at first this did not make me too miserable, for the whole episode was essentially delightful to me. I foresaw that I should have a summer after my own literary heart, and the sense of holding my opportunity was much greater than the sense of losing it. There could be no Venetian business without patience, and since I adored the place I was much more in the spirit of it for having laid in a large provision. That spirit kept me perpetual company and seemed to look out at me from the revived immortal face—in which all his genius shone—of the great poet who was my prompter. I had invoked him and he had come; he hovered before me half the time; it was as if his bright ghost had returned to earth to tell me that he regarded the affair as his own no less than mine and that we should see it fraternally, cheerfully to a conclusion. It was as if he had said, "Poor dear, be easy with her; she has some natural prejudices; only give her time. Strange as it may appear to you she was very attractive in 1820. Meanwhile are we not in Venice together, and what better place is there for the meeting of dear friends? See how it glows with the advancing summer; how the sky and the sea and the rosy air and the marble of the palaces all shimmer and melt together." My eccentric private errand became a part of the general romance and the general glory— I felt even a mystic companionship, a moral fraternity with all those who in the past had been in the service of art. They had worked for beauty, for a devotion; and what else was I doing? That element was in everything that Jeffrey Aspern had written and I was only bringing it to the light.

I lingered in the sala when I went to and fro; I used to watch—as long as I thought decent—the door that led to Miss Bordereau's part of the house. A person observing me might have supposed I was trying to cast a spell upon it or attempting some odd experiment in hypnotism. But I was only praying it would open or thinking what treasure probably lurked behind it. I hold it singular, as I look back, that I should never have doubted for a moment that the sacred relics were there; never have failed to feel a certain joy at being under the same roof with them. After all they were under my hand—they had not escaped me yet; and they made my life continuous, in a fashion, with the illustrious life they had touched at the other end. I lost myself in this satisfaction to the point of assuming—in my quiet extravagance—that poor Miss Tita also went back, went back, as I used to phrase it. She did indeed, the gentle spinster, but not quite so far as Jeffrey Aspern, who was simple hearsay to her, quite as he was to me. Only she had lived for years with Juliana, she had seen and handled the papers and (even though she was stupid) some esoteric knowledge had rubbed off on her. That was what the old woman represented—esoteric knowledge; and this was the idea with which my editorial heart used to thrill. It literally beat faster often, of an evening, when I had been out, as I stopped with my candle in the re-echoing hall on my way up to bed. It was as if at such a moment as that, in the stillness, after the long contradiction of the day, Miss Bordereau's secrets were in the air, the wonder of her survival more palpable. These were the acute impressions. I had them in another form, with more of a certain sort of reciprocity, during the hours that I sat in the garden looking up over the top of my book at the closed windows of my hostess. In these windows no sign of life ever appeared; it was as if, for fear of my catching a glimpse of them, the two ladies passed their days in the dark. But this only proved to me that they had something to conceal; which was what I had wished to demonstrate. Their motionless shutters became as expressive as eyes consciously closed, and I took comfort in thinking that at all events though invisible themselves they saw me between the lashes.

I made a point of spending as much time as possible in the

garden, to justify the picture I had originally given of my horticultural passion. And I not only spent time, but (hang it! as I said) I spent money. As soon as I had got my rooms arranged and could give the proper thought to the matter I surveyed the place with a clever expert and made terms for having it put in order. I was sorry to do this, for personally I liked it better as it was, with its weeds and its wild, rough tangle, its sweet, characteristic Venetian shabbiness. I had to be consistent, to keep my promise that I would smother the house in flowers. Moreover I formed this graceful project that by flowers I would make my way—I would succeed by big nosegays. I would batter the old women with lilies—I would bombard their citadel with roses. Their door would have to yield to the pressure when a mountain of carnations should be piled up against it. The place in truth had been brutally neg-lected. The Venetian capacity for dawdling is of the largest, and for a good many days unlimited litter was all my gardener had to show for his ministrations. There was a great digging of holes and carting about of earth, and after a while I grew so impatient that I had thoughts of sending for my bouquets to the nearest stand. But I reflected that the ladies would see through the chinks of their shutters that they must have been bought and might make up their minds from this that I was a humbug. So I composed myself and finally, though the delay was long, perceived some appearances of bloom. This en-couraged me and I waited serenely enough till they multiplied. Meanwhile the real summer days arrived and began to pass, and as I look back upon them they seem to me almost the happiest of my life. I took more and more care to be in the garden whenever it was not too hot. I had an arbour arranged and a low table and an armchair put into it; and I carried out books and portfolios (I had always some business of writing in hand), and worked and waited and mused and hoped, while the golden hours elapsed and the plants drank in the light and the inscrutable old palace turned pale and then, as the day

waned, began to flush in it and my papers rustled in the
wandering breeze of the Adriatic.

Considering how little satisfaction I got from it at first it is
remarkable that I should not have grown more tired of
wondering what mystic rites of ennui the Misses Bordereau
celebrated in their darkened rooms; whether this had always
been the tenor of their life and how in previous years they had
escaped elbowing their neighbours. It was clear that they
must have had other habits and other circumstances; that they
must once have been young or at least middle-aged. There was
no end to the questions it was possible to ask about them and
no end to the answers it was not possible to frame. I had
known many of my country-people in Europe and was
familiar with the strange ways they were liable to take up
there; but the Misses Bordereau formed altogether a new type
of the American absentee. Indeed it was plain that the American name had ceased to have any application to them—I had
seen this in the ten minutes I spent in the old woman's room.
You could never have said whence they came, from the
appearance of either of them; wherever it was they had long
ago dropped the local accent and fashion. There was nothing
in them that one recognised, and putting the question of speech
aside they might have been Norwegians or Spaniards. Miss
Bordereau, after all, had been in Europe nearly threequarters
of a century; it appeared by some verses addressed to her by
Aspern on the occasion of his own second absence from
America—verses of which Cumnor and I had after infinite
conjecture established solidly enough the date—that she was
even then, as a girl of twenty, on the foreign side of the sea.
There was an implication in the poem (I hope not just for the
phrase) that he had come back for her sake. We had no real
light upon her circumstances at that moment, any more than
we had upon her origin, which we believed to be of the sort
usually spoken of as modest. Cumnor had a theory that she
had been a governess in some family in which the poet visited

and that, in consequence of her position, there was from the
first something unavowed, or rather something positively
clandestine, in their relations. I on the other hand had hatched
a little romance according to which she was the daughter of an
artist, a painter or a sculptor, who had left the western world
when the century was fresh, to study in the ancient schools.
It was essential to my hypothesis that this amiable man should
have lost his wife, should have been poor and unsuccessful
and should have had a second daughter, of a disposition quite
different from Juliana's. It was also indispensable that he
should have been accompanied to Europe by these young
ladies and should have established himself there for the
remainder of a struggling, saddened life. There was a further
implication that Miss Bordereau had had in her youth a perverse and adventurous, albeit a generous and fascinating
character, and that she had passed through some singular
vicissitudes. By what passions had she been ravaged, by what
sufferings had she been blanched, what store of memories had
she laid away for the monotonous future?

I asked myself these things as I sat spinning theories about
her in my arbour and the bees droned in the flowers. It was
incontestable that, whether for right or for wrong, most
readers of certain of Aspern's poems (poems not as ambiguous as the sonnets—scarcely more divine, I think—of Shakespeare) had taken for granted that Juliana had not always
adhered to the steep footway of renunciation. There hovered
about her name a perfume of reckless passion, an intimation
that she had not been exactly as the respectable young person
in general. Was this a sign that her singer had betrayed her,
had given her away, as we say nowadays, to posterity? Certain
it is that it would have been difficult to put one's finger on the
passage in which her fair fame suffered an imputation. Moreover was not any fame fair enough that was so sure of duration
and was associated with works immortal through their beauty?
It was a part of my idea that the young lady had had a foreign

lover (and an unedifying tragical rupture) before her meeting
with Jeffrey Aspern. She had lived with her father and sister
in a queer old-fashioned, expatriated, artistic Bohemia, in the
days when the æsthetic was only the academic and the painters
who knew the best models for a *contadina* and *pifferaro* wore
peaked hats and long hair. It was a society less furnished than
the coteries of to-day (in its ignorance of the wonderful
chances, the opportunities of the early bird, with which its
path was strewn), with tatters of old stuff and fragments of old
crockery; so that Miss Bordereau appeared not to have picked
up or have inherited many objects of importance. There was
no enviable *bric-à-brac*, with its provoking legend of cheap-
ness, in the room in which I had seen her. Such a fact as that
suggested bareness, but none the less it worked happily into
the sentimental interest I had always taken in the early movements of my countrymen as visitors to Europe. When Americans went abroad in 1820 there was something romantic,
almost heroic in it, as compared with the perpetual ferryings
of the present hour, when photography and other conveniences have annihilated surprise. Miss Bordereau sailed with her
family on a tossing brig, in the days of long voyages and sharp
differences; she had her emotions on the top of yellow dili-
gences, passed the night at inns where she dreamed of
travellers' tales, and was struck, on reaching the eternal city,
with the elegance of Roman pearls and scarfs. There was something touching to me in all that and my imagination frequently
went back to the period. If Miss Bordereau carried it there of
course Jeffrey Aspern at other times had done so a great deal
more. It was a much more important fact, if one were looking
at his genius critically, that he had lived in the days before the
general transfusion. It had happened to me to regret that he
had known Europe at all; I should have liked to see what he
would have written without that experience, by which he had
incontestably been enriched. But as his fate had ordered otherwise I went with him—I tried to judge how the old world

would have struck him. It was not only there, however, that I watched him; the relations he had entertained with the new had even a livelier interest. His own country after all had had most of his life, and his muse, as they said at that time, was essentially American. That was originally what I had loved him for: that at a period when our native land was nude and crude and provincial, when the famous "atmosphere" it is supposed to lack was not even missed, when literature was lonely there and art and form almost impossible, he had found means to live and write like one of the first; to be free and general and not at all afraid; to feel, understand and express everything.

V

I was seldom at home in the evening, for when I attempted to occupy myself in my apartments the lamplight brought in a swarm of noxious insects, and it was too hot for closed windows. Accordingly I spent the late hours either on the water (the moonlight of Venice is famous), or in the splendid square which serves as a vast forecourt to the strange old basilica of Saint Mark. I sat in front of Florian's *café*, eating ices, listening to music, talking with acquaintances: the traveller will remember how the immense cluster of tables and little chairs stretches like a promontory into the smooth lake of the Piazza. The whole place, of a summer's evening, under the stars and with all the lamps, all the voices and light footsteps on marble (the only sounds of the arcades that enclose it), is like an open-air saloon dedicated to cooling drinks and to a still finer degustation—that of the exquisite impressions received during the day. When I did not prefer to keep mine to myself there was always a stray tourist, disencumbered of his Bädeker, to discuss them with, or some domesticated painter rejoicing in the return of the season of strong effects. The wonderful church, with its low domes and bristling embroideries, the mystery of its mosaic and sculpture, looked ghostly in the tempered gloom, and the sea-breeze passed between the twin columns of the Piazzetta, the lintels of a door no longer guarded, as gently as if a rich curtain were swaying there. I used sometimes on these occasions to think of the Misses Bordereau and of the pity of their being shut up in apartments which in the Venetian July even Venetian vastness did not prevent from being stuffy. Their life seemed miles away from the life of the Piazza, and no doubt it was really too late to make the austere Juliana change her habits. But poor Miss Tita would have enjoyed one of Florian's ices, I was sure; sometimes I even had thoughts of carrying one home to her. Fortunately my patience bore fruit and I was not obliged to do anything so ridiculous.

One evening about the middle of July I came in earlier than usual—I forget what chance had led to this—and instead of going up to my quarters made my way into the garden. The temperature was very high; it was such a night as one would gladly have spent in the open air and I was in no hurry to go to bed. I had floated home in my gondola, listening to the slow splash of the oar in the narrow dark canals, and now the only thought that solicited me was the vague reflection that it would be pleasant to recline at one's length in the fragrant darkness on a garden bench. The odour of the canal was doubtless at the bottom of that aspiration and the breath of the garden, as I entered it, gave consistency to my purpose. It was delicious—just such an air as must have trembled with Romeo's vows when he stood among the flowers and raised his arms to his mistress's balcony. I looked at the windows of the palace to see if by chance the example of Verona (Verona being not far off) had been followed; but everything was dim, as usual, and everything was still. Juliana, on summer nights in her youth, might have murmured down from open windows at Jeffrey Aspern, but Miss Tita was not a poet's mistress any more than I was a poet. This however did not prevent my gratification from being great as I became aware on reaching the end of the garden that Miss Tita was seated in my little bower. At first I only made out an indistinct figure, not in the least counting on such an overture from one of my hostesses; it even occurred to me that some sentimental maidservant had stolen in to keep a tryst with her sweetheart. I was going to turn away, not to frighten her, when the figure rose to its height and I recognised Miss Bordereau's niece. I must do myself the justice to say that I did not wish to frighten her either, and much as I had longed for some such accident I should have been capable of retreating. It was as if I had laid a trap for her by coming home earlier than usual and adding to that eccentricity by creeping into the garden. As she rose she spoke to me, and then I reflected that perhaps, secure in my almost inveterate absence, it was her nightly practice to take a lonely airing. There was no trap, in truth, because I had had no suspicion. At first I took for granted that the words she uttered expressed discomfiture at my arrival; but as she repeated them—I had not caught them clearly—I had the surprise of hearing her say, "Oh, dear, I'm so very glad you've come!" She and her aunt had in common the property of unexpected speeches. She came out of the arbour almost as if she were going to throw herself into my arms.

I hasten to add that she did nothing of the kind; she did not even shake hands with me. It was a gratification to her to see me and presently she told me why—because she was nervous when she was out-of-doors at night alone. The plants and bushes looked so strange in the dark, and there were all sorts of queer sounds—she could not tell what they were—like the noises of animals. She stood close to me, looking about her with an air of greater security but without any demonstration of interest in me as an individual. Then I guessed that nocturnal prowlings were not in the least her habit, and I was also reminded (I had been struck with the circumstance in talking with her before I took possession) that it was impossible to over-estimate her simplicity.

"You speak as if you were lost in the backwoods," I said, laughing. "How you manage to keep out of this charming place when you have only three steps to take to get into it, is more than I have yet been able to discover. You hide away mighty well so long as I am on the premises, I know; but I had a hope that you peeped out a little at other times. You and your poor aunt are worse off than Carmelite nuns in their cells. Should you mind telling me how you exist without air, without exercise, without any sort of human contact? I don't see how you carry on the common business of life."

She looked at me as if I were talking some strange tongue and her answer was so little of an answer that I was considerably irritated. "We go to bed very early—earlier than you would believe." I was on the point of saying that this only deepened the mystery when she gave me some relief by adding, "Before you came we were not so private. But I never have been out at night."

"Never in these fragrant alleys, blooming here under your nose?"

"Ah," said Miss Tita, "they were never nice till now!" There was an unmistakable reference in this and a flattering comparison, so that it seemed to me I had gained a small advantage. As it would help me to follow it up to establish a sort of grievance I asked her why, since she thought my garden nice, she had never thanked me in any way for the flowers I had been sending up in such quantities for the previous three weeks. I had not been discouraged—there had been, as she would have observed, a daily armful; but I had been brought up in the common forms and a word of recognition now and then would have touched me in the right place.

"Why I didn't know they were for me!"

"They were for both of you. Why should I make a difference?"

Miss Tita reflected as if she might be thinking of a reason for that, but she failed to produce one. Instead of this she asked abruptly, "Why in the world do you want to know us?"

"I ought after all to make a difference," I replied. "That question is your aunt's; it isn't yours. You wouldn't ask it if you hadn't been put up to it."

"She didn't tell me to ask you," Miss Tita replied, without confusion; she was the oddest mixture of the shrinking and the direct.

"Well, she has often wondered about it herself and expressed her wonder to you. She has insisted on it, so that she has put the idea into your head that I am unsufferably pushing. Upon my word I think I have been very discreet. And how completely your aunt must have lost every tradition of sociability, to see anything out of the way in the idea that respectable intelligent people, living as we do under the same roof, should occasionally exchange a remark! What could be more natural? We are of the same country and we have at least some of the same tastes, since, like you, I am intensely fond of Venice."

My interlocutress appeared incapable of grasping more than one clause in any proposition, and she declared quickly, eagerly, as if she were answering my whole speech: "I am not in the least fond of Venice. I should like to go far away!"

"Has she always kept you back so?" I went on, to show her that I could be as irrelevant as herself.

"She told me to come out to-night; she has told me very often," said Miss Tita. "It is I who wouldn't come. I don't like to leave her."

"Is she too weak, is she failing?" I demanded, with more emotion, I think, than I intended to show. I judged this by the way her eyes rested upon me in the darkness. It embarrassed me a little, and to turn the matter off I continued genially: "Do let us sit down together comfortably somewhere and you will tell me all about her."

Miss Tita made no resistance to this. We found a bench less secluded, less confidential, as it were, than the one in the arbour; and we were still sitting there when I heard midnight ring out from those clear bells of Venice which vibrate with a solemnity of their own over the lagoon and hold the air so much more than the chimes of other places. We were together more than an hour and our interview gave, as it struck me, a great lift to my undertaking. Miss Tita accepted the situation without a protest; she had avoided me for three months, yet now she treated me almost as if these three months had made me an old friend. If I had chosen I might have inferred from this that though she had avoided me she had given a good deal of consideration to doing so. She paid no attention to the flight of time—never worried at my keeping her so long away from her aunt. She talked freely, answering questions and asking them and not even taking advantage of certain longish pauses with which they inevitably alternated to say she thought she had better go in. It was almost as if she were waiting for something—something I might say to her—and intended to give me my opportunity. I was the more struck by this as she told me that her aunt had been less well for a good many days and in a way that was rather new. She was weaker; at moments it seemed as if she had no strength at all; yet more than ever before she wished to be left alone. That was why she had told her to come out—not even to remain in her own room, which was alongside; she said her niece irritated her, made her nervous. She sat still for hours to-gether, as if she were asleep; she had always done that, musing and dozing; but at such times formerly she gave at intervals some small sign of life, of interest, liking her companion to be near her with her work. Miss Tita confided to me that at present her aunt was so motionless that she sometimes feared she was dead; moreover she took hardly any food—one couldn't see what she lived on. The great thing was that she still on most days got up; the serious job was to dress her, to wheel her out of her bedroom. She clung to as many of her old habits as possible and she had always, little company as they had received for years, made a point of sitting in the parlour.

I scarcely knew what to think of all this—of Miss Tita's sudden conversion to sociability and of the strange circumstance that the more the old lady appeared to decline toward her end the less she should desire to be looked after. The story did not hang together, and I even asked myself whether it were not a trap laid for me, the result of a design to make me show my hand. I could not have told why my companions (as they could only by courtesy be called) should have this purpose—why they should try to trip up so lucrative a lodger. At any rate I kept on my guard, so that Miss Tita should not have occasion again to ask me if I had an *arrière-pensée*. Poor woman, before we parted for the night my mind was at rest as to *her* capacity for entertaining one.

She told me more about their affairs than I had hoped; there was no need to be prying, for it evidently drew her out simply to feel that I listened, that I cared. She ceased wondering why I cared, and at last, as she spoke of the brilliant life they had led years before, she almost chattered. It was Miss Tita who judged it brilliant; she said that when they first came to live in Venice, years and years before (I saw that her mind was essentially vague about dates and the order in which events had occurred), there was scarcely a week that they had not some visitor or did not make some delightful *passeggio* in the city. They had seen all the curiosities; they had even been to the Lido in a boat (she spoke as if I might think there was a way on foot); they had had a collation there, brought in three baskets and spread out on the grass. I asked her what people they had known and she said, Oh! very nice ones—the Cavaliere Bombicci and the Contessa Altemura, with whom they had had a great friendship. Also English people—the Churtons and the Goldies and Mrs Stock-Stock, whom they had loved dearly; she was dead and gone, poor dear. That was

the case with most of their pleasant circle (this expression was
Miss Tita's own), though a few were left, which was a wonder
considering how they had neglected them. She mentioned the
names of two or three Venetian old women; of a certain
doctor, very clever, who was so kind—he came as a friend, he
had really given up practice; of the *avvocato* Pochintesta, who
wrote beautiful poems and had addressed one to her aunt.
These people came to see them without fail every year, usually
at the *capo d'anno*, and of old her aunt used to make them some
little present—her aunt and she together: small things that she,
Miss Tita, made herself, like paper lamp-shades or mats for
the decanters of wine at dinner or those woollen things that in
cold weather were worn on the wrists. The last few years
there had not been many presents; she could not think what
to make and her aunt had lost her interest and never suggested.
But the people came all the same; if the Venetians liked you
once they liked you for ever.

There was something affecting in the good faith of this
sketch of former social glories; the picnic at the Lido had
remained vivid through the ages and poor Miss Tita evidently
was of the impression that she had had a brilliant youth. She
had in fact had a glimpse of the Venetian world in its gossip-
ing, home-keeping, parsimonious, professional walks; for
I observed for the first time that she had acquired by contact
something of the trick of the familiar, soft-sounding, almost
infantile speech of the place. I judged that she had imbibed
this invertebrate dialect, from the natural way the names of
things and people—mostly purely local—rose to her lips. If
she knew little of what they represented she knew still less of
anything else. Her aunt had drawn in—her failing interest in
the table-mats and lamp-shades was a sign of that—and she
had not been able to mingle in society or to entertain it alone;
so that the matter of her reminiscences struck one as an old
world altogether. If she had not been so decent her references
would have seemed to carry one back to the queer rococo

Venice of Casanova. I found myself falling into the error of thinking of her too as one of Jeffrey Aspern's contemporaries; this came from her having so little in common with my own. It was possible, I said to myself, that she had not even heard of him; it might very well be that Juliana had not cared to lift even for her the veil that covered the temple of her youth. In this case she perhaps would not know of the existence of the papers, and I welcomed that presumption—it made me feel more safe with her—until I remembered that we had believed the letter of disavowal received by Cumnor to be in the handwriting of the niece. If it had been dictated to her she had of course to know what it was about; yet after all the effect of it was to repudiate the idea of any connection with the poet. I held it probable at all events that Miss Tita had not read a word of his poetry. Moreover if, with her companion, she had always escaped the interviewer there was little occasion for her having got it into her head that people were "after" the letters. People had not been after them, inasmuch as they had not heard of them; and Cumnor's fruitless feeler would have been a solitary accident.

When midnight sounded Miss Tita got up; but she stopped at the door of the house only after she had wandered two or three times with me round the garden. "When shall I see you again?" I asked, before she went in; to which she replied with promptness that she should like to come out the next night. She added however that she should not come—she was so far from doing everything she liked.

"You might do a few things that *I* like," I said with a sigh.

"Oh, you—I don't believe you!" she murmured, at this, looking at me with her simple solemnity.

"Why don't you believe me?"

"Because I don't understand you."

"That is just the sort of occasion to have faith." I could not say more, though I should have liked to, as I saw that I only mystified her; for I had no wish to have it on my conscience that I might pass for having made love to her. Nothing less should I have seemed to do had I continued to beg a lady to "believe in me" in an Italian garden on a mid-summer night. There was some merit in my scruples, for Miss Tita lingered and lingered: I perceived that she felt that she should not really soon come down again and wished therefore to protract the present. She insisted too on making the talk between us personal to ourselves; and altogether her behaviour was such as would have been possible only to a completely innocent woman.

"I shall like the flowers better now that I know they are also meant for me."

"How could you have doubted it? If you will tell me the kind you like best I will send a double lot of them."

"Oh, I like them all best!" Then she went on, familiarly: "Shall you study—shall you read and write—when you go up to your rooms?"

"I don't do that at night, at this season. The lamplight brings in the animals."

"You might have known that when you came."

"I did know it!"

"And in winter do you work at night?"

"I read a good deal, but I don't often write." She listened as if these details had a rare interest, and suddenly a temptation quite at variance with the prudence I had been teaching myself associated itself with her plain, mild face. Ah yes, she was safe and I could make her safer! It seemed to me from one moment to another that I could not wait longer—that I really must take a sounding. So I went on: "In general before I go to sleep—very often in bed (it's a bad habit, but I confess to it), I read some great poet. In nine cases out of ten it's a volume of Jeffrey Aspern."

I watched her well as I pronounced that name but I saw nothing wonderful. Why should I indeed—was not Jeffrey Aspern the property of the human race?

"Oh, we read him—we *have* read him," she quietly replied.

"He is my poet of poets—I know him almost by heart."

For an instant Miss Tita hesitated; then her sociability was too much for her.

"Oh, by heart—that's nothing!" she murmured, smiling. "My aunt used to know him—to know him"—she paused an instant and I wondered what she was going to say—"to know him as a visitor."

"As a visitor?" I repeated, staring.

"He used to call on her and take her out."

I continued to stare. "My dear lady, he died a hundred years ago!"

"Well," she said, mirthfully, "my aunt is a hundred and fifty."

"Mercy on us!" I exclaimed; "why didn't you tell me before? I should like so to ask her about him."

"She wouldn't care for that—she wouldn't tell you," Miss Tita replied.

"I don't care what she cares for! She *must* tell me—it's not a chance to be lost."

"Oh, you should have come twenty years ago: then she still talked about him."

"And what did she say?" I asked, eagerly.

"I don't know—that he liked her immensely."

"And she—didn't she like him?"

"She said he was a god." Miss Tita gave me this information flatly, without expression; her tone might have made it a piece of trivial gossip. But it stirred me deeply as she dropped the words into the summer night; it seemed such a direct testimony.

"Fancy, fancy!" I murmured. And then, "Tell me this, please—has she got a portrait of him? They are distressingly rare."

"A portrait? I don't know," said Miss Tita; and now there

was discomfiture in her face. "Well, good-night!" she added; and she turned into the house.

I accompanied her into the wide, dusky, stone-paved passage which on the ground floor corresponded with our grand sala. It opened at one end into the garden, at the other upon the canal, and was lighted now only by the small lamp that was always left for me to take up as I went to bed. An extinguished candle which Miss Tita apparently had brought down with her stood on the same table with it. "Good-night, good-night!" I replied, keeping beside her as she went to get her light. "Surely you would know, shouldn't you, if she had one?"

"If she had what?" the poor lady asked, looking at me queerly over the flame of her candle.

"A portrait of the god. I don't know what I wouldn't give to see it."

"I don't know what she has got. She keeps her things locked up." And Miss Tita went away, toward the staircase, with the sense evidently that she had said too much.

I let her go—I wished not to frighten her—and I contented myself with remarking that Miss Bordereau would not have locked up such a glorious possession as that—a thing a person would be proud of and hang up in a prominent place on the parlour-wall. Therefore of course she had not any portrait. Miss Tita made no direct answer to this and candle in hand, with her back to me, ascended two or three stairs. Then she stopped short and turned round looking at me across the dusky space.

"Do you write—do you write?" There was a shake in her voice—she could scarcely bring out what she wanted to ask.

"Do I write? Oh, don't speak of my writing on the same day with Aspern's!"

"Do you write about *him*—do you pry into his life?"

"Ah, that's your aunt's question; it can't be yours!" I said, in a tone of slightly wounded sensibility.

"All the more reason then that you should answer it. Do you, please?"

I thought I had allowed for the falsehoods I should have to tell; but I found that in fact when it came to the point I had not. Besides, now that I had an opening there was a kind of relief in being frank. Lastly (it was perhaps fanciful, even fatuous), I guessed that Miss Tita personally would not in the last resort be less my friend. So after a moment's hesitation I answered, "Yes, I have written about him and I am looking for more material. In heaven's name have you got any?"

"*Santo Dio!*" she exclaimed, without heeding my question; and she hurried upstairs and out of sight. I might count upon her in the last resort, but for the present she was visibly alarmed. The proof of it was that she began to hide again, so that for a fortnight I never beheld her. I found my patience ebbing and after four or five days of this I told the gardener to stop the flowers.

VI

ONE afternoon, as I came down from my quarters to go out, I found Miss Tita in the sala: it was our first encounter on that ground since I had come to the house. She put on no air of being there by accident; there was an ignorance of such arts in her angular, diffident directness. That I might be quite sure she was waiting for me she informed me of the fact and told me that Miss Bordereau wished to see me: she would take me into the room at that moment if I had time. If I had been late for a love-tryst I would have stayed for this, and I quickly signified that I should be delighted to wait upon the old lady. "She wants to talk with you—to know you," Miss Tita said, smiling as if she herself appreciated that idea; and she led me to the door of her aunt's apartment. I stopped her a moment before she had opened it, looking at her with some curiosity.

I told her that this was a great satisfaction to me and a great honour; but all the same I should like to ask what had made Miss Bordereau change so suddenly. It was only the other day that she wouldn't suffer me near her. Miss Tita was not embarrassed by my question; she had as many little unexpected serenities as if she told fibs, but the odd part of them was that they had on the contrary their source in her truthfulness. "Oh, my aunt changes," she answered; "it's so terribly dull—I suppose she's tired."

"But you told me that she wanted more and more to be alone."

Poor Miss Tita coloured, as if she found me over-insistent. "Well, if you don't believe she wants to see you—I haven't invented it! I think people often are capricious when they are very old."

"That's perfectly true. I only wanted to be clear as to whether you have repeated to her what I told you the other night."

"What you told me?"

"About Jeffrey Aspern—that I am looking for materials."

"If I had told her do you think she would have sent for you?"

"That's exactly what I want to know. If she wants to keep him to herself she might have sent for me to tell me so."

"She won't speak of him," said Miss Tita. Then as she opened the door she added in a lower tone, "I have told her nothing."

The old woman was sitting in the same place in which I had seen her last, in the same position, with the same mystifying bandage over her eyes. Her welcome was to turn her almost invisible face to me and show me that while she sat silent she saw me clearly. I made no motion to shake hands with her; I felt too well on this occasion that that was out of place for ever. It had been sufficiently enjoined upon me that she was too sacred for that sort of reciprocity—too venerable to touch. There was something so grim in her aspect (it was partly the accident of her green shade), as I stood there to be measured, that I ceased on the spot to feel any doubt as to her knowing my secret, though I did not in the least suspect that Miss Tita had not just spoken the truth. She had not betrayed me, but the old woman's brooding instinct had served her; she had turned me over and over in the long, still hours and she had guessed. The worst of it was that she looked terribly like an old woman who at a pinch would burn her papers. Miss Tita pushed a chair forward, saying to me, "This will be a good place for you to sit." As I took possession of it I asked after Miss Bordereau's health; expressed the hope that in spite of the very hot weather it was satisfactory. She replied that it was good enough—good enough; that it was a great thing to be alive.

"Oh, as to that, it depends upon what you compare it with!" I exclaimed, laughing.

"I don't compare—I don't compare. If I did that I should have given everything up long ago."

I liked to think that this was a subtle allusion to the rapture she had known in the society of Jeffrey Aspern—though it was true that such an allusion would have accorded ill with the wish I imputed to her to keep him buried in her soul. What it accorded with was my constant conviction that no human being had ever had a more delightful social gift than his, and what it seemed to convey was that nothing in the world was worth speaking of if one pretended to speak of that. But one did not! Miss Tita sat down beside her aunt, looking as if she had reason to believe some very remarkable conversation would come off between us.

"It's about the beautiful flowers," said the old lady; "you sent us so many—I ought to have thanked you for them before. But I don't write letters and I receive only at long intervals."

She had not thanked me while the flowers continued to

come, but she departed from her custom so far as to send for
me as soon as she began to fear that they would not come any
more. I noted this; I remembered what an acquisitive propen-
sity she had shown when it was a question of extracting gold
from me, and I privately rejoiced at the happy thought I had
had in suspending my tribute. She had missed it and she was
willing to make a concession to bring it back. At the first sign
of this concession I could only go to meet her. "I am afraid
you have not had many, of late, but they shall begin again
immediately—to-morrow, to-night."

"Oh, do send us some to-night!" Miss Tita cried, as if it
were an immense circumstance.

"What else should you do with them? It isn't a manly taste
to make a bower of your room," the old woman remarked.

"I don't make a bower of my room, but I am exceedingly
fond of growing flowers, of watching their ways. There is
nothing unmanly in that: it has been the amusement of philosophers, of statesmen in retirement; even I think of great
captains."

"I suppose you know you can sell them—those you don't
use," Miss Bordereau went on. "I daresay they wouldn't give
you much for them; still, you could make a bargain."

"Oh, I have never made a bargain, as you ought to know.
My gardener disposes of them and I ask no questions."

"I would ask a few, I can promise you!" said Miss Bordereau; and it was the first time I had heard her laugh. I could
not get used to the idea that this vision of pecuniary profit was
what drew out the divine Juliana most.

"Come into the garden yourself and pick them; come as
often as you like; come every day. They are all for you," I
pursued, addressing Miss Tita and carrying off this veracious
statement by treating it as an innocent joke. "I can't imagine
why she doesn't come down," I added, for Miss Bordereau's
benefit.

"You must make her come; you must come up and fetch

her," said the old woman, to my stupefaction. "That odd thing you have made in the corner would be a capital place for her to sit."

The allusion to my arbour was irreverent; it confirmed the impression I had already received that there was a flicker of impertinence in Miss Bordereau's talk, a strange mocking lambency which must have been a part of her adventurous youth and which had outlived passions and faculties. None the less I asked, "Wouldn't it be possible for you to come down there yourself? Wouldn't it do you good to sit there in the shade, in the sweet air?"

"Oh, sir, when I move out of this it won't be to sit in the air, and I'm afraid that any that may be stirring around me won't be particularly sweet! It will be a very dark shade indeed. But that won't be just yet," Miss Bordereau continued, cannily, as if to correct any hopes that this courageous allusion to the last receptacle of her mortality might lead me to entertain. "I have sat here many a day and I have had enough of arbours in my time. But I'm not afraid to wait till I'm called."

Miss Tita had expected some interesting talk, but perhaps she found it less genial on her aunt's side (considering that I had been sent for with a civil intention) than she had hoped. As if to give the conversation a turn that would put our companion in a light more favourable she said to me, "Didn't I tell you the other night that she had sent me out? You see that I can do what I like!"

"Do you pity her—do you teach her to pity herself?" Miss Bordereau demanded, before I had time to answer this appeal. "She has a much easier life than I had when I was her age."

"You must remember that it has been quite open to me to think you rather inhuman."

"Inhuman? That's what the poets used to call the women a hundred years ago. Don't try that; you won't do as well as they!" Juliana declared. "There is no more poetry in the world—that I know of at least. But I won't bandy words with you," she pursued, and I well remember the old-fashioned, artificial sound she gave to the speech. "You have made me talk, talk! It isn't good for me at all." I got up at this and told her I would take no more of her time; but she detained me to ask, "Do you remember, the day I saw you about the rooms, that you offered us the use of your gondola?" And when I assented, promptly, struck again with her disposition to make a "good thing" of being there and wondering what she now had in her eye, she broke out, "Why don't you take that girl out in it and show her the place?"

"Oh dear aunt, what do you want to do with me?" cried the "girl," with a piteous quaver. "I know all about the place!"

"Well then, go with him as a cicerone!" said Miss Bordereau, with an effect of something like cruelty in her implacable power of retort—an incongruous suggestion that she was a sarcastic, profane, cynical old woman. "Haven't we heard that there have been all sorts of changes in all these years? You ought to see them and at your age (I don't mean because you're so young), you ought to take the chances that come. You're old enough, my dear, and this gentleman won't hurt you. He will show you the famous sunsets, if they still go on —do they go on? The sun set for me so long ago. But that's not a reason. Besides, I shall never miss you; you think you are too important. Take her to the Piazza; it used to be very pretty," Miss Bordereau continued, addressing herself to me. "What have they done with the funny old church? I hope it hasn't tumbled down. Let her look at the shops; she may take some money, she may buy what she likes."

Poor Miss Tita had got up, discountenanced and helpless, and as we stood there before her aunt it would certainly have seemed to a spectator of the scene that the old woman was amusing herself at our expense. Miss Tita protested, in a confusion of exclamations and murmurs; but I lost no time in saying that if she would do me the honour to accept the hospitality of my boat I would engage that she should not be bored. Or if she did not want so much of my company the boat itself, with the gondolier, was at her service; he was a capital oar and she might have every confidence. Miss Tita, without definitely answering this speech, looked away from me, out of the window, as if she were going to cry; and I remarked that once we had Miss Bordereau's approval we could easily come to an understanding. We would take an hour, whichever she liked, one of the very next days. As I made my obeisance to the old lady I asked her if she would kindly permit me to see her again.

For a moment she said nothing; then she inquired, "Is it very necessary to your happiness?"

"It diverts me more than I can say."

"You are wonderfully civil. Don't you know it almost kills *me?*"

"How can I believe that when I see you more animated, more brilliant than when I came in?"

"That is very true, aunt," said Miss Tita. "I think it does you good."

"Isn't it touching, the solicitude we each have that the other shall enjoy herself?" sneered Miss Bordereau. "If you think me brilliant to-day you don't know what you are talking about; you have never seen an agreeable woman. Don't try to pay me a compliment; I have been spoiled," she went on. "My door is shut, but you may sometimes knock."

With this she dismissed me and I left the room. The latch closed behind me, but Miss Tita, contrary to my hope, had remained within. I passed slowly across the hall and before taking my way down-stairs I waited a little. My hope was answered; after a minute Miss Tita followed me. "That's a delightful idea about the Piazza," I said. "When will you go —to-night, to-morrow?"

She had been disconcerted, as I have mentioned, but I had

already perceived and I was to observe again that when Miss Tita was embarrassed she did not (as most women would have done) turn away from you and try to escape, but came closer, as it were, with a deprecating, clinging appeal to be spared, to be protected. Her attitude was perpetually a sort of prayer for assistance, for explanation; and yet no woman in the world could have been less of a comedian. From the moment you were kind to her she depended on you absolutely; her self-consciousness dropped from her and she took the greatest intimacy, the innocent intimacy which was the only thing she could conceive, for granted. She told me she did not know what had got into her aunt; she had changed so quickly, she had got some idea. I replied that she must find out what the idea was and then let me know; we would go and have an ice together at Florian's and she should tell me while we listened to the band.

"Oh, it will take me a long time to find out!" she said, rather ruefully; and she could promise me this satisfaction neither for that night nor for the next. I was patient now, however, for I felt that I had only to wait; and in fact at the end of the week, one lovely evening after dinner, she stepped into my gondola, to which in honour of the occasion I had attached a second oar.

We swept in the course of five minutes into the Grand Canal; whereupon she uttered a murmur of ecstasy as fresh as if she had been a tourist just arrived. She had forgotten how splendid the great water-way looked on a clear, hot summer evening, and how the sense of floating between marble palaces and reflected lights disposed the mind to sympathetic talk. We floated long and far, and though Miss Tita gave no high-pitched voice to her satisfaction I felt that she surrendered herself. She was more than pleased, she was transported; the whole thing was an immense liberation. The gondola moved with slow strokes, to give her time to enjoy it, and she listened to the plash of the oars, which grew louder and more musically liquid as we passed into narrow canals, as if it were a revelation of Venice. When I asked her how long it was since she had been in a boat she answered, "Oh, I don't know; a long time —not since my aunt began to be ill." This was not the only example she gave me of her extreme vagueness about the previous years and the line which marked off the period when Miss Bordereau flourished. I was not at liberty to keep her out too long, but we took a considerable *giro* before going to the Piazza. I asked her no questions, keeping the conversation on purpose away from her domestic situation and the things I wanted to know; I poured treasures of information about Venice into her ears, described Florence and Rome, discoursed to her on the charms and advantages of travel. She reclined, receptive, on the deep leather cushions, turned her eyes conscientiously to everything I pointed out to her, and never mentioned to me till some time afterwards that she might be supposed to know Florence better than I, as she had lived there for years with Miss Bordereau. At last she asked, with the shy impatience of a child, "Are we not really going to the Piazza? That's what I want to see!" I immediately gave the order that we should go straight; and then we sat silent with the expectation of arrival. As some time still passed, however, she said suddenly, of her own movement, "I have found out what is the matter with my aunt: she is afraid you will go!"

"What has put that into her head?"

"She has had an idea you have not been happy. That is why she is different now."

"You mean she wants to make me happier?"

"Well, she wants you not to go; she wants you to stay."

"I suppose you mean on account of the rent," I remarked candidly.

Miss Tita's candour showed itself a match for my own. "Yes, you know; so that I shall have more."

"How much does she want you to have?" I asked, laughing.

"She ought to fix the sum, so that I may stay till it's made up."

"Oh, that wouldn't please me," said Miss Tita. "It would be unheard of, your taking that trouble."

"But suppose I should have my own reasons for staying in Venice?"

"Then it would be better for you to stay in some other house."

"And what would your aunt say to that?"

"She wouldn't like it at all. But I should think you would do well to give up your reasons and go away altogether."

"Dear Miss Tita," I said, "it's not so easy to give them up!"

She made no immediate answer to this, but after a moment she broke out: "I think I know what your reasons are!"

"I daresay, because the other night I almost told you how I wish you would help me to make them good."

"I can't do that without being false to my aunt."

"What do you mean, being false to her?"

"Why, she would never consent to what you want. She has been asked, she has been written to. It made her fearfully angry."

"Then she *has* got papers of value?" I demanded, quickly.

"Oh, she has got everything!" sighed Miss Tita, with a curious weariness, a sudden lapse into gloom.

These words caused all my pulses to throb, for I regarded them as precious evidence. For some minutes I was too agitated to speak, and in the interval the gondola approached the Piazzetta. After we had disembarked I asked my companion whether she would rather walk round the square or go and sit at the door of the café; to which she replied that she would do whichever I liked best—I must only remember again how little time she had. I assured her there was plenty to do both, and we made the circuit of the long arcades. Her spirits revived at the sight of the bright shop-windows, and she lingered and stopped, admiring or disapproving of their contents, asking

me what I thought of things, theorising about prices. My
attention wandered from her; her words of a while before,
"Oh, she has got everything!" echoed so in my consciousness. We sat down at last in the crowded circle at Florian's,
finding an unoccupied table among those that were ranged in
the square. It was a splendid night and all the world was out-
of-doors; Miss Tita could not have wished the elements more
auspicious for her return to society. I saw that she enjoyed it
even more than she told; she was agitated with the multitude
of her impressions. She had forgotten what an attractive thing
the world is, and it was coming over her that somehow she
had for the best years of her life been cheated of it. This did
not make her angry; but as she looked all over the charming
scene her face had, in spite of its smile of appreciation, the
flush of a sort of wounded surprise. She became silent, as if
she were thinking with a secret sadness of opportunities, for
ever lost, which ought to have been easy; and this gave me a
chance to say to her, "Did you mean a while ago that your
aunt has a plan of keeping me on by admitting me occasionally
to her presence?"

"She thinks it will make a difference with you if you sometimes see her. She wants you so much to stay that she is
willing to make that concession."

"And what good does she consider that I think it will do
me to see her?"

"I don't know; she thinks it's interesting," said Miss Tita,
simply. "You told her you found it so."

"So I did; but every one doesn't think so."

"No, of course not, or more people would try."

"Well, if she is capable of making that reflection she is
capable also of making this further one," I went on: "that I
must have a particular reason for not doing as others do, in
spite of the interest she offers—for not leaving her alone."
Miss Tita looked as if she failed to grasp this rather complicated proposition; so I continued, "If you have not told her

what I said to you the other night may she not at least have guessed it?"

"I don't know; she is very suspicious."

"But she has not been made so by indiscreet curiosity, by persecution?"

"No, no; it isn't that," said Miss Tita, turning on me a somewhat troubled face. "I don't know how to say it: it's on account of something—ages ago, before I was born—in her life."

"Something? What sort of thing?" I asked, as if I myself could have no idea.

"Oh, she has never told me," Miss Tita answered; and I was sure she was speaking the truth.

Her extreme limpidity was almost provoking, and I felt for the moment that she would have been more satisfactory if she had been less ingenuous. "Do you suppose it's something to which Jeffrey Aspern's letters and papers—I mean the things in her possession—have reference?"

"I daresay it is!" my companion exclaimed, as if this were a very happy suggestion. "I have never looked at any of those things."

"None of them? Then how do you know what they are?"

"I don't," said Miss Tita, placidly. "I have never had them in my hands. But I have seen them when she has had them out."

"Does she have them out often?"

"Not now, but she used to. She is very fond of them."

"In spite of their being compromising?"

"Compromising?" Miss Tita repeated, as if she was ignorant of the meaning of the word. I felt almost as one who corrupts the innocence of youth.

"I mean their containing painful memories."

"Oh, I don't think they are painful."

"You mean you don't think they affect her reputation?"

At this a singular look came into the face of Miss Bordereau's niece—a kind of confession of helplessness, an appeal to me to deal fairly, generously with her. I had brought her to the Piazza, placed her among charming influences, paid her an attention she appreciated, and now I seemed to let her perceive that all this had been a bribe—a bribe to make her turn in some way against her aunt. She was of a yielding nature and capable of doing almost anything to please a person who was kind to her; but the greatest kindness of all would be not to presume too much on this. It was strange enough, as I afterwards thought, that she had not the least air of resenting my want of consideration for her aunt's character, which would have been in the worst possible taste if anything less vital (from my point of view) had been at stake. I don't think she really measured it. "Do you mean that she did something bad?" she asked in a moment.

"Heaven forbid I should say so, and it's none of my business. Besides, if she did," I added, laughing, "it was in other ages, in another world. But why should she not destroy her papers?"

"Oh, she loves them too much."

"Even now, when she may be near her end?"

"Perhaps when she's sure of that she will."

"Well, Miss Tita," I said, "it's just what I should like you to prevent."

"How can I prevent it?"

"Couldn't you get them away from her?"

"And give them to you?"

This put the case very crudely, though I am sure there was no irony in her intention. "Oh, I mean that you might let me see them and look them over. It isn't for myself; there is no personal avidity in my desire. It is simply that they would be of such immense interest to the public, such immeasurable importance as a contribution to Jeffrey Aspern's history."

She listened to me in her usual manner, as if my speech were full of reference to things she had never heard of, and I felt particularly like the reporter of a newspaper who forces his way into a house of mourning. This was especially the case when after a moment she said, "There was a gentleman who some time ago wrote to her in very much those words. He also wanted her papers."

"And did she answer him?" I asked, rather ashamed of myself for not having her rectitude.

"Only when he had written two or three times. He made her very angry."

"And what did she say?"

"She said he was a devil," Miss Tita replied, simply.

"She used that expression in her letter?"

"Oh no; she said it to me. She made me write to him."

"And what did you say?"

"I told him there were no papers at all."

"Ah, poor gentleman!" I exclaimed.

"I knew there were, but I wrote what she bade me."

"Of course you had to do that. But I hope I shall not pass for a devil."

"It will depend upon what you ask me to do for you," said Miss Tita, smiling.

"Oh, if there is a chance of *your* thinking so my affair is in a bad way! I sha'n't ask you to steal for me, nor even to fib—for you can't fib, unless on paper. But the principal thing is this—to prevent her from destroying the papers."

"Why, I have no control of her," said Miss Tita. "It's she who controls me."

"But she doesn't control her own arms and legs, does she? The way she would naturally destroy her letters would be to burn them. Now she can't burn them without fire, and she can't get fire unless you give it to her."

"I have always done everything she has asked," my companion rejoined. "Besides, there's Olimpia."

I was on the point of saying that Olimpia was probably corruptible, but I thought it best not to sound that note. So I simply inquired if that faithful domestic could not be managed.

"Every one can be managed by my aunt," said Miss Tita. And then she observed that her holiday was over; she must go home.

I laid my hand on her arm, across the table, to stay her a moment. "What I want of you is a general promise to help me."

"Oh, how can I—how can I?" she asked, wondering and troubled. She was half surprised, half frightened at my wishing to make her play an active part.

"This is the main thing: to watch her carefully and warn me in time, before she commits that horrible sacrilege."

"I can't watch her when she makes me go out."

"That's very true."

"And when you do too."

"Mercy on us; do you think she will have done anything to-night?"

"I don't know; she is very cunning."

"Are you trying to frighten me?" I asked.

I felt this inquiry sufficiently answered when my companion murmured in a musing, almost envious way, "Oh, but she loves them—she loves them!"

This reflection, repeated with such emphasis, gave me great comfort; but to obtain more of that balm I said, "If she shouldn't intend to destroy the objects we speak of before her death she will probably have made some disposition by will."

"By will?"

"Hasn't she made a will for your benefit?"

"Why, she has so little to leave. That's why she likes money," said Miss Tita.

"Might I ask, since we are really talking things over, what you and she live on?"

"On some money that comes from America, from a lawyer. He sends it every quarter. It isn't much!"

"And won't she have disposed of that?"

My companion hesitated—I saw she was blushing. "I believe it's mine," she said; and the look and tone which accompanied these words betrayed so the absence of the habit of thinking of herself that I almost thought her charming. The next instant she added, "But she had a lawyer once, ever so long ago. And some people came and signed something."

"They were probably witnesses. And you were not asked to sign? Well then," I argued, rapidly and hopefully, "it is because you are the legatee; she has left all her documents to you!"

"If she has it's with very strict conditions," Miss Tita responded, rising quickly, while the movement gave the words a little character of decision. They seemed to imply that the bequest would be accompanied with a command that the articles bequeathed should remain concealed from every inquisitive eye and that I was very much mistaken if I thought she was the person to depart from an injunction so solemn.

"Oh, of course you will have to abide by the terms," I said; and she uttered nothing to mitigate the severity of this conclusion. None the less, later, just before we disembarked at her own door, on our return, which had taken place almost in silence, she said to me abruptly, "I will do what I can to help you." I was grateful for this—it was very well so far as it went; but it did not keep me from remembering that night in a worried waking hour that I now had her word for it to reinforce my own impression that the old woman was very cunning.

VII

THE fear of what this side of her character might have led her to do made me nervous for days afterwards. I waited for an intimation from Miss Tita; I almost figured to myself that it was her duty to keep me informed, to let me know definitely whether or no Miss Bordereau had sacrificed her treasures. But as she gave no sign I lost patience and determined to judge so far as was possible with my own senses. I sent late one afternoon to ask if I might pay the ladies a visit, and my servant came back with surprising news. Miss Bordereau could be approached without the least difficulty; she had been moved out into the sala and was sitting by the window that overlooked the garden. I descended and found this picture correct; the old lady had been wheeled forth into the world and had a certain air, which came mainly perhaps from some brighter element in her dress, of being prepared again to have converse with it. It had not yet, however, begun to flock about her; she was perfectly alone and, though the door leading to her own quarters stood open, I had at first no glimpse of Miss Tita. The window at which she sat had the afternoon shade and, one of the shutters having been pushed back, she could see the pleasant garden, where the summer sun had by this time dried up too many of the plants—she could see the yellow light and the long shadows.

"Have you come to tell me that you will take the rooms for six months more?" she asked, as I approached her, startling me by something coarse in her cupidity almost as much as if she had not already given me a specimen of it. Juliana's desire to make our acquaintance lucrative had been, as I have sufficiently indicated, a false note in my image of the woman who had inspired a great poet with immortal lines; but I may say here definitely that I recognised after all that it behoved me to make a large allowance for her. It was I who had kindled the unholy flame; it was I who had put into her head that she had the means of making money. She appeared never to have thought of that; she had been living wastefully for years, in a house five times too big for her, on a footing that I could explain only by the presumption that, excessive as it was, the space she enjoyed cost her next to nothing and that small as were her revenues they left her, for Venice, an appreciable margin. I had descended on her one day and taught her to calculate, and my almost extravagant comedy on the subject of the garden had presented me irresistibly in the light of a victim. Like all persons who achieve the miracle of changing their point of view when they are old she had been intensely converted; she had seized my hint with a desperate, tremulous clutch.

I invited myself to go and get one of the chairs that stood, at a distance, against the wall (she had given herself no concern as to whether I should sit or stand); and while I placed it near her I began, gaily, "Oh, dear madam, what an imagination you have, what an intellectual sweep! I am a poor devil of a man of letters who lives from day to day. How can I take palaces by the year? My existence is precarious. I don't know whether six months hence I shall have bread to put in my mouth. I have treated myself for once; it has been an immense luxury. But when it comes to going on——!"

"Are your rooms too dear? if they are you can have more for the same money," Juliana responded. "We can arrange, we can *combinare*, as they say here."

"Well yes, since you ask me, they are too dear," I said. "Evidently you suppose me richer than I am."

She looked at me in her barricaded way. "If you write books don't you sell them?"

"Do you mean don't people buy them? A little—not so much as I could wish. Writing books, unless one be a great genius—and even then!—is the last road to fortune. I think there is no more money to be made by literature."

"Perhaps you don't choose good subjects. What do you write about?" Miss Bordereau inquired.

"About the books of other people. I'm a critic, an historian, in a small way." I wondered what she was coming to.

"And what other people, now?"

"Oh, better ones than myself: the great writers mainly—

the great philosophers and poets of the past; those who are dead and gone and can't speak for themselves."

"And what do you say about them?"

"I say they sometimes attached themselves to very clever women!" I answered, laughing. I spoke with great deliberation, but as my words fell upon the air they struck me as imprudent. However, I risked them and I was not sorry, for perhaps after all the old woman would be willing to treat. It seemed to be tolerably obvious that she knew my secret: why therefore drag the matter out? But she did not take what I had said as a confession: she only asked:

"Do you think it's right to rake up the past?"

"I don't know that I know what you mean by raking it up; but how can we get at it unless we dig a little? The present has such a rough way of treading it down."

"Oh, I like the past, but I don't like critics," the old woman declared, with her fine tranquillity.

"Neither do I, but I like their discoveries."

"Aren't they mostly lies?"

"The lies are what they sometimes discover," I said, smiling at the quiet impertinence of this. "They often lay bare the truth."

"The truth is God's, it isn't man's; we had better leave it alone. Who can judge of it—who can say?"

"We are terribly in the dark, I know," I admitted; "but if we give up trying what becomes of all the fine things? What becomes of the work I just mentioned, that of the great philosophers and poets? It is all vain words if there is nothing to measure it by."

"You talk as if you were a tailor," said Miss Bordereau, whimsically; and then she added quickly, in a different manner, "This house is very fine; the proportions are magnificent. To-day I wanted to look at this place again. I made them bring me out here. When your man came, just now, to learn if I would see you, I was on the point of sending for you, to ask if you didn't mean to go on. I wanted to judge what I'm letting you have. This sala is very grand," she pursued, like an auctioneer, moving a little, as I guessed, her invisible eyes. "I don't believe you often have lived in such a house, eh?"

"I can't often afford to!" I said.

"Well then, how much will you give for six months?"

I was on the point of exclaiming—and the air of excruciation in my face would have denoted a moral fact—"Don't, Juliana; for *his* sake, don't!" But I controlled myself and asked less passionately: "Why should I remain so long as that?"

"I thought you liked it," said Miss Bordereau, with her shrivelled dignity.

"So I thought I should."

For a moment she said nothing more, and I left my own words to suggest to her what they might. I half expected her to say, coldly enough, that if I had been disappointed we need not continue the discussion, and this in spite of the fact that I believed her now to have in her mind (however it had come there), what would have told her that my disappointment was natural. But to my extreme surprise she ended by observing: "If you don't think we have treated you well enough perhaps we can discover some way of treating you better." This speech was somehow so incongruous that it made me laugh again, and I excused myself by saying that she talked as if I were a sulky boy, pouting in the corner, to be "brought round." I had not a grain of complaint to make; and could anything have exceeded Miss Tita's graciousness in accompanying me a few nights before to the Piazza? At this the old woman went on: "Well, you brought it on yourself!" And then in a different tone, "She is a very nice girl." I assented cordially to this proposition, and she expressed the hope that I did so not merely to be obliging, but that I really liked her. Meanwhile I wondered still more what Miss Bordereau was coming to. "Except for me, to-day," she said, "she has not a relation in the world." Did she by describing her niece as amiable and unencumbered wish to represent her as a *parti?*

It was perfectly true that I could not afford to go on with my rooms at a fancy price and that I had already devoted to my undertaking almost all the hard cash I had set apart for it. My patience and my time were by no means exhausted, but I should be able to draw upon them only on a more usual Venetian basis. I was willing to pay the venerable woman with whom my pecuniary dealings were such a discord twice as much as any other *padrona di casa* would have asked, but I was not willing to pay her twenty times as much. I told her so plainly, and my plainness appeared to have some success, for she exclaimed, "Very good; you have done what I asked—you have made an offer!"

"Yes, but not for half a year. Only by the month."

"Oh, I must think of that then." She seemed disappointed that I would not tie myself to a period, and I guessed that she wished both to secure me and to discourage me; to say, severely, "Do you dream that you can get off with less than six months? Do you dream that even by the end of that time you will be appreciably nearer your victory?" What was more in my mind was that she had a fancy to play me the trick of making me engage myself when in fact she had annihilated the papers. There was a moment when my suspense on this point was so acute that I all but broke out with the question, and what kept it back was but a kind of instinctive recoil (lest it should be a mistake), from the last violence of self-exposure. She was such a subtle old witch that one could never tell where one stood with her. You may imagine whether it cleared up the puzzle when, just after she had said she would think of my proposal and without any formal transition, she drew out of her pocket with an embarrassed hand a small object wrapped in crumpled white paper. She held it there a moment and then she asked, "Do you know much about curiosities?"

"About curiosities?"

"About antiquities, the old gimcracks that people pay so much for to-day. Do you know the kind of price they bring?"

I thought I saw what was coming, but I said ingenuously, "Do you want to buy something?"

"No, I want to sell. What would an amateur give me for that?" She unfolded the white paper and made a motion for me to take from her a small oval portrait. I possessed myself of it with a hand of which I could only hope that she did not perceive the tremor, and she added, "I would part with it only for a good price."

At the first glance I recognised Jeffrey Aspern, and I was well aware that I flushed with the act. As she was watching me however I had the consistency to exclaim, "What a striking face! Do tell me who it is."

"It's an old friend of mine, a very distinguished man in his day. He gave it to me himself, but I'm afraid to mention his name, lest you never should have heard of him, critic and historian as you are. I know the world goes fast and one generation forgets another. He was all the fashion when I was young."

She was perhaps amazed at my assurance, but I was surprised at hers; at her having the energy, in her state of health and at her time of life, to wish to sport with me that way simply for her private entertainment—the humour to test me and practise on me. This, at least, was the interpretation that I put upon her production of the portrait, for I could not believe that she really desired to sell it or cared for any information I might give her. What she wished was to dangle it before my eyes and put a prohibitive price on it. "The face comes back to me, it torments me," I said, turning the object this way and that and looking at it very critically. It was a careful but not a supreme work of art, larger than the ordinary miniature and representing a young man with a remarkably handsome face, in a high-collared green coat and a buff waist-coat. I judged the picture to have a valuable quality of resemblance and to have been painted when the model was about twenty-five years old. There are, as all the world knows, three other portraits of the poet in existence, but none of them is of so early a date as this elegant production. "I have never seen the original but I have seen other likenesses," I went on. "You expressed doubt of this generation having heard of the gentleman, but he strikes me for all the world as a celebrity. Now who is he? I can't put my finger on him—I can't give him a label. Wasn't he a writer? Surely he's a poet." I was determined that it should be she, not I, who should first pronounce Jeffrey Aspern's name.

My resolution was taken in ignorance of Miss Bordereau's extremely resolute character, and her lips never formed in my hearing the syllables that meant so much for her. She neglected to answer my question but raised her hand to take back the picture, with a gesture which though ineffectual was in a high degree peremptory. "It's only a person who should know for himself that would give me my price," she said with a certain dryness.

"Oh, then, you have a price?" I did not restore the precious thing; not from any vindictive purpose but because I instinctively clung to it. We looked at each other hard while I retained it.

"I know the least I would take. What it occurred to me to ask you about is the most I shall be able to get."

She made a movement, drawing herself together as if, in a spasm of dread at having lost her treasure, she were going to attempt the immense effort of rising to snatch it from me. I instantly placed it in her hand again, saying as I did so, "I should like to have it myself, but with your ideas I could never afford it."

She turned the small oval plate over in her lap, with its face down, and I thought I saw her catch her breath a little, as if she had had a strain or an escape. This however did not prevent her saying in a moment, "You would buy a likeness of a person you don't know, by an artist who has no reputation?"

"The artist may have no reputation, but that thing is wonderfully well painted," I replied, to give myself a reason.

"It's lucky you thought of saying that, because the painter was my father."

"That makes the picture indeed precious!" I exclaimed, laughing; and I may add that a part of my laughter came from my satisfaction in finding that I had been right in my theory of Miss Bordereau's origin. Aspern had of course met the young lady when he went to her father's studio as a sitter. I observed to Miss Bordereau that if she would entrust me with her property for twenty-four hours I should be happy to take advice upon it; but she made no answer to this save to slip it in silence into her pocket. This convinced me still more that she had no sincere intention of selling it during her lifetime, though she may have desired to satisfy herself as to the sum her niece, should she leave it to her, might expect eventually to obtain for it. "Well, at any rate I hope you will not offer it without giving me notice," I said, as she remained irresponsive. "Remember that I am a possible purchaser."

"I should want your money first!" she returned, with unexpected rudeness; and then, as if she bethought herself that I had just cause to complain of such an insinuation and wished to turn the matter off, asked abruptly what I talked about with her niece when I went out with her that way in the evening.

"You speak as if we had set up the habit," I replied. "Certainly I should be very glad if it were to become a habit. But in that case I should feel a still greater scruple at betraying a lady's confidence."

"Her confidence? Has she got confidence?"

"Here she is—she can tell you herself," I said; for Miss Tita now appeared on the threshold of the old woman's parlour. "Have you got confidence, Miss Tita? Your aunt wants very much to know."

"Not in her, not in her!" the younger lady declared, shaking her head with a dolefulness that was neither jocular nor affected. "I don't know what to do with her; she has fits of horrid imprudence. She is so easily tired—and yet she has begun to roam—to drag herself about the house." And she stood looking down at her immemorial companion with a sort of helpless wonder, as if all their years of familiarity had not made her perversities, on occasion, any more easy to follow.

"I know what I'm about. I'm not losing my mind. I daresay you would like to think so," said Miss Bordereau, with a cynical little sigh.

"I don't suppose you came out here yourself. Miss Tita must have had to lend you a hand," I interposed, with a pacifying intention.

"Oh, she insisted that we should push her; and when she insists!" said Miss Tita, in the same tone of apprehension; as if there were no knowing what service that she disapproved of her aunt might force her next to render.

"I have always got most things done I wanted, thank God! The people I have lived with have humoured me," the old woman continued, speaking out of the gray ashes of her vanity.

"I suppose you mean that they have obeyed you."

"Well, whatever it is, when they like you."

"It's just because I like you that I want to resist," said Miss Tita, with a nervous laugh.

"Oh, I suspect you'll bring Miss Bordereau upstairs next, to pay me a visit," I went on; to which the old lady replied:

"Oh no; I can keep an eye on you from here!"

"You are very tired; you will certainly be ill to-night!" cried Miss Tita.

"Nonsense, my dear; I feel better at this moment than I

have done for a month. To-morrow I shall come out again. I want to be where I can see this clever gentleman."

"Shouldn't you perhaps see me better in your sitting-room?" I inquired.

"Don't you mean shouldn't you have a better chance at me?" she returned, fixing me a moment with her green shade. "Ah, I haven't that anywhere! I look at you but I don't see you."

"You excite her dreadfully—and that is not good," said Miss Tita, giving me a reproachful, appealing look.

"I want to watch you—I want to watch you!" the old lady went on.

"Well then, let us spend as much of our time together as possible—I don't care where—and that will give you every facility."

"Oh, I've seen you enough for to-day. I'm satisfied. Now I'll go home." Miss Tita laid her hands on the back of her aunt's chair and began to push, but I begged her to let me take her place. "Oh yes, you may move me this way—you sha'n't in any other!" Miss Bordereau exclaimed, as she felt herself propelled firmly and easily over the smooth, hard floor. Before we reached the door of her own apartment she commanded me to stop, and she took a long, last look up and down the noble sala. "Oh, it's a magnificent house!" she murmured; after which I pushed her forward. When we had entered the parlour Miss Tita told me that she should now be able to manage, and at the same moment the little red-haired *donna* came to meet her mistress. Miss Tita's idea was evidently to get her aunt immediately back to bed. I confess that in spite of this urgency I was guilty of the indiscretion of lingering; it held me there to think that I was nearer the documents I coveted—that they were probably put away somewhere in the faded, unsociable room. The place had indeed a bareness which did not suggest hidden treasures; there were no dusky nooks nor curtained corners, no massive cabinets nor chests with iron bands. Moreover it was possible, it was perhaps even probable that the old lady had consigned her relics to her bedroom, to some battered box that was shoved under the bed, to the drawer of some lame dressing-table, where they would be in the range of vision by the dim night-lamp. None the less I scrutinised every article of furniture, every conceivable cover for a hoard, and noticed that there were half a dozen things with drawers, and in particular a tall old secretary, with brass ornaments of the style of the Empire—a receptacle somewhat rickety but still capable of keeping a great many secrets. I don't know why this article fascinated me so, inasmuch as I certainly had no definite purpose of breaking into it; but I stared at it so hard that Miss Tita noticed me and changed colour. Her doing this made me think I was right and that wherever they might have been before the Aspern papers at that moment languished behind the peevish little lock of the secretary. It was hard to remove my eyes from the dull mahogany front when I reflected that a simple panel divided me from the goal of my hopes; but I remembered my prudence and with an effort took leave of Miss Bordereau. To make the effort graceful I said to her that I should certainly bring her an opinion about the little picture.

"The little picture?" Miss Tita asked, surprised.

"What do *you* know about it, my dear?" the old woman demanded. "You needn't mind. I have fixed my price."

"And what may that be?"

"A thousand pounds."

"Oh Lord!" cried poor Miss Tita, irrepressibly.

"Is that what she talks to you about?" said Miss Bordereau.

"Imagine your aunt's wanting to know!" I had to separate from Miss Tita with only those words, though I should have liked immensely to add, "For heaven's sake meet me to-night in the garden!"

VIII

As it turned out the precaution had not been needed, for three hours later, just as I had finished my dinner, Miss Bordereau's niece appeared, unannounced, in the open doorway of the room in which my simple repasts were served. I remember well that I felt no surprise at seeing her; which is not a proof that I did not believe in her timidity. It was immense, but in a case in which there was a particular reason for boldness it never would have prevented her from running up to my rooms. I saw that she was now quite full of a particular reason; it threw her forward—made her seize me, as I rose to meet her, by the arm.

"My aunt is very ill; I think she is dying!"

"Never in the world," I answered, bitterly. "Don't you be afraid!"

"Do go for a doctor—do, do! Olimpia is gone for the one we always have, but she doesn't come back; I don't know what has happened to her. I told her that if he was not at home she was to follow him where he had gone; but apparently she is following him all over Venice. I don't know what to do—she looks so as if she were sinking."

"May I see her, may I judge?" I asked. "Of course I shall be delighted to bring some one; but hadn't we better send my man instead, so that I may stay with you?"

Miss Tita assented to this and I despatched my servant for the best doctor in the neighbourhood. I hurried downstairs with her, and on the way she told me that an hour after I quitted them in the afternoon Miss Bordereau had had an attack of "oppression," a terrible difficulty in breathing. This had subsided but had left her so exhausted that she did not come up: she seemed all gone. I repeated that she was not gone, that she would not go yet; whereupon Miss Tita gave me a sharper sidelong glance than she had ever directed at me and said, "Really, what do you mean? I suppose you don't accuse her of making-believe!" I forget what reply I made to this, but I grant that in my heart I thought the old woman capable of any weird manœuvre. Miss Tita wanted to know what I had done to her; her aunt had told her that I had made her so angry. I declared I had done nothing—I had been exceedingly careful; to which my companion rejoined that Miss Bordereau had assured her she had had a scene with me —a scene that had upset her. I answered with some resentment that it was a scene of her own making—that I couldn't think what she was angry with me for unless for not seeing my way to give a thousand pounds for the portrait of Jeffrey Aspern. "And did she show you that? Oh gracious—oh deary me!" groaned Miss Tita, who appeared to feel that the situation was passing out of her control and that the elements of her fate were thickening around her. I said that I would give anything to possess it, yet that I had not a thousand pounds; but I stopped when we came to the door of Miss Bordereau's room. I had an immense curiosity to pass it, but I thought it my duty to represent to Miss Tita that if I made the invalid angry she ought perhaps to be spared the sight of me. "The sight of you? Do you think she can *see*?" my companion demanded, almost with indignation. I did think so but forbore to say it, and I softly followed my conductress.

I remember that what I said to her as I stood for a moment beside the old woman's bed was, "Does she never show you her eyes then? Have you never seen them?" Miss Bordereau had been divested of her green shade, but (it was not my fortune to behold Juliana in her nightcap) the upper half of her face was covered by the fall of a piece of dingy lacelike muslin, a sort of extemporised hood which, wound round her head, descended to the end of her nose, leaving nothing visible but her white withered cheeks and puckered mouth, closed

tightly and, as it were, consciously. Miss Tita gave me a
glance of surprise, evidently not seeing a reason for my
impatience. "You mean that she always wears something?
She does it to preserve them."

"Because they are so fine?"

"Oh, to-day, to-day!" And Miss Tita shook her head,
speaking very low. "But they used to be magnificent!"

"Yes indeed, we have Aspern's word for that." And as I
looked again at the old woman's wrappings I could imagine
that she had not wished to allow people a reason to say that
the great poet had overdone it. But I did not waste my time in
considering Miss Bordereau, in whom the appearance of
respiration was so slight as to suggest that no human attention
could ever help her more. I turned my eyes all over the room,
rummaging with them the closets, the chests of drawers, the
tables. Miss Tita met them quickly and read, I think, what was
in them; but she did not answer it, turning away restlessly,
anxiously, so that I felt rebuked, with reason, for a preoccupa-
tion that was almost profane in the presence of our dying companion. All the same I took another look, endeavouring to
pick out mentally the place to try first, for a person who
should wish to put his hand on Miss Bordereau's papers
directly after her death. The room was a dire confusion; it
looked like the room of an old actress. There were clothes
hanging over chairs, odd-looking, shabby bundles here and
there, and various pasteboard boxes piled together, battered,
bulging and discoloured, which might have been fifty years
old. Miss Tita after a moment noticed the direction of my eyes
again and, as if she guessed how I judged the air of the place
(forgetting I had no business to judge it at all), said, perhaps
to defend herself from the imputation of complicity in such
untidiness:

"She likes it this way; we can't move things. There are old
bandboxes she has had most of her life." Then she added, half
taking pity on my real thought, "Those things were *there*."

And she pointed to a small, low trunk which stood under a sofa where there was just room for it. It appeared to be a queer, superannuated coffer, of painted wood, with elaborate handles and shrivelled straps and with the colour (it had last been endued with a coat of light green) much rubbed off. It evidently had travelled with Juliana in the olden time—in the days of her adventures, which it had shared. It would have made a strange figure arriving at a modern hotel.

" *Were* there—they aren't now?" I asked, startled by Miss Tita's implication.

She was going to answer, but at that moment the doctor came in—the doctor whom the little maid had been sent to fetch and whom she had at last overtaken. My servant, going on his own errand, had met her with her companion in tow, and in the sociable Venetian spirit, retracing his steps with them, had also come up to the threshold of Miss Bordereau's room, where I saw him peeping over the doctor's shoulder. I motioned him away the more instantly that the sight of his prying face reminded me that I myself had almost as little to do there—an admonition confirmed by the sharp way the little doctor looked at me, appearing to take me for a rival who had the field before him. He was a short, fat, brisk gentleman who wore the tall hat of his profession and seemed to look at everything but his patient. He looked particularly at me, as if it struck him that I should be better for a dose, so that I bowed to him and left him with the women, going down to smoke a cigar in the garden. I was nervous; I could not go further; I could not leave the place. I don't know exactly what I thought might happen, but it seemed to me important to be there. I wandered about in the alleys—the warm night had come on—smoking cigar after cigar and looking at the light in Miss Bordereau's windows. They were open now, I could see; the situation was different. Sometimes the light moved, but not quickly; it did not suggest the hurry of a crisis. Was the old woman dying or was she already dead? Had the doctor said that there was nothing to be done at her tremendous age but to let her quietly pass away; or had he simply announced with a look a little more conventional that the end of the end had come? Were the other two women moving about to perform the offices that follow in such a case? It made me uneasy not to be nearer, as if I thought the doctor himself might carry away the papers with him. I bit my cigar hard as it came over me again that perhaps there were now no papers to carry!

I wandered about for an hour—for an hour and a half. I looked out for Miss Tita at one of the windows, having a vague idea that she might come there to give me some sign. Would she not see the red tip of my cigar moving about in the dark and feel that I wanted eminently to know what the doctor had said? I am afraid it is a proof my anxieties had made me gross that I should have taken in some degree for granted that at such an hour, in the midst of the greatest change that could take place in her life, they were uppermost also in poor Miss Tita's mind. My servant came down and spoke to me; he knew nothing save that the doctor had gone after a visit of half an hour. If he had stayed half an hour then Miss Bordereau was still alive: it could not have taken so much time as that to enunciate the contrary. I sent the man out of the house; there were moments when the sense of his curiosity annoyed me and this was one of them. *He* had been watching my cigar-tip from an upper window, if Miss Tita had not; he could not know what I was after and I could not tell him, though I was conscious he had fantastic private theories about me which he thought fine and which I, had I known them, should have thought offensive.

I went upstairs at last but I ascended no higher than the sala. The door of Miss Bordereau's apartment was open, showing from the parlour the dimness of a poor candle. I went toward it with a light tread and at the same moment Miss Tita appeared and stood looking at me as I approached. "She's better— she's better," she said, even before I had asked. "The doctor has given her something; she woke up, came back to life while he was there. He says there is no immediate danger."

"No immediate danger? Surely he thinks her condition strange!"

"Yes, because she had been excited. That affects her dreadfully."

"It will do so again then, because she excites herself. She did so this afternoon."

"Yes; she mustn't come out any more," said Miss Tita, with one of her lapses into a deeper placidity.

"What is the use of making such a remark as that if you begin to rattle her about again the first time she bids you?"

"I won't—I won't do it any more."

"You must learn to resist her," I went on.

"Oh yes, I shall; I shall do so better if you tell me it's right."

"You mustn't do it for me; you must do it for yourself. It all comes back to you, if you are frightened."

"Well, I am not frightened now," said Miss Tita, cheerfully. "She is very quiet."

"Is she conscious again—does she speak?"

"No, she doesn't speak, but she takes my hand. She holds it fast."

"Yes," I rejoined, "I can see what force she still has by the way she grabbed that picture this afternoon. But if she holds you fast how comes it that you are here?"

Miss Tita hesitated a moment; though her face was in deep shadow (she had her back to the light in the parlour and I had put down my own candle far off, near the door of the sala), I thought I saw her smile ingenuously. "I came on purpose—I heard your step."

"Why, I came on tiptoe, as inaudibly as possible."

"Well, I heard you," said Miss Tita.

"And is your aunt alone now?"

"Oh no; Olimpia is sitting there."

On my side I hesitated. "Shall we then step in there?" And I nodded at the parlour; I wanted more and more to be on the spot.

"We can't talk there—she will hear us."

I was on the point of replying that in that case we would sit silent, but I was too conscious that this would not do, as there was something I desired immensely to ask her. So I proposed that we should walk a little in the sala, keeping more at the other end, where we should not disturb the old lady. Miss Tita assented unconditionally; the doctor was coming again, she said, and she would be there to meet him at the door. We strolled through the fine superfluous hall, where on the marble floor—particularly as at first we said nothing—our footsteps were more audible than I had expected. When we reached the other end—the wide window, inverterately closed, connecting with the balcony that overhung the canal—I suggested that we should remain there, as she would see the doctor arrive still better. I opened the window and we passed out on the balcony. The air of the canal seemed even heavier, hotter than that of the sala. The place was hushed and void; the quiet neighbourhood had gone to sleep. A lamp, here and there, over the narrow black water, glimmered in double; the voice of a man going homeward singing, with his jacket on his shoulder and his hat on his ear, came to us from a distance. This did not prevent the scene from being very *comme il faut*, as Miss Bordereau had called it the first time I saw her. Presently a gondola passed along the canal with its slow rhythmical plash, and as we listened we watched it in silence. It did not stop, it did not carry the doctor; and after it had gone on I said to Miss Tita:

"And where are they now—the things that were in the trunk?"

"In the trunk?"

"That green box you pointed out to me in her room. You said her papers had been there; you seemed to imply that she had transferred them."

"Oh yes; they are not in the trunk," said Miss Tita.

"May I ask if you have looked?"

"Yes, I have looked—for you."

"How for me, dear Miss Tita? Do you mean you would have given them to me if you had found them?" I asked, almost trembling.

She delayed to reply and I waited. Suddenly she broke out, "I don't know what I would do—what I wouldn't!"

"Would you look again—somewhere else?"

She had spoken with a strange, unexpected emotion, and she went on in the same tone: "I can't—I can't—while she lies there. It isn't decent."

"No, it isn't decent," I replied, gravely. "Let the poor lady rest in peace." And the words, on my lips, were not hypocritical, for I felt reprimanded and shamed.

Miss Tita added in a moment, as if she had guessed this and were sorry for me, but at the same time wished to explain that I did drive her on or at least did insist too much: "I can't deceive her that way. I can't deceive her—perhaps on her deathbed."

"Heaven forbid I should ask you, though I have been guilty myself!"

"You have been guilty?"

"I have sailed under false colours." I felt now as if I must tell her that I had given her an invented name, on account of my fear that her aunt would have heard of me and would refuse to take me in. I explained this and also that I had really been a party to the letter written to them by John Cumnor months before.

She listened with great attention, looking at me with parted lips, and when I had made my confession she said, "Then your real name—what is it?" She repeated it over twice when

I had told her, accompanying it with the exclamation "Gracious, gracious!" Then she added, "I like your own best."

"So do I," I said, laughing. "Ouf! it's a relief to get rid of the other."

"So it was a regular plot—a kind of conspiracy?"

"Oh, a conspiracy—we were only two," I replied, leaving out Mrs Prest of course.

She hesitated; I thought she was perhaps going to say that we had been very base. But she remarked after a moment, in a candid, wondering way, "How much you must want them!"

"Oh, I do, passionately!" I conceded, smiling. And this chance made me go on, forgetting my compunction of a moment before. "How can she possibly have changed their place herself? How can she walk? How can she arrive at that sort of muscular exertion? How can she lift and carry things?"

"Oh, when one wants and when one has so much will!" said Miss Tita, as if she had thought over my question already herself and had simply had no choice but that answer—the idea that in the dead of night, or at some moment when the coast was clear, the old woman had been capable of a miraculous effort.

"Have you questioned Olimpia? Hasn't she helped her—hasn't she done it for her?" I asked; to which Miss Tita replied promptly and positively that their servant had had nothing to do with the matter, though without admitting definitely that she had spoken to her. It was as if she were a little shy, a little ashamed now of letting me see how much she had entered into my uneasiness and had me on her mind. Suddenly she said to me, without any immediate relevance:

"I feel as if you were a new person, now that you have got a new name."

"It isn't a new one; it is a very good old one, thank heaven!"

She looked at me a moment. "I do like it better."

"Oh, if you didn't I would almost go on with the other!"

"Would you really?"

I laughed again, but for all answer to this inquiry I said, "Of course if she can rummage about that way she can perfectly have burnt them."

"You must wait—you must wait," Miss Tita moralised mournfully; and her tone ministered little to my patience, for it seemed after all to accept that wretched possibility. I would teach myself to wait, I declared nevertheless; because in the first place I could not do otherwise and in the second I had her promise, given me the other night, that she would help me.

"Of course if the papers are gone that's no use," she said; not as if she wished to recede, but only to be conscientious.

"Naturally. But if you could only find out!" I groaned, quivering again.

"I thought you said you would wait."

"Oh, you mean wait even for that?"

"For what then?"

"Oh, nothing," I replied, rather foolishly, being ashamed to tell her what had been implied in my submission to delay— the idea that she would do more than merely find out. I know not whether she guessed this; at all events she appeared to become aware of the necessity for being a little more rigid.

"I didn't promise to deceive, did I? I don't think I did."

"It doesn't much matter whether you did or not, for you couldn't!"

I don't think Miss Tita would have contested this even had she not been diverted by our seeing the doctor's gondola shoot into the little canal and approach the house. I noted that he came as fast as if he believed that Miss Bordereau was still in danger. We looked down at him while he disembarked and then went back into the sala to meet him. When he came up however I naturally left Miss Tita to go off with him alone, only asking her leave to come back later for news.

I went out of the house and took a long walk, as far as the

Piazza, where my restlessness declined to quit me. I was unable to sit down (it was very late now but there were people still at the little tables in front of the cafés); I could only walk round and round, and I did so half a dozen times. I was uncomfortable, but it gave me a certain pleasure to have told Miss Tita who I really was. At last I took my way home again, slowly getting all but inextricably lost, as I did whenever I went out in Venice: so that it was considerably past midnight when I reached my door. The sala, upstairs, was as dark as usual and my lamp as I crossed it found nothing satisfactory to show me. I was disappointed, for I had notified Miss Tita that I would come back for a report, and I thought she might have left a light there as a sign. The door of the ladies' apartment was closed; which seemed an intimation that my faltering friend had gone to bed, tired of waiting for me. I stood in the middle of the place, considering, hoping she would hear me and perhaps peep out, saying to myself too that she would never go to bed with her aunt in a state so critical; she would sit up and watch—she would be in a chair, in her dressing-gown. I went nearer the door; I stopped there and listened. I heard nothing at all and at last I tapped gently. No answer came and after another minute I turned the handle. There was no light in the room; this ought to have prevented me from going in, but it had no such effect. If I have candidly narrated the importunities, the indelicacies, of which my desire to possess myself of Jeffrey Aspern's papers had rendered me capable I need not shrink from confessing this last indiscretion. I think it was the worst thing I did; yet there were extenuating circumstances. I was deeply though doubtless not disinterestedly anxious for more news of the old lady, and Miss Tita had accepted from me, as it were, a rendezvous which it might have been a point of honour with me to keep. It may be said that her leaving the place dark was a positive sign that she released me, and to this I can only reply that I desired not to be released.

The door of Miss Bordereau's room was open and I could see beyond it the faintness of a taper. There was no sound— my footstep caused no one to stir. I came further into the room; I lingered there with my lamp in my hand. I wanted to give Miss Tita a chance to come to me if she were with her aunt, as she must be. I made no noise to call her; I only waited to see if she would not notice my light. She did not, and I explained this (I found afterwards I was right) by the idea that she had fallen asleep. If she had fallen asleep her aunt was not on her mind, and my explanation ought to have led me to go out as I had come. I must repeat again that it did not, for I found myself at the same moment thinking of something else. I had no definite purpose, no bad intention, but I felt myself held to the spot by an acute, though absurd, sense of opportunity. For what I could not have said, inasmuch as it was not in my mind that I might commit a theft. Even if it had been I was confronted with the evident fact that Miss Bordereau did not leave her secretary, her cupboard and the drawers of her tables gaping. I had no keys, no tools and no ambition to smash her furniture. None the less it came to me that I was now, perhaps alone, unmolested, at the hour of temptation and secrecy, nearer to the tormenting treasure than I had ever been. I held up my lamp, let the light play on the different objects as if it could tell me something. Still there came no movement from the other room. If Miss Tita was sleeping she was sleeping sound. Was she doing so—generous creature—on purpose to leave me the field? Did she know I was there and was she just keeping quiet to see what I would do—what I *could* do? But what could I do, when it came to that? She herself knew even better than I how little.

I stopped in front of the secretary, looking at it very idiotically; for what had it to say to me after all? In the first place it was locked, and in the second it almost surely contained nothing in which I was interested. Ten to one the papers had been destroyed; and even if they had not been destroyed the old woman would not have put them in such a place as that after removing them from the green trunk—would not have transferred them, if she had the idea of their safety on her brain, from the better hiding-place to the worse. The secretary was more conspicuous, more accessible in a room in which she could no longer mount guard. It opened with a key, but there was a little brass handle, like a button, as well; I saw this as I played my lamp over it. I did something more than this at that moment: I caught a glimpse of the possibility that Miss Tita wished me really to understand. If she did not wish me to understand, if she wished me to keep away, why had she not locked the door of communication between the sitting-room and the sala? That would have been a definite sign that I was to leave them alone. If I did not leave them alone she meant me to come for a purpose—a purpose now indicated by the quick, fantastic idea that to oblige me she had unlocked the secretary. She had not left the key, but the lid would probably move if I touched the button. This theory fascinated me, and I bent over very close to judge. I did not propose to do anything, not even—not in the least—to let down the lid; I only wanted to test my theory, to see if the cover *would* move. I touched the button with my hand—a mere touch would tell me; and as I did so (it is embarrassing for me to relate it), I looked over my shoulder. It was a chance, an instinct, for I had not heard anything. I almost let my luminary drop and certainly I stepped back, straightening myself up at what I saw. Miss Bordereau stood there in her night-dress, in the doorway of her room, watching me; her hands were raised, she had lifted the everlasting curtain that covered half her face, and for the first, the last, the only time I beheld her extraordinary eyes. They glared at me, they made me horribly ashamed. I never shall forget her strange little bent white tottering figure, with its lifted head, her attitude, her expression; neither shall I forget the tone in which as I turned, looking at her, she hissed out passionately, furiously:

"Ah, you publishing scoundrel!"

I know not what I stammered, to excuse myself, to explain; but I went towards her, to tell her I meant no harm. She waved me off with her old hands, retreating before me in horror; and the next thing I knew she had fallen back with a quick spasm, as if death had descended on her, into Miss Tita's arms.

IX

I LEFT Venice the next morning, as soon as I learnt that the old lady had not succumbed, as I feared at the moment, to the shock I had given her—the shock I may also say she had given me. How in the world could I have supposed her capable of getting out of bed by herself? I failed to see Miss Tita before going; I only saw the *donna*, whom I entrusted with a note for her younger mistress. In this note I mentioned that I should be absent but for a few days. I went to Treviso, to Bassano, to Castelfranco; I took walks and drives and looked at musty old churches with ill-lighted pictures and spent hours seated smoking at the doors of cafés, where there were flies and yellow curtains, on the shady side of sleepy little squares. In spite of these pastimes, which were mechanical and perfunctory, I scantily enjoyed my journey: there was too strong a taste of the disagreeable in my life. It had been devilish awkward, as the young men say, to be found by Miss Bordereau in the dead of night examining the attachment of her bureau; and it had not been less so to have to believe for a good many hours afterward that it was highly probable I had killed her. In writing to Miss Tita I attempted to minimise these irregularities; but as she gave me no word of answer I could not know what impression I made upon her. It rankled in my mind that I had been called a publishing scoundrel, for certainly I did publish and certainly I had not been very delicate. There was a moment when I stood convinced that the only way to make up for this latter fault was to take myself away altogether on the instant; to sacrifice my hopes and relieve the two poor women for ever of the oppression of my intercourse. Then I reflected that I had better try a short absence first, for I must already have had a sense (unexpressed and dim) that in disappearing completely it would not be merely my own hopes that I should condemn to extinction. It would perhaps be sufficient if I stayed away long enough to give the elder lady time to think she was rid of me. That she would wish to be rid of me after this (if I was not rid of her) was now not to be doubted: that nocturnal scene would have cured her of the disposition to put up with my company for the sake of my dollars. I said to myself that after all I could not abandon Miss Tita, and I continued to say this even while I observed that she quite failed to comply with my earnest request (I had given her two or three addresses, at little towns, *poste restante*) that she would let me know how she was getting on. I would have made my servant write to me but that he was unable to manage a pen. It struck me there was a kind of scorn in Miss Tita's silence (little disdainful as she had ever been), so that I was uncomfortable and sore. I had scruples about going back and yet I had others about not doing so, for I wanted to put myself on a better footing. The end of it was that I did return to Venice on the twelfth day; and as my gondola gently bumped against Miss Bordereau's steps a certain palpitation of suspense told me that I had done myself a violence in holding off so long.

I had faced about so abruptly that I had not telegraphed to my servant. He was therefore not at the station to meet me, but he poked out his head from an upper window when I reached the house. "They have put her into the earth, *la vecchia*," he said to me in the lower hall, while he shouldered my valise; and he grinned and almost winked, as if he knew I should be pleased at the news.

"She's dead!" I exclaimed, giving him a very different look.

"So it appears, since they have buried her."

"It's all over? When was the funeral?"

"The other yesterday. But a funeral you could scarcely call it, signore; it was a dull little passeggio of two gondolas. Poveretta!" the man continued, referring apparently to Miss Tita. His conception of funerals was apparently that they were mainly to amuse the living.

I wanted to know about Miss Tita—how she was and where she was—but I asked him no more questions till we had got upstairs. Now that the fact had met me I took a bad view of it, especially of the idea that poor Miss Tita had had to manage by herself after the end. What did she know about arrangements, about the steps to take in such a case? Poveretta indeed! I could only hope that the doctor had given her assistance and that she had not been neglected by the old friends of whom she had told me, the little band of the faithful whose fidelity consisted in coming to the house once a year. I elicited from my servant that two old ladies and an old gentleman had in fact rallied round Miss Tita and had supported her (they had come for her in a gondola of their own) during the journey to the cemetery, the little red-walled island of tombs which lies to the north of the town, on the way to Murano. It appeared from these circumstances that the Misses Bordereau were Catholics, a discovery I had never made, as the old woman could not go to church and her niece, so far as I perceived, either did not or went only to early mass in the parish, before I was stirring. Certainly even the priests respected their seclusion; I had never caught the whisk of the curato's skirt. That evening, an hour later, I sent my servant down with five words written on a card, to ask Miss Tita if she would see me for a few moments. She was not in the house, where he had sought her, he told me when he came back, but in the garden walking about to refresh herself and gathering flowers. He had found her there and she would be very happy to see me.

I went down and passed half an hour with poor Miss Tita. She had always had a look of musty mourning (as if she were wearing out old robes of sorrow that would not come to an end), and in this respect there was no appreciable change in her appearance. But she evidently had been crying, crying a great deal—simply, satisfyingly, refreshingly, with a sort of primitive, retarded sense of loneliness and violence. But she had none of the formalism or the self-consciousness of grief, and I was almost surprised to see her standing there in the first dusk with her hands full of flowers, smiling at me with her reddened eyes. Her white face, in the frame of her mantilla, looked longer, leaner than usual. I had had an idea that she would be a good deal disgusted with me—would consider that I ought to have been on the spot to advise her, to help her; and, though I was sure there was no rancour in her composition and no great conviction of the importance of her affairs, I had prepared myself for a difference in her manner, for some little injured look, half familiar, half estranged, which should say to my conscience, "Well, you are a nice person to have professed things!" But historic truth compels me to declare that Tita Bordereau's countenance expressed unqualified pleasure in seeing her late aunt's lodger. That touched him extremely and he thought it simplified his situation until he found it did not. I was as kind to her that evening as I knew how to be, and I walked about the garden with her for half an hour. There was no explanation of any sort between us; I did not ask her why she had not answered my letter. Still less did I repeat what I had said to her in that communication; if she chose to let me suppose that she had forgotten the position in which Miss Bordereau surprised me that night and the effect of the discovery on the old woman I was quite willing to take it that way: I was grateful to her for not treating me as if I had killed her aunt.

We strolled and strolled and really not much passed between us save the recognition of her bereavement, conveyed in my manner and in a visible air that she had of depending on me now, since I let her see that I took an interest in her. Miss Tita had none of the pride that makes a person wish to preserve the look of independence; she did not in the least pretend that she knew at present what would become of her. I forbore to touch particularly on that however, for I certainly was not prepared to say that I would take charge of her. I was cautious; not ignobly, I think, for I felt that her knowledge of life was so small that in her unsophisticated vision there would be no reason why—since I seemed to pity her—I should not look after her. She told me how her aunt had died, very peacefully at the last, and how everything had been done afterwards by the care of her good friends (fortunately, thanks to me, she said, smiling, there was money in the house; and she repeated that when once the Italians like you they are your friends for life); and when we had gone into this she asked me about my *giro*, my impressions, the places I had seen. I told her what I could, making it up partly, I am afraid, as in my depression I had not seen much; and after she had heard me she exclaimed, quite as if she had forgotten her aunt and her sorrow, "Dear, dear, how much I should like to do such things—to take a little journey!" It came over me for the moment that I ought to propose some tour, say I would take her anywhere she liked; and I remarked at any rate that some excursion—to give her a change—might be managed: we would think of it, talk it over. I said never a word to her about the Aspern documents; asked no questions as to what she had ascertained or what had otherwise happened with regard to them before Miss Bordereau's death. It was not that I was not on pins and needles to know, but that I thought it more decent not to betray my anxiety so soon after the catastrophe. I hoped she herself would say something, but she never glanced that way, and I thought this natural at the time. Later however, that night, it occurred to me that her silence was somewhat strange; for if she had talked of my movements, of anything so detached as the Giorgione at Castelfranco, she might have alluded to what she could easily remember was in my mind. It was not to be supposed that the emotion produced by her aunt's death had blotted out the recollection that I was interested in that lady's relics, and I fidgeted afterwards as it came to me that her reticence might very possibly mean simply that nothing had been found. We separated in the garden (it was she who said she must go in); now that she was alone in the rooms I felt that (judged, at any rate, by Venetian ideas) I was on rather a different footing in regard to visiting her there. As I shook hands with her for good-night I asked her if she had any general plan—had thought over what she had better do. "Oh yes, oh yes, but I haven't settled anything yet," she replied, quite cheerfully. Was her cheerfulness explained by the impression that I would settle for her?

I was glad the next morning that we had neglected practical questions, for this gave me a pretext for seeing her again immediately. There was a very practical question to be touched upon. I owed it to her to let her know formally that of course I did not expect her to keep me on as a lodger, and also to show some interest in her own tenure, what she might have on her hands in the way of a lease. But I was not destined, as it happened, to converse with her for more than an instant on either of these points. I sent her no message; I simply went down to the sala and walked to and fro there. I knew she would come out; she would very soon discover I was there. Somehow I preferred not to be shut up with her; gardens and big halls seemed better places to talk. It was a splendid morning, with something in the air that told of the waning of the long Venetian summer; a freshness from the sea which stirred the flowers in the garden and made a pleasant draught in the house, less shuttered and darkened now than when the old woman was alive. It was the beginning of autumn, of the end of the golden months. With this it was the end of my experiment—or would be in the course of half an hour, when I should really have learned that the papers had been reduced to ashes. After that there would be nothing left for me but to go to the station; for seriously (and as it struck me in the morning light) I could not linger there to act as guardian to a piece of middle-aged female helplessness. If she had not saved the papers wherein should I be indebted to her? I think I winced a little as I asked myself how much, if she *had* saved them, I should have to recognise and, as it were, to reward such a courtesy. Might not that circumstance after all saddle me with a guardianship? If this idea did not make me more uncomfortable as I walked up and down it was because I was convinced I had nothing to look to. If the old woman had not destroyed everything before she pounced upon me in the parlour she had done so afterwards.

It took Miss Tita rather longer than I had expected to guess that I was there; but when at last she came out she looked at me without surprise. I said to her that I had been waiting for her and she asked why I had not let her know. I was glad the next day that I had checked myself before remarking that I had wished to see if a friendly intuition would not tell her: it became a satisfaction to me that I had not indulged in that rather tender joke. What I did say was virtually the truth—that I was too nervous, since I expected her now to settle my fate.

"Your fate?" said Miss Tita, giving me a queer look; and as she spoke I noticed a rare change in her. She was different from what she had been the evening before—less natural, less quiet. She had been crying the day before and she was not crying now, and yet she struck me as less confident. It was as if something had happened to her during the night, or at least as if she had thought of something that troubled her—something in particular that affected her relations with me, made them more embarrassing and complicated. Had she simply perceived that her aunt's not being there now altered my position?

"I mean about our papers. *Are* there any? You must know now."

"Yes, there are a great many; more than I supposed." I was struck with the way her voice trembled as she told me this.

"Do you mean that you have got them in there—and that I may see them?"

"I don't think you can see them," said Miss Tita, with an extraordinary expression of entreaty in her eyes, as if the dearest hope she had in the world now was that I would not take them from her. But how could she expect me to make such a sacrifice as that after all that had passed between us? What had I come back to Venice for but to see them, to take them? My delight at learning they were still in existence was such that if the poor woman had gone down on her knees to beseech me never to mention them again I would have treated the proceeding as a bad joke. "I have got them but I can't show them," she added.

"Not even to me? Ah, Miss Tita!" I groaned, with a voice of infinite remonstrance and reproach.

She coloured and the tears came back to her eyes; I saw that it cost her a kind of anguish to take such a stand but that a dreadful sense of duty had descended upon her. It made me quite sick to find myself confronted with that particular obstacle; all the more that it appeared to me I had been extremely encouraged to leave it out of account. I almost considered that Miss Tita had assured me that if she had no greater hindrance than that——! "You don't mean to say you made her a deathbed promise? It was precisely against your doing anything of that sort that I thought I was safe. Oh, I would rather she had burned the papers outright than that!"

"No, it isn't a promise," said Miss Tita.

"Pray what is it then?"

She hesitated and then she said, "She tried to burn them, but I prevented it. She had hid them in her bed."

"In her bed?"

"Between the mattresses. That's where she put them when she took them out of the trunk. I can't understand how she did it, because Olimpia didn't help her. She tells me so and I believe her. My aunt only told her afterwards, so that she shouldn't touch the bed—anything but the sheets. So it was badly made," added Miss Tita, simply.

"I should think so! And how did she try to burn them?"

"She didn't try much; she was too weak, those last days. But she told me—she charged me. Oh, it was terrible! She couldn't speak after that night; she could only make signs."

"And what did you do?"

"I took them away. I locked them up."

"In the secretary?"

"Yes, in the secretary," said Miss Tita, reddening again.

"Did you tell her you would burn them?"

"No, I didn't—on purpose."

"On purpose to gratify me?"

"Yes, only for that."

"And what good will you have done me if after all you won't show them?"

"Oh, none; I know that—I know that."

"And did she believe you had destroyed them?"

"I don't know what she believed at the last. I couldn't tell —she was too far gone."

"Then if there was no promise and no assurance I can't see what ties you."

"Oh, she hated it so—she hated it so! She was so jealous. But here's the portrait—you may have that," Miss Tita announced, taking the little picture, wrapped up in the same manner in which her aunt had wrapped it, out of her pocket.

"I may have it—do you mean you give it to me?" I questioned, staring, as it passed into my hand.

"Oh yes."

"But it's worth money—a large sum."

"Well!" said Miss Tita, still with her strange look.

I did not know what to make of it, for it could scarcely mean that she wanted to bargain like her aunt. She spoke as if she wished to make me a present. "I can't take it from you as a gift," I said, "and yet I can't afford to pay you for it according to the ideas Miss Bordereau had of its value. She rated it at a thousand pounds."

"Couldn't we sell it?" asked Miss Tita.

"God forbid! I prefer the picture to the money."

"Well then keep it."

"You are very generous."

"So are you."

"I don't know why you should think so," I replied, and this was a truthful speech, for the singular creature appeared to have some very fine reference in her mind, which I did not in the least seize.

"Well, you have made a great difference for me," said Miss Tita.

I looked at Jeffrey Aspern's face in the little picture, partly in order not to look at that of my interlocutress, which had begun to trouble me, even to frighten me a little—it was so self-conscious, so unnatural. I made no answer to this last declaration; I only privately consulted Jeffrey Aspern's delightful eyes with my own (they were so young and brilliant, and yet so wise, so full of vision); I asked him what on earth was the matter with Miss Tita. He seemed to smile at me with friendly mockery, as if he were amused at my case. I had got into a pickle for him—as if he needed it! He was unsatisfactory, for the only moment since I had known him. Nevertheless, now that I held the little picture in my hand I felt that it would be a precious possession. "Is this a bribe to make me give up the papers?" I demanded in a moment, perversely. "Much as I value it, if I were to be obliged to choose, the papers are what I should prefer. Ah, but ever so much!"

"How can you choose—how can you choose?" Miss Tita asked, slowly, lamentably.

"I see! Of course there is nothing to be said, if you regard the interdiction that rests upon you as quite insurmountable. In this case it must seem to you that to part with them would be an impiety of the worst kind, a simple sacrilege!"

Miss Tita shook her head, full of her dolefulness. "You would understand if you had known her. I'm afraid," she quavered suddenly—"I'm afraid! She was terrible when she was angry."

"Yes, I saw something of that, that night. She was terrible. Then I saw her eyes. Lord, they were fine!"

"I see them—they stare at me in the dark!" said Miss Tita.

"You are nervous, with all you have been through."

"Oh yes, very—very!"

"You mustn't mind; that will pass away," I said, kindly. Then I added, resignedly, for it really seemed to me that I must accept the situation, "Well, so it is, and it can't be helped. I must renounce." Miss Tita, at this, looking at me, gave a low, soft moan, and I went on: "I only wish to heaven she had destroyed them; then there would be nothing more to say. And I can't understand why, with her ideas, she didn't."

"Oh, she lived on them!" said Miss Tita.

"You can imagine whether that makes me want less to see them," I answered, smiling. "But don't let me stand here as if I had it in my soul to tempt you to do anything base. Naturally you will understand I give up my rooms. I leave Venice immediately." And I took up my hat, which I had placed on a chair. We were still there rather awkwardly, on our feet, in the middle of the sala. She had left the door of the apartments open behind her but she had not led me that way.

A kind of spasm came into her face as she saw me take my hat. "Immediately—do you mean to-day?" The tone of the words was tragical—they were a cry of desolation.

"Oh no; not so long as I can be of the least service to you."

"Well, just a day or two more—just two or three days," she panted. Then controlling herself she added in another

manner, "She wanted to say something to me—the last day—
something very particular, but she couldn't."

"Something very particular?"

"Something more about the papers."

"And did you guess—have you any idea?"

"No, I have thought—but I don't know. I have thought
all kinds of things."

"And for instance?"

"Well, that if you were a relation it would be different."

"If I were a relation?"

"If you were not a stranger. Then it would be the same for
you as for me. Anything that is mine—would be yours, and
you could do what you like. I couldn't prevent you—and you
would have no responsibility."

She brought out this droll explanation with a little nervous
rush, as if she were speaking words she had got by heart.
They gave me an impression of subtlety and at first I failed to
follow. But after a moment her face helped me to see further,
and then a light came into my mind. It was embarrassing, and
I bent my head over Jeffrey Aspern's portrait. What an odd
expression was in his face! "Get out of it as you can, my dear
fellow!" I put the picture into the pocket of my coat and said
to Miss Tita, "Yes, I'll sell it for you. I sha'n't get a thousand
pounds by any means, but I shall get something good."

She looked at me with tears in her eyes, but she seemed to
try to smile as she remarked, "We can divide the money."

"No, no, it shall be all yours." Then I went on, "I think
I know what your poor aunt wanted to say. She wanted to
give directions that her papers should be buried with her."

Miss Tita appeared to consider this suggestion for a
moment; after which she declared, with striking decision,
"Oh no, she wouldn't have thought that safe!"

"It seems to me nothing could be safer."

"She had an idea that when people want to publish they
are capable——" And she paused, blushing.

"Of violating a tomb? Mercy on us, what must she have thought of me!"

"She was not just, she was not generous!" Miss Tita cried with sudden passion.

The light that had come into my mind a moment before increased. "Ah, don't say that, for we *are* a dreadful race." Then I pursued, "If she left a will, that may give you some idea."

"I have found nothing of the sort—she destroyed it. She was very fond of me," Miss Tita added, incongruously. "She wanted me to be happy. And if any person should be kind to me—she wanted to speak of that."

I was almost awestricken at the astuteness with which the good lady found herself inspired, transparent astuteness as it was and sewn, as the phrase is, with white thread. "Depend upon it she didn't want to make any provision that would be agreeable to me."

"No, not to you but to me. She knew I should like it if you could carry out your idea. Not because she cared for you but because she did think of me," Miss Tita went on, with her unexpected, persuasive volubility. "You could see them—you could use them." She stopped, seeing that I perceived the sense of that conditional—stopped long enough for me to give some sign which I did not give. She must have been conscious however that though my face showed the greatest embarrassment that was ever painted on a human countenance it was not set as a stone, it was also full of compassion. It was a comfort to me a long time afterwards to consider that she could not have seen in me the smallest symptom of disrespect. "I don't know what to do; I'm too tormented, I'm too ashamed!" she continued, with vehemence. Then turning away from me and burying her face in her hands she burst into a flood of tears. If she did not know what to do it may be imagined whether I did any better. I stood there dumb, watching her while her sobs resounded in the great empty hall. In a moment she was facing me again, with her streaming eyes. "I would give you everything—and she would understand, where she is—she would forgive me!"

"Ah, Miss Tita—ah, Miss Tita," I stammered, for all reply. I did not know what to do, as I say, but at a venture I made a wild, vague movement, in consequence of which I found myself at the door. I remember standing there and saying, "It wouldn't do—it wouldn't do!" pensively, awkwardly, grotesquely, while I looked away to the opposite end of the sala as if there were a beautiful view there. The next thing I remember is that I was downstairs and out of the house. My gondola was there and my gondolier, reclining on the cushions, sprang up as soon as he saw me. I jumped in and to his usual "*Dove commanda?*" I replied, in a tone that made him stare, "Anywhere, anywhere; out into the lagoon!"

He rowed me away and I sat there prostrate, groaning softly to myself, with my hat pulled over my face. What in the name of the preposterous did she mean if she did not mean to offer me her hand? That was the price—that was the price! And did she think I wanted it, poor deluded, infatuated, extravagant lady? My gondolier, behind me, must have seen my ears red as I wondered, sitting there under the fluttering *tenda*, with my hidden face, noticing nothing as we passed—wondered whether her delusion, her infatuation had been my own reckless work. Did she think I had made love to her, even to get the papers? I had not, I had not; I repeated that over to myself for an hour, for two hours, till I was wearied if not convinced. I don't know where my gondolier took me; we floated aimlessly about on the lagoon, with slow, rare strokes. At last I became conscious that we were near the Lido, far up, on the right hand, as you turn your back to Venice, and I made him put me ashore. I wanted to walk, to move, to shed some of my bewilderment. I crossed the narrow strip and got to the sea-beach—I took my way toward Malamocco. But presently I flung myself down again on the warm sand, in the breeze, on the coarse dry grass. It took it out of me to think I had been so much at fault, that I had unwittingly but none the less deplorably trifled. But I had not given her cause—distinctly I had not. I had said to Mrs Prest that I would make love to her; but it had been a joke without consequences and I had never said it to Tita Bordereau. I had been as kind as possible, because I really liked her; but since when had that become a crime where a woman of such an age and such an appearance was concerned? I am far from remembering clearly the succession of events and feelings during this long day of confusion, which I spent entirely in wandering about, without going home, until late at night; it only comes back to me that there were moments when I pacified my conscience and others when I lashed it into pain. I did not laugh all day—that I do recollect; the case, however it might have struck others, seemed to me so little amusing. It would have been better perhaps for me to feel the comic side of it. At any rate, whether I had given cause or not it went without saying that I could not pay the price. I could not accept. I could not, for a bundle of tattered papers, marry a ridiculous, pathetic, provincial old woman. It was a proof that she did not think the idea would come to me, her having determined to suggest it herself in that practical, argumentative, heroic way, in which the timidity however had been so much more striking than the boldness that her reasons appeared to come first and her feelings afterward.

As the day went on I grew to wish that I had never heard of Aspern's relics, and I cursed the extravagant curiosity that had put John Cumnor on the scent of them. We had more than enough material without them and my predicament was the just punishment of that most fatal of human follies, our not having known when to stop. It was very well to say it was no predicament, that the way out was simple, that I had only to leave Venice by the first train in the morning, after writing a note to Miss Tita, to be placed in her hand as soon as I got clear of the house; for it was a strong sign that I was embarrassed that when I tried to make up the note in my mind in advance (I would put it on paper as soon as I got home, before going to bed), I could not think of anything but "How can I thank you for the rare confidence you have placed in me?" That would never do; it sounded exactly as if an acceptance were to follow. Of course I might go away without writing a word, but that would be brutal and my idea was still to exclude brutal solutions. As my confusion cooled I was lost in wonder at the importance I had attached to Miss Bordereau's crumpled scraps; the thought of them became odious to me and I was as vexed with the old witch for the superstition that had prevented her from destroying them as I was with myself for having already spent more money than I could afford in attempting to control their fate. I forget what I did, where I went after leaving the Lido and at what hour or with what recovery of composure I made my way back to my boat. I only know that in the afternoon, when the air was aglow with the sunset, I was standing before the church of Saints John and Paul and looking up at the small square-jawed face of Bartolommeo Colleoni, the terrible *condottiere* who sits so sturdily astride of his huge bronze horse, on the high pedestal on which Venetian gratitude maintains him. The statue is incomparable, the finest of all mounted figures, unless that of Marcus Aurelius, who rides benignant before the Roman Capitol, be finer: but I was not thinking of that; I only found myself staring at the triumphant captain as if he had an oracle on his lips. The western light shines into all his grimness at that hour and makes it wonderfully personal. But he continued to look far over my head, at the red immersion of another day —he had seen so many go down into the lagoon through the centuries—and if he were thinking of battles and stratagems they were of a different quality from any I had to tell him of. He could not direct me what to do, gaze up at him as I might. Was it before this or after that I wandered about for an hour in the small canals, to the continued stupefaction of my gondolier, who had never seen me so restless and yet so void of a purpose and could extract from me no order but "Go anywhere—everywhere—all over the place"? He reminded me that I had not lunched and expressed therefore respectfully the hope that I would dine earlier. He had had long periods of leisure during the day, when I had left the boat and rambled, so that I was not obliged to consider him, and I told him that that day, for a change, I would touch no meat. It was an effect of poor Miss Tita's proposal, not altogether auspicious, that I had quite lost my appetite. I don't know why it happened that on this occasion I was more than ever struck with that queer air of sociability, of cousinship and family life, which makes up half the expression of Venice. Without streets and vehicles, the uproar of wheels, the brutality of horses, and with its little winding ways where people crowd together, where voices sound as in the corridors of a house, where the human step circulates as if it skirted the angles of furniture and shoes never wear out, the place has the character of an immense collective apartment, in which Piazza San Marco is the most ornamented corner and palaces and churches, for the rest, play the part of great divans of repose, tables of entertainment, expanses of decoration. And somehow the splendid common domicile, familiar, domestic and resonant, also resembles a theatre, with actors clicking over bridges and, in straggling processions, tripping along fondamentas. As you sit in your gondola the footways that in certain parts edge the canals assume to the eye the importance of a stage, meeting it at the same angle, and the Venetian figures, moving to and fro against the battered scenery of their little houses of comedy, strike you as members of an endless dramatic troupe.

I went to bed that night very tired, without being able to compose a letter to Miss Tita. Was this failure the reason why I became conscious the next morning as soon as I awoke of a determination to see the poor lady again the first moment she would receive me? That had something to do with it, but what had still more was the fact that during my sleep a very odd revulsion had taken place in my spirit. I found myself aware of this almost as soon as I opened my eyes; it made me jump out of my bed with the movement of a man who remembers that he has left the house-door ajar or a candle burning under a shelf. Was I still in time to save my goods? That question was in my heart; for what had now come to pass was that in the unconscious cerebration of sleep I had swung back to a passionate appreciation of Miss Bordereau's papers. They were now more precious than ever and a kind of ferocity had come into my desire to possess them. The condition Miss Tita had attached to the possession of them no longer appeared an obstacle worth thinking of, and for an hour, that morning, my repentant imagination brushed it aside. It was absurd that I should be able to invent nothing; absurd to renounce so easily and turn away helpless from the idea that the only way to get hold of the papers was to unite myself to her for life. I would not unite myself and yet I would have them. I must add that by the time I sent down to ask if she would see me I had invented no alternative, though to do so I had had all the time that I was dressing. This failure was humiliating, yet what could the alternative be? Miss Tita sent back word that I might come; and as I descended the stairs and crossed the sala to her door—this time she received me in her aunt's forlorn parlour—I hoped she would not think my errand was to tell her I accepted her hand. She certainly would have made the day before the reflection that I declined it.

As soon as I came into the room I saw that she had drawn this inference, but I also saw something which had not been in my forecast. Poor Miss Tita's sense of her failure had produced an extraordinary alteration in her, but I had been too full of my literary concupiscence to think of that. Now I perceived it; I can scarcely tell how it startled me. She stood in the middle of the room with a face of mildness bent upon me, and her look of forgiveness, of absolution made her angelic. It beautified her; she was younger; she was not a ridiculous old woman. This optical trick gave her a sort of phantasmagoric brightness, and while I was still the victim of it I heard a whisper somewhere in the depths of my conscience: "Why not, after all—why not?" It seemed to me I was ready to pay the price. Still more distinctly however than the whisper I heard Miss Tita's own voice. I was so struck with the different effect she made upon me that at first I was not clearly aware of what she was saying; then I perceived she had bade me good-bye—she said something about hoping I should be very happy.

"Good-bye—good-bye?" I repeated, with an inflection interrogative and probably foolish.

I saw she did not feel the interrogation, she only heard the words; she had strung herself up to accepting our separation and they fell upon her ear as a proof. "Are you going to-day?" she asked. "But it doesn't matter, for whenever you go I shall not see you again. I don't want to." And she smiled strangely, with an infinite gentleness. She had never doubted that I had left her the day before in horror. How could she, since I had not come back before night to contradict, even as a simple form, such an idea? And now she had the force of soul —Miss Tita with force of soul was a new conception—to smile at me in her humiliation.

"What shall you do—where shall you go?" I asked.

"Oh, I don't know. I have done the great thing. I have destroyed the papers."

"Destroyed them?" I faltered.

"Yes; what was I to keep them for? I burnt them last night, one by one, in the kitchen."

"One by one?" I repeated, mechanically.

"It took a long time—there were so many." The room seemed to go round me as she said this and a real darkness for a moment descended upon my eyes. When it passed Miss Tita was there still, but the transfiguration was over and she had changed back to a plain, dingy, elderly person. It was in this character she spoke as she said, "I can't stay with you longer, I can't;" and it was in this character that she turned her back upon me, as I had turned mine upon her twenty-four hours before, and moved to the door of her room. Here she did what I had not done when I quitted her—she paused long enough to give me one look. I have never forgotten it and I sometimes still suffer from it, though it was not resentful. No, there was no resentment, nothing hard or vindictive in poor Miss Tita; for when, later, I sent her in exchange for the portrait of Jeffrey Aspern a larger sum of money than I had hoped to be able to gather for her, writing to her that I had sold the picture, she kept it with thanks; she never sent it back. I wrote to her that I had sold the picture, but I admitted to Mrs Prest, at the time (I met her in London, in the autumn), that it hangs above my writing-table. When I look at it my chagrin at the loss of the letters becomes almost intolerable.

THE LIAR

I

THE train was half an hour late and the drive from the station longer than he had supposed, so that when he reached the house its inmates had dispersed to dress for dinner and he was conducted straight to his room. The curtains were drawn in this asylum, the candles were lighted, the fire was bright, and when the servant had quickly put out his clothes the comfortable little place became suggestive—seemed to promise a pleasant house, a various party, talks, acquaintances, affinities, to say nothing of very good cheer. He was too occupied with his profession to pay many country visits, but he had heard people who had more time for them speak of establishments where "they do you very well." He foresaw that the proprietors of Stayes would do him very well. In his bedroom at a country house he always looked first at the books on the shelf and the prints on the walls; he considered that these things gave a sort of measure of the culture and even of the character of his hosts. Though he had but little time to devote to them on this occasion a cursory inspection assured him that if the literature, as usual, was mainly American and humorous the art consisted neither of the water-colour studies of the children nor of "goody" engravings. The walls were adorned with old-fashioned lithographs, principally portraits of country gentlemen with high collars and riding gloves: this suggested—and it was encouraging—that the tradition of portraiture was held in esteem. There was the customary novel of Mr Le Fanu, for the bedside; the ideal reading in a country house for the hours after midnight. Oliver Lyon could scarcely forbear beginning it while he buttoned his shirt.

Perhaps that is why he not only found every one assembled in the hall when he went down, but perceived from the way the move to dinner was instantly made that they had been waiting for him. There was no delay, to introduce him to a lady, for he went out in a group of unmatched men, without this appendage. The men, straggling behind, sidled and edged as usual at the door of the dining-room, and the *dénouement* of this little comedy was that he came to his place last of all. This made him think that he was in a sufficiently distinguished company, for if he had been humiliated (which he was not), he could not have consoled himself with the reflection that such a fate was natural to an obscure, struggling young artist. He could no longer think of himself as very young, alas, and if his position was not so brilliant as it ought to be he could no longer justify it by calling it a struggle. He was something of a celebrity and he was apparently in a society of celebrities. This idea added to the curiosity with which he looked up and down the long table as he settled himself in his place.

It was a numerous party—five and twenty people; rather an odd occasion to have proposed to him, as he thought. He would not be surrounded by the quiet that ministers to good work; however, it had never interfered with his work to see the spectacle of human life before him in the intervals. And though he did not know it, it was never quiet at Stayes. When he was working well he found himself in that happy state— the happiest of all for an artist—in which things in general contribute to the particular idea and fall in with it, help it on and justify it, so that he feels for the hour as if nothing in the world can happen to him, even if it come in the guise of disaster or suffering, that will not be an enhancement of his subject. Moreover there was an exhilaration (he had felt it before) in the rapid change of scene—the jump, in the dusk of the afternoon, from foggy London and his familiar studio to a centre of festivity in the middle of Hertfordshire and a drama half acted, a drama of pretty women and noted men and wonderful orchids in silver jars. He observed as a not unimportant fact that one of the pretty women was beside him: a gentleman sat on his other hand. But he went into his neighbours little as yet: he was busy looking out for Sir David, whom he had never seen and about whom he naturally was curious.

Evidently, however, Sir David was not at dinner, a circumstance sufficiently explained by the other circumstance which constituted our friend's principal knowledge of him—his being ninety years of age. Oliver Lyon had looked forward with great pleasure to the chance of painting a nonagenarian, and though the old man's absence from table was something of a disappointment (it was an opportunity the less to observe him before going to work), it seemed a sign that he was rather a sacred and perhaps therefore an impressive relic. Lyon looked at his son with the greater interest—wondered whether the glazed bloom of his cheek had been transmitted from Sir David. That would be jolly to paint, in the old man—the withered ruddiness of a winter apple, especially if the eye were still alive and the white hair carried out the frosty look. Arthur Ashmore's hair had a midsummer glow, but Lyon was glad his commission had been to delineate the father rather than the son, in spite of his never having seen the one and of the other being seated there before him now in the happy expansion of liberal hospitality.

Arthur Ashmore was a fresh-coloured, thick-necked English gentleman, but he was just not a subject; he might have been a farmer and he might have been a banker: you could scarcely paint him in characters. His wife did not make up the amount; she was a large, bright, negative woman, who had the same air as her husband of being somehow tremendously new; a sort of appearance of fresh varnish (Lyon could scarcely tell whether it came from her complexion or from her clothes), so that one felt she ought to sit in a gilt frame, suggesting reference to a catalogue or a price-list. It was as if she were already rather a bad though expensive portrait, knocked off by an eminent hand, and Lyon had no wish to copy that work. The pretty woman on his right was engaged with her neighbour and the gentleman on his other side looked shrinking and scared, so that he had time to lose himself in his favourite diversion of watching face after face. This amusement gave him the greatest pleasure he knew, and he often thought it a mercy that the human mask did interest him and that it was not less vivid than it was (sometimes it ran its success in this line very close), since he was to make his living by reproducing it. Even if Arthur Ashmore would not be inspiring to paint (a certain anxiety rose in him lest if he should make a hit with her father-in-law Mrs Arthur should take it into her head that he had now proved himself worthy to *aborder* her husband); even if he had looked a little less like a page (fine as to print and margin) without punctuation, he would still be a refreshing, iridescent surface. But the gentleman four persons off—what was he? Would he be a subject, or was his face only the legible door-plate of his identity, burnished with punctual washing and shaving—the least thing that was decent that you would know him by?

This face arrested Oliver Lyon: it struck him at first as very handsome. The gentleman might still be called young, and his features were regular: he had a plentiful, fair moustache that curled up at the ends, a brilliant, gallant, almost adventurous air, and a big shining breastpin in the middle of his shirt. He appeared a fine satisfied soul, and Lyon perceived that wherever he rested his friendly eye there fell an influence as pleasant as the September sun—as if he could make grapes and pears or even human affection ripen by looking at them. What was odd in him was a certain mixture of the correct and the extravagant: as if he were an adventurer imitating a gentleman with rare perfection or a gentleman who had taken a fancy to go about with hidden arms. He might have been a dethroned prince or the war-correspondent of a newspaper: he represented both enterprise and tradition, good manners and bad taste. Lyon at length fell into conversation with the lady beside him —they dispensed, as he had had to dispense at dinner-parties before, with an introduction—by asking who this personage might be.

"Oh, he's Colonel Capadose, don't you know?" Lyon didn't know and he asked for further information. His neighbour had a sociable manner and evidently was accustomed to quick transitions; she turned from her other interlocutor with a methodical air, as a good cook lifts the cover of the next sauce-pan. "He has been a great deal in India—isn't he rather celebrated?" she inquired. Lyon confessed he had never heard of him, and she went on, "Well, perhaps he isn't; but he says he is, and if you think it, that's just the same, isn't it?"

"If *you* think it?"

"I mean if he thinks it—that's just as good, I suppose."

"Do you mean that he says that which is not?"

"Oh dear, no—because I never know. He is exceedingly clever and amusing—quite the cleverest person in the house, unless indeed you are more so. But that I can't tell yet, can I? I only know about the people I know; I think that's celebrity enough!"

"Enough for them?"

"Oh, I see you're clever. Enough for me! But I have heard of you," the lady went on. "I know your pictures; I admire them. But I don't think you look like them."

"They are mostly portraits," Lyon said; ' and what I usually try for is not my own resemblance."

"I see what you mean. But they have much more colour. And now you are going to do some one here?"

"I have been invited to do Sir David. I'm rather disappointed at not seeing him this evening."

"Oh, he goes to bed at some unnatural hour—eight o'clock or something of that sort. You know he's rather an old mummy."

"An old mummy?" Oliver Lyon repeated.

"I mean he wears half a dozen waistcoats, and that sort of thing. He's always cold."

"I have never seen him and never seen any portrait or photograph of him," Lyon said. "I'm surprised at his never having had anything done—at their waiting all these years."

"Ah, that's because he was afraid, you know; it was a kind of superstition. He was sure that if anything were done he would die directly afterwards. He has only consented to-day."

"He's ready to die then?"

"Oh, now he's so old he doesn't care."

"Well, I hope I shan't kill him," said Lyon. "It was rather unnatural in his son to send for me."

"Oh, they have nothing to gain—everything is theirs already!" his companion rejoined, as if she took this speech quite literally. Her talkativeness was systematic—she fraternised as seriously as she might have played whist. "They do as they like—they fill the house with people—they have *carte blanche*."

"I see—but there's still the title."

"Yes, but what is it?"

Our artist broke into laughter at this, whereat his companion stared. Before he had recovered himself she was scouring the plain with her other neighbour. The gentleman on his left at last risked an observation, and they had some fragmentary talk. This personage played his part with difficulty: he uttered a remark as a lady fires a pistol, looking the other way. To catch the ball Lyon had to bend his ear, and this movement led to his observing a handsome creature who was seated on the same side, beyond his interlocutor. Her profile was presented to him and at first he was only struck with its beauty; then it produced an impression still more agreeable—a sense of undimmed remembrance and intimate association. He had not recognised her on the instant only because he had so little expected to see her there; he had not seen her anywhere for so long, and no news of her ever came to him. She was often in his thoughts, but she had passed out of his life. He thought of her twice a week; that may be called often in relation to a person one has not seen for twelve years. The moment after he recognised her he felt how true it was that it was only she who could look like that: of the most charming head in the world (and this lady had it) there could never be a replica. She was leaning forward a little; she remained in profile, apparently listening to some one on the other side of her. She was listening, but she was also looking, and after a moment Lyon followed the direction of her eyes. They rested upon the gentleman who had been described to him as Colonel Capadose—rested, as it appeared to him, with a kind of habitual, visible complacency. This was not strange, for the Colonel was unmistakably formed to attract the sympathetic gaze of woman; but Lyon was slightly disappointed that she could let *him* look at her so long without giving him a glance. There was nothing between them to-day and he had no rights, but she must have known he was coming (it was of course not such a tremendous event, but she could not have been staying in the house without hearing of it), and it was not natural that that should absolutely fail to affect her.

She was looking at Colonel Capadose as if she were in love with him—a queer accident for the proudest, most reserved of women. But doubtless it was all right, if her husband liked it or didn't notice it: he had heard indefinitely, years before, that she was married, and he took for granted (as he had not heard that she had become a widow) the presence of the happy man on whom she had conferred what she had refused to *him*, the poor art-student at Munich. Colonel Capadose appeared to be aware of nothing, and this circumstance, incongruously enough, rather irritated Lyon than gratified him. Suddenly the lady turned her head, showing her full face to our hero. He was so prepared with a greeting that he instantly smiled, as a shaken jug overflows; but she gave him no response, turned away again and sank back in her chair. All that her face said in that instant was, "You see I'm as handsome as ever." To which he mentally subjoined, "Yes, and as much good it does me!" He asked the young man beside him if he knew who that beautiful being was—the fifth person beyond him. The young man leaned forward, considered and then said, "I think she's Mrs Capadose."

"Do you mean his wife—that fellow's?" And Lyon indicated the subject of the information given him by his other neighbour.

"Oh, is *he* Mr Capadose?" said the young man, who appeared very vague. He admitted his vagueness and explained it by saying that there were so many people and he had come only the day before. What was definite to Lyon was that Mrs Capadose was in love with her husband; so that he wished more than ever that he had married her.

"She's very faithful," he found himself saying three minutes later to the lady on his right. He added that he meant Mrs Capadose.

"Ah, you know her then?"

"I knew her once upon a time—when I was living abroad."

"Why then were you asking me about her husband?"

"Precisely for that reason. She married after that—I didn't even know her present name."

"How then do you know it now?"

"This gentleman has just told me—he appears to know."

"I didn't know he knew anything," said the lady, glancing forward.

"I don't think he knows anything but that."

"Then you have found out for yourself that she is faithful. What do you mean by that?"

"Ah, you mustn't question me—I want to question you," Lyon said. "How do you all like her here?"

"You ask too much! I can only speak for myself. I think she's hard."

"That's only because she's honest and straightforward."

"Do you mean I like people in proportion as they deceive?"

"I think we all do, so long as we don't find them out," Lyon said. "And then there's something in her face—a sort of Roman type, in spite of her having such an English eye. In fact, she's English down to the ground; but her complexion, her low forehead and that beautiful close little wave in her dark hair make her look like a glorified *contadina*."

"Yes, and she always sticks pins and daggers into her head, to increase that effect. I must say I like her husband better: he is so clever."

"Well, when I knew her there was no comparison that could injure her. She was altogether the most delightful thing in Munich."

"In Munich?"

"Her people lived there; they were not rich—in pursuit of economy in fact, and Munich was very cheap. Her father was the younger son of some noble house; he had married a second time and had a lot of little mouths to feed. She was the child of the first wife and she didn't like her stepmother, but she was charming to her little brothers and sisters. I once made a sketch of her as Werther's Charlotte, cutting bread and butter while they clustered all round her. All the artists in the place were in love with her but she wouldn't look at 'the likes' of us. She was too proud—I grant you that; but she wasn't stuck up nor young ladyish; she was simple and frank and kind about it. She used to remind me of Thackeray's Ethel Newcome. She told me she must marry well: it was the one thing she could do for her family. I suppose you would say that she *has* married well."

"She told *you?*" smiled Lyon's neighbour.

"Oh, of course I proposed to her too. But she evidently thinks so herself!" he added.

When the ladies left the table the host as usual bade the

gentlemen draw together, so that Lyon found himself opposite
to Colonel Capadose. The conversation was mainly about
the "run," for it had apparently been a great day in the
hunting-field. Most of the gentlemen communicated their
adventures and opinions, but Colonel Capadose's pleasant
voice was the most audible in the chorus. It was a bright and
fresh but masculine organ, just such a voice as, to Lyon's
sense, such a "fine man" ought to have had. It appeared from
his remarks that he was a very straight rider, which was also
very much what Lyon would have expected. Not that he
swaggered, for his allusions were very quietly and casually
made; but they were all too dangerous experiments and close
shaves. Lyon perceived after a little that the attention paid by
the company to the Colonel's remarks was not in direct relation to the interest they seemed to offer; the result of which
was that the speaker, who noticed that *he* at least was listening,
began to treat him as his particular auditor and to fix his eyes
on him as he talked. Lyon had nothing to do but to look sympathetic and assent—Colonel Capadose appeared to take so
much sympathy and assent for granted. A neighbouring
squire had had an accident; he had come a cropper in an
awkward place—just at the finish—with consequences that
looked grave. He had struck his head; he remained insensible,
up to the last accounts: there had evidently been concussion of
the brain. There was some exchange of views as to his recovery—how soon it would take place or whether it would take
place at all; which led the Colonel to confide to our artist
across the table that *he* shouldn't despair of a fellow even if he
didn't come round for weeks—for weeks and weeks and
weeks—for months, almost for years. He leaned forward;
Lyon leaned forward to listen, and Colonel Capadose mentioned that he knew from personal experience that there was
really no limit to the time one might lie unconscious without
being any the worse for it. It had happened to him in Ireland,
years before; he had been pitched out of a dogcart, had turned

a sheer somersault and landed on his head. They thought he was dead, but he wasn't; they carried him first to the nearest cabin, where he lay for some days with the pigs, and then to an inn in a neighbouring town—it was a near thing they didn't put him under ground. He had been completely insensible—without a ray of recognition of any human thing—for three whole months; had not a glimmer of consciousness of any blessed thing. It was touch and go to that degree that they couldn't come near him, they couldn't feed him, they could scarcely look at him. Then one day he had opened his eyes—as fit as a flea!

"I give you my honour it had done me good—it rested my brain." He appeared to intimate that with an intelligence so active as his these periods of repose were providential. Lyon thought his story very striking, but he wanted to ask him whether he had not shammed a little—not in relating it, but in keeping so quiet. He hesitated however, in time, to imply a doubt—he was so impressed with the tone in which Colonel Capadose said that it was the turn of a hair that they hadn't buried him alive. That had happened to a friend of his in India—a fellow who was supposed to have died of jungle fever—they clapped him into a coffin. He was going on to recite the further fate of this unfortunate gentleman when Mr Ashmore made a move and every one got up to adjourn to the drawing-room. Lyon noticed that by this time no one was heeding what his new friend said to him. They came round on cither side of the table and met while the gentlemen dawdled before going out.

"And do you mean that your friend was literally buried alive?" asked Lyon, in some suspense.

Colonel Capadose looked at him a moment, as if he had already lost the thread of the conversation. Then his face brightened—and when it brightened it was doubly handsome. "Upon my soul he was chucked into the ground!"

"And was he left there?"

"He was left there till I came and hauled him out."

"*You* came?"

"I dreamed about him—it's the most extraordinary story: I heard him calling to me in the night. I took upon myself to dig him up. You know there are people in India—a kind of beastly race, the ghouls—who violate graves. I had a sort of presentiment that they would get at him first. I rode straight, I can tell you; and, by Jove, a couple of them had just broken ground! Crack—crack, from a couple of barrels, and they showed me their heels, as you may believe. Would you credit that I took him out myself? The air brought him to and he was none the worse. He has got his pension—he came home the other day; he would do anything for me."

"He called to you in the night?" said Lyon, much startled.

"That's the interesting point. Now *what was it?* It wasn't his ghost, because he wasn't dead. It wasn't himself, because he couldn't. It was something or other! You see India's a strange country—there's an element of the mysterious: the air is full of things you can't explain."

They passed out of the dining-room, and Colonel Capadose, who went among the first, was separated from Lyon; but a minute later, before they reached the drawing-room, he joined him again. "Ashmore tells me who you are. Of course I have often heard of you—I'm very glad to make your acquaintance; my wife used to know you."

"I'm glad she remembers me. I recognised her at dinner and I was afraid she didn't."

"Ah, I daresay she was ashamed," said the Colonel, with indulgent humour.

"Ashamed of me?" Lyon replied, in the same key.

"Wasn't there something about a picture? Yes; you painted her portrait."

"Many times," said the artist; "and she may very well have been ashamed of what I made of her."

"Well, I wasn't, my dear sir; it was the sight of that picture, which you were so good as to present to her, that made me first fall in love with her."

"Do you mean that one with the children—cutting bread and butter?"

"Bread and butter? Bless me, no—vine leaves and a leopard skin—a kind of Bacchante."

"Ah, yes," said Lyon; "I remember. It was the first decent portrait I painted. I should be curious to see it to-day."

"Don't ask her to show it to you—she'll be mortified!" the Colonel exclaimed.

"Mortified?"

"We parted with it—in the most disinterested manner," he laughed. "An old friend of my wife's—her family had known him intimately when they lived in Germany—took the most extraordinary fancy to it: the Grand Duke of Silberstadt-Schreckenstein, don't you know? He came out to Bombay while we were there and he spotted your picture (you know he's one of the greatest collectors in Europe), and made such eyes at it that, upon my word—it happened to be his birthday —she told him he might have it, to get rid of him. He was perfectly enchanted—but we miss the picture."

"It is very good of you," Lyon said. "If it's in a great collection—a work of my incompetent youth—I am infinitely honoured."

"Oh, he has got it in one of his castles; I don't know which —you know he has so many. He sent us, before he left India— to return the compliment—a magnificent old vase."

"That was more than the thing was worth," Lyon remarked.

Colonel Capadose gave no heed to this observation; he seemed to be thinking of something. After a moment he said, "If you'll come and see us in town she'll show you the vase." And as they passed into the drawing-room he gave the artist a friendly propulsion. "Go and speak to her; there she is— she'll be delighted."

Oliver Lyon took but a few steps into the wide saloon; he stood there a moment looking at the bright composition of the lamplit group of fair women, the single figures, the great setting of white and gold, the panels of old damask, in the centre of each of which was a single celebrated picture. There was a subdued lustre in the scene and an air as of the shining trains of dresses tumbled over the carpet. At the furthest end of the room sat Mrs Capadose, rather isolated; she was on a small sofa, with an empty place beside her. Lyon could not flatter himself she had been keeping it for him; her failure to respond to his recognition at table contradicted that, but he felt an extreme desire to go and occupy it. Moreover he had her husband's sanction; so he crossed the room, stepping over the tails of gowns, and stood before his old friend.

"I hope you don't mean to repudiate me," he said.

She looked up at him with an expression of unalloyed pleasure. "I am so glad to see you. I was delighted when I heard you were coming."

"I tried to get a smile from you at dinner—but I couldn't."

"I didn't see—I didn't understand. Besides, I hate smirking and telegraphing. Also I'm very shy—you won't have forgotten that. Now we can communicate comfortably." And she made a better place for him on the little sofa. He sat down and they had a talk that he enjoyed, while the reason for which he used to like her so came back to him, as well as a good deal of the very same old liking. She was still the least spoiled beauty he had ever seen, with an absence of coquetry or any insinuating art that seemed almost like an omitted faculty; there were moments when she struck her interlocutor as some fine creature from an asylum—a surprising deaf-mute or one of the operative blind. Her noble pagan head gave her privileges that she neglected, and when people were admiring her brow she was wondering whether there were a good fire in her bedroom. She was simple, kind and good; inexpressive but not inhuman or stupid. Now and again she dropped something that had a sifted, selected air—the sound of an impression at first hand. She had no imagination, but she had added up her feelings, some of her reflections, about life. Lyon talked of the old days in Munich, reminded her of incidents, pleasures and pains, asked her about her father and the others; and she told him in return that she was so impressed with his own fame, his brilliant position in the world, that she had not felt very sure he would speak to her or that his little sign at table was meant for her. This was plainly a perfectly truthful speech —she was incapable of any other—and he was affected by such humility on the part of a woman whose grand line was unique. Her father was dead; one of her brothers was in the navy and the other on a ranch in America; two of her sisters were married and the youngest was just coming out and very pretty. She didn't mention her stepmother. She asked him about his own personal history and he said that the principal thing that had happened to him was that he had never married.

"Oh, you ought to," she answered. "It's the best thing."

"I like that—from you!" he returned.

"Why not from me? I am very happy."

"That's just why I can't be. It's cruel of you to praise your state. But I have had the pleasure of making the acquaintance of your husband. We had a good bit of talk in the other room."

"You must know him better—you must know him really well," said Mrs Capadose.

"I am sure that the further you go the more you find. But he makes a fine show, too."

She rested her good gray eyes on Lyon. "Don't you think he's handsome?"

"Handsome and clever and entertaining. You see I'm generous."

"Yes; you must know him well," Mrs Capadose repeated.

"He has seen a great deal of life," said her companion.

"Yes, we have been in so many places. You must see my little girl. She is nine years old—she's too beautiful."

"You must bring her to my studio some day—I should like to paint her."

"Ah, don't speak of that," said Mrs Capadose. "It reminds me of something so distressing."

"I hope you don't mean when *you* used to sit to me—though that may well have bored you."

"It's not what you did—it's what we have done. It's a confession I must make—it's a weight on my mind! I mean about that beautiful picture you gave me—it used to be so much admired. When you come to see me in London (I count on your doing that very soon) I shall see you looking all round. I can't tell you I keep it in my own room because I love it so, for the simple reason——" And she paused a moment.

"Because you can't tell wicked lies," said Lyon.

"No, I can't. So before you ask for it——"

"Oh, I know you parted with it—the blow has already fallen," Lyon interrupted.

"Ah then, you have heard? I was sure you would! But do you know what we got for it? Two hundred pounds."

"You might have got much more," said Lyon, smiling.

"That seemed a great deal at the time. We were in want of the money—it was a good while ago, when we first married. Our means were very small then, but fortunately that has changed rather for the better. We had the chance; it really seemed a big sum, and I am afraid we jumped at it. My husband had expectations which have partly come into effect, so that now we do well enough. But meanwhile the picture went."

"Fortunately the original remained. But do you mean that two hundred was the value of the vase?" Lyon asked.

"Of the vase?"

"The beautiful old Indian vase—the Grand Duke's offering."

"The Grand Duke?"

"What's his name?—Silberstadt-Schreckenstein. Your husband mentioned the transaction."

"Oh, my husband," said Mrs Capadose; and Lyon saw that she coloured a little.

Not to add to her embarrassment, but to clear up the ambiguity, which he perceived the next moment he had better have left alone, he went on: "He tells me it's now in his collection."

"In the Grand Duke's? Ah, you know its reputation? I believe it contains treasures." She was bewildered, but she recovered herself, and Lyon made the mental reflection that for some reason which would seem good when he knew it the husband and the wife had prepared different versions of the same incident. It was true that he did not exactly see Everina Brant preparing a version; that was not her line of old, and indeed it was not in her eyes to-day. At any rate they both had the matter too much on their conscience. He changed the subject, said Mrs Capadose must really bring the little girl. He sat with her some time longer and thought—perhaps it was only a fancy—that she was rather absent, as if she were annoyed at their having been even for a moment at cross-purposes. This did not prevent him from saying to her at the last, just as the ladies began to gather themselves together to go to bed: "You seem much impressed, from what you say, with my renown and my prosperity, and you are so good as greatly to exaggerate them. Would you have married me if you had known that I was destined to success?"

"I did know it."

"Well, I didn't."

"You were too modest."

"You didn't think so when I proposed to you."

"Well, if I had married you I couldn't have married *him*— and he's so nice," Mrs Capadose said. Lyon knew she thought it—he had learned that at dinner—but it vexed him a little to hear her say it. The gentleman designated by the pronoun came up, amid the prolonged hand-shaking for good-night, and Mrs Capadose remarked to her husband as she turned away, "He wants to paint Amy."

"Ah, she's a charming child, a most interesting little creature," the Colonel said to Lyon. "She does the most remarkable things."

Mrs Capadose stopped, in the rustling procession that followed the hostess out of the room. "Don't tell him, please don't," she said.

"Don't tell him what?"

"Why, what she does. Let him find out for himself." And she passed on.

"She thinks I swagger about the child—that I bore people," said the Colonel. "I hope you smoke." He appeared ten minutes later in the smoking-room, in a brilliant equipment, a suit of crimson foulard covered with little white spots. He gratified Lyon's eye, made him feel that the modern age has its splendour too and its opportunities for costume. If his wife was an antique he was a fine specimen of the period of colour: he might have passed for a Venetian of the sixteenth century. They were a remarkable couple, Lyon thought, and as he looked at the Colonel standing in bright erectness before the chimney-piece while he emitted great smoke-puffs he did not wonder that Everina could not regret she had not married *him*. All the gentlemen collected at Stayes were not smokers and some of them had gone to bed. Colonel Capadose remarked that there probably would be a smallish muster, they had had such a hard day's work. That was the worst of a hunting house—the men were so sleepy after dinner; it was devilish stupid for the ladies, even for those who.hunted themselves—for women were so extraordinary, they never showed it. But most fellows revived under the stimulating influences of the smoking-room, and some of them, in this confidence, would turn up yet. Some of the grounds of their confidence—not all of them—might have been seen in a cluster of glasses and bottles on a table near the fire, which made the great salver and its contents twinkle sociably. The others lurked as yet in various improper corners of the minds of the most loquacious. Lyon was alone with Colonel Capadose for some moments before their companions, in varied eccentricities of uniform, straggled in, and he perceived that this wonderful man had but little loss of vital tissue to repair.

They talked about the house, Lyon having noticed an oddity of construction in the smoking-room; and the Colonel explained that it consisted of two distinct parts, one of which was of very great antiquity. They were two complete houses in short, the old one and the new, each of great extent and each very fine in its way. The two formed together an enormous structure—Lyon must make a point of going all over it. The modern portion had been erected by the old man when he bought the property; oh yes, he had bought it, forty years before—it hadn't been in the family: there hadn't been any particular family for it to be in. He had had the good taste not to spoil the original house—he had not touched it beyond what was just necessary for joining it on. It was very curious indeed—a most irregular, rambling, mysterious pile, where they every now and then discovered a walled-up room or a secret staircase. To his mind it was essentially gloomy, however; even the modern additions, splendid as they were, failed to make it cheerful. There was some story about a skeleton having been found years before, during some repairs under a stone slab of the floor of one of the passages; but the family were rather shy of its being talked about. The place they were in was of course in the old part, which contained after all some of the best rooms: he had an idea it had been the primitive kitchen, half modernised at some intermediate period.

"My room is in the old part too then—I'm very glad," Lyon said. "It's very comfortable and contains all the latest conveniences, but I observed the depth of the recess of the door and the evident antiquity of the corridor and staircase—

the first short one—after I came out. That panelled corridor is admirable; it looks as if it stretched away, in its brown dimness (the lamps didn't seem to me to make much impression on it), for half a mile."

"Oh, don't go to the end of it!" exclaimed the Colonel, smiling.

"Does it lead to the haunted room?" Lyon asked.

His companion looked at him a moment. "Ah, you know about that?"

"No, I don't speak from knowledge, only from hope. I have never had any luck—I have never stayed in a dangerous house. The places I go to are always as safe as Charing Cross. I want to see—whatever there is, the regular thing. *Is* there a ghost here?"

"Of course there is—a rattling good one."

"And have you seen him?"

"Oh, don't ask me what *I've* seen—I should tax your credulity. I don't like to talk of these things. But there are two or three as bad—that is, as good!—rooms as you'll find anywhere."

"Do you mean in my corridor?" Lyon asked.

"I believe the worst is at the far end. But you would be ill-advised to sleep there."

"Ill-advised?"

"Until you've finished your job. You'll get letters of importance the next morning, and you'll take the 10.20."

"Do you mean I will invent a pretext for running away?"

"Unless you are braver than almost any one has ever been. They don't often put people to sleep there, but sometimes the house is so crowded that they have to. The same thing always happens—ill-concealed agitation at the breakfast-table and letters of the greatest importance. Of course it's a bachelor's room, and my wife and I are at the other end of the house. But we saw the comedy three days ago—the day after we got here. A young fellow had been put there—I forget his name

—the house was so full; and the usual consequence followed. Letters at breakfast—an awfully queer face—an urgent call to town—so very sorry his visit was cut short. Ashmore and his wife looked at each other, and off the poor devil went."

"Ah, that wouldn't suit me; I must paint my picture," said Lyon. "But do they mind your speaking of it? Some people who have a good ghost are very proud of it, you know."

What answer Colonel Capadose was on the point of making to this inquiry our hero was not to learn, for at that moment their host had walked into the room accompanied by three or four gentlemen. Lyon was conscious that he was partly answered by the Colonel's not going on with the subject. This however on the other hand was rendered natural by the fact that one of the gentlemen appealed to him for an opinion on a point under discussion, something to do with the everlasting history of the day's run. To Lyon himself Mr Ashmore began to talk, expressing his regret at having had so little direct conversation with him as yet. The topic that suggested itself was naturally that most closely connected with the motive of the artist's visit. Lyon remarked that it was a great disadvantage to him not to have had some preliminary acquaintance with Sir David—in most cases he found that so important. But the present sitter was so far advanced in life that there was doubtless no time to lose. "Oh, I can tell you all about him," said Mr Ashmore; and for half an hour he told him a good deal. It was very interesting as well as very eulogistic, and Lyon could see that he was a very nice old man, to have endeared himself so to a son who was evidently not a gusher. At last he got up—he said he must go to bed if he wished to be fresh for his work in the morning. To which his host replied, "Then you must take your candle; the lights are out; I don't keep my servants up."

In a moment Lyon had his glimmering taper in hand, and as he was leaving the room (he did not disturb the others with a good-night; they were absorbed in the lemon-squeezer and

the soda-water cork) he remembered other occasions on which
he had made his way to bed alone through a darkened country-
house; such occasions had not been rare, for he was almost
always the first to leave the smoking-room. If he had not
stayed in houses conspicuously haunted he had, none the less
(having the artistic temperament), sometimes found the great
black halls and staircases rather "creepy": there had been
often a sinister effect, to his imagination, in the sound of his
tread in the long passages or the way the winter moon peeped
into tall windows on landings. It occurred to him that if
houses without supernatural pretensions could look so wicked
at night, the old corridors of Stayes would certainly give him
a sensation. He didn't know whether the proprietors were
sensitive; very often, as he had said to Colonel Capadose,
people enjoyed the impeachment. What determined him to
speak, with a certain sense of the risk, was the impression that
the Colonel told queer stories. As he had his hand on the door
he said to Arthur Ashmore, "I hope I shan't meet any ghosts."

"Any ghosts?"

"You ought to have some—in this fine old part."

"We do our best, but *que voulez-vous?*" said Mr Ashmore.
"I don't think they like the hot-water pipes."

"They remind them too much of their own climate? But
haven't you a haunted room—at the end of my passage?"

"Oh, there are stories—we try to keep them up."

"I should like very much to sleep there," Lyon said.

"Well, you can move there to-morrow if you like."

"Perhaps I had better wait till I have done my work."

"Very good; but you won't work there, you know. My
father will sit to you in his own apartments."

"Oh, it isn't that; it's the fear of running away, like that
gentleman three days ago."

"Three days ago? What gentleman?" Mr Ashmore asked.

"The one who got urgent letters at breakfast and fled by
the 10.20. Did he stand more than one night?"

"I don't know what you are talking about. There was no such gentleman—three days ago."

"Ah, so much the better," said Lyon, nodding good-night and departing. He took his course, as he remembered it, with his wavering candle, and, though he encountered a great many gruesome objects, safely reached the passage out of which his room opened. In the complete darkness it seemed to stretch away still further, but he followed it, for the curiosity of the thing, to the end. He passed several doors with the name of the room painted upon them, but he found nothing else. He was tempted to try the last door—to look into the room of evil fame; but he reflected that this would be indiscreet, since Colonel Capadose handled the brush—as a *raconteur*—with such freedom. There might be a ghost and there might not; but the Colonel himself, he inclined to think, was the most mystifying figure in the house.

II

LYON found Sir David Ashmore a capital subject and a very comfortable sitter into the bargain. Moreover he was a very agreeable old man, tremendously puckered but not in the least dim; and he wore exactly the furred dressing-gown that Lyon would have chosen. He was proud of his age but ashamed of his infirmities, which however he greatly exaggerated and which did not prevent him from sitting there as submissive as if portraiture in oils had been a branch of surgery. He demolished the legend of his having feared the operation would be fatal, giving an explanation which pleased our friend much better. He held that a gentleman should be painted but once in his life—that it was eager and fatuous to be hung up all over the place. That was good for women, who made a pretty wall-pattern; but the male face didn't lend itself to decorative repetition. The proper time for the likeness was at the last, when the whole man was there—you got the totality of his experience. Lyon could not reply that that period was not a real compendium—you had to allow so for leakage; for there had been no crack in Sir David's crystallisation. He spoke of his portrait as a plain map of the country, to be consulted by his children in a case of uncertainty. A proper map could be drawn up only when the country had been travelled. He gave Lyon his mornings, till luncheon, and they talked of many things, not neglecting, as a stimulus to gossip, the people in the house. Now that he did not "go out," as he said, he saw much less of the visitors at Stayes: people came and went whom he knew nothing about, and he liked to hear Lyon describe them. The artist sketched with a fine point and did not caricature, and it usually befell that when Sir David did not know the sons and daughters he had known the fathers and mothers. He was one of those terrible old gentlemen who are a repository of antecedents. But in the case of the Capadose family, at whom they arrived by an easy stage, his knowledge embraced two, or even three, generations. General Capadose was an old crony, and he remembered his father before him. The general was rather a smart soldier, but in private life of too speculative a turn—always sneaking into the City to put his money into some rotten thing. He married a girl who brought him something and they had half a dozen children. He scarcely knew what had become of the rest of them, except that one was in the Church and had found preferment—wasn't he Dean of Rockingham? Clement, the fellow who was at Stayes, had some military talent; he had served in the East, he had married a pretty girl. He had been at Eton with his son, and he used to come to Stayes in his holidays. Lately, coming back to England, he had turned up with his wife again; that was before he—the old man—had been put to grass. He was a taking dog, but he had a monstrous foible.

"A monstrous foible?" said Lyon.

"He's a thumping liar."

Lyon's brush stopped short, while he repeated, for somehow the formula startled him, "A thumping liar?"

"You are very lucky not to have found it out."

"Well, I confess I have noticed a romantic tinge——"

"Oh, it isn't always romantic. He'll lie about the time of day, about the name of his hatter. It appears there are people like that."

"Well, they are precious scoundrels," Lyon declared, his voice trembling a little with the thought of what Everina Brant had done with herself.

"Oh, not always," said the old man. "This fellow isn't in the least a scoundrel. There is no harm in him and no bad intention; he doesn't steal nor cheat nor gamble nor drink; he's very kind—he sticks to his wife, is fond of his children. He simply can't give you a straight answer."

"Then everything he told me last night, I suppose, was mendacious: he delivered himself of a series of the stiffest statements. They stuck, when I tried to swallow them, but I never thought of so simple an explanation."

"No doubt he was in the vein," Sir David went on. "It's a natural peculiarity—as you might limp or stutter or be left-handed. I believe it comes and goes, like intermittent fever. My son tells me that his friends usually understand it and don't haul him up—for the sake of his wife."

"Oh, his wife—his wife!" Lyon murmured, painting fast.

"I daresay she's used to it."

"Never in the world, Sir David. How can she be used to it?"

"Why, my dear sir, when a woman's fond!—And don't they mostly handle the long bow themselves? They are connoisseurs—they have a sympathy for a fellow performer."

Lyon was silent a moment; he had no ground for denying

that Mrs Capadose was attached to her husband. But after a
little he rejoined: "Oh, not this one! I knew her years ago—
before her marriage; knew her well and admired her. She was
as clear as a bell."

"I like her very much," Sir David said, "but I have seen
her back him up."

Lyon considered Sir David for a moment, not in the light
of a model. "Are you very sure?"

The old man hesitated; then he answered, smiling, "You're
in love with her."

"Very likely. God knows I used to be!"

"She must help him out—she can't expose him."

"She can hold her tongue," Lyon remarked.

"Well, before you probably she will."

"That's what I am curious to see." And Lyon added,
privately, "Mercy on us, what he must have made of her!"
He kept this reflection to himself, for he considered that he
had sufficiently betrayed his state of mind with regard to Mrs
Capadose. None the less it occupied him now immensely, the
question of how such a woman would arrange herself in such
a predicament. He watched her with an interest deeply quickened when he mingled with the company; he had had his own
troubles in life, but he had rarely been so anxious about anything as he was now to see what the loyalty of a wife and the
infection of an example would have made of an absolutely
truthful mind. Oh, he held it as immutably established that
whatever other women might be prone to do she, of old, had
been perfectly incapable of a deviation. Even if she had not
been too simple to deceive she would have been too proud;
and if she had not had too much conscience she would have
had too little eagerness. It was the last thing she would have
endured or condoned—the particular thing she would not
have forgiven. Did she sit in torment while her husband
turned his somersaults, or was she now too so perverse that
she thought it a fine thing to be striking at the expense of one's

honour? It would have taken a wondrous alchemy—working backwards, as it were—to produce this latter result. Besides these two alternatives (that she suffered tortures in silence and that she was so much in love that her husband's humiliating idiosyncrasy seemed to her only an added richness—a proof of life and talent), there was still the possibility that she had not found him out, that she took his false pieces at his own valuation. A little reflection rendered this hypothesis untenable; it was too evident that the account he gave of things must repeatedly have contradicted her own knowledge. Within an hour or two of his meeting them Lyon had seen her confronted with that perfectly gratuitous invention about the profit they had made off his early picture. Even then indeed she had not, so far as he could see, smarted, and—but for the present he could only contemplate the case.

Even if it had not been interfused, through his uneradicated tenderness for Mrs Capadose, with an element of suspense, the question would still have presented itself to him as a very curious problem, for he had not painted portraits during so many years without becoming something of a psychologist. His inquiry was limited for the moment to the opportunity that the following three days might yield, as the Colonel and his wife were going on to another house. It fixed itself largely of course upon the Colonel too—this gentleman was such a rare anomaly. Moreover it had to go on very quickly. Lyon was too scrupulous to ask other people what they thought of the business—he was too afraid of exposing the woman he once had loved. It was probable also that light would come to him from the talk of the rest of the company: the Colonel's queer habit, both as it affected his own situation and as it affected his wife, would be a familiar theme in any house in which he was in the habit of staying. Lyon had not observed in the circles in which he visited any marked abstention from comment on the singularities of their members. It interfered with his progress that the Colonel hunted all day, while he plied his brushes and chatted with Sir David; but a Sunday intervened and that partly made it up. Mrs Capadose fortunately did not hunt, and when his work was over she was not inaccessible. He took a couple of longish walks with her (she was fond of that), and beguiled her at tea into a friendly nook in the hall. Regard her as he might he could not make out to himself that she was consumed by a hidden shame; the sense of being married to a man whose word had no worth was not, in her spirit, so far as he could guess, the canker within the rose. Her mind appeared to have nothing on it but its own placid frankness, and when he looked into her eyes (deeply, as he occasionally permitted himself to do), they had no uncomfortable consciousness. He talked to her again and still again of the dear old days—reminded her of things that he had not (before this reunion) the least idea that he remembered. Then he spoke to her of her husband, praised his appearance, his talent for conversation, professed to have felt a quick friendship for him and asked (with an inward audacity at which he trembled a little) what manner of man he was. "What manner?" said Mrs Capadose. "Dear me, how can one describe one's husband? I like him very much."

"Ah, you have told me that already!" Lyon exclaimed, with exaggerated ruefulness.

"Then why do you ask me again?" She added in a moment, as if she were so happy that she could afford to take pity on him, "He is everything that's good and kind. He's a soldier—and a gentleman—and a dear! He hasn't a fault. And he has great ability."

"Yes; he strikes one as having great ability. But of course I can't think him a dear."

"I don't care what you think him!" said Mrs Capadose, looking, it seemed to him, as she smiled, handsomer than he had ever seen her. She was either deeply cynical or still more deeply impenetrable, and he had little prospect of winning from her the intimation that he longed for—some hint that it had come over her that after all she had better have married a man who was not a by-word for the most contemptible, the least heroic, of vices. Had she not seen—had she not felt—the smile go round when her husband executed some especially characteristic conversational caper? How could a woman of her quality endure that day after day, year after year, except by her quality's altering? But he would believe in the alteration only when he should have heard *her* lie. He was fascinated by his problem and yet half exasperated, and he asked himself all kinds of questions. Did she not lie, after all, when she let his falsehoods pass without a protest? Was not her life a perpetual complicity, and did she not aid and abet him by the simple fact that she was not disgusted with him? Then again perhaps she *was* disgusted and it was the mere desperation of her pride that had given her an inscrutable mask. Perhaps she protested in private, passionately; perhaps every night, in their own apartments, after the day's hideous performance, she made him the most scorching scene. But if such scenes were of no avail and he took no more trouble to cure himself, how could she regard him, and after so many years of marriage too, with the perfectly artless complacency that Lyon had surprised in her in the course of the first day's dinner? If our friend had not been in love with her he could have taken the diverting view of the Colonel's delinquencies; but as it was they turned to the tragical in his mind, even while he had a sense that his solicitude might also have been laughed at.

The observation of those three days showed him that if Capadose was an abundant he was not a malignant liar and that his fine faculty exercised itself mainly on subjects of small direct importance. "He is the liar platonic," he said to himself; "he is disinterested, he doesn't operate with a hope of gain or with a desire to injure. It is art for art and he is prompted by the love of beauty. He has an inner vision of what might have been, of what ought to be, and he helps on the good cause by the simple substitution of a *nuance*. He paints, as it were, and so do I!" His manifestations had a considerable variety, but a family likeness ran through them, which consisted mainly of their singular futility. It was this that made them offensive; they encumbered the field of conversation, took up valuable space, converted it into a sort of brilliant sun-shot fog. For a fib told under pressure a convenient place can usually be found, as for a person who presents himself with an author's order at the first night of a play. But the supererogatory lie is the gentleman without a voucher or a ticket who accommodates himself with a stool in the passage.

In one particular Lyon acquitted his successful rival; it had puzzled him that irrepressible as he was he had not got into a mess in the service. But he perceived that he respected the service—that august institution was sacred from his depredations. Moreover though there was a great deal of swagger in his talk it was, oddly enough, rarely swagger about his military exploits. He had a passion for the chase, he had followed it in far countries and some of his finest flowers were reminiscences of lonely danger and escape. The more solitary the scene the bigger of course the flower. A new acquaintance, with the Colonel, always received the tribute of a bouquet: that generalisation Lyon very promptly made. And this extraordinary man had inconsistencies and unexpected lapses— lapses into flat veracity. Lyon recognised what Sir David had told him, that his aberrations came in fits or periods—that he would sometimes keep the truce of God for a month at a time. The muse breathed upon him at her pleasure; she often left him alone. He would neglect the finest openings and then set sail in the teeth of the breeze. As a general thing he affirmed the false rather than denied the true; yet this proportion was sometimes strikingly reversed. Very often he joined in the laugh against himself—he admitted that he was trying it on and that a good many of his anecdotes had an experimental character. Still he never completely retracted nor retreated—

he dived and came up in another place. Lyon divined that he was capable at intervals of defending his position with violence, but only when it was a very bad one. Then he might easily be dangerous—then he would hit out and become calumnious. Such occasions would test his wife's equanimity —Lyon would have liked to see her there. In the smoking-room and elsewhere the company, so far as it was composed of his familiars, had an hilarious protest always at hand; but among the men who had known him long his rich tone was an old story, so old that they had ceased to talk about it, and Lyon did not care, as I have said, to elicit the judgment of those who might have shared his own surprise.

The oddest thing of all was that neither surprise nor familiarity prevented the Colonel's being liked; his largest drafts on a sceptical attention passed for an overflow of life and gaiety—almost of good looks. He was fond of portraying his bravery and used a very big brush, and yet he was unmistakably brave. He was a capital rider and shot, in spite of his fund of anecdote illustrating these accomplishments: in short he was very nearly as clever and his career had been very nearly as wonderful as he pretended. His best quality however remained that indiscriminate sociability which took interest and credulity for granted and about which he bragged least. It made him cheap, it made him even in a manner vulgar; but it was so contagious that his listener was more or less on his side as against the probabilities. It was a private reflection of Oliver Lyon's that he not only lied but made one feel one's self a bit of a liar, even (or especially) if one contradicted him. In the evening, at dinner and afterwards, our friend watched his wife's face to see if some faint shade or spasm never passed over it. But she showed nothing, and the wonder was that when he spoke she almost always listened. That was her pride: she wished not to be even suspected of not facing the music. Lyon had none the less an importunate vision of a veiled figure coming the next day in the dusk to certain places to repair the Colonel's ravages, as the relatives of kleptomaniacs punctually call at the shops that have suffered from their pilferings.

"I must apologise, of course it wasn't true, I hope no harm is done, it is only his incorrigible——" Oh, to hear that woman's voice in that deep abasement! Lyon had no nefarious plan, no conscious wish to practise upon her shame or her loyalty; but he did say to himself that he should like to bring her round to feel that there would have been more dignity in a union with a certain other person. He even dreamed of the hour when, with a burning face, she would ask *him* not to take it up. Then he should be almost consoled—he would be magnanimous.

Lyon finished his picture and took his departure, after having worked in a glow of interest which made him believe in his success, until he found he had pleased every one, especially Mr and Mrs Ashmore, when he began to be sceptical. The party at any rate changed: Colonel and Mrs Capadose went their way. He was able to say to himself however that his separation from the lady was not so much an end as a beginning, and he called on her soon after his return to town. She had told him the hours she was at home—she seemed to like him. If she liked him why had she not married him or at any rate why was she not sorry she had not? If she was sorry she concealed it too well. Lyon's curiosity on this point may strike the reader as fatuous, but something must be allowed to a disappointed man. He did not ask much after all; not that she should love him to-day or that she should allow him to tell her that he loved her, but only that she should give him some sign she was sorry. Instead of this, for the present, she contented herself with exhibiting her little daughter to him. The child was beautiful and had the prettiest eyes of innocence he had ever seen: which did not prevent him from wondering whether she told horrid fibs. This idea gave him much entertainment— the picture of the anxiety with which her mother would watch as she grew older for the symptoms of heredity. That was a nice occupation for Everina Brant! Did she lie to the child herself, about her father—was that necessary, when she pressed her daughter to her bosom, to cover up his tracks? Did he control himself before the little girl—so that she might not hear him say things she knew to be other than he said? Lyon doubted this: his genius would be too strong for him, and the only safety for the child would be in her being too stupid to analyse. One couldn't judge yet—she was too young. If she should grow up clever she would be sure to tread in his steps—a delightful improvement in her mother's situation! Her little face was not shifty, but neither was her father's big one: so that proved nothing.

Lyon reminded his friends more than once of their promise that Amy should sit to him, and it was only a question of his leisure. The desire grew in him to paint the Colonel also—an operation from which he promised himself a rich private satisfaction. He would draw him out, he would set him up in that totality about which he had talked with Sir David, and none but the initiated would know. They, however, would rank the picture high, and it would be indeed six rows deep—a masterpiece of subtle characterisation, of legitimate treachery. He had dreamed for years of producing something which should bear the stamp of the psychologist as well as of the painter, and here at last was his subject. It was a pity it was not better, but that was not *his* fault. It was his impression that already no one drew the Colonel out more than he, and he did it not only by instinct but on a plan. There were moments when he was almost frightened at the success of his plan—the poor gentleman went so terribly far. He would pull up some day, look at Lyon between the eyes—guess he was being played upon—which would lead to his wife's guessing it also. Not that Lyon cared much for that however, so long as she failed to suppose (as she must) that *she* was a part of his joke. He formed such a habit now of going to see her of a Sunday afternoon that he was angry when she went out of town. This occurred often, as the couple were great visitors and the Colonel was always looking for sport, which he liked best when it could be had at other people's expense. Lyon would have supposed that this sort of life was particularly little to her taste, for he had an idea that it was in country-houses that her husband came out strongest. To let him go off without her, not to see him expose himself—that ought properly to have been a relief and a luxury to her. She told Lyon in fact that she preferred staying at home; but she neglected to say it was because in other people's houses she was on the rack: the reason she gave was that she liked so to be with the child. It was not perhaps criminal to draw such a bow, but it was vulgar: poor Lyon was delighted when he arrived at that formula. Certainly some day too he would cross the line—he would become a noxious animal. Yes, in the meantime he was vulgar, in spite of his talents, his fine person, his impunity. Twice, by exception, toward the end of the winter, when he left town for a few days' hunting, his wife remained at home. Lyon had not yet reached the point of asking himself whether the desire not to miss two of his visits had something to do with her immobility. That inquiry would perhaps have been more in place later, when he began to paint the child and she always came with her. But it was not in her to give the wrong name, to pretend, and Lyon could see that she had the maternal passion, in spite of the bad blood in the little girl's veins.

She came inveterately, though Lyon multiplied the sittings: Amy was never entrusted to the governess or the maid. He had knocked off poor old Sir David in ten days, but the portrait of the simple-faced child bade fair to stretch over into the following year. He asked for sitting after sitting, and it would have struck any one who might have witnessed the affair that he was wearing the little girl out. He knew better however and Mrs Capadose also knew: they were present together at the long intermissions he gave her, when she left her pose and roamed about the great studio, amusing herself with its curiosities, playing with the old draperies and costumes, having unlimited leave to handle. Then her mother and Mr Lyon sat and talked; he laid aside his brushes and leaned back in his chair; he always gave her tea. What Mrs Capadose did not know was the way that during these weeks he neglected other orders: women have no faculty of imagination with regard to a man's work beyond a vague idea that it doesn't matter. In fact Lyon put off everything and made several celebrities wait. There were half-hours of silence, when he plied his brushes, during which he was mainly conscious that Everina was sitting there. She easily fell into that if he did not insist on talking, and she was not embarrassed nor bored by it. Sometimes she took up a book—there were plenty of them about; sometimes, a little way off, in her chair, she watched his progress (though without in the least advising or correcting), as if she cared for every stroke that represented her daughter. These strokes were occasionally a little wild; he was thinking so much more of his heart than of his hand. He was not more embarrassed than she was, but he was agitated: it was as if in the sittings (for the child, too, was beautifully quiet) something was growing between them or had already grown—a tacit confidence, an inexpressible secret. He felt it that way; but after all he could not be sure that she did. What he wanted her to do for him was very little; it was not even to confess that she was unhappy. He would be superabundantly gratified if she should simply let him know, even by a silent sign, that she recognised that with him her life would have been finer. Sometimes he guessed—his presumption went so far—that he might see this sign in her contentedly sitting there.

III

AT last he broached the question of painting the Colonel: it was now very late in the season—there would be little time before the general dispersal. He said they must make the most of it; the great thing was to begin; then in the autumn, with the resumption of their London life, they could go forward. Mrs Capadose objected to this that she really could not consent to accept another present of such value. Lyon had given her the portrait of herself of old, and he had seen what they had had the indelicacy to do with it. Now he had offered her this beautiful memorial of the child—beautiful it would evidently be when it was finished, if he could ever satisfy himself; a precious possession which they would cherish for ever. But his generosity must stop there—they couldn't be so tremendously "beholden" to him. They couldn't order the picture— of course he would understand that, without her explaining: it was a luxury beyond their reach, for they knew the great prices he received. Besides, what had they ever done—what above all had *she* ever done, that he should overload them with benefits? No, he was too dreadfully good; it was really impossible that Clement should sit. Lyon listened to her without protest, without interruption, while he bent forward at his work, and at last he said: "Well, if you won't take it why not let him sit for me for my own pleasure and profit? Let it be a favour, a service I ask of him. It will do me a lot of good to paint him and the picture will remain in my hands."

"How will it do you a lot of good?" Mrs Capadose asked.

"Why, he's such a rare model—such an interesting subject. He has such an expressive face. It will teach me no end of things."

"Expressive of what?" said Mrs Capadose.

"Why, of his nature."

"And do you want to paint his nature?"

"Of course I do. That's what a great portrait gives you, and I shall make the Colonel's a great one. It will put me up high. So you see my request is eminently interested."

"How can you be higher than you are?"

"Oh, I'm insatiable! Do consent," said Lyon.

"Well, his nature is very noble," Mrs Capadose remarked.

"Ah, trust me, I shall bring it out!" Lyon exclaimed, feeling a little ashamed of himself.

Mrs Capadose said before she went away that her husband would probably comply with his invitation, but she added, "Nothing would induce me to let you pry into *me* that way!"

"Oh, you," Lyon laughed—"I could do you in the dark!"

The Colonel shortly afterwards placed his leisure at the painter's disposal and by the end of July had paid him several visits. Lyon was disappointed neither in the quality of his sitter nor in the degree to which he himself rose to the occasion; he felt really confident that he should produce a fine thing. He was in the humour; he was charmed with his *motif* and deeply interested in his problem. The only point that troubled him was the idea that when he should send his picture to the Academy he should not be able to give the title, for the catalogue, simply as "The Liar." However, it little mattered, for he had now determined that this character should be perceptible even to the meanest intelligence—as overtopping as it had become to his own sense in the living man. As he saw nothing else in the Colonel to-day, so he gave himself up to the joy of painting nothing else. How he did it he could not have told you, but it seemed to him that the mystery of how to do it was revealed to him afresh every time he sat down to his work. It was in the eyes and it was in the mouth, it was in every line of the face and every fact of the attitude, in the indentation of the chin, in the way the hair was planted, the

moustache was twisted, the smile came and went, the breath
rose and fell. It was in the way he looked out at a bam-
boozled world in short—the way he would look out for ever.
There were half a dozen portraits in Europe that Lyon rated
as supreme; he regarded them as immortal, for they were as
perfectly preserved as they were consummately painted. It
was to this small exemplary group that he aspired to annex the
canvas on which he was now engaged. One of the productions
that helped to compose it was the magnificent Moroni of the
National Gallery—the young tailor, in the white jacket, at his
board with his shears. The Colonel was not a tailor, nor was
Moroni's model, unlike many tailors, a liar; but as regards the
masterly clearness with which the individual should be rendered his work would be on the same line as that. He had to a
degree in which he had rarely had it before the satisfaction of
feeling life grow and grow under his brush. The Colonel, as it
turned out, liked to sit and he liked to talk while he was
sitting: which was very fortunate, as his talk largely constituted Lyon's inspiration. Lyon put into practice that idea of
drawing him out which he had been nursing for so many
weeks: he could not possibly have been in a better relation to
him for the purpose. He encouraged, beguiled, excited him,
manifested an unfathomable credulity, and his only interrup-
tions were when the Colonel did not respond to it. He had his
intermissions, his hours of sterility, and then Lyon felt that the
picture also languished. The higher his companion soared, the
more gyrations he executed, in the blue, the better he painted;
he couldn't make his flights long enough. He lashed him on
when he flagged; his apprehension became great at moments
that the Colonel would discover his game. But he never did,
apparently; he basked and expanded in the fine steady light of
the painter's attention. In this way the picture grew very fast;
it was astonishing what a short business it was, compared with
the little girl's. By the fifth of August it was pretty well
finished: that was the date of the last sitting the Colonel was

for the present able to give, as he was leaving town the next day with his wife. Lyon was amply content—he saw his way so clear: he should be able to do at his convenience what remained, with or without his friend's attendance. At any rate, as there was no hurry, he would let the thing stand over till his own return to London, in November, when he would come back to it with a fresh eye. On the Colonel's asking him if his wife might come and see it the next day, if she should find a minute—this was so greatly her desire—Lyon begged as a special favour that she would wait: he was so far from satisfied as yet. This was the repetition of a proposal Mrs Capadose had made on the occasion of his last visit to her, and he had then asked for a delay—declared that he was by no means content. He was really delighted, and he was again a little ashamed of himself.

By the fifth of August the weather was very warm, and on that day, while the Colonel sat straight and gossiped, Lyon opened for the sake of ventilation a little subsidiary door which led directly from his studio into the garden and sometimes served as an entrance and an exit for models and for visitors of the humbler sort, and as a passage for canvases, frames, packing-boxes, and other professional gear. The main entrance was through the house and his own apartments, and this approach had the charming effect of admitting you first to a high gallery, from which a crooked picturesque staircase enabled you to descend to the wide, decorated, encumbered room. The view of this room, beneath them, with all its artistic ingenuities and the objects of value that Lyon had collected, never failed to elicit exclamations of delight from persons stepping into the gallery. The way from the garden was plainer and at once more practicable and more private. Lyon's domain, in St John's Wood, was not vast, but when the door stood open of a summer's day it offered a glimpse of flowers and trees, you smelt something sweet and you heard the birds. On this particular morning the side-door had been found convenient by an unannounced visitor, a youngish woman who stood in the room before the Colonel perceived her and whom he perceived before she was noticed by his friend. She was very quiet, and she looked from one of the men to the other. "Oh, dear, here's another!" Lyon exclaimed, as soon as his eyes rested on her. She belonged, in fact, to a somewhat importunate class—the model in search of employment, and she explained that she had ventured to come straight in, that way, because very often when she went to call upon gentlemen the servants played her tricks, turned her off and wouldn't take in her name.

"But how did you get into the garden?" Lyon asked.

"The gate was open, sir—the servants' gate. The butcher's cart was there."

"The butcher ought to have closed it," said Lyon.

"Then you don't require me, sir?" the lady continued.

Lyon went on with his painting; he had given her a sharp look at first, but now his eyes lighted on her no more. The Colonel, however, examined her with interest. She was a person of whom you could scarcely say whether being young she looked old or old she looked young; she had at any rate evidently rounded several of the corners of life and had a face that was rosy but that somehow failed to suggest freshness. Nevertheless she was pretty and even looked as if at one time she might have sat for the complexion. She wore a hat with many feathers, a dress with many bugles, long black gloves, encircled with silver bracelets, and very bad shoes. There was something about her that was not exactly of the governess out of place nor completely of the actress seeking an engagement, but that savoured of an interrupted profession or even of a blighted career. She was rather soiled and tarnished, and after she had been in the room a few moments the air, or at any rate the nostril, became acquainted with a certain alcoholic waft. She was unpractised in the *h*, and when Lyon at last thanked her and said he didn't want her—he was doing nothing for which she could be useful—she replied with rather a wounded manner, "Well, you know you 'ave 'ad me!"

"I don't remember you," Lyon answered.

"Well, I daresay the people that saw your pictures do! I haven't much time, but I thought I would look in."

"I am much obliged to you."

"If ever you should require me, if you just send me a postcard——"

"I never send postcards," said Lyon.

"Oh well, I should value a private letter! Anything to Miss Geraldine, Mortimer Terrace Mews, Notting 'ill——"

"Very good; I'll remember," said Lyon.

Miss Geraldine lingered. "I thought I'd just stop, on the chance."

"I'm afraid I can't hold out hopes, I'm so busy with portraits," Lyon continued.

"Yes; I see you are. I wish I was in the gentleman's place."

"I'm afraid in that case it wouldn't look like me," said the Colonel, laughing.

"Oh, of course it couldn't compare—it wouldn't be so 'andsome! But I do hate them portraits!" Miss Geraldine declared. "It's so much bread out of our mouths."

"Well, there are many who can't paint them," Lyon suggested, comfortingly.

"Oh, I've sat to the very first—and only to the first! There's many that couldn't do anything without me."

"I'm glad you're in such demand." Lyon was beginning to be bored and he added that he wouldn't detain her—he would send for her in case of need.

"Very well; remember it's the Mews—more's the pity! You don't sit so well as us!" Miss Geraldine pursued, looking at the Colonel. "If you should require me, sir——"

"You put him out; you embarrass him," said Lyon.

"Embarrass him, oh gracious!" the visitor cried, with a

laugh which diffused a fragrance. "Perhaps *you* send post-cards, eh?" she went on to the Colonel; and then she retreated with a wavering step. She passed out into the garden as she had come.

"How very dreadful—she's drunk!" said Lyon. He was painting hard, but he looked up, checking himself: Miss Geraldine, in the open doorway, had thrust back her head.

"Yes, I do hate it—that sort of thing!" she cried with an explosion of mirth which confirmed Lyon's declaration. And then she disappeared.

"What sort of thing—what does she mean?" the Colonel asked.

"Oh, my painting you, when I might be painting her."

"And have you ever painted her?"

"Never in the world; I have never seen her. She is quite mistaken."

The Colonel was silent a moment; then he remarked, "She was very pretty—ten years ago."

"I daresay, but she's quite ruined. For me the least drop too much spoils them; I shouldn't care for her at all."

"My dear fellow, she's not a model," said the Colonel, laughing.

"To-day, no doubt, she's not worthy of the name; but she has been one."

"*Jamais de la vie!* That's all a pretext."

"A pretext?" Lyon pricked up his ears—he began to wonder what was coming now.

"She didn't want you—she wanted me."

"I noticed she paid you some attention. What does she want of you?"

"Oh, to do me an ill turn. She hates me—lots of women do. She's watching me—she follows me."

Lyon leaned back in his chair—he didn't believe a word of this. He was all the more delighted with it and with the Colonel's bright, candid manner. The story had bloomed, fragrant, on the spot. "My dear Colonel!" he murmured, with friendly interest and commiseration.

"I was annoyed when she came in—but I wasn't startled," his sitter continued.

"You concealed it very well, if you were."

"Ah, when one has been through what I have! To-day however I confess I was half prepared. I have seen her hanging about—she knows my movements. She was near my house this morning—she must have followed me."

"But who is she then—with such a *toupet?*"

"Yes, she has that," said the Colonel; "but as you observe she was primed. Still, there was a cheek, as they say, in her coming in. Oh, she's a bad one! She isn't a model and she never was; no doubt she has known some of those women and picked up their form. She had hold of a friend of mine ten years ago—a stupid young gander who might have been left to be plucked but whom I was obliged to take an interest in for family reasons. It's a long story—I had really forgotten all about it. She's thirty-seven if she's a day. I cut in and made him get rid of her—I sent her about her business. She knew it was me she had to thank. She has never forgiven me—I think she's off her head. Her name isn't Geraldine at all and I doubt very much if that's her address."

"Ah, what is her name?" Lyon asked, most attentive. The details always began to multiply, to abound, when once his companion was well launched—they flowed forth in battalions.

"It's Pearson—Harriet Pearson; but she used to call herself Grenadine—wasn't that a rum appellation? Grenadine—Geraldine—the jump was easy." Lyon was charmed with the promptitude of this response, and his interlocutor went on: "I hadn't thought of her for years—I had quite lost sight of her. I don't know what her idea is, but practically she's harmless. As I came in I thought I saw her a little way up the road. She must have found out I come here and have arrived before me. I daresay—or rather I'm sure—she is waiting for me there now."

"Hadn't you better have protection?" Lyon asked, laughing.

"The best protection is five shillings—I'm willing to go that length. Unless indeed she has a bottle of vitriol. But they only throw vitriol on the men who have deceived them, and I never deceived her—I told her the first time I saw her that it wouldn't do. Oh, if she's there we'll walk a little way together and talk it over and, as I say, I'll go as far as five shillings."

"Well," said Lyon, "I'll contribute another five." He felt that this was little to pay for his entertainment.

That entertainment was interrupted however for the time by the Colonel's departure. Lyon hoped for a letter recounting the fictive sequel; but apparently his brilliant sitter did not operate with the pen. At any rate he left town without writing; they had taken a rendezvous for three months later. Oliver Lyon always passed the holidays in the same way; during the first weeks he paid a visit to his elder brother, the happy possessor, in the south of England, of a rambling old house with formal gardens, in which he delighted, and then he went abroad—usually to Italy or Spain. This year he carried out his custom after taking a last look at his all but finished work and feeling as nearly pleased with it as he ever felt with the translation of the idea by the hand—always, as it seemed to him, a pitiful compromise. One yellow afternoon, in the country, as he was smoking his pipe on one of the old terraces he was seized with the desire to see it again and do two or three things more to it: he had thought of it so often while he lounged there. The impulse was too strong to be dismissed, and though he expected to return to town in the course of another week he was unable to face the delay. To look at the picture for five minutes would be enough—it would clear up certain questions which hummed in his brain; so that the next morning, to give himself this luxury, he took the train for

London. He sent no word in advance; he would lunch at his club and probably return into Sussex by the 5.45.

In St John's Wood the tide of human life flows at no time very fast, and in the first days of September Lyon found unmitigated emptiness in the straight sunny roads where the little plastered garden-walls, with their incommunicative doors, looked slightly Oriental. There was definite stillness in his own house, to which he admitted himself by his pass-key, having a theory that it was well sometimes to take servants unprepared. The good woman who was mainly in charge and who cumulated the functions of cook and housekeeper was, however, quickly summoned by his step, and (he cultivated frankness of intercourse with his domestics) received him without the confusion of surprise. He told her that she needn't mind the place being not quite straight, he had only come up for a few hours—he should be busy in the studio. To this she replied that he was just in time to see a lady and a gentleman who were there at the moment—they had arrived five minutes before. She had told them he was away from home but they said it was all right; they only wanted to look at a picture and would be very careful of everything. "I hope it is all right, sir," the housekeeper concluded. "The gentleman says he's a sitter and he gave me his name—rather an odd name; I think it's military. The lady's a very fine lady, sir; at any rate there they are."

"Oh, it's all right," Lyon said, the identity of his visitors being clear. The good woman couldn't know, for she usually had little to do with the comings and goings; his man, who showed people in and out, had accompanied him to the country. He was a good deal surprised at Mrs Capadose's having come to see her husband's portrait when she knew that the artist himself wished her to forbear; but it was a familiar truth to him that she was a woman of a high spirit. Besides, perhaps the lady was not Mrs Capadose; the Colonel might have brought some inquisitive friend, a person who wanted a portrait of *her* husband. What were they doing in town, at any rate, at that moment? Lyon made his way to the studio with a certain curiosity; he wondered vaguely what his friends were "up to." He pushed aside the curtain that hung in the door of communication—the door opening upon the gallery which it had been found convenient to construct at the time the studio was added to the house. When I say he pushed it aside I should amend my phrase; he laid his hand upon it, but at that moment he was arrested by a very singular sound. It came from the floor of the room beneath him and it startled him extremely, consisting apparently as it did of a passionate wail—a sort of smothered shriek—accompanied by a violent burst of tears. Oliver Lyon listened intently a moment, and then he passed out upon the balcony, which was covered with an old thick Moorish rug. His step was noiseless, though he had not endeavoured to make it so, and after that first instant he found himself profiting irresistibly by the accident of his not having attracted the attention of the two persons in the studio, who were some twenty feet below him. In truth they were so deeply and so strangely engaged that their unconsciousness of observation was explained. The scene that took place before Lyon's eyes was one of the most extraordinary they had ever rested upon. Delicacy and the failure to comprehend kept him at first from interrupting it—for what he saw was a woman who had thrown herself in a flood of tears on her companion's bosom—and these influences were succeeded after a minute (the minutes were very few and very short) by a definite motive which presently had the force to make him step back behind the curtain. I may add that it also had the force to make him avail himself for further contemplation of a crevice formed by his gathering together the two halves of the *portière*. He was perfectly aware of what he was about—he was for the moment an eavesdropper, a spy; but he was also aware that a very odd business, in which his confidence had been trifled with, was going forward, and that if in a measure it didn't concern him, in a measure it very definitely did. His observation, his reflections, accomplished themselves in a flash.

His visitors were in the middle of the room; Mrs Capadose clung to her husband, weeping, sobbing as if her heart would break. Her distress was horrible to Oliver Lyon but his astonishment was greater than his horror when he heard the Colonel respond to it by the words, vehemently uttered, "Damn him, damn him, damn him!" What in the world had happened? why was she sobbing and whom was he damning? What had happened, Lyon saw the next instant, was that the Colonel had finally rummaged out his unfinished portrait (he knew the corner where the artist usually placed it, out of the way, with its face to the wall) and had set it up before his wife on an empty easel. She had looked at it a few moments and then—apparently—what she saw in it had produced an explosion of dismay and resentment. She was too busy sobbing and the Colonel was too busy holding her and reiterating his objurgation, to look round or look up. The scene was so unexpected to Lyon that he could not take it, on the spot, as a proof of the triumph of his hand—of a tremendous hit: he could only wonder what on earth was the matter. The idea of the triumph came a little later. Yet he could see the portrait from where he stood; he was startled with its look of life—he had not thought it so masterly. Mrs Capadose flung herself away from her husband—she dropped into the nearest chair, buried her face in her arms, leaning on a table. Her weeping suddenly ceased to be audible, but she shuddered there as if she were overwhelmed with anguish and shame. Her husband remained a moment staring at the picture; then he went to her, bent over her, took hold of her again, soothed her. "What is it, darling, what the devil is it?" he demanded.

Lyon heard her answer. "It's cruel—oh, it's too cruel!"

"Damn him—damn him—damn him!" the Colonel repeated.

"It's all there—it's all there!" Mrs Capadose went on.

"Hang it, what's all there?"

"Everything there oughtn't to be—everything he has seen —it's too dreadful!"

"Everything he has seen? Why, ain't I a good-looking fellow? He has made me rather handsome."

Mrs Capadose had sprung up again; she had darted another glance at the painted betrayal. "Handsome? Hideous, hideous! Not that—never, never!"

"Not *what*, in heaven's name?" the Colonel almost shouted. Lyon could see his flushed, bewildered face.

"What he has made of you—what you know! *He* knows —he has seen. Every one will know—every one will see. Fancy that thing in the Academy!"

"You're going wild, darling; but if you hate it so it needn't go."

"Oh, he'll send it—it's so good! Come away—come away!" Mrs Capadose wailed, seizing her husband.

"It's so good?" the poor man cried.

"Come away—come away," she only repeated; and she turned toward the staircase that ascended to the gallery.

"Not that way—not through the house, in the state you're in," Lyon heard the Colonel object. "This way—we can pass," he added; and he drew his wife to the small door that opened into the garden. It was bolted, but he pushed the bolt and opened the door. She passed out quickly, but he stood there looking back into the room. "Wait for me a moment!" he cried out to her; and with an excited stride he re-entered the studio. He came up to the picture again, and again he stood looking at it. "Damn him—damn him—damn him!" he broke out once more. It was not clear to Lyon whether this malediction had for its object the original or the painter of the portrait. The Colonel turned away and moved rapidly about the room, as if he were looking for something; Lyon was unable for the instant to guess his intention. Then the artist said to himself, below his breath, "He's going to do it a harm!" His first impulse was to rush down and stop him; but he paused, with the sound of Everina Brant's sobs still in his ears. The Colonel found what he was looking for—found it among some odds and ends on a small table and rushed back with it to the easel. At one and the same moment Lyon perceived that the object he had seized was a small Eastern dagger and that he had plunged it into the canvas. He seemed animated by a sudden fury, for with extreme vigour of hand he dragged the instrument down (Lyon knew it to have no very fine edge) making a long, abominable gash. Then he plucked it out and dashed it again several times into the face of the likeness, exactly as if he were stabbing a human victim: it had the oddest effect—that of a sort of figurative suicide. In a few seconds more the Colonel had tossed the dagger away—he looked at it as he did so, as if he expected it to reek with blood—and hurried out of the place, closing the door after him.

The strangest part of all was—as will doubtless appear—that Oliver Lyon made no movement to save his picture. But he did not feel as if he were losing it or cared not if he were, so much more did he feel that he was gaining a certitude. His old friend *was* ashamed of her husband, and he had made her so, and he had scored a great success, even though the picture had been reduced to rags. The revelation excited him so—as indeed the whole scene did—that when he came down the steps after the Colonel had gone he trembled with his happy agitation; he was dizzy and had to sit down a moment. The portrait had a dozen jagged wounds—the Colonel literally had hacked it to death. Lyon left it where it was, never touched it, scarcely looked at it; he only walked up and down his studio, still excited, for an hour. At the end of this time his good woman came to recommend that he should have some luncheon; there was a passage under the staircase from the offices.

"Ah, the lady and gentleman have gone, sir? I didn't hear them."

"Yes; they went by the garden."

But she had stopped, staring at the picture on the easel. "Gracious, how you 'ave served it, sir!"

Lyon imitated the Colonel. "Yes, I cut it up—in a fit of disgust."

"Mercy, after all your trouble! Because they weren't pleased, sir?"

"Yes; they weren't pleased."

"Well, they must be very grand! Blessed if I would!"

"Have it chopped up; it will do to light fires," Lyon said.

He returned to the country by the 3.30 and a few days later passed over to France. During the two months that he was absent from England he expected something—he could hardly have said what; a manifestation of some sort on the Colonel's part. Wouldn't he write, wouldn't he explain, wouldn't he take for granted Lyon had discovered the way he had, as the cook said, served him and deem it only decent to take pity in some fashion or other on his mystification? Would he plead guilty or would he repudiate suspicion? The latter course would be difficult and make a considerable draft upon his genius, in view of the certain testimony of Lyon's house-keeper, who had admitted the visitors and would establish the connection between their presence and the violence wrought. Would the Colonel proffer some apology or some amends, or would any word from him be only a further expression of that destructive petulance which our friend had seen his wife so suddenly and so potently communicate to him? He would have either to declare that he had not touched the picture or to admit that he had, and in either case he would have to tell a fine story. Lyon was impatient for the story and, as no letter came, disappointed that it was not produced. His impatience however was much greater in respect to Mrs Capadose's ver-

sion, if version there was to be; for certainly that would be the
real test, would show how far she would go for her husband,
on the one side, or for him, Oliver Lyon, on the other. He
could scarcely wait to see what line she would take; whether
she would simply adopt the Colonel's, whatever it might be.
He wanted to draw her out without waiting, to get an idea in
advance. He wrote to her, to this end, from Venice, in the tone
of their established friendship, asking for news, narrating his
wanderings, hoping they should soon meet in town and not
saying a word about the picture. Day followed day, after the
time, and he received no answer; upon which he reflected that
she couldn't trust herself to write—was still too much under
the influence of the emotion produced by his "betrayal." Her
husband had espoused that emotion and she had espoused the
action he had taken in consequence of it, and it was a complete
rupture and everything was at an end. Lyon considered this
prospect rather ruefully, at the same time that he thought it
deplorable that such charming people should have put themselves so grossly in the wrong. He was at last cheered, though
little further enlightened, by the arrival of a letter, brief but
breathing good-humour and hinting neither at a grievance nor
at a bad conscience. The most interesting part of it to Lyon
was the postscript, which consisted of these words: "I have a
confession to make to you. We were in town for a couple of
days, the 1st of September, and I took the occasion to defy
your authority—it was very bad of me but I couldn't help it.
I made Clement take me to your studio—I wanted so dreadfully to see what you had done with him, your wishes to the
contrary notwithstanding. We made your servants let us in
and I took a good look at the picture. It is really wonderful!"
"Wonderful" was non-committal, but at least with this letter
there was no rupture.

The third day after Lyon's return to London was a Sunday,
so that he could go and ask Mrs Capadose for luncheon. She
had given him in the spring a general invitation to do so and

he had availed himself of it several times. These had been the occasions (before he sat to him) when he saw the Colonel most familiarly. Directly after the meal his host disappeared (he went out, as he said, to call on *his* women) and the second half-hour was the best, even when there were other people. Now, in the first days of December, Lyon had the luck to find the pair alone, without even Amy, who appeared but little in public. They were in the drawing-room, waiting for the repast to be announced, and as soon as he came in the Colonel broke out, "My dear fellow, I'm delighted to see you! I'm so keen to begin again."

"Oh, do go on, it's so beautiful," Mrs Capadose said, as she gave him her hand.

Lyon looked from one to the other; he didn't know what he had expected, but he had not expected this. "Ah, then, you think I've got something?"

"You've got everything," said Mrs Capadose, smiling from her golden-brown eyes.

"She wrote you of our little crime?" her husband asked. "She dragged me there—I had to go." Lyon wondered for a moment whether he meant by their little crime the assault on the canvas; but the Colonel's next words didn't confirm this interpretation. "You know I like to sit—it gives such a chance to my *bavardise*. And just now I have time."

"You must remember I had almost finished," Lyon remarked.

"So you had. More's the pity. I should like you to begin again."

"My dear fellow, I shall have to begin again!" said Oliver Lyon with a laugh, looking at Mrs Capadose. She did not meet his eyes—she had got up to ring for luncheon. "The picture has been smashed," Lyon continued.

"Smashed? Ah, what did you do that for?" Mrs Capadose asked, standing there before him in all her clear, rich beauty. Now that she looked at him she was impenetrable.

"I didn't—I found it so—with a dozen holes punched in it!"

"I say!" cried the Colonel.

Lyon turned his eyes to him, smiling. "I hope *you* didn't do it?"

"Is it ruined?" the Colonel inquired. He was as brightly true as his wife and he looked simply as if Lyon's question could not be serious. "For the love of sitting to you? My dear fellow, if I had thought of it I would!"

"Nor you either?" the painter demanded of Mrs Capadose. Before she had time to reply her husband had seized her arm, as if a highly suggestive idea had come to him. "I say, my dear, that woman—that woman!"

"That woman?" Mrs Capadose repeated; and Lyon too wondered what woman he meant.

"Don't you remember when we came out, she was at the door—or a little way from it? I spoke to you of her—I told you about her. Geraldine—Grenadine—the one who burst in that day," he explained to Lyon. "We saw her hanging about —I called Everina's attention to her."

"Do you mean she got at my picture?"

"Ah yes, I remember," said Mrs Capadose, with a sigh.

"She burst in again—she had learned the way—she was waiting for her chance," the Colonel continued. "Ah, the little brute!"

Lyon looked down; he felt himself colouring. This was what he had been waiting for—the day the Colonel should wantonly sacrifice some innocent person. And could his wife be a party to that final atrocity? Lyon had reminded himself repeatedly during the previous weeks that when the Colonel perpetrated his misdeed she had already quitted the room; but he had argued none the less—it was a virtual certainty—that he had on rejoining her immediately made his achievement plain to her. He was in the flush of performance; and even if he had not mentioned what he had done she would have guessed it. He did not for an instant believe that poor Miss Geraldine had been hovering about his door, nor had the account given by the Colonel the summer before of his relations with this lady deceived him in the slightest degree. Lyon had never seen her before the day she planted herself in his studio; but he knew her and classified her as if he had made her. He was acquainted with the London female model in all her varieties—in every phase of her development and every step of her decay. When he entered his house that September morning just after the arrival of his two friends there had been no symptoms whatever, up and down the road, of Miss Geraldine's reappearance. That fact had been fixed in his mind by his recollecting the vacancy of the prospect when his cook told him that a lady and a gentleman were in his studio: he had wondered there was not a carriage nor a cab at his door. Then he had reflected that they would have come by the underground railway; he was close to the Marlborough Road station and he knew the Colonel, coming to his sittings, more than once had availed himself of that convenience. "How in the world did she get in?" He addressed the question to his companions indifferently.

"Let us go down to luncheon," said Mrs Capadose, passing out of the room.

"We went by the garden—without troubling your servant —I wanted to show my wife." Lyon followed his hostess with her husband and the Colonel stopped him at the top of the stairs. "My dear fellow, I *can't* have been guilty of the folly of not fastening the door?"

"I am sure I don't know, Colonel," Lyon said as they went down. "It was a very determined hand—a perfect wild-cat."

"Well, she *is* a wild-cat—confound her! That's why I wanted to get him away from her."

"But I don't understand her motive."

"She's off her head—and she hates me; that was her motive."

"But she doesn't hate me, my dear fellow!" Lyon said, laughing.

"She hated the picture—don't you remember she said so? The more portraits there are the less employment for such as her."

"Yes; but if she is not really the model she pretends to be, how can that hurt her?" Lyon asked.

The inquiry baffled the Colonel an instant—but only an instant. "Ah, she was in a vicious muddle! As I say, she's off her head."

They went into the dining-room, where Mrs Capadose was taking her place. "It's too bad, it's too horrid!" she said. "You see the fates are against you. Providence won't let you be so disinterested—painting masterpieces for nothing."

"Did *you* see the woman?" Lyon demanded, with something like a sternness that he could not mitigate.

Mrs Capadose appeared not to perceive it or not to heed it if she did. "There was a person, not far from your door, whom Clement called my attention to. He told me something about her but we were going the other way."

"And do you think she did it?"

"How can I tell? If she did she was mad, poor wretch."

"I should like very much to get hold of her," said Lyon. This was a false statement, for he had no desire for any further conversation with Miss Geraldine. He had exposed his friends to himself, but he had no desire to expose them to any one else, least of all to themselves.

"Oh, depend upon it she will never show again. You're safe!" the Colonel exclaimed.

"But I remember her address—Mortimer Terrace Mews, Notting Hill."

"Oh, that's pure humbug; there isn't any such place."

"Lord, what a deceiver!" said Lyon.

"Is there any one else you suspect?" the Colonel went on.

"Not a creature."

"And what do your servants say?"

"They say it wasn't *them*, and I reply that I never said it was. That's about the substance of our conferences."

"And when did they discover the havoc?"

"They never discovered it at all. I noticed it first—when I came back."

"Well, she could easily have stepped in," said the Colonel. "Don't you remember how she turned up that day, like the clown in the ring?"

"Yes, yes; she could have done the job in three seconds, except that the picture wasn't out."

"My dear fellow, don't curse me!—but of course I dragged it out."

"You didn't put it back?" Lyon asked tragically.

"Ah, Clement, Clement, didn't I tell you to?" Mrs Capadose exclaimed in a tone of exquisite reproach.

The Colonel groaned, dramatically; he covered his face with his hands. His wife's words were for Lyon the finishing touch; they made his whole vision crumble—his theory that she had secretly kept herself true. Even to her old lover she wouldn't be so! He was sick; he couldn't eat; he knew that he looked very strange. He murmured something about it being useless to cry over spilled milk—he tried to turn the conversation to other things. But it was a horrid effort and he wondered whether they felt it as much as he. He wondered all sorts of things: whether they guessed he disbelieved them (that he had seen them of course they would never guess); whether they had arranged their story in advance or it was only an inspiration of the moment; whether she had resisted, protested, when the Colonel proposed it to her, and then had been borne down by him; whether in short she didn't loathe herself as she sat there. The cruelty, the cowardice of fastening their unholy act upon the wretched woman struck him as monstrous—no less monstrous indeed than the levity that could make them run the risk of her giving them, in her righteous indignation, the lie. Of course that risk could only exculpate her and not inculpate them—the probabilities protected them so perfectly; and what the Colonel counted on (what he would have counted upon the day he delivered himself, after first seeing her, at the studio, if he had thought about the matter then at all and not spoken from the pure spontaneity of his genius) was simply that Miss Geraldine had really vanished for ever into her native unknown. Lyon wanted so much to quit the subject that when after a little Mrs Capadose said to him, "But can nothing be done, can't the picture be repaired? You know they do such wonders in that way now," he only replied, "I don't know, I don't care, it's all over, n'en parlons plus!" Her hypocrisy revolted him. And yet, by way of plucking off the last veil of her shame, he broke out to her again, shortly afterward, "And you did like it, really?" To which she returned, looking him straight in his face, without a blush, a pallor, an evasion, "Oh, I loved it!" Truly her husband had trained her well. After that Lyon said no more and his companions forbore temporarily to insist, like people of tact and sympathy aware that the odious accident had made him sore.

When they quitted the table the Colonel went away without coming upstairs; but Lyon returned to the drawing-room with his hostess, remarking to her however on the way that he could remain but a moment. He spent that moment—it prolonged itself a little—standing with her before the chimney-piece. She neither sat down nor asked him to; her manner denoted that she intended to go out. Yes, her husband had trained her well; yet Lyon dreamed for a moment that now he was alone with her she would perhaps break down, retract, apologise, confide, say to him, "My dear old friend, forgive this hideous comedy—you understand!" And then how he would have loved her and pitied her, guarded her, helped her always! If she were not ready to do something of that sort why had she treated him as if he were a dear old friend; why had she let him for months suppose certain things—or almost; why had she come to his studio day after day to sit near him on the pretext of her child's portrait, as if she liked to think what might have been? Why had she come so near a tacit confession, in a word, if she was not willing to go an inch further? And she was not willing—she was not; he could see that as he lingered there. She moved about the room a little, rearranging two or three objects on the tables, but she did nothing more. Suddenly he said to her: "Which way was she going, when you came out?"

"She—the woman we saw?"

"Yes, your husband's strange friend. It's a clew worth following." He had no desire to frighten her; he only wanted to communicate the impulse which would make her say, "Ah, spare me—and spare *him!* There was no such person."

Instead of this Mrs Capadose replied, "She was going away from us—she crossed the road. We were coming towards the station."

"And did she appear to recognise the Colonel—did she look round?"

"Yes; she looked round, but I didn't notice much. A hansom came along and we got into it. It was not till then that Clement told me who she was: I remember he said that she was there for no good. I suppose we ought to have gone back."

"Yes; you would have saved the picture."

For a moment she said nothing; then she smiled. "For you, I am very sorry. But you must remember that I possess the original!"

At this Lyon turned away. "Well, I must go," he said; and he left her without any other farewell and made his way out of the house. As he went slowly up the street the sense came back to him of that first glimpse of her he had had at Stayes—the way he had seen her gaze across the table at her husband. Lyon stopped at the corner, looking vaguely up and down. He would never go back—he couldn't. She was still in love with the Colonel—he had trained her too well.

A NOTE ON THE TEXT

In preparing these tales for publication, the editor had to choose between James's original magazine texts, those published in book form soon afterwards and those revised and rewritten for the New York Edition. The obvious choice, it seemed to him, was the original book form of the story where there was one. In that form it had the benefit of revision from magazine to volume; and in that form it was best known to James's generation. It seemed to the editor that in a chronological edition of James's shorter fictions, the New York Edition texts had no relevance. They belong exclusively to the edition for which they were designed; particularly since the revisions were often made several decades after the original publication.

The original magazine publications of the tales in this volume were as follows:

"Georgina's Reasons," *New York Sun*, 20 and 27 July, 3 August 1884.

"A New England Winter," *Century Magazine*, August–September 1884.

"The Path of Duty," *English Illustrated Magazine*, December 1884.

"Mrs Temperly," *Harper's Weekly*, 6–20 August 1887 (entitled "Cousin Maria").

"Louisa Pallant," *Harper's New Monthly Magazine*, February 1888.

"The Aspern Papers," *Atlantic Monthly*, March–May 1888.

"The Liar," *Century Magazine*, May–June 1888.

"A New England Winter" was reprinted first in Boston

and then in London in *Tales of Three Cities* in 1884. "Georgina's Reasons" and "The Path of Duty" were reprinted first in Boston in *The Author of Beltraffio* and then in London in *Stories Revived* in 1885. For these three tales the London text has been preferred to that which appeared in Boston three or four months earlier and with less supervision by the author. The texts of the remaining four tales follow those of their first book publication, "Mrs Temperly" and "The Liar" in *A London Life* (London, 1889), and "Louisa Pallant" and "The Aspern Papers" in *The Aspern Papers* (London, 1888).

For the complete bibliography of the tales the reader is referred to *A Bibliography of the Writings of Henry James* by Leon Edel and Dan H. Laurence (second edition, revised, London, 1961) in the Soho Bibliographies published by Rupert Hart-Davis.